DANGEROUS GIRL

FAÎTE FALLING
BOOK ELEVEN

MARY E. TWOMEY

MARY E. TWOMEY

Dangerous Girl
Book Eleven in the Faîte Falling Series

By

Mary E. Twomey

COPYRIGHT

DEDICATION

For Liz Holland.

Who picks me up
when I'm certain all I'm capable of is falling.

ACKNOWLEDGMENTS

Thank you to my editor, Ruth Gross, for sticking with me through eleven books.

Thank you to my Beta readers, Laura Velarde and Brandy Crosson, who set me straight when I went off on tangents.

I have a stellar ARC team. They encourage me, send me any typos, and are pretty much the best wombats a girl could ask for.

Thank you to Powerhouse and Write Club. I honestly don't know how you rein me in and keep me focused, but whatever magical dwarf you've got tucked away in your pockets to grant you the power to keep me tethered to reality, kudos to him (and you).

Thank you to my assistant (and brother) Brian Androsian. You kept your eye-rolling to a minimum every time I handed you a new task. Well done on not murdering me.

Thank you to Jamie Burnham, for letting me get a peek at the rock star life. You made Lugh far more glamorous and mysterious.

Thank you to Madeline Freeman, who reminds me to be a person, when we all know I'm a perfectly good robot.

1

BEWARE THE JABBERWOCK

*B*eing alone with your thoughts is a thing most people pay good money for during yoga classes or meditation retreats. I didn't have to spend a dime on the dungeon I'd been thrown in, thanks to the fangs I hadn't asked for. When the lost magic escaped into Faîte, it infected some people with a Vampire curse, and others with a Werewolf curse. I learned that if I touched the Werewolves or the *Farouche* Vampires, I could cure them, sucking the poison back to where it came from, inside my ring.

I was an *Attelage* Vampire, though, and because Uncle Dub was thorough, I couldn't cure myself or my kind. I'd used my fangs to weaken the Werewolves I'd been fighting, in an attempt to get close enough to cure them. It had worked, but when the villagers saw me chomp down and drink the blood, my "thank you for saving our village" card must've gotten lost in the mail. I was swiftly kidnapped and taken to this stinking bunker, where the vigilantes of Éireland were desperately trying to free their land of the higher magic that had seized them so abruptly.

It was a solid plan, except that *Attelage* Vampires like myself didn't usually feed off random victims, like the *Farouche* Vampires did. Those dudes had gone rabid, and fed on their victims until the last drop of blood was drained. *Attelage* Vamps only fed on the blood of the person they'd had their first drink from. We had rational thought, and were still pretty much ourselves, while the *Farouche* were rabid and didn't have language. Bastien was my mate, and we'd made our peace with the situation nearly two years ago when it all hit the fan.

The rest of the world? Not so much. My father disowned me, and turned me out of the kingdom I'd restored to him. Now Duke Lot was in charge of District 1, so that I could live a peaceful life in Common – the earth we all know and love. Ice cream. Indoor plumbing. Fast food. Grad school. All the things I needed and missed, and had given up to be back here in Faîte, sucking the lost magic out of the land as best I could.

I didn't expect to be abducted, or that people were still so set in their ways that they couldn't evaluate the situation and see that *Attelage* Vamps weren't a danger to the public. It didn't matter, though. People love being right more than they love justice, I'd learned. Now I was on the docket to be burned so they didn't have to reevaluate what they were doing.

That was how I landed myself in the dungeon of gnashing teeth and endless tears. Around every six hours or so, two burly men would come in and yank a Vampire out of their cell, taking them to the furnace, where they were burned alive. Their bodies heated the bunker, which was supposed to be their way of being useful to society, since apparently once we were infected, we had no purpose in Faîte anymore.

The flying ability Dub had introduced me to wasn't all that stellar or reliable, but I still kicked myself for not at least trying to levitate off the horse they rode me in on. A dozen other possible escape plans dawned on me far too late. I sympathized with all the movie characters I'd ever shouted at because I knew better than they did.

Now I was stuck in a cage, trying not to lose my shiz.

Three Vampires had been taken from the dark dungeon and escorted to the furnace while I waited in hopes that Rudy – the dude who'd carried me inside – would tell the up-and-ups that there was an Untouchable in their dungeon. That shouldn't really be happening, under the highest law of the land. It was supposed to be my Get Out of Jail Free card, yet here I sat, encased behind iron bars as I waited out my doom. This time he'd left us with a lantern. I'd thought it was a mercy to keep us from the dark, but I quickly learned the dim light only amped up the fear. The concrete walls of the windowless basement dungeon we were kept in was one long rectangle, with dozens of cells running down both walls. It was cold here, despite our fellow citizens' bodies being burned to warm the place. The whole place stank of urine and terror. I wasn't sure which was worse as both stenches seemed to seep into my pores.

I sat with my legs crossed, trying to will calm into my soul by my body setting the precedent. Other than the fact that my arms were still tied behind my back, I looked the picture of poise, ready for the cover of any yoga magazine. Well, I was bloody and bruised from the fight with the Werewolves, but other than that, totally Zen.

I sent out positive vibes into the universe – both universes, I hoped. I wished good things for Reyn, who'd married my Aunt Lane, the woman who raised me as her daughter. I wished a lifetime of giggles and smiles for Lucas, their adorable one-year-old son, who had probably long forgotten all about me.

I wished nothing but happiness for Lane, but knew that if I didn't return to her, that would be a wasted wish. We were two of a kind, and needed each other to find our way through the mess of both worlds. Girlfriends to our core, it tore me up inside that I might die in here in a matter of days or hours, and she would never know. She would live in wait, hoping that I would come back to her, putting her smiles on hold until I burst through the front door, belting out the Spice Girls just to make her twerk and laugh. She would be a mother, forever without her daughter. I knew she would never be able to properly let me go if she didn't see my body.

I switched from that dead end of misery to Draper, my adopted brother who loved me, even when I was wrong, even when I was a mess. He didn't care if I was the Awesome Queen Rosie or not, he'd loved me from the beginning. We'd doted on each other, protected each other, and kept an eye out from the first time we'd met as adults. I hoped he was having fun, and that when the time came, he would help Lane move on from her grief.

Judah could help with that, too. My BFF could make anyone smile. He was probably married by now, making an honest woman out of his high school sweetheart. My chin hung, marring my perfect yoga pose as the Vampires wailed all around me, screaming and rattling their cages in the dark. I wouldn't see Judah get married. I was supposed to be his best man, to kick him down the aisle when he got cold feet. I was supposed to make sure Jill had her something old, something new, something borrowed, and all that. Judah would never remember the details, and Jill deserved every frill and bow for waiting for him to get it together for as long as she did.

Judah had promised he wouldn't get married without me. How long would he be expected to keep that promise? It had already been months, if not more than half a year I'd been back in Faîte, trying to right the things that had gone so very wrong. I tried to hear Judah's voice as he rapped out the periodic chart for me, but it was hard to focus on dropping killer beats when the background noise was a constant loop of wailing and screaming for mercy.

I gulped at the thought of Bastien. My husband had been so patient with me, waiting for me to get my act together, and then staying with me when Dub had taken away my sight. It was then that I truly saw Bastien, ironically enough. I saw how gentle he was, despite his burly and scarred exterior. I saw his kindness and patience as he guided me through each narrow doorway, and through our home, where we'd made so many happy memories.

My heart sank at the knowledge that he'd be just like Lane if he didn't have my body to confirm that I'd died. He'd tear apart whole cities to unearth me, but if I was pure ash, there wouldn't be anything left of me to find. He would drive himself to madness, drinking heavily again, and undoing all the hard work he'd accomplished in AA. I wanted so badly for Bastien to have a good life, but part of that desire was for me to be there to watch it all happen. I wanted to observe and celebrate every moment. I'd spent so long not seeing him. Above all else, I desperately wanted that, and only that. To see my husband again.

"Why are ye so calm?" someone screeched at me from my left.

I opened my eyes and turned to the woman in the cell next to me. She was easily in her late fifties, but the madness of terror had twisted what might have been a demure deportment into a harried mess. Her brown hair had streaks of gray, and it stuck out at all ends, having come loose from her bun ages ago.

"Hi," I said, not bothering to answer her question. I didn't want to admit to her that I wasn't calm. Inside, I was screaming with the rest of them. "I'm Rosie. What's your name?"

She gaped at me, and then seemed to remember herself by small degrees. She had stains on her apron, and a *Little House on the Prairie* calico dress. She gripped the bars that divided our cages and moved her face between two of them, her nose and chin poking into my space. "Marcia. I'm Marcia of the Green Marsh."

It was probably the worst time for my stupid sense of humor to rear its immature head, but a small smile tugged the corner of my mouth upward. "Marcia from the Marsh? That's funny. That's like if I was Rosie from the Rose Gardens. Totally cute."

"What do ye have tha ye aren't scared? Do ye have a plan?"

"I wish. I don't have anything," I admitted, and that truth sank deep inside of me. "But I don't want to die screaming. That's not me."

"You've lost your mind, then. This is the end for us! My mate's out there, and I can feel the last of her blood leaving me. I've been four days without her blood! I need blood!" Her eyes had a ring of crazy around them, which I could only just make out through the dim lantern's light.

I inhaled through my nose, welcoming the acrid stench

of released body fluids. "You can make it six days, Marcia. You'll be okay for another couple of days. It just feels terrible, but it's possible."

"You're mad. No one's coming for us, ye know. We're in here until the coals go cold, and they need us to warm them." She let out a cry of anguish that matched the others'.

My head moved back and forth to a beat only I heard. I knew that if I cried, there would be no way to stop the insanity that rocketed around inside my bones. If I gave in for even a second, I would lose what little I had of myself forever. Somehow that last straw seemed like one push too far. So I bopped, as I always did when I needed to find the answer on a test, and it eluded me. Eventually, a song would come alongside me and swoop me away, taking my mind from everything that overwhelmed me, putting me on a higher plane of existence.

I couldn't imagine what song might suit this situation, what miracle might pull me from the muck, but I knew I needed something. I wouldn't bring Lost and Forgotten into this dismal place. Lugh's masterpieces deserved better than a dungeon. I'd clung to his music when I'd been trapped in the well, but somehow this seemed worse.

Judah had set Lewis Carroll's poem "Jabberwocky" to a rap beat in honor of Tupac, so that I would remember it for our ninth-grade presentation on poetry. We'd received an A on that project. Even though most of our classmates rolled their eyes at our dorkiness, we did Tupac and Carroll proud.

My head moved back and forth, finding my groove (and myself) in the gravest of places. If this would be how my great adventure of life came to a close, I would end it on a note that *I* chose. I didn't bother being quiet, but projected from my diaphragm as if I was performing for a whole audience.

""'Twas brillig, and the slithy toves

Did gyre and gimble in the wabe:

All mimsy were the borogoves,

And the mome raths outgrabe.'"

I ignored Marcia's wails that the new Vamp had gone insane, and bent my head back to let out a cry of my own, shouting it to the heavens, if indeed Heaven could hear me in a place as forsaken as this.

My voice was that of a protester, crying out my fearsome wail that I was a person, and I wouldn't devolve into the monster they claimed I was. And if I did, oh, the wrath that would rain down on them.

"'Beware the Jabberwock, my son!'" I screamed, scaring a few of the Vampires into stunned silence. Their own cries had been fueling each other on to madness. My madness was different. It was a calculated insanity that would make them rue the day they'd trapped me.

"'The jaws that bite, the claws that catch!

Beware the Jubjub bird,

and shun the frumious Bandersnatch!'"

A few cheered me on, with their jaws that bit and claws that – well, they were just hands, but to us, they were weapons. We were weapons, and somewhere along the lines, we'd identified either too much or not enough with that. We'd been shunted aside by society, to the point where all we were expected to be was scared or incoherent kindling. If they wanted to call us monsters, I would not become one. They didn't know who I was, but I knew. Oh, I knew.

My voice was so loud, only a few sniffles and the wails from the rabid *Farouche* Vamps could be heard echoing around the dungeon. The *Attelage* Vampires calmed, leaning in to listen.

"'He took his vorpal sword in hand;
Long time the manxome foe he sought.
So rested he by the Tumtum tree,
and stood while in thought.'"

I was still cross-legged, the picture of repose tinged with psychosis. My hands were tied behind my back, while most of them were free to move their arms as a last mercy before there were no mercies left. Though I didn't have to compete with the noise anymore, my volume raged onward, furious that I'd tried to heal this world, yet here I was – bound in a cage. I didn't do well with cages, so I shouted the injustice to the tune of Tupac, who'd known his fair share of injustice, too.

"And, as in uffish thought he stood,
The Jabberwock, with eyes of flame,

Came whiffling through the tulgey wood,

And burbled as it came!'"

This brought out cries of unity among the ranks, and soon they were all on their feet with their hands clutching the bars to listen in on the next few lines of nonsense.

I banged my forehead against the bars to keep the beat as I counted out the gangsta rhythm. My voice broke with screamed passion as the words echoed off the walls and pinged each of our ravaged hearts.

"'One, two! One, Two! And through and through.

The vorpal blade went snicker-snack!

He left it dead, and with its head,

He went galumphing back.

'And hast though slain the Jabberwock?'"

At this, everyone screamed a hearty, "No!" Tears welled in my eyes at the ferocity in our newfound unity. We were people, alright, and we wouldn't go begging. We would make them regret attempting to turn us into the monsters they feared. My voice warbled, but I persisted, pushing my point to the very end.

"'Come to my arms, my beanish boy!

O frabjous day! Callooh! Callay!'

he chortled in his joy.

'Twas brillib, and the slithy toves

Did gyre and gimble in the wabe:

All mimsy were the borogoves,

and the mome raths outgrabe!'"

I hung my head, letting a rare slice of serenity fall

among the sniffles. My heart pounded out the rhythm of our war cry, assuring me that though I was trapped in a cell, they would never take me away from myself. I had me, and that would have to be enough.

"What do we do now?" Marcia asked. "How do we make them fear the Jabberwock?"

I remained silent for a few beats, and then kept my eyes on the bars before me as I answered loud enough for everyone to hear over the nonsensical screeching of the *Farouche.* "We aren't the Jabberwock. We aren't monsters. You're a woman, Marcia. You'll die as you lived, and they won't take that from you. I won't let them turn me into a monster. They'll feed me into the fire as a person. My face will haunt them, and that's how I'll live on through this terrible day. They'll fear something far worse than the Jabberwock before this is all said and done. They'll be the monsters, and they'll have no choice but to fear themselves."

2

FINNEGAN'S GRAND MISTAKES

I struggled fruitlessly against my bindings, but didn't squirm around or whimper, lest I undo the calm I'd instilled in my fellow prisoners. When the door opened far too soon for the fire to have died down, my breath came in nervous pants when Rudy's boots stalked down death row. The piercing stench of feces, vomit and urine was pungent in my nose, pushing out any other smells. Rudy skipped over the dozens of cells before mine, and paused in front of my small gate, peering inside. *It's not my time yet!* I wanted to protest, my lower lip wavering in the line of fire as my chin rose in defiance.

"What's going on in here tha you're all so quiet?"

None of us answered, and I knew we were all trying to retain what little dignity we could. The poor *Farouche* couldn't help themselves, and they threw their bodies against the bars like animals at the fresh blood Rudy had in his veins. There were ten *Farouche*, and the rest of us were *Attelage*.

"No one's chatty today? Can't say I miss the screaming." He turned to me and said, "Congratulations," with that same absence of malice in his tone. He sounded like a man resigned to put abandoned puppies down at the pound – a dirty job, but someone had to do it. "Your plea intrigued Finnegan. I can't make no promises, but he wants to meet with ye."

I drew in a quavering breath and did my best to scramble to my feet without the use of my hands. The screeching picked up around me as everyone started to plead for mercy, for justice, for an audience, for under-standing. They assumed I was being taken early to the slaughter, which meant that the system of going down the row wasn't something they could depend on for a few extra hours of a chance. That's all any of us could hope for anymore – just a chance that anyone might remember we were people, and we weren't done contributing to the world just yet.

I dug my heels in before Rudy dragged me out, so I could turn to the others. "No! We won't go down like this. They fear the Jabberwock, but make them understand that they're murdering their countrymen! If they can't hear us, then let them see who you are. Who are you?" I demanded of each of them. "If you were husbands, wives, workers, children, and friends before this day, then be who you are! You are not the Jabberwock! You are Éireland!"

The crying stopped abruptly from the sentient ones, and almost as one, each chest puffed out to reclaim the dignity that had been stripped from us. My shoulders rolled back as I looked on my fellow prisoners with nothing short of pride.

"Tha's enough, now," Rudy said uncertainly, tugging on my bicep. He shot me an apologetic look before sliding the black sack over my head. It was for his own protection, to keep me from being able to bite him. "Easy, lass," he warned as I whimpered. I didn't like being blinded.

A fearful shiver ran through me, but I kept my head up. The inside of the bag stank like bile from who knows how many other Vampires losing their lunch out of fear when they'd been kidnapped in broad daylight. I wonder how many of their family members had stood by and watched, offering up no protest when their loved one was taken away. We were the diseased, the lepers. We were the problem, when moments before we'd been people.

Somewhere inside of me, a steadiness anchored my fluttering heartrate. I knew who I was, and it wasn't a screeching Vampire. I was a person, and live or die, they would remember that about me – that they'd murdered a person, and not a monster.

My steps somehow managed to find their steadiness, taking one after the other with a calmness that settled deep down in my bones. My chin leveled, and my chest broadened, as if it was my choice to hold my hands behind my back, and not the rope that kept them imprisoned.

As long as I had me, nothing could keep me in prison.

After a few beats, *I* set the pace that Rudy followed along with, and in that, I found a small victory. If I could make Rudy slow his steps for me, there was a chance that I could make him see me as a person. This wasn't about just my freedom anymore; there was a whole dungeon, and beyond that, a whole world that was teeming with the misunderstood, and I was their queen.

If these were my people, what a queen I would be. I was determined not to let them down.

Rudy didn't warn me of the stairs. My foot caught on the first one, and I pitched forward, banging my chin on the stone so hard that my teeth rattled. "Oh, tha sounded painful. Up ye get, now. We don't want to keep Finnegan waiting."

I didn't speak to him, but righted myself and moved up the steps, my body aching head to toe from Faîte jarring everything that had once been painless and carefree. I refused to gag at the stench of the black sack over my head. I refused to stumble over my stubbed toes. I refused to speak to someone who had no desire or ability to help me.

We paused, and Rudy muttered a professional, "I've got the prisoner for Finnegan. He's expecting this one."

"Alright. He's got two guards in there with him, so she shouldn't be a problem." A heavy door swung open, and I was escorted inside, my feet sliding over smoother poured concrete, instead of the uneven stone steps.

"This is her, Captain Finnegan. Something's

happening with the prisoners down there, so I should probably get back to them."

"More helpless pleas for mercy?" Finnegan's voice was gravelly. It sounded like he gargled with shards of glass just for the heck of it.

"No. The opposite, actually. The *Attelage* are quiet, just standing around with these angry looks."

Finnegan made a pfft sound, like he couldn't care less, so long as the business of burning people was operational. "Go ahead. I think my men can protect me against this wee pixie."

"Yes, sir."

Rudy yanked the black sack from my head, and fresh air filled my lungs. Well, it was fresher than the vomit and blood stench, having the scent of damp rocks to it as I inhaled. I kept my chin raised, reminding myself that I was Lane's daughter, and we didn't waste our time letting the world tell us who we were.

Captain Finnegan winced at my appearance. My face was streaked with dried blood, which I would not try to conceal. The captain had a rust-colored mustache that looked recently oiled and trimmed. His slate eyes were small, and looked impervious to empathy, so I knew not to try that tact. Even sitting down in his makeshift throne – it was too decorative a chair to be anything else – he was enormous. Muscular, thick and tall, I guessed he would tower over me, and could easily tie me into a pretzel if I vexed him too much. He stared at me, squinting through the dim shadows that the solitary lantern hanging from a hook in the corner cast between us. "So, I hear ye have some wild stories. Entertain me, wee pixie."

I kept my voice low and level, ironing out any quakes that might give away how scared I was beneath my determination. Of the two emotions, I willed determination to win out, and stuffed the fear down where it hopefully wouldn't be seen by Finnegan and the two gargoyles who flanked him. "Sure, I can tell you a story. I've got all kinds. Would you like to hear about Duchess Elaine, who adopted and raised me, and would have your heads if she saw me tied like this? How about the one where Duke Lot and I share a castle, ruling Avalon together with King Urien, my father? Or perhaps you'd like to hear the story about my husband, Bastien the Bold, who would love to see what accommodations you've given his Untouchable wife. I've got a great story about the time some of Morgan le Fae's soldiers messed with me, and Link the Terrifying slit their throats in vengeance for breaking the highest law." I met Finnegan's eyes without a snarl and without a plea, so he didn't feel like I'd handed him control over my fate. My hands were bound, and I was truthfully without a prayer, but I didn't want him to feel that. I wanted him to know he was trying to hold back a tidal wave. Sooner or later, I would crush him.

Finnegan didn't get up, but leaned back in his oversized wooden chair. "Those are some mighty tales. Got any proof?"

"You could let me summon Kerdik here as my witness. I'm not sure you've seen the fountain he made for me in Avalon. I could show you the ring he put on my finger, and the one Bastien gave me, too."

"Well, you've got the accent down. We've not had any Avalonians in here before." Finnegan studied my face, no doubt hoping I would fidget and give away my nerves. I remained steady, meeting his gaze with a steely one of my own. "If you're the Avalon Rose, then what are ye doing in Éireland?"

"Healing the Werewolves. I assume you want that problem taken care of."

He scoffed at me. "Ye can't heal a Werewolf."

"I can't heal ignorance, and yours runs deep. Werewolves are easy." The insult rolled off my tongue, and I wondered if it would cost me. "If you want a good show, bring in a Werewolf. Bring him in alive and unharmed, and I'll show you they can be healed."

His squint didn't waver, even as he clicked his fingers and pointed to the door. His guard obeyed the unspoken command, and left to send more vigilantes on a mission that I hoped wouldn't end in bloodshed. "Tha's all well and good, but it'll only buy you as many hours as it takes to get the Were creature here. If your little trick doesn't work, I'm moving ye up the row."

"Fine by me. If I'm wrong, you can even slam some salmon on my head to give yourselves a nice little barbecue when you throw me in."

Finnegan let slip a little smirk at my grim humor, but quickly covered it with his stoic almost-scowl. "Ye don't seem as worried as ye should be."

"You know, you're like, the tenth dumbass who's said that to me. I think picturing what Bastien, Link and Madigan are going to do to your carcass is what gives me that confident glow. Or maybe it's the screams of the damned down there. I dunno."

"You've got a mouth on ye, tha's for sure."

"Believe me, if I thought I could talk actual sense into you, I'd be jawing away. I have no interest in wasting my breath trying to fix your stupidity."

Finnegan stood, and I had to remind myself not to stumble backwards. He was almost as tall as Mad, and nearly as beefy. "I'd heard the Avalon Rose turned Vamp, but to see it with my own eyes? Ye aren't how I pictured ye."

"And how do you spend your time thinking about me?" I asked with a maudlin smile.

He cleared the gap with two strides, his remaining guard watching the exchange with boredom. It was clear Finnegan didn't need a guard; they just looked good to the opposition.

Finnegan took my hair in his fist and jerked my head to the side, eyeing my bandage curiously. His whisper in my ear had the stench of creep to it, but I didn't give him the satisfaction of a cringe. "I pictured ye in a gown with a grand crown on your head. Yet ye come to me like this –

bloody, bandaged, and with a scowl tha could make any man want to kiss away your pout."

"Put that on the list of things to tell my husband you said to me when he tears off your balls and feeds them to you."

He chuckled, though I couldn't tell you why. His thick finger felt like leather as it peeled the bandage away from my neck. "If you're marked, tha's something."

"I am, but my neck tattoo was burned by the Nain Rouge. My wrist tattoo's still intact, though."

Finnegan frowned at the skin that I could hear crinkling with its blackened edges. "Well, there's something there, but it's hard to make out. The Nain Rouge, ye say? Tha's another tall tale. The Nain's been locked…"

"Inside Cailleach's cane, I know. But he escaped. We locked him back inside, though. Now the only monsters who set nonsensical fire to innocent people are you guys."

Finnegan's hand latched onto my chin, squeezing to let me know he didn't appreciate my lip. His grip was bruising, but I fought with everything in me not to let out a whimper. Those would do no good in here. His mouth was a mere two inches from mine when he bent over to get in my face. "Tha's enough out of ye." He examined my eyes, as if searching for signs of flight or fear.

I refused to cower, instead raising my eyebrow in a "Is this really your best move, dude?" kind of way.

"I'll admit, you've got that royal way about ye. Everyone else tha comes in pleads with us to let them go. They've got family. They've got friends. They're harmless." He sighed, letting his breath cover my face. "It's tiresome. To see ye come in here without the usual tears is a sight for sore eyes, tha's for sure."

When he removed his hand, giving my face a shove to the side, I made a point not to flex my jaw and open my mouth to test for damage. If there was damage, there wasn't a lick of help for me, so there was no use confirming it. "How inconvenient, the tears of the damned."

"Aye." I didn't like it when Finnegan drew his knife from its sheath on his belt. I liked the situation even less when he coiled his arms around me, as if we were slow dancing. His breath was hot on my forehead, and his smile at my unconcealed discomfort at having him so near set my teeth on edge. My breasts were smashed to his torso, so I tried not to breathe. He leaned in to whisper sweet nothings in my ear, making panic rise in my chest. "I want to get a look at tha wrist of yours to see if your tattoo is really there. If ye try to escape, what do ye think's going to happen?"

I ran through the list of things I'd already endured at the hands of Faîte, and tried not to tremble as his body engulfed mine. "I won't live long enough to regret it. Blah, blah, blah. I know the drill." I tried to sound as if I didn't give a crap, but my quickened breath and my uncontrollable shudder didn't fool anyone.

"Tha's a good girl." Even after he'd cut my wrists free, he didn't pull back. Instead I remained in his embrace, stuck in limbo where I was too afraid to draw in a breath. "Have ye been a good girl?"

My skin crawled with ripples of disgust. "I think you should ask my husband that question. Make sure you're holding me just like this when you do."

He backed me up against the wall, and I had to fight at the panic with an imaginary steel sword so I didn't freak out and give him exactly what he wanted. He tugged my arms to the sides, pressing his massive body to mine so that I was pinned to the cold wall.

"Let's have a look, then." He peered down at my wrists, clearly seeing the tattoo that marked me as Untouchable. He swore, not in surprise, but in defeat. "She's telling the truth," he said over his shoulder to his guard. "We can't kill her without breaking the highest law. Vampire or not, we can't burn her."

3

FINNEGAN'S MISSION

I should've felt vindicated, but all I felt was sick. The only reason I was being allowed to live was because of who my husband was, not because of who I was. I knew I should take the victory and run, but all I'd managed to save was my own life. Marcia was still down there, as were the others who didn't have an Untouchable to care about their plight.

Finnegan sent his guards out to track down the Untouchables, and to fetch me some water to wash my face. He downed a glass of something amber in color that made him wince before he spoke to me. He stood next to his throne, though this time without the air of ownership. "When your husband comes, you'd do well to remember tha I didn't lay a hand on ye."

"I'm guessing the bruises on my face from when you grabbed my jaw will do the tattling for me. You know, I don't get you. You respect the Untouchables, but you don't have any decency for your fellow countrymen? How's that measure out?" Now that I wasn't as afraid I'd be offed on the spot, my tongue loosened to argue for Marcia's case. I pressed my ring to my chest and muttered Kerdik's name three times. Then for good measure, I did the same ritual to call Cailleach. Might as well bring in the entire arsenal.

Now that my arms were free, I knew what to do. I held up my hands and tried to shoot out ice from my palms. Dread made my heart sink when I realized that my mojo Cailleach had granted me was failing. No more than a puff of cool air wafted from my palms, bringing too many cuss words to my brain. She'd warned me the magic she was granting me would fade. It was her hope we'd have this all wrapped up before her gift drifted away.

If only.

Finnegan didn't even notice my attempt to freeze him, so ineffectual was my borrowed magic. "I'm fighting for redemption in Éireland. The Vampire curse is pure evil. There's not a lick of good in any of the Vamps. They tear through villages and leave no survivors."

"That's the *Farouche* Vamps, which I can cure."

Finnegan eyed me with skepticism. "I heard wind of the *Farouche* Vampires in Avalon being cured. I didn't put much hope in it, I'll admit."

"What about me? I'm an *Attelage* Vamp, and I'm clearly not ripping through villages. We mate with one person, and that's that."

"Oh, so we're supposed to look the other way because you've confined your hunger to one person? What about tha person's rights? And ye know tha when their mate dies, the Vamp can move onto another. They can just as easily drain a village as a *Farouche* can."

"In theory, sure, but we're all in our right minds. I'm standing here right now, having a rational conversation with you. I'm clearly not going to drain you on the spot."

"But ye could. I've seen it happen."

I studied the weightiness in his small eyes, and the untold anger he kept barricaded inside. "Who did you lose to an *Attelage* Vampire?"

I took a shot, and when his eyes widened, I knew I'd hit the right nerve.

He drew in several weighted breaths before he replied in a low voice. "My wife was picking wheat in the fields when an *Attelage* scum happened upon her. He was starving, and took a bite before she could escape."

"What happened to her?"

"After she left me for him, her body was found not a week later. She was happy with me before he came along, and now she's dead."

I nodded, giving his confession a little space to breathe in the open air. It seemed like it had been bottled up inside of him for far too long. "What was her name?"

"It doesn't matter. I gave her a good life, and she left me for a creature with no soul."

I didn't bother arguing that last point. "It's a strange

thing, the bond between an *Attelage* Vampire and her mate. I was lucky that my husband happened to be the one I mated with. It made everything far more intense than either of us were prepared for. I can't imagine going through that with a stranger. Both of them must've been so confused."

He slammed his glass down on the end table with all the finality of a king. "I don't care about their confusion. She left me for a monster – a monster who ended up killing her. I can't kill ye because of your mark and the fact tha you're the Avalon Rose, but if those things weren't true, I'd chuck ye into the fire with the rest of them. Make no mistake, tha's where ye belong."

I didn't know what to say to that. I mean, I wasn't exactly spotless in all of this. I'd almost killed Bastien once in a feeding frenzy. I loved him with all my heart, but in the mess of the moment, I hadn't been able to see him. I'd only seen the blood. "I get what you're saying, but this isn't the way."

"Should we do what Province 10 did? Just cast out the Vampires and hope they don't find their way back in? How solid did tha plan work for ye?"

"That was King Urien's mistake. You think I have no soul? Really? My dad kicked me out of my home – the home I gave back to him after I helped resurrect him from Morgan le Fae's spellwork. He threw me out, but even he knows I have a soul."

"Ye couldn't possibly. I looked into my wife's eyes the

day she told me she was leaving with tha creature, and I couldn't see none of what I loved about her. She wasn't there anymore. She'd been replaced by something heartless. It's the only way to explain why she left."

I looked on Finnegan's hard expression with a sadness I couldn't brush aside. If I'd known him under different circumstances, I'd have hugged him and let him tell me everything that weighed him down. As I was still his prisoner, I kept the hugging to a minimum. "It's addiction," I explained. "When we feed, it releases a chemical that makes us crave our mate, and our mate gets that same high. It's crazy powerful, but it's not a soul-eraser. All the same, though, I'm sorry she left you. I'd like to think you didn't deserve that. Though, you're a mass-murderer now, so maybe you did. Maybe she got out just in time."

"You're too mouthy for a woman on death row."

"You're too broken to be making decisions that affect hundreds of people."

"More than hundreds," he corrected me with a superior glint in his eyes. "We burned our thousandth body last week."

"Mazel tov," I replied dryly.

One of his guards came back in with a pitcher halfway filled with water, and a basin with a washcloth. He set it on the table and spoke quietly to Finnegan. "I sent out two of our fastest riders in the direction we found her. Word's already spreading tha we kidnapped the Avalon Rose."

"Spreading how?"

"Word's been sent overseas from the Untouchables to King Urien and Duke Lot. If this thing comes down on us, ye won't keep your head. Best smooth things over before Duke Lot sends his army to get her back."

Finnegan cursed, pulling out a piece of parchment and a pot of ink with a quill. Hurriedly, he scrawled out who knows what and shoved it at his guard. "Send this to Avalon. I'll not start a war over this." He glared at me. "Are ye happy now?"

I poured out a little water and started washing my face. Having the blood and grime wiped from my skin felt almost as good as the luxurious bath I truly craved. "I'm jumping for joy on the inside. Enjoy your little operation here. Once the army comes for me, your vigilante days are over."

"They're coming to free ye, not the Vamps. Those are destined for the fire, and there's nothing ye can do about it. Ye aren't our queen. Ye don't cast orders in Éireland over what we do with our people. Queen Shavon okayed our operation, and tha's who we answer to."

"Show me to your furnace," I demanded once my face was clean enough.

"You'll stay right here."

"Actually, I'm the Queen of Avalon, so I'm fairly certain I'm allowed to go wherever I friggin' feel like. The accommodations you've offered left something to be desired. I'd like to see the furnace. Warm my cold hands a bit."

Finnegan's lips tightened beneath his mustache. "Fine. Right this way, your majesty."

He made to grab my arm, but I responded with a sharp punch to his bicep. "I'm Untouchable," I reminded him with a growl. "I can walk without being manhandled, and you can show me the way without breaking the highest law."

It was at that moment I saw the wheels of doom turning in his mind. He'd put his hands on me. I'd been bound by his men. I'd been shoved in a cage. He'd broken the highest law several times over, and there was no escaping that fact. Perhaps without the blood streaking my face I looked a little more myself, and not like a prisoner they could walk all over. Dread began to wipe away the in-control bravado he'd worn, and he opened the door without his signature sneer. "Right this way, your majesty."

It was the one time I was grateful for my royalty card. With my shoulders rolled back, I wore my jeans as if they were the finest gown, my steps heavy with purpose as he led me through the compound to the place where too many had met their untimely end.

I felt the heat before I saw the room. Sweat began to bead on my forehead, though it wasn't just from the flames that licked at the circular iron door inside the furnace room. I could practically hear the sounds of the many people who'd been burned alive, their shouts for mercy falling on willfully deaf and ignorant ears. I wondered how often that same deafness struck me, and did a quick evaluation to be sure I wasn't condemning anyone who hadn't been given their fair chance.

"You've seen it. Now come to the bunkers. It's nicer up there."

I turned slowly, digging my heels into a fight I hadn't been born for, but life itself had pushed me into. "When the Untouchables get here, or Duke Lot or whoever, you can send them down here for me. I'm not moving from this spot until they come and take me away."

Finnegan sighed. "Ye can't stay here. It's far too hot for more than a few minutes."

I peered into the window of the furnace room, knowing I had no other choice. "If you want to burn any other bodies, you'll have to forcibly remove me, which violates the highest law. I'm not sure if you've seen Madigan the Formidable's victims, but he tends to deconstruct before he lets them die. He doesn't much care for people breaking the highest law. I'd send your men out with axes if you want to keep this place good and heated.

"Ye don't have the authority to enforce your laws here! This is Éireland, not Avalon. We deal with monsters in our own way."

"Well, this is how I deal with monsters, and since my Untouchable card trumps your megalomaniac card, I get to win this one."

He was at a loss for words, stammering and fuming until he jabbed his finger at me, a bull backing down in front of a bunny. "Bastien the Bold must be a masochist, marrying ye. You're a right pill, ye are."

"I'll be sure to tell him you said so." When he didn't move from his spot, I quirked my eyebrow at him. "Don't you have some squirrels to yell at or something?"

"This isn't over!"

A delicious thought occurred to me, brushing a wicked smile across my face. "Isn't one of the perks of being an Untouchable that I get to take whatever land I want for myself?"

Finnegan's eyes grew wide. "Ye can't do tha without Queen Shavon here to sign over the deed."

I snapped my fingers a few times just to be a jerk. "Chop, chop, then. Go summon Queen Shavon. I'd like this deed in my name by tomorrow morning. I think I'll redo the dungeon, too, since I'll have no use for it in the traditional sense. Prisoners aren't people, correct? We're just property? In that case, I'll be seizing that, too."

Finnegan sneered at me, furious that I made him play by the rules of his own land, and I'd won. "I'll send for Queen Shavon in the morning. Until the deed is signed over, the prisoners and this property belong to me."

I crossed my arms over my chest, ready to stand my ground all friggin' day. "Enjoy your last moments, Princess," I snarled as Finnegan stomped away.

4

PIMP DADDY TO THE RESCUE

Day three of standing my ground felt a little like slowly melting, and going through the worst detox of my life. No spa on earth could squeeze the impurities from my pores like the furnace could. They'd been burning a body every six hours, but they'd been overestimating how long the flames could last in the giant abyss. They'd tried to coax me out of the way with food, and then blood. I'd rolled my eyes at the ridiculous attempt, and how little knowledge they actually had about *Attelage* Vampires.

I was starving, that was for sure. I wanted Bastien's blood like you wouldn't believe. The heat made me sweat out the nourishment I'd taken from him the last time I'd fed, making my four days of being without blood seem like the full seven.

Nevertheless, I stood my ground. I'd sweat through the

same clothes I'd been wearing for more than half a week, but I refused to give them an inch, knowing if I did, they'd have the next body ready to go. When I felt the waves of hunger and exhaustion, I pictured Marcia's terrified face as she'd clung to my cell's bars. Her fear became my touchstone, emboldening me to stand my ground.

My brain began to drift, talking in roundabout swirls as the hours stretched on. The heat made me loopy, and each time the guys came to check and see if I'd moved an inch, I laughed like a madwoman. After everything I'd endured, maybe I was finally cracking. I was trying to right a system that wasn't even mine, and put order to anarchy with no backup. I prayed my royalty card would hold, but there was no guarantee that one thing or another wouldn't send them over the edge.

In my heated haze, I saw Judah standing next to me, leaning on the door. I frowned at him. "Don't do that, Pimp Daddy. It's too hot there. Stand over here."

"What for? I'm not real. I can stand wherever I feel like. I can even do this." Judah started doing the Macarena, making me laugh at the outdated and exaggerated moves. "It's good to hear your laugh, Hot Mama." He slapped his knee and mimed laughing. "Get it? Because it's so hot in here." He stood straight and smiled. "Miss you."

"I miss you, too. Man, was it a million years ago we used to live together? Because it feels like way too long. This grownup stuff? Sucks super way bad."

Judah snorted. "Let me check my calendar." He

pretended to flip through his day planner. "Why yes, it's right here. Exactly one million years to the date. Happy anniversary, roomie."

"I'm thinking your life in Tulsa is slightly more glamorous than this." I motioned around the bare walls of the long hallway that separated the furnace from the rest of the place. As great as it was to see Judah, the comfort of my BFF made me weepy for the real thing. Now that there was someone to whine to, I let myself feel the misery in my bones. "I'm hungry, and I don't feel so good."

He motioned around the hallway. "This thing you're doing here. Is it important?"

I nodded, morose in that truth.

"More important than food?"

"More important than me. There are dozens in there, and probably tons more that'll be brought in to fill those cells and be burned alive." My throat was beyond dry. My lips were cracked from dehydration. Even my eyeballs felt parched. "Burned alive, Judah."

"I can watch the door for a while, you know."

Hope sprang in my chest, though a niggling voice in the back of my brain warned me about... something. "Really? I just need to sleep for a little bit. Get some distance from the heat. I'm not doing so hot, Judah."

"Go on. I've got this." His voice started to sound like Bastien's, and his face mutated to the man I needed to see more than anyone else. His cadence deepened, and the geektastic t-shirt Judah had been rocking changed into flannel. "Daisy, you don't look so good."

"I don't... Bastien, I..." I wanted to gracefully collapse into his arms, but somehow I fell right through his grip. Sleep covered me like a blanket, and as much as I tried to keep up the good fight, my body decided it was quite finished. Bastien and Judah disappeared from my vision, and the world faded from view, plunging me into a deep sleep.

5

MARCIA, MARCIA, MARCIA

I awoke to the smell of roast beef, my stomach raging to get at anything that might satiate the starvation that was set in deep. Though I didn't want to consume meat, my stomach felt like it was eating itself. There was blood in my mouth, and I licked at the source greedily. It was only then I realized I'd bitten through the skin on my knuckle, and was suckling on the digit like a baby sucking her thumb.

I sat up, groaning as every bone in my body protested the movement. There was a plate of dinner on the side table, and a pitcher of water with a basin. The room was small, no larger than the quaintest dorm, but it was quiet, and I was alone. I cracked my neck and twisted my waist, but both those simple acts made me want to climb back into the bed.

The roll looked safe, so I munched on the hard crust. I

knew it wouldn't sustain me, but it couldn't hurt to take in a few calories. The water was room temperature, and felt like the best thing in the world, apart from blood. My body screamed at the liquid to be thicker and red. It howled for the tasteless nothing to be one hundred percent pure Bastien. I talked myself down as best I could, reminding my stomach that there just weren't any other options right now. I was... somewhere.

I glanced around, taking a few minutes to recall where I was, and what I was supposed to be doing. A guilty gasp ripped from my cracked lips, and as much as I wanted to lie back down and cry through the pain that felt etched deep inside my body, I knew I shouldn't be here. I downed the rest of the water, splashed some on my face, swallowed the rest of the vegetarian portions of the meal, and moved cautiously from the room.

I wasn't expecting a roadblock the second I opened the door, but there he was – Rudy, with a submissive tilt to his head. "Good morning, your majesty. Can I get ye anything?"

"You can step aside, so I can get back to the furnace. How'd I even get up here?"

"Ye passed out. Conked your head pretty bad. Do ye want me to send the doc up to look at ye again? He bandaged up your neck while ye were out."

"No, thanks. How long have I been out?"

"It's been about twelve hours since we found ye passed out."

I bit down on my lower lip, perplexed. Where was Kerdik? He didn't have to travel through the snow, as the others did. He could port in and save the day, only he hadn't. My eyebrows pushed together in consternation, wondering why he hadn't come for me. Had he written me off, finally deciding that it was too much to keep me in his life? Would he let me suffer like this? If my Untouchable card hadn't worked, would he have let me burn? The ache in my chest felt like a bowling ball's worth of weight that I knew I'd carry around for a good, long while. Kerdik was gone, and I was on my own.

I did my best to appear in control. "Excuse me, Rudy. I've got a date with a furnace."

"It won't do ye no good, your majesty. They're all gone."

I quirked my eyebrow at him. "Finnegan left you alone in charge of all the Vampires? That sounds like a recipe for a mutiny if I ever saw one."

"The Vampires," he clarified. "We ran them each through while ye were sleeping. We'll burn them on the schedule as needed to heat the building, but the deed is done." He had the grace to lower his head to me. "Apologies, your majesty."

My mouth fell open in stunned silence. "I didn't mean to faint. I didn't mean to sleep! No! It can't be over! I did everything I could!"

"Aye, it was a valiant effort, but this is our way. You're in Éireland, not Avalon." His words were a gentle scolding, as if I was a child.

"I want to see the cells," I said without hesitation. Every movement felt like my bones were being jarred from their sockets, but this was something I had to do. I brushed past Rudy, but made it only five steps before I was winded. My body was wussing out on me, and I wasn't even sure which way the dungeon was. My gut was too hungry for my Compass to give me proper directions.

Rudy took pity on me, gently taking my elbow to guide me back to my room. "Now, now. Ye look barely upright. I don't think stairs are the right choice for ye. There's nothing to be done about it. They're all long gone."

I turned and pounded my fists to his chest, though the effort hurt me more than it did him. I felt how ineffectual my fight was, and I let out a bleat of shame. My brilliant plan had saved only me. Stupid Remedial Rosie, who couldn't stay awake long enough to save people who couldn't speak for themselves. There had to have been a better way. I'd failed them, every last one of them.

"You killed them all! What makes me any different? You have no clue how the world works. All you're getting is a bunch of broken families who are missing whole chunks now because they don't understand what's happened! They don't know that we can be normal! I'm normal! I still have something to contribute to society! I'm still a person! This is not my great adventure!" My fragile fists wailed on his chest, and he let me, barely flinching at my attack.

"Avalon can deal with ye as they see fit. If they haven't removed ye from your throne, we can't make tha call. But for our own kinsmen, we have tha authority. As much as it upsets ye, this is the way it is."

"What if you were the one infected? What song would you sing then? Would you roll over, or would you fight a broken system?"

I didn't realize he'd corralled me to my bedside until the backs of my thighs hit the straw mattress. "Get some rest, your majesty. Our fastest riders were sent out to find Bastien the Bold, and others sent word to Avalon. Someone will be here to collect ye soon enough."

I glanced at the bed, not wanting a lick of comfort after all I'd been through. "Take me to the dungeon. The Queen of Avalon issued a command. Are you really so dense as to ignore it?" I grimaced at sounding exactly like my mother's daughter.

Rudy sighed, knowing he had very little choice in the matter. "Aye. I'll take ye. But I don't think ye should be out of bed. Ye look sickly."

I didn't respond, but I did let him take my hand. His other arm curved around my waist to ensure I didn't fall, which I was on the verge of doing. I kept my mouth shut through the agony that the simple act of walking pushed through my body. Everything in me wanted to give up and let unconsciousness take me all over again, but I knew that if I succumbed, it was anyone's guess who else might die. There would be more Vampires brought in, and they would need someone to block the furnace. Though I was fairly certain a stiff breeze might knock me over at this point, a waif in the way was better than nothing.

The only good the water did me was give me a fresh supply of tears that dripped down my face when I took in the row of lifeless bodies. There they were, lining the hallway like Legos, freshly killed and stacked three high all the way down on each side. My vision blurred with the red I couldn't dismiss.

Rudy dropped his grip on me and jumped back, crying out in horror. "What's happened to your face? Why are ye... are ye bleeding from your eyes? Ah!"

"They're tears. I cry blood now. Kerdik blessed me, and it did funky things to my body." I inched painfully down the row, searching for Marcia's body. She'd been wearing a stained beige apron, and a simple calico dress that looked like she was ready for days on the prairie.

Rudy came alongside me again and supported my elbow. "Come now, you've seen the bodies. Tha's enough. Let's get ye back to your room."

"You killed Marcia." My eyes scanned the hallway until I saw the hem of a blue dress sticking out from one of the rows. I hobbled over to her, yelping at the sight of the woman I'd done my best to save. Now she was tucked inside a pile of dead bodies. "You killed Marcia!"

"Who?"

"You didn't even learn their names?"

"They're not people, so no. It makes it easier if we don't know their names."

I knelt next to her and held her head, crying out at the pain this simple action caused me. I wept over her body, crying for a woman I didn't truly know, but I'd failed all the same. "You're not a Jabberwocky," I whispered. "I know you're not a monster. I'm so sorry, sister." I kissed her bloodstained forehead, tears trickling down my cheeks and adding to the mess that probably had been a lovely face, once upon a better time. "I tried, but I didn't... I'm so sorry."

Rudy sighed. "I don't need to see this, and neither do ye. Let's get out of here, and get ye to a more comfortable room."

"You'll take others," I said, my voice gravelly and deadly with intent. "This won't be the end of it."

"We'll keep going until the land is purged."

I allowed his hands to hoist me up, but when we reached the row of cells on our way toward the stairs that led to the livable parts of the compound, I paused. "Here," I said, pointing to the first cell on the block. "I'll stay here until someone comes for me."

"Ye can't stay in a cell. We moved one of the lads out so ye could have a room all to yourself. See? We obey the law." He said this as if to push a vote in his favor for when the Untouchables came to clean house.

I gripped the iron rungs of the cell and pushed the door open. Letting go of his arm, I stepped inside, sinking to the floor and sitting in the murky puddle of blood, vomit and urine. "This is where you put me when you brought me in, so I think I'll stay where I belong. The next person to die so you don't have to chop wood will be me. No one else dies for this."

Rudy made like he wanted to snatch me up, but hesitated, knowing he couldn't put his hands on me without permission, on pain of death. "Finnegan's not going to like this."

"Well, it sounds like you've got an awkward conversation coming your way, pal. Now, if you'll excuse me, I've got some decorating to do in my new room." I took a fistful of the vomit and blood, and started painting the bars of my cell with it, just to gross him out and show him that I meant business.

Rudy stepped away from the crazy lady, which was one point in favor of his cognitive reasoning. Rudy looked as if he feared my insanity might be airborne, and would find its way into him. "I'll, um, I'll be back with some water and some... I'll be back."

I listened to his footsteps echo down the lifeless cell-block, and up the stairs into the bustle that was kept from me. In hindsight, sitting in the filth probably wasn't my best move, but I didn't get up. I was too tired, my body too sore for normal movements. I'd wanted to save them, but I could only save myself. If help didn't find me soon, I wouldn't even be able to pull *that* off. Dozens had died because I was weak.

I hadn't been able to think up a solution to save them, confirming that I was every bit as dumb as my test scores claimed. I was Remedial Rosie, as I'd always suspected.

My eyes drifted shut, giving the cruelty in the world free reign to run amuck, since I was powerless to stop it. I didn't lift my head, but sank down into the sick, my breathing shallow and pained. I didn't stand when Finnegan's boots thundered down the steps.

I didn't even rouse enough for words when I felt rough hands try to shake me awake however many hours or days later.

"No! No! What have you done to her?" Water was poured over my face, and the flies that had made my body their perch of preference buzzed away at the intrusion. "Bastien, she needs blood. Hurry!" I felt my body being carried out of the cell, but my eyes wouldn't open to confirm it. I was floating, whether in death or in life, I wasn't sure, and couldn't find the wherewithal to care. Everything was an abyss of floating realities, and I wasn't sure which one I was stuck in this time.

Warm liquid was dribbled into my pried-open mouth, and my parched throat swallowed on reflex. A trickle of life shot through me, but it wasn't enough to get me to sit up on my own. I couldn't even lift my head, but that small swallow helped to clear a little of the fog that had trapped my brain for so long. I tried to ask where I was, but my vocal chords were useless – raw strands that might as well have puffed out dust when rubbed together.

More water, more disparate voices that made no sense

to me. I wasn't even sure if they were speaking the same language. All I knew was that there was food nearby. Someone was rinsing my hair, and wiping my face with a wet washrag. The material felt bristly as it swept over my cheeks. My skin felt so thin and papery that I wondered if the cloth might cut me.

I heard a man's voice roaring with some crazy command that I couldn't decipher, and then lots of shouts that sounded like grown men whimpering.

That was all I could make out before I lost consciousness again.

6

BASTIEN'S TEARS

felt my body being rocked as if I was in a cradle, the gentle motion moving me back and forth like a lullaby I didn't want to wake from. I imagined André René Roussimoff was holding me in his giant arms, singing to me with his odd voice that always made me smile. In my dream, he wasn't dead, and I wasn't on the verge. Or perhaps I was also dead, and this was my version of Heaven.

But I didn't deserve such comforts. The Vampires had died because of me. Because I was weak. Because I hadn't found a way to save them. Because I was nothing more than the Stupid Girl.

I went back to sleep, though as I shifted in Andre's burly arms, my body didn't hurt as much. I could move without wincing. I could only hope that with a few more hours, I might be able to sleep away my whole life, and put the sordid details of my cockroach-like survival behind me. I could rest in André Roussimoff's arms, and let him do the heavy lifting of the world's problems. He was built for it, after all.

"Honey, I need you to try to swallow," Bastien's voice said to me. It sounded like he was speaking through a funnel, from too far away. Even so, I did as he requested. Really, he'd asked precious little of me in the last year. This seemed to be the least I could do.

My throat ached, but as I swallowed, the funnel shortened, bringing his voice nearer. "Good, babe. A little more."

My throat constricted, and warmth slid down my esophagus, coating my insides with a glow that healed as it oozed through me like honey. I shifted in Andre's arms, and felt soft flannel rub across my bare breasts. The scent of Bastien filled my lungs, making me dizzy with sensation. My lips parted, silently asking for more.

"Daisy, can you hear me? Open your eyes. Tell me you can hear me." His voice was desperate, but my eyelids still felt too heavy to commit to the effort of opening for him. I wanted to see my husband, but my body wasn't cooperating.

I let out a small mewl that I hoped communicated something like, "I totally hear you. I'm alright, or I'm dead. Not sure. Either way, you're hot, and I'd do you right now if I could lift my head."

"Rosie! Honey, wake up. Open your eyes for me. Please,

baby. Have some more blood." Warmth dribbled into my mouth, but hot tears also splashed down on my face, pooling in the corners of my eyes, as if his tears were my own. I didn't like him being in pain. There were so many times I'd broken down, but he hadn't. The only times I'd ever seen him cry were when I was beyond repair.

I didn't want to be the Broken Girl, yet here I was, unable to lift my hand to comfort the man I loved. I swallowed, determined to get better so he never had to weep again.

"We're almost to shore," a man's voice I didn't recognize said. "My house is closer than the castle, if you'd rather take her there until she's better. You can stay with me as long as you'd like."

There was a pause, and then Bastien said through his tears, "What if she doesn't get better?"

The second voice was kind, and drew near to us, as if moving forward to pat Bastien on the back to rally him. "Vampires can withstand more than a week of starvation. It's been not too much more than that. It's going to take time to bring her back, but don't you worry, Son. She'll come back. We've got seals that are tugging us back to Avalon far faster than the wind alone could take us." There was a long pause, and then the man said, "I admit, I never thought I'd see you in love. When you agreed to marry my Rachelle, part of me was grateful, but the other part was unbearably sad for you."

My ears perked up as my muddled brain pushed

together the facts. *Reyn's dad.* If this was Reyn's father, then he was technically my grandfather. I strained to lift my chin, but my body was too stiff for pleasantries.

I worked down five more gulps of blood before unconsciousness claimed me again.

7

A TASTE OF BASTIEN

"Get back, old man, or so help me, I'll knock you on your ass if you come near her."

It wasn't the best way to be roused, but my eyes opened finally, letting the interior of the lantern-lit castle flood my vision. I gasped at being able to see again. Each time I opened my eyes felt like a miracle I didn't take for granted. The ceiling passed overhead, the solid beams painted gold to reflect the light and show off Morgan's opulence. It was *my* opulence now, I guess, but it didn't feel like it. I hadn't taken the time to Scrooge McDuck my way through a roomful of gold, swimming in the wealth with a grin on my face. I tried to picture myself doing the back-stroke through an ocean of coins, but it was too much a caricature to look like me in the daydream.

"She's my daughter, Bastien, and you'll not keep me from her."

"The only reason we're here is because Kerwin didn't have the herbs Remy needed to heal her. The rules haven't changed. You turned your back on her, so enjoy the view of her life at a distance. She doesn't so much as hear a peep from your mouth when she finally wakes up, understand? I don't want her to ever see your face again. You live under her roof because she's a better person than either of us are."

"I guess I deserved that."

"Shut up and move. Go do whatever it is that kept you from crossing the ocean to claim your only daughter."

"You understand nothing. You're a boy still. You're responsible for one woman, and that's all. I'm responsible for my entire province. I can't just leave them. And what's the meaning of letting Dullahan into the castle? We have standards, Bastien."

"She sets the rules for this place, not you! Remy and Demi risked their necks for her, so they can stay as long as they feel like it. And don't give me the whole 'can't be pulled away from my job' bit. Lot left Avalon to find Rosie! Lot didn't blink, and she's not his daughter. She gave you your life back, and you can't take a few sick days to rescue hers? You're Morgan's husband, till your last pathetic breath!"

"Enough, now." Lugh's interjection made me rally, but I couldn't find my voice. "Bastien, I've got her. Ye can duke this out with the king all ye like, but Rosie's bones are fragile. Tha boat trip didn't do her no favors. Remy said she needs to lie down."

"Fine. I'll be up in a second. Careful not to let her arms swing. It hurts her when they move too much."

Lugh sounded confused, but hopeful. "Did she tell you tha? Has she woken up?"

"I can tell because I'm her husband! I'm her *Guardien*. If she's in pain, I know about it. I found her in those godforsaken barracks because it's her *lueur* inside of me! I know my wife!"

"Alright, alright. Settle, Bastien. I was only asking. Come on, Remy. Demi, can ye grab the gear and bring it into the castle?"

"Yes, of course. Malone, stay with Rosie. Make sure her room is well-guarded." Demi's voice gave commands easily, as if needing to establish that he wasn't here as a slave any longer. I couldn't imagine how difficult it must've been for Demi to walk back into the place he'd been a slave in for so many years.

It wasn't until my body felt the luxury of the queenly plush sheets beneath it did my limbs stop groaning, protesting any and all movement.

"Rosie, can you hear me?" Remy said, his two fingers pressing on my wrist to fish for a pulse.

I opened my eyes, which was my grandest feat, my show-stopping circus trick.

He clapped his hands to gain Lugh's attention. *"She's awake!"*

Lugh rushed to my side, scooping up my hand so he could see my amazing accomplishment. "Prim, can ye hear us? Can ye see? It's Lugh, and you're in your castle. Talk to me, lass."

"*Her skin is still cold. Up, Malone.*" Remy clicked his fingers at my wolf, and patted the mattress.

The soft warmth of Malone pressed up against me, like an oversized teddy bear I couldn't help but snuggle. I wanted to pet him, but couldn't lift my hand to commit to the effort. "*Queen Rosie, you're safe. Ye don't have to worry about a thing now. I'll watch over ye.*"

There were too many voices, and I couldn't answer any of them if I tried.

"*More blankets!*" Remy called, tugging on the comforter so Lugh understood. Remy bent over and opened his bag of tricks, digging in the bottom for some magical cure that I hoped he had buried in there somewhere. "*The only thing that'll cure you is more blood. Bastien will be up in a moment, I'm sure. Until then, I can make you a little more comfortable. Tell me where it hurts, and I can rub some numbing cream on the area.*"

I wanted to tell him, but my throat was too dry. There seemed to be a disconnect from my brain to my mouth, like whatever monkey up there was pulling the levers had fallen asleep at the wheel or something. Instead I blinked at him, wishing I could speak to tell him my legs ached so badly, I wanted to cry.

When Demi came in, it was with two thick blankets,

and the air of taking charge. "I thought she might need these. She's awake? Juliet, are you alright?"

My heart felt like it was being squeezed for all the emotion I had left in me. Demi's head rested against his chest in its sling, his eyes locking in on mine with an earnest plea for me to speak to him. I wanted to, but I couldn't.

"I'll draw her a bath. That should soothe the ache in her legs."

Remy's eyebrows scrunched together. *"Well, how did he guess that? Did I miss something?"*

I knew how. Demi had loved me. He was the best at his job, which had been to anticipate my needs. Even cut in two pieces as he was, he was ever himself, and after all he'd been put through, that was a beautiful thing.

Remy rubbed cream into my feet, my ankles, and my knees, each stroke taking away the ache that felt like it was set in too deep to ever fully heal. *"There. Is that a little better?"*

Soon enough, the room was filled with the scent of the rose oil Demi used to draw my baths with when we'd lived under this very roof and shared a room. It was so long ago. I felt like a different person now – or not a person, as the case may be.

When Bastien came into the room however long later, Lugh gave him the rundown while Demi fished through my drawers to find me something clean to wear. "What are you doing?" Bastien asked with an edge in his tone.

Demi shrugged. "Drawing a bath and laying out clothes for Rosie."

The moment the words hit the air, I knew they were the wrong ones. Bastien's slow seethe was already on tap after dealing with Urien. "You don't do anything that involves my naked wife."

Demi set the clothes on the foot of the bed and raised his hands. "You can see she's fully clothed. I wouldn't bed your wife, unless she specifically asked me to." Demi looked triumphant in spouting out the wrong words, choosing them carefully to dig under Bastien's skin.

"Malone, get him out of here before I throw his head into the moat!" Bastien roared, and I heard something crash outside of my view. Malone let loose an internal groan and hopped off the mattress, corralling Demi out of my bedroom.

Bastien's hands quaked as he shooed out the others with slightly less acid in his tone. He climbed into the bed and coiled his body around mine, warming us both. Then he pulled out his knife and cut a slit across the palm of his hand. "Here, Daisy. Drink a little more, then I'll let you go back to sleep."

Fighting with my languid body to stay awake was a chore, but I managed a few more minutes before my eyelids drifted shut. Bastien's arms around me soothed the ache the dungeon had bred into me. After being swelteringly hot for so long, it felt wrong to be cold. His breath on my shoulder lulled me to a haven I never wanted to leave as he spooned me into a dreamless sleep.

"I've got you, Daisy," he assured me as his breathing evened out. His body began to relax, now that we were together and safely tangled in the luxurious bed. "I've got you."

I AWOKE TO THE SUNLIGHT DANCING ON MY FACE, AND Bastien's hand palming my hip. I rolled onto my back, yawning and stretching under his watchful eye. He studied my movements to see how hurt I still was. My muscles were stiff and sore, but my limbs were mobile now, which was a vast improvement.

There were so many things I wanted to tell him – about the dungeon, about my suspected Gancanagh heritage, about Marcia. The only thing I could utter when my mouth finally opened was a woeful and passionate, "I missed you."

Bastien seemed to need to hear those simple words more than any other explanation about the harrowing events I could give him. He cupped my cheek and leaned down to brush a kiss to my lips. "I drove myself crazy trying to find you. What I wouldn't give for a little piece of your Compass. What kills me is we weren't all that far away. I followed the tug on the *lueur*. If I started to grow more restless, we changed directions. It was a slow, frustrating process, but we never stopped looking. I'm so, so sorry it took that long to find you."

My eyelids swept shut, relishing the peacefulness of the moment. It was a thing of sadness that there were so few to cling to these days. "You found me. I'm not in the dungeon."

"No, you're not in the dungeon."

"I'm in bed with my husband," I said, hinting at the need that never seemed to go away.

A low rumble vibrated Bastien's chest, and I knew I'd said the very right thing. His fingers danced on the collar of the flannel he'd wrapped me in while I'd slept, and now was desperate to peel off my body. He gazed down at my breasts, and I could feel his exhale warming my skin, caressing my form as only he could. "You have to get better, baby. This thing we've got going here? I can't turn it off. I'm barely holding on. I'm afraid I... Link and Mad are still in Éireland with Nicholai. I left them there so they could deal with the compound."

"How are they dealing with it?"

"Finnegan's dead. Link and Mad don't pull punches with stuff like that. It's safe to say that anyone who knew you were locked in that compound is now six feet under. I heard Link saying that he was going to drop the bodies off on Queen Shavon's doorstep to make a statement that the objectives of the compound were out of line." His hand trailed down my body, inciting more heat than either of us could deal with responsibly. "I need someone who can pull me off you if I start to lose my mind, or if you can't stop yourself when you're full. You need to feed more than a few drops."

I found the strength to nod, wondering what sort of solution he was hoping to come up with. He placed a kiss atop both my breasts, and I knew the flannel wouldn't last more than a minute on my body once we got started.

Bastien got up and popped his head out of the door. "Where's Remy? Fine. I guess you'll have to do."

When Lugh came back in, I didn't totally understand what was going to happen next. Bastien spoke to Lugh in hushed, assertive whispers that I couldn't decipher. Then Lugh nodded, his eyes wide as his gaze darted to me. "Um, sure. I can help with tha. Go ahead. Do what ye need to."

Bastien was shaking with longing as he climbed atop the mattress, and rolled on his side next to me. "Bite me, Daisy. I need it. I'm going crazy without you, and I know you need to feed." He moved my hair away from my forehead, and the simple touch made my body arch for him. "Lugh can pull you off me if you can't stop."

I was hesitant, mostly because I was afraid we would start dry humping in front of Lugh. After a gentle kiss to my lips, the need won out. My chin angled toward my prey, my nose stinging with the heady aroma of Bastien's natural scent. My hunter's senses led me to the crook of his neck, where the smell was concentrated, hitting me in waves of attraction that made my mouth water. I could barely move, but I rooted around until I found my favorite spot. When my teeth did what Vampire teeth do, a flood of warmth and delicious desire coated my tongue and ran down my throat. There was nothing else in my mind except for Bastien when I drew him past my lips. Everything in me screamed for more, so I took in all I could, my eyes livening with new light.

Bastien called out my name in the same way he did when we were in the throes, along with a string of curse words that flew out from his delirious lips. He grabbed a handful of my backside, squeezing and kneading, as if using the grip to hold himself back.

My bones stopped screaming at me the more I drank. I could inhale a full breath without effort now, and my clumsy fingers found their purpose as they combed through Bastien's hair and ran over his chest. His blood was bringing my body to life, giving pleasure to parts that mere minutes ago couldn't remember anything past the pain. I didn't want to live in agony, but needed a heavy dose of euphoria, which my husband gave to me in droves.

"Lugh, it's about to get Rated-R in here real quick. Would you mind waiting outside?" I asked, unable to tear my eyes from the wonder that was Bastien.

"Aye. Bastien, are ye alright for me to step out?"

"What she said." Bastien's nostrils were flared, and I knew he was seconds away from pouncing.

"Grand. Have fun, kids. Call if ye need me."

The moment the door shut, Bastien's hips found mine in a frenzied rhythm that was more teenager than grown man, but my fragile body was just as rabid for him. He cried out again and again, telling the castle by his moans and hurried grunts that we knew exactly what to do with a mattress all to ourselves.

My limbs finally found the strength to roll my body atop his, pinning him beneath me so I could strip what I wanted from his willing body. He'd awoken the beast, and I was ready to take what was mine.

Bastien was all mine, and I was his.

Lugh was standing just outside the door as our clothes were shed so we could comfort each other as only we knew how.

8

THE TRUTH IN THE MUTATIONS

When Lugh tore me off of Bastien, I'd reclaimed enough strength to claw clumsily at the hands that kept me from my guy. "Bastien!" I cried out, my heart rending in two at the small gap between our bodies.

"I'm alright, baby. Good call, Lugh. You got her off me before she took too much. Just give me a minute, and I can help you with her."

"More!" I demanded like the infant I was in that moment. It was lucky for Lugh that my muscles weren't fully operational. He was able to pin my arms to my sides and sweep my legs out from under me, making me kneel down with my back anchored to his heaving chest. I was wrapped in the sheet, and sorely wished we were far enough along with the whole cravings thing to where we didn't need a chaperone to listen outside the door to make sure things didn't get out of hand.

"Tha was a sight to see, Prim, but I think your man might need a few minutes to recoup. Breathe through it, now. Deep breaths."

The next few minutes were a series of labored inhales and exhales heard around the room. "I'm okay now," I assured Lugh, but he wasn't hearing it.

"Grand. I'm not sure your husband's up for round two, though."

Bastien managed to sit up and pull on pants. He picked his shirt up off the floor so he could use it to stem the flow of blood on his neck. He shot me a breathy smile, followed by a chuckle that we were together again. "We did it. I thought you might die in my arms, Daisy. I tried feeding you my blood, but you could barely swallow. What happened? I got you out of there before I heard any straight answers. Left Link and Mad to deal with the prisoners. They seemed geared up for tearing the place apart."

My voice was a little raspy, but the blood had done my body a world of good. I didn't realize I could stand until Lugh helped me up, and I walked unsteadily to the bed with only a little help. He handed me a t-shirt, underwear and jeans, and then turned around so Bastien could help me figure out how to clothe my clumsy form.

"Sorry about all that," I offered to Lugh, unable to make eye contact.

Lugh held up his hand to stave off my apology. "Don't think on it, Prim. We're in this together, aye?"

I blinked up at him, his words sticking into the vulnerable crevices of my heart. We were in this together, this double-long life. That he was intent on keeping me from accidentally killing my husband during our married time spoke volumes of just how lucky I was to have someone so decent in my corner. "Thank you. Truly."

"Are ye feeling better?"

"A hundred times better."

"Then it's all grand." He leaned against the wall and crossed his arms over his chest. "While Bastien's catching his breath, I want to know more about how ye got to the state we found ye in. We're all a little desperate for information. Start from the beginning."

It took a few false starts as I struggled to find the words, but eventually I was able to explain what the vigilantes had been doing, and my part in it all. The guilt was at the forefront, which couldn't be helped. "Her name was Marcia," I told them, the grief washing over me afresh. "They slaughtered them all because I passed out, and couldn't block the furnace door anymore. It's all my fault, Bastien! I had this great plan, but I couldn't stay awake long enough to make it stick."

"It doesn't sound like there was anything you could've done, short of calling Kerdik to clean house." Bastien added that last note begrudgingly, and I could tell how much it cost his pride.

My voice was quiet when I finally spoke. "I did call him, but he didn't come. Neither did Cailleach. Kerdik and I had a talk before he left. I told you. He said he's out."

Lugh looked worried. "No, he's not. If Kerdik didn't answer, something's wrong."

I shook my head. "He said he needed to put some distance between us. Watching me be married was too hard for him, so he needed to leave for a while. I'm thinking it's more the decades version of 'a while' than the few days to clear his head."

Bastien's face kept shifting from elated to dismayed. "But we're here to fix Avalon. We're fixing his nation, and he just bails? That's not right."

"How long did you expect he'd be cool with our arrangement? When he asked for space, it felt more like the permanent kind. I'm telling you, I paged him, but he didn't come. We're on our own with this."

Lugh leaned on the wall, facing us but looking miles away in his mind. "Did he say where he was going?"

"Just that he was off with Brìghde, going after Dother."

"I don't like it," Lugh ruled, as if that would change anything.

"How patient did we all assume Kerdik could be? I think he did pretty good, considering everything. How patient would you be if you had to watch the person you wanted to be with getting it on with her husband?" I wrapped my arms around myself, hoping that might cover my shame. "Kerdik wanted space, so we'll respect that. He's dealing with his dad, who's a pretty bad guy. Best case scenario, he kills his own father. I think life's put Kerdik through enough. I'll not add to his misery."

Lugh let my words sink in, but just as soon as he digested them, he spat them out. "Misery? Do ye really think it's not worth it to him to hold out for ye? Sure, maybe he wanted a breather from watching ye be so in love with Bastien, but there's no way he wouldn't come when ye called, unless he couldn't." His eyes clouded over with concern.

Bastien shook his head. "We're swimming in our own problems. Even if Kerdik was having trouble tracking down Dother, there's nothing we can do about it."

I sat up a little straighter, dragging the rose-scented air into my lungs and appreciating how my room here smelled nothing like the stank of the dungeon. "But I can. I can find anything. I can find Dother for him."

Bastien pinched the bridge of his nose. "See, that's where I'll pause you. He gave you that ability as your birth blessing, which means he had it to give. You can find things because he taught you how as a baby. So whatever's lost, he should be able to find it just as easily as you can."

Lugh and I shook our heads as if they were tied to the same string. "Tha's not how it works."

"And how would you know?"

Lugh shoved his hands in his pockets, his shoulders hunched inward as he refused to meet our eyes. "Because Brighde misses her mark on occasion, but I never have.

When they gave us blessings, our DNA took the gift and ran with it. Mutated it to be our own."

Bastien harrumphed. "The Nain Rouge is a liar, then. He told me Rosie shouldn't use her Compass again, because Kerdik can just use his."

"Speaking of mutations." I licked my lips, feeling the dryness starting to alleviate from my body after drinking from the delicious well of Bastien. I didn't want to have this conversation, but knew I couldn't keep it from Bastien. My heart thudded unevenly as my gut jerked away from the conversation, warning me this was a bad idea. "I'm not sure if this is a good time to mention this, but the Nain Rouge said something to me before he was trapped. Said he knew my grandfather."

"That's not unsurprising."

"He said my grandfather was Gancanagh, which was how he landed my grandma, who was apparently a total bombshell, and an awesome ruler. Said there was no way the two would've ended up together if he hadn't been Gancanagh and seduced her. He was a farmer, and homely looking, I guess."

Bastien shrugged. "That's not a huge leap. Sure. I can get onboard with that. But so what? It worked out. They had nine daughters together, so I'm guessing they were happy."

My voice came out quiet, and I wished Bastien didn't have to hear my confession. "The Nain Rouge said my grandparents found a way to pass the Gancanagh trait down to their daughters, to a lesser degree. That's how they held the power in Avalon for so long." I picked at my nails, not ready to look up at the guys. "He said it was in me, too, and that's why you're with me, Bastien. Because I bewitched you, so you have no choice. Same with Kerdik, and probably Demi. It's not as strong as it would be if Lugh twisted someone to want him, but it's there. More subtle, but definitely there." I couldn't bring myself to look at Bastien, though I longed to see any hint of "The Nain Rouge is a d-bag for lying to you like that" in his eyes.

I'm fairly certain no one breathed for the next minute. The entire earth most likely stopped turning on its axis, bending whole laws of nature so that the only thing happening in the universe was this conversation, and the fissure that started cracking at my resolve. There was no immediate denial. There was no blowing off my words.

In their silence, I knew I was right.

9

GONE

I didn't need them to confirm it with words. It was written all over Bastien's stunned face that this would be the straw that broke us. He tugged on a shirt in pure flabbergast, making me guess at where he would land on the whole issue. He started and stopped his sentence several times before he spoke, avoiding my gaze the whole time. "I'm going out for a while. Stay in the castle, alright?"

"Bastien, wait! Please don't leave like this. I didn't know!"

"It's fine. I get it. It's just a lot to process. I need some air. You'll be safe here with Lugh, Remy and Malone." He tugged on a flannel over his shirt, and put on socks and his boots without looking at me.

In that simple act, I felt him start to slip through my fingers. "No! Bastien, we have to talk about this!"

"There's nothing to talk about. You put a spell on me!" he shouted, his confusion shifting to anger in a hot second. "All this time, all I feel for you – it was a lie?"

"No! I love you! I didn't mean to do any of that! I didn't even know until the Nain Rouge told me!"

"Fine. Whatever. I'm heading out. I need to clear my head."

"Don't clear your head! Don't run out on us!" I stumbled toward him, tugging on his hand in desperation. Part of me knew that if he walked out that door, he wasn't coming back. I didn't want to be the wife who begged her husband to stick around, but here I was, making love to him one minute, and pleading with him not to leave me in the next.

Bastien shook off my grip, his chin turning from left to right as his nostrils flared. "There is no us! There's a fake us, and that's it! I can't believe after all this time, Roland was right!"

I stumbled backward, stunned. "What?"

"Roland said you'd bewitched me, and it was true! You're Gancanagh! Roland died because he was right about you!"

"But I didn't mean to do anything like that! This was all real for me! Wasn't it real for you? Our whole marriage, everything we are to each other, don't you trust all we've built?"

"Leave me alone, Rosie! I need to get my head around

this." I heard the growl of fury that sounded nothing like the man who'd helped nurse me back to life.

"Okay, take a few hours to mull it over. When are you coming back?"

Bastien slowly shook his head, looking at me with utter disgust that pushed out all of the love he'd lavished on me. "It was a lie. All of it."

"No! I meant every word of us!"

The look he shot me before he fisted the door handle was one of sheer betrayal and loathing – hurt and hatred wrapped into one long glare. "I'll stay somewhere else until..." There was no end to that sentence, only an end to us.

"Bastien, wait! Don't leave!" Before I could stop him, the door opened and shut with a finality that broke my heart. After everything, my heart had remained stalwart in my chest, beating despite the calamity that wreaked havoc on my life. This was the final straw, though. This would be the thing that destroyed that something precious in me that I needed to survive.

I stood there in stunned silence, forgetting to breathe – forgetting so many things. I don't know how many seconds ticked by, stacking up into whole minutes and worlds that divided me from my husband, pushing us apart into two separate sides.

My husband left me.

When my feet started to move toward the door, Lugh intercepted me. His sturdy hug stopped me from running after Bastien, and forfeiting what was left of my self-respect. "Give him some time, Prim. It's a lot, and he doesn't need either of us telling him how to feel about it."

"He left," I choked, letting my fight die in Lugh's arms. "He left me."

"Now, now. Let's not make it as dramatic as all tha. A little space isn't always an ocean of it." He rubbed his hand up and down my spine. "I've been giving the whole thing some thought. I don't know how your grandparents did it, but the men who were taken in by your mammy and your aunts didn't love them when the bewitching would've worn off. It doesn't last a lifetime, understand, unless you're giving out a consistent dose. Tha's probably why your Da had no problem separating from Morgan after he woke. She probably hadn't touched him in two decades, so his addiction to her wore off, and he could see her clearly." Lugh rubbed my back and kissed my nose. "It also explains why I danced with ye *after* I danced with Molly, and she got infected, but ye didn't. A Gancanagh can't bewitch another of its own kind, nor his family, so the good news is tha I can sweat all over ye, and ye won't get your mind bent for me, nor me for you."

"But we're married! Bastien's my husband!"

"Aye. And you'll still be married after this. It's a spat, is all. A new development. But it won't change how Bastien feels about ye. He loves ye, Prim, and tha's been a long time coming, from what I've heard."

I shook my head angrily. "No! When I had a hump and

a lazy eye, no one ever asked me out. It's only when all that got fixed and I got boobs that any dude paid me the time of day. If I was full-on Gancanagh, wouldn't my looks not have mattered? I still should've been able to bewitch dudes if it was based in magic, no matter what I looked like."

"Ah, but you're forgetting that most magic doesn't translate to Common. Some does, but most keeps itself in Faîte. Tha's why ye had such a strong upbringing. Nothing was handed to ye, and ye had to grow a personality. Morgan le Fae didn't have to, apparently, and look what tha got her."

I clenched my fist. "I hate that Nain Rouge! I thought Demi loved me because we had a connection. I thought Bastien married me because we're good together. And I thought Kerdik loved me because finally the universe was throwing me a bone and letting the sexy guy look my way. But it was all a lie?"

Of all things, Lugh smiled at me. It was almost paternal, the affection in his eyes. They twinkled with knowledge I hadn't lived long enough to acquire. "The lie wears off. I daresay Molly might forget all about me in a few more months. Ye and Kerdik were apart for a year or two when ye lived in Common, right? And he still had the glad eye for ye when ye came back. Tha's love, Prim."

"There's a hole in your logic, Sherlock. Brighde's still got the burning loins for you, and she hadn't seen you in years."

Lugh's face twisted at the solid reasoning. "Yeah, well.

Immortals have always been tricky. And Brìghde and I were married. We were together for years. I'm not sure tha wears off as easily. Plus, I'm first-generation pureblood Gancanagh. Tha's gotta mean my poison's more powerful."

I closed my eyes and rested my forehead to his neck. "I stole them. They weren't mine to begin with. My husband isn't mine. Now that I'm thinking about it all, it makes no sense how we even got together. We're from totally different worlds, and he was basically a hermit in the woods before I sank my hooks in. Now his life is completely different! He has a cell phone, and babysits our nephew with me. He goes bowling, Lugh! I made Bastien the Bold go bowling!"

Lugh tucked a lock of hair behind my ear before he tightened his arm around my back to kiss my cheek. "And I'm sure he loved every moment of it. Ye aren't manipulating him into a life of servitude. The poison makes him want to be with ye, so he's not suffering."

My mouth fell open. "That's the worst thing you could've said to me! I don't want to poison the man I love!"

"Your Vampire venom does exactly tha every time ye feed. He gets more and more addicted to ye. It's just the way of nature. No point in fighting it, Prim. He's doubly addicted – once from your Gancanagh poison, and once from your Vampire venom."

"My whole marriage is a lie. My life is a lie!"

Lugh held me, choosing silence and solidarity as opposed to anything that might be geared toward cheering me up. We stayed like that as the minutes piled up, giving me precious time to punish myself and beat my can-do spirit down into a pit of despair.

After the long minutes had quieted my panic as much as they were able, Lugh kissed my forehead, his arms not loosening their hold on me. Slowly Lugh started swaying our hips to a languid rhythm, humming in my ear a song I'd never heard. He had one arm slung low around my hips, and the other held my hand to his heart. "I know the waters are rocking now, but soon enough, I'll take ye home."

We turned in a precious circle, my heart beating and breaking against his. I silently begged for someone to make sense of the mess.

When the next words of sweetness came from him, they were sung to a tune I didn't recognize. "Look for me when your car breaks down, when your heart breaks down, when your life breaks down. Soon enough, I'll take ye home." His low voice was too spectacular to be in the same room as a mess like me, but I clung to the beauty all the same.

Hot tears fell down my cheeks, embarrassing me as they stained his shirt. "I'm sorry! I'm ruining your life!"

Lugh had the presence of mind to chuckle. "Hush, now. I'm composing on the fly. Let me get it out."

I sniffled, my temple resting on his collarbone as his rich, dulcet timbre melted over us like chocolate. "Take me, break me, ruin me for anyone who might want to make me their home. I'll take the midnight calls, the slips and falls. I'll take it all, if you'll let me take ye home."

His fingers started strumming across the swell of my backside, as if I was his instrument. He held my hand out to the side, using my wrist as the neck of his bass guitar. His fingers found the chords on my body easily – a musician in his basest form. I did my best to be a good instrument, sighing out my fear when he found the right chords to suit his song. He hummed a melody with his eyes closed, so I submitted to the music, surrendering a portion of my anxiety to the song. He was utterly striking in his element, and I didn't guess he needed Gancanagh abilities at all to lure every woman on whichever planet he found himself in.

Something beautiful shifted in my heart when his song tickled my ear. Part of me registered that I was in the arms of Lou Van Guarden, and he was composing a song on my body that was inspired by this terrible day. The other part was grateful he kept me from going after Bastien, from tugging on my husband when he'd asked for space to figure things out. That would've been me purposefully controlling Bastien, dismissing his request. Lugh held me together when my marriage was falling apart. We were the same animal – Gancanagh at our cores.

"Thanks, Prim," he whispered, his lips tickling the shell of my ear. "I haven't written a song in absolute ages. I needed tha."

"It was beautiful. A surefire hit."

He smirked at me. "All the lasses say tha." He ran his hand up my spine, across my shoulder, and down my side, tracing the curve of my hip to draw me out of my funk. His eyes danced with the promise that soon enough, the drama would settle, and everything would be okay. "You're bewitching even without using Gancanagh abilities. It'll be alright, Prim. I'll stay with ye until Bastien comes back."

I pulled out of his embrace, my heart slowly frosting over as the magic of the music drifted away. "I'm going to take a bath."

"Alright. Tha's good. Unwind for a bit. He'll be back before the sun goes down."

I gave Lugh a small shake of my head. "We've been through this before. Bastien won't come back. I know him. He'll find his way to the bar, and into some stranger's bed." I tried to keep my breathing even, so I didn't have a panic attack. "He'll go back to his cabin in the woods, and that'll be that."

Lugh held tight to my hand. "He can't. He's your mate. Ye won't survive without him."

I offered up a grim sliver of a smile that was laced with self-loathing. "Yet another way I trapped him." I waved off Lugh's insistence that I was off the mark, and called Rigby in to draw me a bath.

Rigby tried to get stories out of me of my harrowing adventures in Éireland, but I had nothing for him. I waited until he left to shut myself in my bedroom so I could breathe through my heartbreak without an audience.

My legs were just strong enough to get myself to the partition. Slowly, I peeled my clothes off and stepped into the tub. The warm water soothed my aching limbs, but the weight in my chest wasn't quite as buoyant. I felt heavy, and though I wanted to believe Lugh, I knew Bastien. I knew his patterns.

I knew in my broken heart that I was right, and Bastien was gone.

10

KERDIK'S WARNING

I let my tears fall freely in the privacy of the little bathing area until Lugh came back however long later with a tray of food. My chest felt tight with guilt and utter rejection. I heard him murmur something from the other side of the partition, but I was lost in my devastation.

Everything about this totally sucked. I knew who I was, which was why it was so strange that Bastien married me. I was Remedial Rosie. I was the Humpback Whale. I was Baby Got Too Much Back. I was Lazy-Eyed Susan.

My neck tattoo was damaged, and now so was my marriage. The thing is, *I* hadn't broken us this time – or I hadn't meant to, anyway. I'd been me, and that had been enough to break us. I was the Dangerous Girl now, and needed to be careful who I let get close to me.

After my tears were finished, I vowed to suck it up and

deal. I wasn't sure how to do that, and I didn't have any sort of plan, but that was what I knew I had to aim for, at least. I was just about to get out when I heard a pop. Brìghde's voice broke the silence Lugh had allowed me as he'd penned down the lyrics he'd composed on my body. "Lugh? Ye called for me? Finally, ye called for me."

I grimaced at the longing in her tone, wishing I could be a fly on the wall of any other room in the house.

"It's not like tha, Brìg. I've got some questions, and we might have a problem."

"Very well. What do ye need?"

"Is Kerdik alright? Rosie called for him, but he didn't come. She was in danger, but he left her to fend for herself."

Brìghde paused, her voice turning sheepish. "I can't speak to his private life, but he and I split up a couple weeks back. We thought we'd cover more ground tha way. Find Dother faster. Once we find him, we can fix this whole thing. It's just taking longer than we thought. Dother should've shown his cards by now, but he's still lying low."

I stepped out of the tub and toweled off, shoving fresh jeans and a tank top on so I could lend a helping hand to the mix. So help me, I wasn't going to sulk and pine for Bastien. He needed to figure out who he was and where he fit in all of this. Well, I already knew my place. I was supposed to help Avalon, which I could do without him. "I can help find Dother," I offered, coming out from behind the partition, toweling my damp hair. "I've got my Compass back, so I think it's time we put it to good use."

Brìghde gawked at me, going mute when I thought my idea would've put a cherry on the cake for her. "Ye were in the bath?"

"Yeah. Just got back from Éireland. Feels nice to get the dungeon off me."

"Ye were in the bath, alone with Lugh? Where's Bastien?"

"He left me," I said with my head high, defiance shining in my eyes to replace the tears.

"Bastien left ye, and now you're in the tub with my Lugh?"

My nose crinkled in time with Lugh's shoulders slumping. "What? No! I'm not hooking up with Lugh."

"I'm keeping an eye on her, is all, just like Kerdik asked me to. Nothing's going on, Brìghde. Do ye think I'd summon ye here just to shove another woman in your face? I'm worried something's happened to Kerdik. When was the last time ye saw him?"

Brìghde proceeded to throw herself into an emotional rant. "Ye had sex with her! You've got that content look about ye. Don't tell me different."

Lugh threw his hands in the air in exasperation. "I didn't have sex with her. She belongs to Bastien and Kerdik. I don't have a death wish, Brìg." He pinched the bridge of his nose. "I need your help. Ye told me to call if I needed ye, and now I am. I'm telling ye, something's wrong with Kerdik. He wouldn't have blown off Prim like tha."

"Prim? Ye call your girlfriend 'Prim' now? Is it because she's so proper? Is tha what ye like now? Proper girls?"

I raised my eyebrows, but refused to intervene.

Lugh glowered at her, and I could tell he despised the juvenile nature of the fight. "Focus, Brìghde. If no one's seen Kerdik, then we have to find him. It was foolish of the two of ye to split up like tha. Sending Kerdik to face his father, after all Dother did to him as a boy? Why do ye not have his back on this? How can ye not see tha he can't handle something like this alone? Everyone assumes Kerdik's invincible, but he's not!"

Brìghde threw her hands in the air. "It was his idea!"

Lugh's eyes moved from left to right, factoring in this new information with what he knew of his oldest friend. "He knows he's going to die, then. He knows tha whatever happens in the fight, he's not going to come out on top. It's the only reason he'd send ye away." He met my eyes with panic that grew. "He told me to get ye out of Faîte. I thought he was just worrying, but maybe he was warning me. Maybe he was telling me tha something was about to go down tha he couldn't stop. I was going to wait until ye cured the Werewolves in Éireland, but then ye went and got yourself abducted."

"Well, I didn't get kidnapped on purpose," I grumbled.

"I wasn't paying attention. I thought he was just

worrying too much because he's overprotective of ye. I didn't realize... But now I see it."

I shook my head slowly. "You can't be serious. Kerdik wouldn't set himself up to die. He would fight for Avalon until his last breath."

"I'm sure tha's exactly what he's doing. Dother's always been the most horrible of the three Sons of Carman. He put Kerdik through the worst of everything to make sure his boy didn't turn out weak, so his legacy didn't dwindle. Dother wanted to prove to Carman tha he could handle a second child. He wanted a daughter."

"Why?"

"Because this world runs on a matriarchal society. Raising Kerdik's not as satisfying to a megalomaniac as having a daughter would've been."

I shook my head, worried at Kerdik's secret plea to Lugh. "Dude, how do you know all this?"

"Kerdik doesn't have many people to tell his secrets to. I'm done with secrets now. If Kerdik dies, Dother will rule Faîte." Lugh locked his eyes on me. "Prim, pack a bag. We need your Compass to find him."

I nodded, my adrenaline pumping new purpose into my veins. If Kerdik was lost, I wouldn't stop until I found him.

11

NOT GOOD ENOUGH

My feet were unsteady, but with Lugh's help, I made it down the stairs. Brìghde huffed every time he touched me, so we made it a point not to be too near, unless there was danger of me falling. Finally it was decided that Brìghde would make herself useful in Éireland, rounding up the Werewolves so that I could cure them when I had time. She only agreed to leave Lugh's side when he indulged her in a lengthy kiss with plenty of tongue. I blanched at what a weird couple they made, but trusted Lugh to do whatever it took to get the job done. He promised her another kiss if she let us go to find Kerdik. He even vowed to page her when we did, so she could help extract Kerdik from whatever mess he was in.

After she disappeared, I grimaced. "Dude, she licks the outside of your lips when she kisses you. Gross. It's like your chin and mouth are a lollipop to her or something."

"I know. It's her thing." He wiped his mouth off on his shirt.

I had a bag slung over my shoulder with the bare essentials, but needed to stock up on food and water before we left. Malone trotted in and ran his furry side along my leg, and I paused only to bend down and ruffle his hair. "Hey, babe. Missed you."

"I'm here. Are you feeling better?"

"No." I didn't have it in me to lie. "No better than you're doing, I'd guess." He was missing his deceased brother, and there was no fixing that.

I didn't make eye contact with Urien, whose face I hadn't seen in so very long. He was speaking with Remy at the counter, while Fabrice rolled out a long sheet of dough with his pin. "Hello, Rosie. Is everything alright?"

I tried not to let the sound of his voice distract me with the sadness that came when I heard my estranged father say my name. "No." I fished through the cupboards for a wineskin, which Lugh took from me and began to fill with water. "Kerdik might be in trouble, so I'm taking Lugh to go find him."

"What kind of trouble? Do we need to send soldiers?"

I shook my head. "Anyone who comes with us is a mark. The soldiers could be better put to use rounding up the Werewolves, storing them in the dungeon until I get back, and can cure them. Malone can help. He can call out to them in their minds using pack-speak." I bent over and kissed Malone on the top of his head, letting him know I heard his whine about being separated from me.

It was too much. For whatever reason, I dropped to my knees and threw my arms around Malone's neck. We didn't know each other all that well, but he'd been loyal to me when I needed help. I squeezed his furry neck, smiling when he sighed contentedly with his maw on my shoulder.

It was then I realized that his loyalty might've been forced. Had I sweat on him? It was possible. In the fray of trying to escape their clashing jaws, maybe I'd touched them with my damp palms. Maybe Malone wouldn't have felt loyal to me, were he not addicted. Maybe he'd be at home with his parents. Maybe Nolan wouldn't have died at all. I swallowed down the bile that rose up in me, sickened at who I was, and all the lives I was ruining with a simple touch.

"Thank you, Malone. Thank you for everything. After the Werewolves are rounded up, go on back to Éireland. If Brìghde still needs help over there finding all the Werewolves, give her a hand. After that, go back to your family."

"What? No, Rosie. I told ye, I'm in this. I'm your guard."

I kissed him, and then shook my head. "You've given me enough of your life. I won't take any more."

I released him and stood, my heart feeling pierced open. My whole life seemed like a series of well-constructed lies. The only person I felt safe around was Lugh, because I couldn't infect him.

Remy eyed my shifting mood curiously. *"What's going on with Bastien? He had me take some of his blood to store for you. Said he was going out for a few days, but didn't say anything else."*

I tried not to hide from the truth, but put it out there without apology. I kept my eyes on the apples that I stuffed into my bag as I spoke. "Bastien's gone. Our marriage is over. Good to know he isn't going to let me starve. If he brings back more blood, could you store it here for me? I'll come back when I run out."

Urien inhaled sharply, his nostrils flaring. "He did no such thing. I don't believe it. Bastien's completely loyal to you."

I slammed my bag on the counter and glared at my father – locking eyes with him for the first time in over a year. He had more gray streaking through the brown now, but his gaze was no less focused. "Maybe he's decided to take a page out of your book."

Urien inhaled sharply, but didn't argue his case. Remy took a step back, and Fabrice found something utterly fascinating in the cupboard, so he could keep his back to us and pretend he couldn't hear our drama.

I decided not to keep my horrible secret. "Morgan's father was Gancanagh." I guessed by his nonplussed reaction to this, that he already knew as much. "They found a way to pass the gene on through their daughters, which is how you got taken in by Morgan, and were snowed by her so thoroughly."

"You'll watch your tone, young lady."

"I recently found out that it's in me," I told the room, letting that sit in the air for everyone to deal with. "It's less than a first-generation Gancanagh of course, but it's there. I told Bastien, and he flipped. His whole life with me is a lie, apparently, so he left to figure out where to go from here. If he can keep me alive with his blood long enough to rescue Kerdik, heal the Werewolves and help get rid of Dother, great. If not, that's the plan, and whatever I don't figure out, you'll have to deal with."

Urien's guffaw matched his scrunched nose. "Rosalie, this is ludicrous! Sure, Morgan's father was Gancanagh, but Morgan wasn't. Only men carry that trait."

"Oh, no? Think it through. Tell me how normal it is for her to have you so tricked through the years. Tell me how someone like Bastien or Kerdik are anywhere in the realm of possibility for someone like me." I turned to Remy. "Please explain things to Demi, Remy. Tell him I didn't know. That I'm sorry, and I never would've poisoned him on purpose. I'd tell him myself, but this Dother thing is more important than my drama."

Lugh grabbed a few more things from the pantry and shoved them in his pack. "We should go, Prim."

"I... Of course. Anything you need. Rosie, I... I'm so sorry."

"No, I'm sorry, Remy. You probably wouldn't have sworn yourself to me as my knight if I hadn't poisoned you." My voice caught, but I pushed through the painful parts as best I could to give him the full apology he deserved. "You wouldn't have died, if you hadn't been following me."

I ignored Remy's stuttered response, not needing him to try to make me feel better through all of this. Somehow that would just make it all worse.

Urien softened with a father's love. It made me want to puke all over him. "They love you. That's how you ended up catching the eye of Kerdik and Bastien. You're a prize, darling."

I don't know why, but that was the moment I lost my shiz. I picked up a roll from the counter and launched it at Urien, livid that he would say something so untrue to me. "No, I'm not! I'm a Vampire, and that's all I am!" I threw another hard roll at him, satisfied when it dinged him in the head. "You made it clear that nothing else about me mattered! Don't you dare call me a prize! They're addicted to me, which is why they didn't care that I was an abomination. Nothing in my life is real! You can see me clearly because we're related, so I can't poison you with my Gancanagh mojo. You saw me clearly, and you threw me out! I was leaveable! After everything I did for you, I wasn't good enough for my own father!" I threw an apple at his head, and then another. "Of course I'd need magic to make a man marry me. Of course I'd need to bewitch them. There's no other way someone could know me and still love me. You made that crystal clear, Urien."

"I was wrong!" Urien cried, emotion thick in his voice. "I was so very wrong, Rosalie. I was raised hearing stories of only one kind of Vampire. The *Attelage* were before my time. I didn't know any other way existed."

"Then you should've made a way! You should've fought for me, just like I fought for you! They said there was no way you would ever wake up, but I fought for you and made a way! You should've loved me enough to bend physics and upend the laws of gravity, but you didn't!"

"You're right! I should've tried harder."

"You should've tried at all!"

After my fifth angry throw, Lugh tackled me in a hug I didn't deserve. "Easy, darling. It's not going to all make sense now. There's no use making him pay for all he's done. He's drowning in his bad choice. Losing ye was the worst thing tha could happen to a father. Don't let his sadness be yours. Let him have it all."

Urien's head was bowed. "Rosalie, I..."

"Don't say my name!" I raged, furious more with myself that part of me wanted to hear my father call my name.

Lugh held me tight until I calmed down, finally letting my arms go limp around him as the fight left me. "I can see ye clearly, Prim," Lugh whispered. "You're a prize, if ever I saw one. Don't let them tell ye who ye are."

I nodded, though I didn't feel the old me rattling around inside anymore. I felt empty, bereft of the good I'd thought I'd always travel around with.

Lugh kissed my cheek, and then brought my knuckles to his lips. "I'll finish packing up, and I'll leave a note for Duke Lot and Bastien. It'll all be alright." He tipped my chin up so I couldn't hide from his eyes. "Tell me ye believe me, Prim."

I met his eyes with my hollow gaze. I wanted to believe Lugh, to hope that everything would work out in the end, but I just didn't have optimism I could believe in anymore. I'd been surrounded by lies for far too long.

Lugh seemed to understand, and gave me a quiet nod. He brought me in for another hug, cupping the back of my head to anchor it to his collar. "Tha's alright. I'll believe it enough for the both of us. You'll see."

WHERE I KNEW I'D FIND BASTIEN

I didn't want to stop by the tavern on the way out of the city, but the tug in my gut led me there. I needed one more thing before I could leave, and I knew just where to find it. Even without my Compass, I knew where Bastien would be. Beneath my depression, I was saddened most that I was right.

Halfway through enough alcohol to knock a horse on his butt, Bastien was hunched on a barstool at the pub. He had storm clouds practically circling his head, his eyebrows bunched together as he thought through all the ways he'd gone wrong.

I was his problem, and here I was, coming back for more.

"Rally, Prim. We'll be in and out. Chin up."

I didn't think I could feel any lower, but seeing Bastien recoil from me when I took the stool next to him was the punch in the gut I couldn't recover from. "What do you want? I asked you for space. I don't think a night counts."

"You said you're out. I get it. I need my *lueur* back if you're gone."

Bastien didn't argue. He didn't even pretend like he might change his mind. He simply nodded, and then turned in his stool. Wrapping his fist in the front of my shirt, he crashed his warm lips on mine in a punishing kiss that was meant to show me just how broken I'd made him, and that there would be no forgiveness. His tongue found mine, giving me one last kiss to savor and keep in my broken psyche for all of eternity. He had enough facial hair to prick my skin, making my lips search for his. I knew that I would search forever for him, wishing I could find a way to make him stay, to make him mine in the same way I'd been his from the beginning.

When my *lueur* slipped from his lips to mine, I began to cough uncontrollably, ending the kiss I wished could've somehow lasted forever. Of all the things I expected to fade with time, I hadn't known our marriage wouldn't even hit the five-year mark. I choked on the light as it took its sweet time slithering back down inside of me, my eyes watering as I fought for air when the *lueur* lodged itself in my throat.

Lugh slapped me hard on the back until I got it all down, glaring at Bastien. "Ye could've offered her your pint. She didn't know about any of this, mate. She didn't trick ye. She doesn't deserve your hatred."

"She doesn't deserve my ring, either. I don't know how I didn't see it. This is nothing like the life I wanted! I was fine before I met you!"

My fingers shook as I slid my wedding ring off my finger. With the last of my courage, I set the most beautiful diamond on the counter next to his beer. "I'm sorry I put you through this. I honestly thought we were happy together."

Bastien eyed the ring as his vision misted over. "I'll stop by once a week to the castle and drop off some blood to Remy. I won't let you starve. I just can't... I can't live in a lie, Rosie."

"Thank you."

"Here, take some for the road. I can tell you aren't totally one hundred percent yet." Instead of letting me bite him, Bastien used his knife to puncture a small spot on his forearm. When the bartender wasn't looking, he squeezed the wound over his drink, letting the crimson fall into the amber, and mix like a cloud of sadness and beauty. We'd been beautiful, once upon a time. Now we were only sadness.

Bastien slid his beer to me without looking at my face, and then took a napkin and slapped it to the wound. "Drink up. Does Kerdik know?"

"Not yet. But I'm going to tell him."

"Don't. Let him be happy. I wouldn't wish this feeling on anybody. Not even him."

I didn't need to hear any more. I downed the drink,

letting the blood heal the unimportant parts of me – the physical parts. There was no cure for the ache in my chest.

When I finally spoke, my voice was quiet and so very, very small. "I hope you have a good life. No matter what you think, I didn't mean for this to happen. I fell in love with you, and that's as complicated as my side of things ever got."

"Alright. I heard you, so you can go now."

My heart felt like everything good inside might be gone forever. My husband couldn't see me. I'd waited for so long to see him, but now that I could, he couldn't look me in the eye to see who I truly was beneath the magic. "Goodbye, Bastien."

13

SANS SOUCI

I'm not sure how long we walked through the day and on into the dead of night before I realized Lugh was talking. "Are ye sure this is the way?"

I checked back in with my gut, which was a ball of angst. "Yeah. We're nowhere near him, but this is the way." We were walking through a patch of forest, the trees lending nothing to soothe the ache in my chest.

"We need horses. Something to get us there faster."

"Horses? Sure. We can ride horses. Whatever you like."

After a long pause, Lugh prodded with the obvious. "Can ye ask your feathered friends to find us a couple of horses?"

I didn't even realize there were birds following me, chatting their little beaks off until Lugh brought them to my attention. Before I could answer, my right hand started trembling. A shock that zapped me out of my stupor shot through my arm and dinged my chest so hard, I felt my teeth rattle. I tripped and fell, faceplanting oh-so-gracefully on the forest floor.

It wasn't until Lugh cried out that my vision began to clear of the stars that danced in my eyes from the fall. "How did ye do tha?"

Lugh helped me to sit up, brushing off my arms and face while I gawked at the enormous horse that pawed at the earth in front of us. He was black as midnight, and taller than any horse I'd ever seen. He was thick around the middle, and had gray eyes that seemed to see through any bull crap life could throw his way. "I didn't do anything. Where did you come from?" I asked the horse.

"From your ring, stupid girl. Dub sent me to take you wherever you need to go."

My jaw dropped, still taking in the girth of the surly horse. He looked mean, even without the proof of him calling me stupid. "A gift from Dub," I informed Lugh. "What's your name?" I asked the horse, who answered with nothing more than a dismissive snort.

"It's Sans Souci." Lugh was mesmerized. "One of the Sons of Carman sent ye Sans Souci? Do ye understand what this means?"

"Sure, it means Dub can send stuff out of the ring whenever he wants."

"It means we'll be riding on Sans Souci!"

"Quit saying his name like that."

"Like what?"

"Like how people call you Lou Van Guarden." I stood, trying to figure out just what this could mean for our mission. "Dub really sent you? What's he holding over your head? What'd he promise you if you helped me?"

"He promised I could have my chance at killing Dother. That's what we're doing, right?"

Lugh tugged on my sleeve. "What'd he say? What'd he say?"

I ignored Lugh, who kept hitting my arm like a five-year-old asking for ice cream. "Um, yeah. And we could definitely use some help with that. What'd Dother do to you, that you'd want to kill him so badly?"

Sans' eyes turned impossibly colder as he glared at me. *"Before I was sucked into Cailleach's cane, and then got transferred to your ring, I was his son's horse. Dother did a great many things to torture my master."*

My jaw dropped. "You're Kerdik's horse? Like, legit, his horse?"

Sans sneered at me. *"Is that a problem? Dub told me I could avenge my master and kill Dother, who tortured us both."*

"I don't understand. Kerdik created the ring. He trapped all the higher magic inside. Why would he trap you in, too, if you were on his side?"

"I was the lure," Sans confessed. *"Dother and Dian wanted me tortured, since they couldn't kill me. Petulant fools. I knew they'd never leave Kerdik alone, so we came up with a plan to tempt them into a trap. I'm just glad Dub kept me safely*

hidden in the ring from the brothers once we were locked inside. Dother and Dian are psychopaths. Dub's not so bad."

"You gave up your freedom to be trapped inside a ring for decades? Why?"

"If you loved my master as I do, you wouldn't have to ask that. Kerdik gave me many lives to be by his side. It was the least I could do to save him from his tormentors. I was the bait, and Dub sealed us all inside. Dub gave up his freedom too so Faîte could have a chance."

I didn't think I could fit any more new information into my brain. "You're going to help us? Do you have some sort of voodoo that can actually kill Dother?"

"Leave it to me. You bring your ring, and I'll take care of the rest."

14

BELIEVING IN GINGERBREAD HOUSES

Sans Souci was born to ride hard. Lugh was behind me on the horse, his arms encircling me as he gripped braids we'd tied into Sans' mane to use as reins, so we didn't fall off the back end. He rode faster than any horse I'd ever been on, including the Cheval Mallet. He never seemed to tire, either. Of course, he was an immortal horse who'd been blessed by Kerdik, so I guessed there was a whole litany of things I couldn't even begin to imagine Sans was capable of.

Sans wasn't a fan of people, so we galloped through the woods of Province 1, which basically was all of Avalon now. It had taken too much warfare and far too many leaders dying to make it happen, but we were finally one nation. I decided to take that as a win.

"Careful, Sans!" Lugh called when a branch nearly knocked us both off his back.

"If Kerdik's in trouble, I don't care if I lose you both. Hold on and shut up. Are we going in the right direction?"

"Yes, keep going this way." I pressed my chest all the way down to rest on Sans' flank, making myself as flat as I could so we didn't get decapitated. "Duck, Lugh! He's not going to slow down."

Lugh covered my body with his, caging me in while we clung to Sans' barreled midsection with our knees. My thighs were parted wide to accommodate Sans' larger frame. I only hoped we didn't do any long jumps like this. I feared Lugh might go flying off.

"We're okay," Lugh chanted just as much to himself as he meant to reassure me. "Just hold on tight. We'll be there in no time."

Contrary to Lugh's word, the journey was long. It gave me plenty of time to mull over all the many things I would miss about my former husband. He wouldn't come back to Common with me, which meant he might not see Reyn again... ever. The life we'd built together was gone now.

The nasty girl voice inside of me lectured how she wasn't really all that surprised he'd left. It had taken us so long to get together in the first place. Perhaps he had been subconsciously trying to fight the poison I'd infected him with. Maybe he was trying to be the crotchety hermit he'd insisted he was from the very beginning – a man who wanted to live alone in the woods. I'd taken the island of a man and forced him against his will to live in a family. We were practically a commune – sharing one plot of land, pooling our resources and taking care of each other.

My tears drooled down Sans' side, but I didn't care. I had no privacy, and no space to mourn the loss of something that was precious to me. Lugh peppered my cheek with kisses and patted my arm. "Let it out, Prim. No one's going to judge ye out here."

"I will. Don't distract me with whatever lady issues you're dealing with. I'm on a mission, and you should be, too. If you had half a brain in your head, you'd see that whatever you're blubbering about isn't nearly as important as saving Kerdik from Dother. If Kerdik falls, Avalon has nothing. She'll have no watchman to care for her borders. She'll fall without Kerdik to make the crops come in. Selfish people, thinking the world simply turns without effort, because someone else is breaking their back behind the scenes. But please, by all means, go ahead and cry about the terrible tale of you breaking a nail or whatever."

I squinched my eyes shut and prayed for courage, for amnesia, for... something. I didn't know how to get through this. Lane had never taught me how to be divorced gracefully. She'd never been divorced. She was married to the love of her life, after a long time of waiting for the right one. She would never fail at marriage, and when I went home after all this ended, and told her what we were, Reyn wouldn't leave her. There was nothing Lane could do that would make Reyn leave her side.

I remembered their first flirt. It was in Common when

Reyn was smitten, which was before she could've Gancanaghed him into thinking she was the shiz. Reyn knew at first glance that Lane was worth a wild and bloody adventure through Avalon, and he never went back on that.

I was leaveable. My dad knew it, Bastien confirmed it, and now I knew the truth of who I was. I was nothing special. I was Remedial Rosie. Despite the trappings, I was still the ugly girl.

Lugh pressed his cheek to mine in lieu of a hug as he held onto the horse and me for dear life. "Don't go anywhere in your mind. I can see ye drifting to the bad place. Tell me about Christmas. Tell me what we'll do when life is boring again, and we're far, far away from this place."

"I don't believe in gingerbread houses anymore," I confessed. And with those simple words, I knew my heart would remain broken for a very long time.

"Then I guess I'll just have to believe in them for the both of us." He kissed my temple again, as if his sweetness might remind me that there was still good in the world. As if that was all it took for puppies and kitties to play under the glow of rainbows again.

I knew the truth about rainbows, though. During one very depressing science class, I learned they were nothing more than gas and refracted lights. I was smarter after that class, but I wasn't happier. There was no magic in the color anymore. There was no dance in the sky after the rain. The more I figured out life, the less magical I became. Now that I knew why Bastien had loved me so passionately, the rainbow lost a little of its color. I wondered at what point I would settle for a black, white and gray existence simply because it's real.

My gut tugged me toward the right, so I pulled on Sans' mane, steering him in the correct direction. "I don't want to live this long," I admitted. "It feels like it's been too many years already. After we rescue Kerdik and the Werewolves are healed, I'm going to the Forgotten Forest."

Lugh sacrificed his hold on Sans to cover my mouth with his palm. "Tha's enough. There's plenty more to life than Bastien, and he'll come back around once he's finished being an arse. He loves ye."

"He's addicted to me. Not the same."

"Hush, now. When we get back to Common, you'll come on tour with me. We'll be so busy, ye won't have time to feel all of this. Ye can see Europe. We'll write more songs together. We'll kick this, Prim. We'll bury it." He swallowed against my face. "We'll bury it all. Just let it hurt now. Tha's what it's supposed to do when the cut's this fresh."

"*Kerdik, Kerdik,*" Sans chanted, relentless in his fight to reach our destination.

I paused, considering Lugh's offer before answering. It seemed a heck of a lot better to sleep on a bus with him than to go home and face the king-sized bed that had a Bastien-shaped dent on the right side. "We can run away to Europe?"

"Absolutely. We'll leave our heartaches in Avalon, and be nothing but irresponsible on tour. Ye won't run away to the Forgotten Forest. You'll run away with me instead. We'll be frivolous and foolish and fun."

I blinked, hoping my tears had reached a decrescendo. "Okay. It's a deal. Thank you."

He exhaled atop me, letting his weight press me down farther onto Sans Souci. Lugh was good medicine for everything that was broken inside, so I let him cover the parts of me that felt raw and naked.

15

THE CALM BEFORE THE STORM

"*I don't care that you're tired. Stop whining already.*"

I tugged a twig out of my hair and pitched it into the wind as we whipped through the field. "I didn't whine. I asked politely if we could stop for a rest. Lugh and I haven't eaten since yesterday. We've been riding for four days now! We need a break."

"*How Kerdik hasn't wiped your entire race off the face of Faîte is beyond me. Fae are such babies.*"

"Dude, not for nothing, but if you were Kerdik's only friend as a kid, I feel super bad for him. You're a tool."

"*Better that than a whiner.*"

I refused to reply. Sans Souci's tongue was pure acid, and everything that slid through his lips was an insult.

"*Kerdik, Kerdik,*" he chanted, reminding me that he had

his good points, too. He was so singular in his focus; it was impressive.

Lugh's stomach growled. I could feel the rumble from his abdomen that was flexed against my back. I tangled my fingers through his, wishing I could do something to make the ride easier on the dude who'd given up his rock star life to save Kerdik's.

Twilight was rolling in by the time my gut screamed that we were nearing our goal. I tugged on Sans Souci's mane. "Slow down. I think we're close."

"Kerdik! Kerdik!" Sans shouted, letting out a whinny that I'm pretty sure would've blown our cover, had Dother known to keep an ear out for this horse.

We hadn't seen civilization during most of the journey, and this place was no exception. There was plenty of green-ery, but it was all weeds and tangled overgrowth. Each tree looked weary with no one around to appreciate its majesty. They all seemed to mutter, "What's the point?" to us as we passed. The shrubs seemed like miniature gargoyles, daring anyone to step on them and ruin the peace and quiet they'd acquired in the middle of nowhere. Every segment of nature should have been beautiful, but they all had grumpy, frumpy frowns pulling at the knotty surfaces.

Finally, Sans stopped his trot. Lugh slid off and fell in a heap, his legs bowed and not terribly useful after the over-long ride. His voice was scratchy from inhaling too much wind and not stopping for water along the way. He finally found his footing and pawed at the canteen, guzzling a few mouthfuls of water before offering up his arms to help me down.

My legs were similarly useless, and I had no grand delusions of standing, now that I could be free of the crabby horse. I collapsed in Lugh's arms, and after much useless efforts to tough it out and walk, we both decided to lay on the forest floor. We stared up at the ceiling of green and brown, our eyes flitting over the cracks in the branches that let a little of the fading sunlight through.

"I can't feel my legs," I admitted, taking a roll from Lugh that he'd dug out of the pack.

"Legs are overrated. I think my whole body's turned into one giant bruise. Is it possible for one's balls to cry? I feel like mine are weeping right now."

I let out a short laugh, ignoring Sans, who griped that we were being overly dramatic, since he'd done all the work of getting us here. "I dunno. If we're complaining about body parts, I'd like to register for new arms. Remind me to hit the gym when we get back to Common."

"Ye can have the gym. I'll be in the pool, soaking my boys."

"Poor Lugh's testicles," I pouted, sitting up on my elbows. I fished around for the wineskin of blood, unscrewing the cap to take a small swig. Though I wanted to guzzle it, I knew I had to ration. There was enough to last me a month in there, if I only drank the bare minimum. I didn't know how long Bastien would be super invested in keeping me alive, and didn't want to be caught unprepared if he didn't go back to the castle to donate blood next week. I had to be smart about this.

Bastien running down my throat was a sweet form of torture. I craved him – every part of him, but as I swallowed, emptiness filled my soul once again, perhaps even more than it had before I drank his essence. "We should go. Kerdik's not far from here."

"What about Dother? Can ye tune in with your Compass and locate him?"

I closed my eyes and did a quick check. "Yeah. He's in the same location as Kerdik. Hold on. Let me check for Cailleach. She was supposed to be helping him." Sure enough, I felt Cailleach ping in that general area, as well. "She's there with him."

We heard an explosion that sounded a bit like fireworks, and then saw a spark of light flash above us in the distance. Lugh sat up and cursed. "Tha'll be them. Good thinking to keep this fight away from the Fae. No telling what kind of damage they'll do to the area."

"I'm not sure what to do once we're there. I mean, I've got the ring to try and suck Dother inside, but I don't actually know how to do that. The ring does what it does. I just carry it around."

"I don't know, either. I was kind of hoping Kerdik would be the one in control of the fight, and he could direct me to help with whatever he needed, but truly, I have no idea what help I'll be against Dother, if he's on top." He splashed a little water on his hands, and then reached over to wash the dried blood off my cheeks. "Tha's better. Now I can see the face tha Kerdik would fight to the death for. Give him something to rally the man in his loins."

"But it's a lie," I whispered, guilt tainting my tone. "I bewitched him into feeling that way."

Lugh shushed me. "Tha's neither here nor there. All he needs to know is tha ye came to help him. Let him love ye for now."

For now. Those words weighed heavy on my heart. "Okay. That sounds pragmatic."

Lugh cupped my chin, and despite the fact that we both stank of horse and had spent far too many days in too close of quarters, Lugh brought me in for a light, closed-mouth kiss to my lips. "It'll all work out, Prim. I've been Gancanagh far longer than ye have. Trust me tha Kerdik won't care. He'll only care tha ye love him."

I nodded, closing my eyes at the sweetness Lugh lavished on me. "Home stretch, right? After this, we can finish up with the Werewolves, and be done with Faîte."

"Europe, sweetheart. We'll be gone faster than they can throw more problems at us." He fished in his pack and unhooked his bow from the latch on his backpack, running his hand along the curve, and testing the tension with a pluck of his finger on the string before he set it in the grass. The arrows were bound with a thin rope, so they didn't fall all over the place as we rode. He exhaled when he untied them, as if binding them up had somehow strangled him. "Hand me Mathews."

"Huh?" I looked around, and he motioned to his bow as he lined up his arrows. "You named your bow? That's totally precious."

"It's the brand, so it seemed fitting. Mathews has been with me through many a fight. Always has my back." He placed a kiss to the top when I handed it to him. "Missed ye, old boy."

"That won't do anything. Do you really expect to overthrow Dother with a few arrows? You have no idea how immortals work. Idiot."

I glowered at Sans and turned to Lugh. "Mr. Ed is wondering if the arrows will actually slow down Dother at all. I mean, he's immortal, right?"

"Oh, ye of little faith." Lugh tugged a small pot out of the bottom of the quiver and unscrewed the Mason jar lid. He dipped the tip of the arrows one by one into the gooey gray glop inside, and propped them up on the weeds to the left. "It's almost like ye have no idea who my only friend was. Kerdik taught me many things, including how to incapacitate him if he ever got too out of control. It's temporary, but enough to knock him out for a little while."

"Whoa. That's a lot of trust. How'd you come across that? In the beginning, it seemed like if I blinked wrong he'd throw an elemental fit."

"I've had decades to show him my true colors. It's why he trusts me with ye. This is hard to make, too. I didn't have all the stuff when we went up against Dian and Dother before, so Dian was barely stunned. I'm prepared this time, though." He dipped the last arrow into the goo, and screwed the cap back on.

"Wow. That's seriously impressive. I'm glad Kerdik has you. I don't like the thought of him being so lonely."

"Kerdik's only as lonely as he wants to be. He's got a stigma, sure, but he's got me, if he ever reaches out. Before he and Urien had the falling out, they were pretty tight. Plus, there are the other immortals, whenever they get their heads out of their arses. And he's got ye to fill his days with, so tha's a definite plus."

Another explosion made us stand up, shaking off our sore limbs that, seconds ago, had seemed debilitating. Sans Souci looked gruff, his eyes narrowed to slits as he stared into the sky for signs of the fight. *"Enough idle chatter. If Kerdik's in trouble, I'll go after Dother. You two get Kerdik out of there."*

I relayed the plan to Lugh.

"I can help with Dother," Lugh offered, slinging his freshly filled quiver over his shoulder and gripping the bow at his side.

"I can get Kerdik out," I offered, rolling back my shoulders to face the problem head-on. I pushed my personal problems and exhaustion out of my mind, focusing on the task at hand. Sans Souci hadn't been much of a conversationalist, but he'd talked the entire way pretty much, chanting Kerdik's name over and over. Conversing with animals had the drawback of making me sleepy, and I was long overdue. Plus, I was an *Attelage* Vampire, and we required sleep. He'd stopped only twice in four days to let me rest, and I was starting to feel the drag in my limbs.

Lugh reached out and took my hand, letting me know that no matter what, we were in this together. Despite everything, that was a comfort I didn't take for granted. I squeezed his grip, offering up a small representation of a smile as we followed behind Sans Souci, welcoming the fight we'd been searching for.

16

KERDIK'S LAST STAND

When we neared the area my Compass led us to, Lugh dropped my hand and readied his bow and arrow. My knife felt useless, but I clutched it just the same, hoping it would make me feel bolder, and that it might make my knees stop trembling.

Lugh's boot crunched on the dry underbrush, so I paused him with my hand on his arm. "Fly," I whispered. "We don't want to give ourselves away." I turned him to face me, waiting for him to holster his arrow and wrap his arms around my torso, smooshing me to him. We managed to levitate a solid foot without too much trouble. I knew this was draining my magic faster than merely walking, but I didn't want to give our location away before we got close enough to be useful. We were both a little unpracticed at the whole flying thing, so we clung to each other to keep steady.

Sans craned his long neck to look at us when the sounds of our footsteps disappeared. *"Huh. I guess you're not completely useless."*

I shot Sans my middle finger, knowing it was foolish to let him bait me. We flew like that for nearly half an hour, keeping a languid pace so we didn't fly headfirst into a situation we were unprepared for. The explosions grew nearer, and as much as I wanted to run into the fray, I worried what we might find when the gap between us was finally closed.

Slowly, I could see a great valley reveal itself in the distance. The earth seemed to drop off, and the green of nature vanished into a chalky reddish dirt. There were no birds or any other forest creatures – there hadn't been for hours. They wanted nothing to do with the area, and I couldn't blame them.

Clear as day, I heard Cailleach scream, making the hairs on the back of my neck stand at attention. My flight path went wonky, and I accidentally flew us too high, nearly bumping Lugh's head on a branch. "Cailleach," I whispered to Lugh, who nodded, gripping me tight.

"I think we can land, Prim," Lugh whispered. "I don't need to get much closer. Just a bird's-eye view is all I need."

I glanced around and searched for higher ground, whooshing us to a small plateau about the size of a pitcher's mound. Lugh let go of me and coasted down atop the mound, which was angled so that we could hide a bit if we laid flat. He readied his bow and arrow, and then we crawled forward to peer over the edge, like children peeking at what the adults were watching on TV late at night.

Visibility was terrible, since the sun was setting, but the explosions that went off gave a bit of brilliance to the scene. The fireworks show lit the devastation below, causing both Lugh and me to gasp with a shared horror.

Dother was in his glory, grandstanding in the middle of the immortal-carved arena, as if declaring himself the champion gladiator of the match he'd orchestrated. Complete with an evil villain's smile and black cloak, he stood in the center, his arms raised either in victory or in preparation, I wasn't sure.

Cailleach was cowering, hugging the wall of the canyon, looking every bit like the old crone she'd been described as. If I hadn't seen it with my own wide eyes, I wouldn't have believed it. She'd always seemed so unstoppable. Even in the fight with Dian and Dother, she'd been vivacious and filled with venom and fight.

I wasn't expecting Brìghde to have beaten us there, since she was supposed to be in Éireland. I sucked in a breath when I saw her motionless, laying with her eyes skyward and her arms splayed, a black soot mark billowing across her chest.

Kerdik was hovered over Brìghde, protecting the downed soldier with his own body. He bore many of the same soot marks on his arms. His shirt was torn and untucked, his sky-blue hair wildly mussed as his gaze focused on Dother. "It's enough! She doesn't have anything. She can't open the cane, either!"

"Oh, my boy. This is why you're weak. It's never enough until you get the results you're after. This is why your little Avalon never thrived on its own, why you constantly have to be picking up the pieces of your failed experiment." Dother's palms pointed at Brìghde, and despite Kerdik's attempt to shield her, the blast that shot out landed square on her legs, lighting them on fire with flames Kerdik couldn't put out fast enough.

"Enough!" Kerdik bellowed.

Dother merely laughed, looking exactly like his son, but with pale, sallow skin that made me cringe. "I'll bet you wish you could port out of here. I'll bet you're thinking of all the ways you'd like to escape my fly trap. Poor, short-sighted Kerdik. Just like your mother, thinking only of the now, instead of the possible pitfalls of the future."

The second blast was aimed at Kerdik, who gritted his teeth through the pain – too stubborn to cry out. He returned his father's assault with one of his own, sending out a stream of grayish air that made Dother howl when it reached him.

"Foolish boy! Don't you know it's a wasted effort to attack me? I've had decades to perfect my magic, fine-tuning it inside the ring you trapped me in. Well, now who's trapped, Son? I've used your own magic against you. How does it feel to fight an eternal battle against me? Your fight is nothing more than an inconvenience. Once I crack open the Hag's cane, I'll have Carman back. She can deal with your insolence far better than I."

"Try it all day, old man! Try it for years! I've got nothing but time to waste, watching you exhaust yourself trying to best us."

"There is no 'us' here!" Dother countered, motioning to Cailleach, who was shuddering against the wall of the valley. "Brìghde was easy enough to incapacitate, impetuous as she's always been. Cailleach will break. I can already see her weakness for her sister crumbling her fight." He smacked the back of his hand into his palm as he addressed Kerdik. "This is how to get things done, Son. This is why having sentimental attachments makes a man weak."

"Keep fighting us, but we'll never break open the cane!" Kerdik roared, ferocious in his vehemence. "You can spend every second of your newfound freedom struggling against us, because we'll never give you what you want!" He beat his fist to his chest, looking wild and unhinged. "*I* win this time! It's my turn to torment you until you can't bear it. *Now* who's in control of their destiny?"

Dother shot a blast of something that looked like a bowling ball of fire at Kerdik. It knocked him backward without mercy as Dother seethed. "After I get my mother back, I'll break Dian and Dub out of the stone you trapped them in. I hope you enjoyed ruling your little Avalon. I hope it was all you dreamed it could be, because soon enough, you'll be shoved into the stone you lured me into.

I'll smile every day, knowing you're screaming for freedom that you'll never be strong enough to take for yourself!"

My eyes flitted to Sans, who stood in the remaining cover of trees near the edge, looking down on the arena with nostrils flared. I could tell by the anxiety in his slate eyes that he wanted to run down to rescue Kerdik, but the drop was far too steep for a horse. I knew he wouldn't be able to make it down without breaking his ankles, thick as they were.

I clutched Lugh's wrist, my temple pressed to his as we watched the scene like scared children. "I think I can fly Sans down into the valley. If I can just get him down there, then Kerdik has help."

"No, Prim. You'll stay by my side. T'won't do for ye to be captured. If there's one thing Kerdik won't stand a minute of, it's ye being tortured. Kerdik's holding out. We'll help from up here."

I shook my head. "I can do it. It's not like lifting a horse. It'd just be a little more difficult than flying a person." Even as I said this, I wasn't sure how true it was. "I have to help Kerdik. He can't do this much longer."

"No!" Lugh gripped my wrist, but I shrugged out of the hold easily.

"If I don't make it back, you can have all my Lost and Forgotten albums." I kissed his cheek before I lifted my torso from the rock.

I wasn't expecting my ring finger to start burning, but the gold stung me like a hornet, over and over until the giant aquamarine started to tremble in the setting. I flipped over onto my back, my spine pressed to the angled plateau we were perched on, holding my right hand with my left. "Something's wrong!" I whispered. "My ring's heating up!"

"What?"

Before I could offer up another description, a blue fog shot out from the gemstone, and in the next breath, I was face-to-face with Darkness.

17

NO TURNING BACK NOW

*D*ub stared at me, his hand palming my mouth before I could scream as he hovered over my body, hidden from view of the others down below. His free hand shot out and pressed Lugh's temple to the rock, pinning him in place. "Quiet, children," he whispered. "I'm on your side."

In my struggle, my knees parted, giving Dub the space to sink down atop me to make sure he wasn't seen. I tried to speak, but Dub's hand over my mouth kept me quiet.

Lugh was livid, his eyes wide with a note of fear. "Take me. Leave the girl alone."

Dub quirked an eyebrow at Lugh. "How noble, and completely unnecessary. My niece won't come to harm at my hands." He met my eyes, his long nose hovering an inch above mine. It was surreal to see him in this place, marrying my two realities. "Your plan was foolish, so I'm intervening. You aren't practiced enough to fly with the horse, but I am. You exhausted too much magic on the way here. You got me to the cane, which was all I've needed you to do this entire time. I can break it open without letting Carman out and retrieve the onyx. After I bathe in the Síocháin, I can even close up the cane with Dother inside."

I shook my head, since Dub wouldn't move his hand to allow me to speak.

"You don't have a choice," Dub ruled. "You must've realized when I let Sans Souci out and that Kelpie, that surely I could let myself out at any time, no?"

I nodded, wishing I'd finally snapped and gone crazy, so I could pretend this whole scene wasn't happening. Dub was a danger, blinding me and manipulating every situation he could to suit his master plan.

"I knew you were smart. Not to worry. I've put Dian in a deep sleep inside the ring. He doesn't know how to escape, anyway." Dub leaned down and pressed his cheek to mine, his eyes closed in a whispered promise. "Before the sun rises, Dian and Dother will be locked away, never to bother Faîte again. I will rescue my nephew, as I've always tried to do when Dother grew too zealous. Trust me in this, little flower."

I shut my eyes, torn, but ultimately and utterly powerless. When he finally released my mouth from his grip, I wrapped my arms around Dub in a hug. I could scarcely understand why I was embracing him, but after all the nights we'd shared, I couldn't hold back my gratitude for showing up when we didn't have a solid plan. I didn't trust him to do what was best for me, but I was willing to gamble my final chips that he was ready to go to the mat for Kerdik.

"Please, Dub," I whispered in his ear. It was a plea for so many things, but mostly to end the madness – to let me go home. I wanted peace for Faîte, but I had no way to keep my hands wrapped around it when it finally flitted my way. "Please."

Dub nodded, seeming to understand all that I wanted to say. He turned his face to Lugh, gripping one of the arrows in his fist. He brought it near and sniffed the tip, nodding his approval. "That's clever, though it's not enough. You'll need to hit Dother at least three times with your arrows to knock him out for a few minutes."

"How long do ye need?"

"As many minutes as you can get me. Keep Rosie with you. Let me take care of the rest."

"Grand." Lugh got up on his knees and readied his bow, taking aim without needing any further information on the scene. He was named Cross Shot for a reason, and he didn't disappoint. He didn't require the tedious aiming and setting up a shot I'd seen in movies. He picked his point, gave a little nod to himself, and let Mathews do the dirty work. The arrow flew out from the plateau and soared straight into the meat of Dother's shoulder, causing him to cry out. The immortal jag didn't sound like he was in pain, only angry that he'd been sneaked up on.

Dub was on his feet and running toward Sans Souci, letting his evil brother see him, so we weren't the culprits.

Lugh ducked back down and grabbed my hand, sliding me away from the rock that had been our perch. "Let's stay down here. We'll keep out of sight as long as we can. Let the immortals hash this out."

We scrambled left toward the forest and ducked behind a thick tree, where we backed up two whole feet from the edge, but could still keep an eye on the fight. My mouth fell open when I caught sight of the strangest thing I would ever witness (I hope). There was Sans Souci, leaping out from the edge of the valley like a ballerina going for a high jump. His mane whipped through the air as Dub rode atop the horse's back, his legs wrapped to lower the two slowly, and without the dreaded crash I feared when they reached the bottom of the valley.

Dother's mouth was open in shock, taking in the brother he no doubt feared he wouldn't see for quite some time, and the horse he'd loathed almost as much as he'd hated his own son.

"Hit him now, while he's distracted!" I urged Lugh.

Cross Shot himself angled the bow next to the tree, taking no more than two seconds to set up his shot before he let the arrow ring true.

There would be no mistaking the assault this time. Dub was in plain sight with no weapons to speak of, yet Dother had been hit again.

Lugh was quick to duck behind the thick trunk of the

tree with me, but it was too late. Dother gathered his wits about him and blasted out a small inferno, hitting the tree we were huddled behind. I squeaked my fear, jumping as Lugh grabbed my wrist and dragged us farther back.

I was scared, knowing we'd been seen. Lugh's pant leg was on fire, and he cried out when I lowered him to the ground so he didn't run around, like his wild eyes were hinting at. I smacked my pack down on his leg, smothering the fire as best I could. We both whimpered like the scared kids we pretended not to be most the time.

It took far longer to extinguish the flame, making Lugh cry out all over again when the cinders were reborn just as soon as we were certain they were dead. Lugh's hands were unsteady, fumbling with his belt buckle as we fought to think rationally in the midst of the chaos. Instead of risking the greedy fire seeping through and latching onto his hairy leg, Lugh wiggled out of his pants, which were now set on spontaneous combustion mode, no matter how many times I tried to snuff out the hungry flames.

I took a chance and rolled the pants, letting the fire eat away at the material. Lugh pressed his hand to his heart, catching his breath while I ran to the edge of the canyon and chucked the problem pants into the valley.

I locked eyes with Dother, who sneered at me.

It was Kerdik's voice that brought me out of my Mexican standoff with Dother. "Rosie, no! Run, honey! Get out of here!" His voice cracked with desperation, letting me know he was honestly afraid, which meant I was in some very real danger.

"Get her, brother! She holds our prison!" Dother called to Dub, whose horse had finally touched down on the powdery red dust of the valley. Dother's movements were drunken and slow from the arrows' poison, but he was still upright.

It was anybody's guess whose side Dub was truly on, but I held tight to what I knew to be the truth. Dub was always on his own side, whether moral or not. He fought for his agenda at the expense of all else. I only prayed I understood his master plan, and that there were no other bombs about to be dropped.

Dub leaped off the horse, landing without staining his black pants and shirt on the red dirt of the canyon. His black cloak billowed out behind him, his hood pushed back to reveal his stony expression. His upright posture was unaffected by the fray, ignoring all else except his brother. "Dother, this isn't the way. Look at your son. You're teaching him nothing, as usual, except that you are cruel – a lesson he learned ages ago."

I ducked down, watching as Dother pointed to Cailleach's staff, held by the Hag herself as she shuddered off to the side. I saw part of her as the old woman with a hump and wonky eye, but when she shifted in the moonlight, I saw her true form – beauty as she was. The unimpressive brown cane was clutched to her chest like a precious teddy bear she was unwilling to part with on pain of much unfixable damage. "Let me out of this place!" she raged at Dother when Dub turned to her and began to approach.

"Give me the cane, Cailleach. It's far simpler if you comply. Either way, it'll come into my hands. I'd rather not harm you if I don't have to."

"Tear her apart!" Dother raged like a petulant two-year-old, staggering to the side as he gripped his shoulder.

Kerdik took his window and lunged with clumsy limbs in the direction of his father, tackling him to the ground. Then Kerdik backed up, pressing his hands to the earth at the foot of the man who'd tortured him for far too long. The earth began to rumble and break beneath Kerdik's palms, the fissure in the dirt spreading forward seven feet from where he knelt. It took a few seconds of me watching with my mouth hanging open, but finally I realized that Kerdik was digging a shallow grave. Dother was powerless to rise out of it, injured as he was by Lugh's arrows.

As soon as his father was six feet deep, Kerdik filled the space with more dirt, burying his father, who was still very much alive. Over the dirt Kerdik choked whole boulders from his palms, raining them down over the grave as he stood on quaking legs. "Finish it, Dub! We can't get out of here. He's trapped us inside. Help us get him back into Rosie's ring. I can't... It's been too much. I need help."

"Quick, Son," Dub agreed. "Dother's not out."

"I'm coming!" I called to Kerdik, waiting for his nod as I stepped to the edge of the canyon. It took a few breaths, but I eventually willed myself to get over my fear of heights already. I closed my eyes like a baby, sucked in my scream and took a two-step leap off the edge, hoping I remembered all the basics of how to fly.

I floated down into Dub's outstretched arms, letting out my bleat of fear once I landed safely. "Easy, hun," Dub said as he placed my feet on the ground.

No sooner did my legs support my weight did they take off in Kerdik's direction. Though he was battle-torn and weary, there was no more beautiful sight than Kerdik, alive and upright. He limped toward me, meeting me in a hug we both needed. "I told you to run," he growled as he kissed my lips angrily.

"And you were wrong. You need me."

Kerdik chuckled into my mouth. "Indeed, I do. Always my queen. Come. Help me put an end to this madness."

I drew my arm around his waist, supporting his weight so I could be his crutch as he hobbled over to the mound of rocks. They were beginning to shake with Dother's uncontrolled rage. "How do I get him back inside?"

"You need to touch him with the gemstone. Uncle Dub and I will do the rest."

A few of the rocks rolled off the mound ominously, worrying me that I'd stepped into a battle that wasn't quite over. "Lugh!" I cried when a hand burst through the ground like some horrid B monster movie. The fingers were tensed and angry, but they were my only opportunity.

I reached out and gripped Dother's hand in what I hoped was a stern handshake. "Lugh, shoot him again!"

Kerdik gripped his father's wrist with sweaty and clumsy fingers, and then turned in Dub's direction. "Uncle, help me!"

But Dub wasn't anywhere near us, nor did he intend on offering us a hand. He had his palm on Cailleach's forehead, and a serene look on his face. Her gaze was a million miles away, a frozen scream on her face. Easy as arresting a walking stick from an old woman, Dub parted the cane from Cailleach's covetous grip. "That's a good girl," he cooed. He hadn't needed blasts of fire and a whole canyon-sized prison. He was calm in his attack, taking what he wanted without apology or explanation, as usual. I shuddered to think at what tragic and sadistic sights he must've used to plague her sight.

"Dub, no!" Kerdik shouted. "This isn't the way! Carman will escape, and it'll be over for Faîte!"

That was all the time Kerdik's grave afforded us to regroup. Our breather from Dother was officially over. The rocks rolled off him, and he stood up, gripping my hand so tight, I knew there was no escaping the mess I'd stepped in now.

I was face-to-face with my future father-in-law, fear on my features and an evil grin on his. "Hello, daughter," he snarled.

I knew in that moment that there was no turning back.

18

TRUSTING DUB

I knew screaming would do me no good, but when Dother burned the skin on my hand just to punish me for getting in the way, I couldn't help the anguished sound that broke from my lips.

"My, my, what have we here? Could this be the prison that's trapping Dian? The one that kept all three of us locked up for so long? And attached to so lovely a hand."

"Let her go, and I'll do whatever you want!" Kerdik offered, panicking at my fruitless fight.

"Silly boy, you'll already do whatever I want. Such a useless attachment, loving a mortal like this. I could break her so very easily."

I fought to focus through the burning sensation on my wrist, landing kick after kick to his legs, his feet and his groin, but nothing affected him more than a butterfly's effort.

Dub's voice echoed across the canyon, controlled and even, despite the dire situation. "I've got the cane, Dother. Let the girl go. We've got bigger battles ahead." With an awful finality in his voice, he said, "Mother is calling."

Simple as that, Dother dropped his hold on me, moving away from us toward his older brother, who looked the epitome of composure. "How? How did you pry it out of her hands? I've tried everything."

"Cailleach doesn't respond to torture. I know how to deal with pests like her. After much brutality of battle, she thinks Kerdik's saved the day, so she's resting. I changed her vision to see what I wanted her to see, so she won't be a problem anymore." Dub met Kerdik's eyes with a grave nod. "Get Rosie out of sight, but don't take her far. Dother, let them out. If I'm to set Carman free, I don't want the girl nearby."

"Let Mother trap her. For all the trouble the girl's ring has caused us? I hope Carman draws out the spectacle of her torture as long as possible."

Kerdik's weary arms wrapped around me, cooling my burning wrist with icy water that came in sporadic spurts from his palm. He was barely upright, but he was thinking of me.

I had to get him out of there.

Dub was in control, as always, not showing a sign of distress at the thought of my demise. Not sure how much acting was involved in that feat, though. "We can't risk

Rosie touching Carman. If she does, Mother might be sucked from one prison to another."

Dother stumbled to the side, his knees weak from Lugh's arrows. "Good thinking. She'll stay here, though, and watch it all." He flung his arm out in my direction, causing me to flinch. Vines shot from his palm, wrapping around me quicker than I could run from them, though believe me, I tried. I toppled forward, hitting my chin on the floor of the canyon.

A second blast from his father knocked Kerdik back with that same unextinguishable fire that had burned Lugh's leg, giving Kerdik something to deal with that would take a considerable amount of time and effort. Dother turned to his brother with a drunken smile on his face. "Very well. Let's give Mother the welcome she deserves."

Dub was serene as he handed the cane to Dother, delivering the Holy Grail without hesitation. "You earned it, brother. I know how to crack it open. Only Rosie's ring is strong enough to break Cailleach's cane. I'll hold the girl's hand out. You need to bring the end down hard on the ring, as if you mean to break the stick." Dub smirked at me as I screamed from my supine position on the floor. "Or the girl's hand. Break them both; I don't care."

I gulped as I struggled fruitlessly against the bindings that wouldn't let me go. I was tied firmly to the floor of the canyon as the vines took root on either side of me. I was afraid that even my best efforts wouldn't be enough to free myself. The vines snaked more securely around my ribs, squeezing like dozens of thin boa constrictors, making my ribs ache.

Dother shook his head. "No! That's what happened to Dian to suck him back in. He attacked her ring."

Dub was irate at being argued with. "*I* escaped! I just came out and broke the seal. I destroyed the ring's defenses from the inside. Do it now, before the ring repairs itself!"

When the vines snaked around my throat, I let out one last panicked scream, hoping someone was on my side. I'd given it my all, and bet on the wrong horse – who, incidentally was doing his best to help Kerdik to his feet. Good old Sans.

I'd trusted Dub to help us, against my better judgment, and had made the wrong call. I was Remedial Rosie, and it would be the thing that ended Faîte for everyone. Avalon had gambled on the wrong girl, trusting me to save them, and take up their long-fought battles in hopes that I could end the suffering for them all.

I struggled and choked out my best obscenities at Dub, letting him know just how badly he'd betrayed me. My future father-in-law freed only my right arm from the vines, and moved it out to the side, flattening my hand on the dirt and securing my wrist with yet another sinister vine.

Dother didn't waste a moment, knowing the poison he'd been shot with wasn't going to make swinging the cane any easier. Trusting Dub – the true wild card in the bunch – Dother brought the staff down hard like an axe, bashing my hand with abandon.

The arrow came a second too late to stop my hand from taking the brunt of Dother's frustration in life, but I forgave Lugh when Dother took in an ominous pained breath, clutching his chest before his knees buckled. I braced myself for the blow of his body crashing down across mine, but my vision blurred, and before I could make sense of the scene, Dother had vanished completely, my throbbing hand howling with an electric zing that zipped through my body. My entire back tensed, because it had no space for my spine to bow with the painful static shock.

I couldn't breathe, so the world distorted yet again. In the back of my mind, I guessed that Dub had tricked his brother into thinking the ring's defenses were broken, when they weren't. The halo around my vision closed a little more, and in my last moments of stored oxygen, I hoped that Dother had been sucked back into the ring, where he couldn't hurt Kerdik ever again.

My eyes glazed over when smoke began to emanate from the end of Cailleach's cane. Dub grinned at me, not bothering to untangle me from the vines in his moment of triumph.

It was then that I was certain I'd trusted the wrong man. Dub let out a howl of ecstasy when Cailleach's cane split in two, and a putrid, black gas billowed from the wreckage.

19

WHAT I WOULDN'T DO FOR KERDIK

I came to when my lungs finally were able to inflate. Air was pushed into me, and my ribs rejoiced with each contraction. Kerdik's filthy and frightened face moved back from mine with relief that flew from his features in the next breath. "Up you get now, before it's too late!"

Dub's laugh could be heard above the whirring in my ears, which threatened to distance me from the danger of my surroundings. "It's too late, nephew. It's been too long since you've seen your dear grandmother. Why don't you introduce her to your fiancée?"

Kerdik's head whipped back to look at me in horror. He was scared, which was saying something. Instead of porting me out of there, which I guessed he was too weak to do, he gathered me in his arms, covering me with his body to shield me from the ensuing chaos. "No matter what happens, know that I love you," he whispered, his voice pinched and weighted with palpable pain.

I couldn't lift my busted hand to comfort him. My body was too weak from lacking oxygen to do much more than lean into his embrace, hiding in the arms that used their last efforts to shield me.

When my gaze tried to drift to the black abyss that started to form the shape of a tall person, Kerdik turned my chin, so that I could focus only on his face. "Don't look away," he instructed with all the fervency of a beloved teacher. "It's only you, and it's only me. No one else. We go down together."

I studied the fear etched into his wet eyes, wondering if I'd ever seen Kerdik weep before. As his tears fell, I understood that there would be no happily ever after for us. We had this moment, and no more after this. It took all the effort my crushed throat could muster, but I managed to eke out a wavy, "If yours is the last face I see, I can't imagine a more beautiful sight. I love you, Kerdik."

He let out a bitten-off sob before his lips descended on mine, plunging me in the sensation of a connection not many understood. Kerdik needed to be beautiful to someone, and I needed to be someone to a person who was as beautiful as him. We ignored the ticking timeclock that pounded out our last moments, and finally lived out the romance we'd put on hold for far too long.

Kerdik kissed me over and over with desperate, slick and trembling lips until a woman's deep voice made his fingers bite into me. "Well, well. Isn't that a sweet sight? My, my. It's been too long, Kerdik. Don't you want to give your old grandmother a hug?"

He paused and snapped his fingers at Sans Souci. "Guard Rosie, old friend. When you can escape, take her to Lugh." Kerdik cupped my cheek. "Lugh will be good to you."

"Kerdik," I protested, but I had no well-constructed plea that might make a way for us to survive this.

"Do what you like to me," Kerdik said to Carman, releasing me so he could stand between myself and his wrinkleless grandmother, facing the monster head-on. "I'm the one who locked you up for so long. Do what you need to." His fists were clenched, but he didn't close his eyes against the punishment we all knew was coming.

Carman was giant, easily seven feet tall, with muscular arms and thick thighs. She wore a simple black sheath dress that sort of looked like a dark toga. She didn't look older than forty, but I supposed that was the way of most of the immortals. The coveted onyx was the size of a child's fist. It was heart-shaped, and hung nestled between her breasts on a gold chain. She had the same high, sharply-cut cheekbones as her sons and grandson, and the piercing eyes to match. With a simple glance at me, I felt small and incapable of greatness.

Wait. That's not me, I argued with the insecurity that washed through my mind. I'd managed to play and fight with the big kids on the playground this entire time.

Carman was no different. The stakes were no higher: survival or death. It was a constant for me in Faîte. Carman was simply the latest threat. I was Lane's daughter, and that alone was enough to push my fear to the backburner.

I brushed the red dirt off me with my left hand (my right one was too agonized to move. I didn't want to test to see if my fingers were broken). When I stood at Kerdik's side, my calm presence in the face of such grave danger made his chest puff out. The defeat and terror that clouded his handsome features mere seconds ago cleared away, like so many storms rolling away from him. He postured, revealing the man who made a nation out of thin air and used sheer determination to do something great. Avalon had survived, despite all it had been through; I had to believe the same possibility existed for us.

Kerdik's voice came out with a thunderous crack of authority. "I trust you enjoyed your little nap in there? Perhaps it made you wiser. Gave you time to think. Of course, if you need more time, I'm happy to oblige."

Carman's smile looked like an upside-down triangle, her red lips finding the humor in the showdown she'd been waiting for. "I see you've found a girl you could bewitch into looking past your appearances."

"I see you've found no one," Kerdik replied, steadfast in his fight. "Always and only no one – except your sycophant sons. Well done on that, I guess." He glared at Dub, who stood by his mother's side with that same veiled expression of perceived superior intelligence.

Carman tilted her head back and laughed, her enormous braless breasts shaking like two bowls of loose Jell-O. "Oh, Kerdik. You always knew how to entertain me." With no further warning, she mimed throwing a javelin at her grandson, her midnight skirt flying out in the back.

I let out a loud scream when an actual spear pierced Kerdik through the middle, knocking him back and pinning him to the ground. Kerdik's eyes were wide with panic and shock, his fingers scraping against the wood that jutted out from his navel. He was in too much pain to let out a single cry, instead gasping a guttural breath every few seconds when he couldn't free himself.

My palms were slick as they tried to yank the spear from Kerdik's body, but the spearhead had been jagged, and caught on his bones, refusing to let its captive go free.

"Up and over! Quick, Rosie!" Cailleach ran to us, finally coming back to her senses. She stood in between Kerdik's parted legs and lifted his hips, motioning for me to grab his top half. I mentally smacked myself in the forehead, and lifted Kerdik's shoulders as best I could. My right hand was badly bruised, but the bones seemed to be in working order, allowing me to put enough pressure on it to hoist Kerdik up and over the butt of the javelin.

We laid Kerdik in the dirt, and I cradled my love's cheek to my breast as he bled and bled. "I'll fix this!" I promised, not knowing how to make such a thing true.

Cailleach put her hand atop my head to calm my tears that dripped onto Kerdik's chest. "He'll be alright, love.

Tha was just a warmup. Kerdik was built to endure unending torment. This is merely a scratch."

Her attempt to soothe me made me see red when I glared at Carman. "I'm not bewitched to love him! What kind of a dummy are you that you can't see the one bright spot in your terrible family tree? You want your revenge on him for locking you up? Fine. You just had it. You wanted your freedom so badly? Well, you've got it finally, so do something with it! Why are you wasting your time on hurting him? I thought you were supposed to be this big badass. Revenge? Really? You've got all the power in Faîte, and you're wasting it on revenge?" I clutched Kerdik, shaking with rage as I shouted through the canyon at Carman. "I'm never not disappointed in the childish, short-sighted behavior of you stupid immortals!"

"Enough, Rosie," Dub retorted, his jaw tense and his eyes warning me to shut up.

We were way beyond that.

"Don't you talk to me. I've finally got you out of my head! Of all the things that went wrong today, that's the one good thing. Go terrorize some kittens, or kick a puppy. I'm so done with you!"

Sans Souci sensed I'd gone too far, so he moved in front of us, blocking me and Kerdik from view. *"If you're interested in a quick death, that's the way to go about it,"* he muttered to me.

"Shut up, Sans."

Carman's eyebrow quirked as she looked between me

and the horse. "You can hear each other? You can converse with Kerdik's churlish horse?"

I rolled my eyes that this was what we were discussing. But hey, if it gave Kerdik more time to heal, sure, we could talk about that.

Cailleach lit up, her crone features fading into that of her youthful self, her skin smoothing out and her posture straightening. "This is Rosie of Avalon, daughter of Morgan le Fae and King Urien. Kerdik blessed her as a baby, so now she can hear the voices of animals."

Carman froze, taking in the new information. Slowly, a smile swept across her features, though it was clear she was unpracticed in any sort of levity that didn't have the touch of sinister intent to it. She reached out and clutched Dub's hand, who covered it with his other one, clasping her grip with fervent devotion. "Interesting. Tell Sans Souci to stand on his hind legs. I want a demonstration."

Sans snorted derisively, swishing his tail and flaring his nostrils to let his opinion on taking orders be made perfectly clear. Didn't need my birth blessing for that one.

I wiped the tears from my face, but I'm pretty sure that just smeared blood across my cheek. Kerdik tensed and gasped in my arms, but I held him still, refusing to let go of the treasure everyone else had cast aside. "It doesn't work like that. I don't control animals. I can have conversations with them. Life isn't always about domination, you psychopath."

Carman chortled at my lip. "Oh, little girl. Yes, it is."

She took a step forward. "It's your lucky day. I've many uses for someone who can speak with the creatures of Faîte. Can you decipher the pack-speak of the Loup Garoup?"

"The what?" My nose scrunched.

"The Werewolves," Cailleach explained. "She can, but only when they're in their wolf form. During the day, she can't read their minds."

"You can read minds? Hear thoughts, not just intended conversation?"

I squirmed at the attention. I'd been gearing myself up for a showdown, not a show-and-tell. "Yeah. So what? It's not as cool as say, stabbing your grandson with a javelin, but it keeps me entertained."

Carman rolled her shoulders back, and I could see a greed rising up in her eyes. "Oh, child. The plans I have for you."

"Oh, bitch," I echoed her condescending tone. "I couldn't care less about your plans. I'm here for Kerdik, not you." I turned my gaze back to Kerdik, who was still gasping, trying to warn me to run, when we both knew that just wasn't me. Bracing his shoulders so his head lolled in the crook of my arm, I pressed his cheek to my chest. I ran my fingers through his hair, bestowing upon him a gesture of love that hopefully might give him something tender to hold onto, so he might be distracted from his pain. "I'm here," I promised. "I won't leave you."

Sans snorted at Carman and pawed at the dirt. *"Back up, witch! Back up. Don't you dare come near my master."*

When Carman spoke again, she was much closer than I anticipated. Her voice was soft with a manipulative coo. "Rosie, is it? I can see you love my little Kerdik. He's an idealist, that one. Despite that shortcoming, he kept his country going, which is more than I expected of him. I wouldn't be opposed to sparing his life, letting him go free, if you could help me in return."

I stiffened, taking in the warning in Kerdik's eyes as he pawed at my arm to stop me from considering the offer. I scowled at her, anger rising to the surface, surpassing my fear. "What do you want me to do? I can't control the animals."

Sans Souci bucked at the ground and farted in my direction, angry that I was negotiating terms. *"Carman's evil!"*

Carman's tone turned syrupy, moving her pitch up an octave, as if that would make her appear nicer. As if she hadn't just stabbed my love in the stomach. My palms were dripping with Kerdik's blood, and I didn't bother wiping them off as I whipped my head up to scowl at her. "You think I don't know I could get more for my end of the deal? I want your word that Cailleach, Brighde, Sans Souci, Lugh and Kerdik all go free – as in, they could spit in your face, and you'd still let them go. You do all that, and I'll give you a week of my time." I spoke like I was in possession of some grand treasure, which was an odd way to feel about being able to talk to bunnies.

Carman didn't appear to have taken in a word of my

counteroffer. Her mouth fell open as she gaped at my face, surprise rolling off her like a wafting stench. "You're crying blood. That means Kerdik... I didn't anticipate, but I guess it's possible. He gave you a double-portion of life. He intends to keep you."

I didn't have anything to say to this, so I flipped her a nice, juicy shot of my middle finger. I turned my attention back to Kerdik, managing a wan smile as he warned me with gasps and wheezing that I couldn't make this deal. "I'd do anything for you," I reminded him, kissing his sweaty lips. "It's one week. I can handle myself."

Carman sounded perplexed. "He's not forcing you to be his mate? You're here because you... you love him? Even though he's green?"

Kerdik finally let out a cry of anguish, and I heard the rupture of the tender heart everyone else assumed was made of stone. I whipped my head in her direction, seething. "How could you say something so terrible? Kerdik is gorgeous! And even if he didn't have the sexiest skin I've ever seen, I see him – more than you ever bothered to."

Carman threw her arms into the air, speaking over her shoulder to Dub. "Fat lot of good an isolation curse does if she fancies the mutation. Must be something wrong with her brain."

"Don't listen to her, sweetheart," I whispered, willing my voice to be the only thing Kerdik heard. "What can I do? How can I make it better? Can you port out of here?"

Kerdik moved his damp chin from side to side. "Run," he choked out, gripping my shirt with arthritic hands. "Leave me and run!"

I kissed his lips, savoring the taste of Kerdik. I couldn't imagine a world where I stopped loving him – I'd been on this track for so long. I closed my eyes and pressed my forehead to his, willing myself not to break down. I knew if I wavered, Carman would see the upper hand and snatch it from me.

"Cailleach," I called, not moving my face from Kerdik's. "When Carman lifts the spell, I need you to take Kerdik somewhere safe so he can heal. Please."

Cailleach gaped at me, unsure what the right move was. Darned if I knew. "You're certain?"

"I'm not staying behind to watch you get turned into dog food," Sans groused.

I angled my chin to Sans. "I don't expect you to stay with me. Sans, you need to carry Brìghde and get Lugh out of here. Go with them. Kerdik needs someone who loves him, so stay with him, okay?"

Sans snorted, not giving me the satisfaction of a response for several seconds. *"Of course I'll stay with my master. I'll watch over him for you."*

I nodded, and carefully pried my unwilling hands loose from Kerdik, handing him to Cailleach, who was reticent to lift him off the ground.

"No," Kerdik protested, fire in his eyes and venom in

his voice. "I'll end you if you take me from her, Cailleach. Rosie, this is suicide. Callie, take Rosie and run!"

I met Cailleach's eyes until I was certain she understood *I* was the expendable one in this situation. It took everything in me to stand and walk away from Kerdik, but by now I'd learned that if you don't give your everything for what and who you love, it's not worth a whole lot in the long run. I wanted my love to count, so I put my cards on the table, ignoring Kerdik's strangled cries. If this would be the end of my great adventure, then so be it. I squared my shoulders at Carman, who looked at me like I was the first Twinkie cake that ever was.

Dub was not as thrilled, looking down his nose at me as if I was day-old cheese. "You're certain we need her?"

"Need? Maybe not. But *want*, Son. Want."

Suddenly, Dub's nostrils flared, and he took a menacing step toward me. "I know what you're doing. You're trying to get close to my mother, so you can come between us!" Dub's indignation was shrill and childish, and sounded nothing like him. It was almost like he was playing a role – or had been playing one this entire time. If this was who he'd been underneath the cool façade, then mazel tov on the stellar acting chops.

I rolled my eyes. "Yes, that's exactly right, Norman Bates. I've got the burning loins for your mom." I scoffed, flipping my hair over my shoulders. "She's all yours, dude. You can ride shotgun, and I'll be in the backseat. Banner day for you."

Dub was livid, his arm moving around his mother's shoulders, as if she needed protection from little old me. He gesticulated like he was conducting an orchestra with his other hand. "She means to manipulate you, Mother. She means to get close to you, so she can get under your skin in the same way she took down Kerdik."

"Took him down? Carman's the one who's trying to take him out! You are so off on this, Drama Queen."

Carman shushed her son, doing her best to pacify the brat. "She can't manipulate me, Dub. You're such a good boy, freeing me like you did. You'll be the only one at my side."

When she turned toward him, it was with a loving expression that looked foreign on her features. With harsh eyebrows and a sneer that was too deeply engrained to change now, she attempted a smile that had no malice in it, and failed miserably.

Dub's hand moved up, almost in a lover's caress across her front – slow and tender. It wasn't until his hand wrapped around the giant onyx hanging around her neck that I realized Dub was, perhaps, the greatest actor of them all.

20

BUTTERSCOTCH AND KNITTING NEEDLES

"Now, Lugh!" Dub cried out, his voice cracking across the dark canyon. The moon's light shone down on his hand as it gripped the enormous onyx on the chain around Carman's neck, and ripped it from her.

An arrow flew from above, soaring like a missile from severe heights above us until it landed with a *thwunk* through Carman's shoulder. I didn't understand, but when the second arrow followed behind not five seconds later, I backed away to give Lugh a clearer shot.

Carman shrieked in fury at her son for the assault that had caught every single one of us off-guard (except for Lugh, who had apparently been waiting with his arrows ready). She had two arrows jutting out of her, and grabbed at the one piercing her side to yank it out and slice it through the side of her son's neck.

Dub scrambled to stab Carman through the chest with the tip of the heart-shaped onyx, but his usually composed face was awash in pain and shock. He flailed, disoriented as he fought to hit his mark with clumsy hands.

I didn't know if he would be able to stab her through, ending Kerdik's torment for good. I didn't have the patience to wait it all out and hope for the best. I knew what false hope got a girl in Faîte, and I was determined not to let my destiny be decided by two immortals who were basically so drunk with the poison, that they could barely land a proper punch.

I didn't weigh the pros and cons. I didn't think at all, actually – I only ran. Bolting toward the two, I yanked the stone from Dub. My goal-winning shooting foot kicked out, catching Carman in the stomach. She keeled over, and before I could work out a solid plan, I landed a swift uppercut to the bottom of her jaw. The onyx that was clutched in my fist gouged a line across her chin.

It didn't shock me that I'd spilled a little of her blood. What made me stumble back instead of deliver another blow was the fact that her blood was black as pitch. It oozed from her chin like car oil, staining her creamy skin and ruining the pretty canvas.

"Finish it!" Dub shouted, stumbling toward us, as if that would be helpful.

I clocked Carman across the face with my busted hand, crying out at the pain I should've expected. My ring didn't scrape her at all, which gave me the hint that the onyx was my only weapon in this fight. My right hook that knocked her sideways was helped, of course, by the two arrows that impaired her dexterity. I kicked out her legs with a simple sweep, and shoved her backwards. Carman landed with a thud on the hard ground, her shoulders skipping twice before her body settled with a groan.

I glanced at Kerdik, who couldn't sit up without Cailleach's help, asking silent permission to do the unthinkable, and murder a member of his family.

"Do it!" Dub growled, falling to his knees with the arrow still sticking out of his neck. He looked like a grotesque Trick-or-Treater, complete with red corn syrup spilling down his collar.

I took in Kerdik's mangled body, determination steeling inside of me as I clutched the onyx in my trembling fist. Without getting the "go ahead" from Kerdik that I needed, I dropped to my knees at Carman's side and raised the onyx high.

"Wait!" she gasped. "I need... a warrior... like you."

Lane didn't need me to be a warrior. She needed me to love the Spice Girls, and to do my best in school and on the field. She needed me to be me, and in that moment, I understood that I was enough for my true mother. More importantly, I was enough for myself. My greatest adventure would be with myself, not with anyone else. In the grand story of my life, *I* held the onyx.

With a shriek of triumph mingled with fear, I brought the onyx down hard onto Carman's chest. The pointed bottom of the heart seemed just as livid at its owner as I was, and sliced without apology for all she had put it through.

"Not deep enough!" Dub shouted. "Pierce the heart!"

Again, I stabbed down, hoping this was the worst act my hands would ever commit. I was murdering a grandmother in cold blood. Granted, she wasn't the butterscotch and knitting kind, but still, she was a grandmother. If Kerdik still wanted me after all was said and done, this would've been *my* grandmother.

I'd never had one of those.

Just like Morgan, Carman was out to use me, exploiting my gifts of happenstance to further her kingdom. I'd decided I had enough people like that in my life, and the world didn't need any more. Faîte had been through enough. Faîte had put me through enough, and it was up to me to put an end to the torment we'd both suffered at the hands of such selfish rulers.

I was about to bring the onyx down a third time, when Carman burst into flames. Though she was on her last leg, she had the wherewithal to conjure up a controlled inferno that would burn me if I dared to finish the job. Smart girl.

I smiled down at her, meeting her crazy eyes with a calm that settled over me like a cozy blanket. She was beginning to understand that perhaps I was, in fact, the more unbalanced one of the two of us, unafraid of certain doom. "That little fire trick might've worked, but see, I've been burned before. And would you look at that? I'm still here." I clutched the onyx, willing my fury to be bigger than hers, my mission grander. The fire rippled over her body, leaving her unburned, but threatening me with its unforgiving heat.

When I brought the stone down into the deep cut the third time, a shriek ripped from Carman. The fire caught on my sleeves, but I didn't pull back. My skin was screaming, begging with an unintelligible wail for mercy. I leaned my weight onto the onyx, welcoming the heat with my sadistic smile.

Carman batted at my body, but I was unmovable in my conviction. Her fight began to fall away like a dying star – once great, but now irrelevant. She gasped, then let out a sickly gurgle. Then finally, at long last, there was nothing.

21

HUNGRY

Cailleach was on top of me, her body weighted and battle-worn, but determined to put out the fire with her many layers of the billowing dress I loved. It was then that I felt the flames, and the damage they had done. I'd stabbed Carman fairly quickly, so I didn't think the skin would be blackened, but my nerve endings screamed their dismal plight all the same.

Cailleach drenched me with her freezing water that came in unsteady spurts, turning me over and over like a rolling pin. She didn't slow until the flames were extinguished, and I was nauseous from being rolled for so long. "There. It's over. It's actually over! Ye did it, Rosie. Ye..." She looked down at me in wonder. "Carman's dead!"

In lieu of a response, I blinked up at the moon, wondering just how long it had been watching us get it wrong this many times. Though the dust was settling and the fire was out, the victory didn't hit me as a thing to be celebrated just yet.

Dub crawled over to me, batting Cailleach out of the way so he could hover over me, his wobbly arms on either side of my head. "Open up," he commanded.

"How did you... And then with the necklace... That was your plan?" I spoke between coughs.

"Never mind about that. Open your mouth."

I stapled my lips shut, too turned around by all of his flip-flopping to take him at his word.

The arrow was missing from his neck, but the blood still drooled down his shirt. He kept blinking, willing his vision to comply, his heart racing against the drug that fought to impair the functions of his higher faculties. His slick palm slapped against my cheek, making me gasp. He took his opportunity and shoved his finger in my mouth. The acrid rust taste told me there was blood on his finger, and it was definitely nothing as sweet as Bastien's. "That's my girl." He reached over and swiped his hand over his mother, drenching his hand in the black oil that coated her chest and chin. He spoke tenderly to me, wooing me with his gentle tone. "A little more, now. Open up for me."

"I don't understand," I admitted, so very lost in the night.

Dub painted the inside of my mouth with the blood, stroking my tongue with the pad of his filthy finger. When he seemed satisfied with that, he turned to look over his shoulder at Cailleach. "All of you, take some of

Carman's blood on your tongue. Kerdik, I'm coming, Son." He left me to stumble over to Kerdik, dipping his blacked finger into his nephew's mouth next. "Carman's blood can heal you in minutes. Cailleach, take some to Brìghde, and then port up to Lugh. He deserves a piece of the prize, too."

I blinked up at the moon again, taking a few moments to let everyone else scramble while I laid there, bereft of duty for once. I felt weightless at having no pressing plight. No one would take me away from my life. No one would take Kerdik away from me.

After a few minutes, I took inventory of my faculties, noting with surprise that the sting of the burns had gone away completely. I glanced down and noted with a gasp that my arms, which should at least have been red and starting to blister, were my familiar shade of peachiness. I turned my hands over, and even flexed my right fist, shocked that there was no hesitation in the movement.

"Dub, was that your plan all along?" I questioned, not understanding the full scope of what I'd just partaken in.

Dub let out a nervous chuckle, and walked back to me without the drunken stupor of the poison. Carman's blood could have been used all this time to cure so many things. "Indeed. I'm not sure it was my best idea to go off on my own tangent, but you not knowing certainly made your performance believable." He helped me to my feet slowly, letting my legs regain their confidence with plenty of support. He met my eyes with a question in his own that seemed to speak to his very core. "You gave yourself up for Kerdik."

For a few beats, the two of us simply inhaled and exhaled, sharing the same air as we began to digest all the implications of my offer to Carman. "I love him," I stated simply. It truly wasn't any more complicated than that.

Dub smiled at me. It was a slow-spreading expression that melted away the whining and petulance he'd displayed to manipulate his mother. It was Dub, and I was grateful he gave me the opportunity to see his true self, however jaded that man might be. "Then let's get you back to him, shall we?"

I nodded, and he escorted me over to Kerdik, who was sitting up, still in shock. He touched his stomach over and over, confused and looking like he was totally behind on everything. "Stabbed through the stomach, then Rosie and Callie got the spear out of me. Then..." He recounted the events, as if that would make the leaps of magic fit into the confines of logic.

I let Kerdik puzzle through without interruption, relieved to be able to stand up on my own. The battle was over. Carman was dead. That was all my brain could handle. I didn't have the oomph left in me to celebrate, but the relief was there. No one would hurt Faîte like Carman was aiming to. No one would control the Werewolves, or me. No one would torment Kerdik anymore, except...

Except for his father and his other uncle. If Dub could crack his way out of the ring, it was only a matter of time until those two jackholes snaked their way out. I clenched my fists, not willing to tolerate an ounce of that nonsense. This noise would end tonight, and that's the name of that tune.

"My ring. Dub, your brothers are still inside, and they have to go. I'm not risking one of them escaping down the road. We have to get them out." I met his eyes with a promise. "We have to kill them."

Dub was focused on Lugh, who was at the edge of the canyon, peering down at us. "Empty out your water vessels and fill them with Carman's blood. Quick, now."

"Lugh's got my stuff up there. I'll go get him." I wanted this over with. I wanted Faîte to be settled already. I wanted... food?

I was hungry, and not for blood. My eyebrows pushed together as I glanced down at my stomach, curious as to what could possibly make me want to eat food, of all things. Giving the others a moment to regroup, I bent my knees, and then pushed off the ground, soaring higher than my limited tolerance for heights usually permitted. I clawed at the canyon walls, using them to anchor myself as I flitted up the side. My fingers were coated in the red dirt and black blood, but I didn't care. My stomach was screaming for food. "Lugh?" I called into the woods. The hunger was reaching full-on panic, so my Compass wasn't all that reliable, shooting in all directions with its hunger-induced ADD.

"Aye. Are ye alright, Prim?" He trotted toward me, bow

and quiver slung over his shoulder. His eyes were wide with the desire to celebrate, but his senses were still on high alert, just in case he'd misread the victory from his high vantage point. "I'm thinking ye deserve a backstage pass to all my shows until the end of time for tha. I didn't know ye had tha in ye. You're always such a softy for the Werewolves."

I should've answered him with anything relevant, but the only thing in my brain was a throaty cry of starvation. "I need food! In the packs. Do we have apples? Rolls? Anything, please!"

Lugh's thick eyebrows shot into his hairline. "Who needs food?" he asked, knowing he was the only person who craved people food in the mix.

"I do! Something's shifting in me, and... Please, Lugh!"

Lugh grabbed my hand and darted to where he'd stashed our packs. I nearly cried when his fingers fumbled on the baguette he pulled out like a freaking beautiful magician. I barely had it in my hands before I was tearing apart the bread with insatiable bites.

After my tenth ravenous bite, I used my tongue to fish around inside my mouth, touching the edges of the fangs that were still there, but somehow didn't feel quite so predatory. I knew better than to trust a cure by this point in the journey, but my hunger for people food had me curi-ous. "I don't understand." That was all the pausing I could do for talking. Food needed to be consumed. I demolished the baguette, and my stomach screamed in angst for more

– eternally more. "I have to eat, Lugh! Seriously, everything we've got. I can't... It's painful!"

Lugh didn't know what to make of my manic state. I was the one who insisted on shallow gulps of the blood to draw out the supply. I was the vegetarian, who chose death at the bottom of the well rather than eat the meat that was thrown down at me. Something had shifted in my body, and I couldn't turn it off. I was shaking as Lugh dumped out the contents of the pack, revealing enough provisions for himself and me – a solid week of travel cuisine. "At least let me cut some of this cheese and make ye a sandwich."

"No time. Can't stop." I inhaled three apples before he could slap together a cheese sandwich for me, and then I demolished that, too. He didn't know what to make of my craziness, so he simply wrapped his arms around me, holding me to his chest while I shook as I scarfed down the second baguette with cheese.

I didn't feel more than a passing wave of guilt as I tore through the entire store of food. "Tha's all of it. Ye can't eat the bag, Prim."

My stomach had the nerve to growl, but I did my best to stifle my whimper through the hunger pangs that were still clawing at me. "We need your canteen. Let's grab it all and fly down. How immortal are you feeling tonight?"

"Just enough to finish the job."

Lugh found my gaze in the moonlight, and though I wanted to get everything done and over with so we could get home, we both took the time to exhale in unison. There was something special about the air that expelled from our lungs. It felt like a sort of purging – pushing out the things that had taunted us so often. Avalon and Éireland had pulled us down and defined most of our missions in Faîte. After this, it would be mostly over. We could leave the magic behind us, and breathe in the car fumes and coffee shops of modern life in Common.

I reached out and squeezed Lugh's hand. "Tell me how quick we'll be out of here when this is all over with. Lightning speed, right?"

"So quick, they won't know what hit them. We'll stop by your mum's in the Americas, and then we'll be gone – off to Europe to lounge away and do a whopping, blissful nothing. Can ye picture it, Prim? Can ye picture the beautiful nothing?"

I leaned back, resting my head on his shoulder. Closing my eyes, I envisioned myself without Avalon, without Faîte. I was sipping from a coconut (why not?), wearing a bikini, with no tattoos or scars anywhere in sight. I was standing with a volleyball tucked under my arm, readying to go back out on the sand and play.

Play. I couldn't think of anything more incredible. "I can see it. Tell me it's real."

Lugh pulled my fist to his mouth so he could bless it with a quick kiss to seal the deal. "Very real. All this will be a distant dream."

"Some parts were a good dream," I agreed, recalling

the incredible places I'd been, the people I'd befriended, the animals I'd loved, and the boys I'd kissed.

"Aye. And ye have many more good dreams inside of ye." Lugh nuzzled his nose to mine, and then pressed a secret kiss to my closed lips. It was sweet, just like him. It was the perfect thing for a friendship between two people who would have many years to keep tabs on each other. "Mm," he mewled contentedly. "Shall we?"

"Let's end this." I stood to my feet, and then helped Lugh up. We grabbed our provisions and walked toward the edge, stopping a few feet from the precipice. I reached out for his hand and linked my fingers through his. Without needing to discuss it, we took the jump at a run, bolting over the edge and leaping off the cliff. We soared down together into the canyon below with shrieks of glee and trepidation on our lips.

22

LITTLE BROTHERS

"Shouldn't Dub have come out by now?" Brìghde said the thing we were all thinking.

I scratched a spot on my elbow, amazed at how clearheaded and strong I felt after the couple of weeks I'd survived. "How long does something like this typically take? I mean, Dub's just got to go in the ring, call his brothers, and pop on out, right? It's been hours."

I should've known better than to speak. Brìghde's neutral gaze mutated into a piercing glare when her eyes cut to me. "I didn't ask for your opinion. What would ye know about any of this?"

"Easy, sister," Cailleach said, her hand on Brìghde's shoulder to talk her down from pouncing. "Rosie doesn't love Lugh. She's no threat to ye."

The canyon walls shook with Brìghde's sudden wrath, alerting the wee hours of the almost-dawn that immortals were big, giant babies. Not a huge surprise. "Then why is she standing so close to him?"

I jumped away from Lugh, who'd been standing next to Kerdik, facing me with six feet of space between us, his bow and arrow hanging at his side. He'd had it aimed at me for a good twenty minutes until it began to dawn on all of us that Dub going in to get his brothers out might take more time than an episode of *Saved by the Bell.*

Kerdik moved closer to me, frowning at Brìghde for her eighth irrational comment that morning. "Enough. You're drunk on the spell of the Gancanagh. Let Lugh go. He knows better than to fall for a woman who's taken twice over." Kerdik's eyes darted to my left hand. The barely-there light of the sun that was a mere slice over the horizon illuminated my naked finger. His eyebrows pushed together in confusion, and then worry. "Don't panic *Fleur,* but your wedding ring's fallen off." His head darted around, searching the ground around us, truly concerned about a piece of jewelry that had probably hurt him more than most objects in his long life. "Not to worry; I'll find it. It probably slipped off in the fight. I'm sure it's around here somewhere."

I held my chin high, not really wanting to have this conversation with so many ears. I took a few more steps back, jerking my chin to the side to silently ask Kerdik to come with me for a semi-private conversation. "Yeah, about that. Bastien and I sort of split up." I tried to make it all sound like no big deal – like Bastien had chosen to go home from the carnival early to beat the crowd, and I'd opted to stay.

Kerdik's eyebrows shot up into his hairline. "What?" he nearly shouted. He caught himself and lowered his voice, glancing at the others to make sure our exchange was granted the privacy I'd been hoping for. "What are you saying? What do you mean, 'split up?'"

I shrugged, not wanting to get into the big, bad reason I was going to be a Ms. instead of a Mrs. Divorced at twenty-four. Right on track. "I can't really get into the specifics now, but I did something unforgivable, so he decided we were done."

Kerdik put his hand over his mouth, and to his credit, did not give off any hints of joy. "Darling, I'm so sorry. What could you possibly have done that was so dreadful?"

I shook my head. "I'll tell you after this is all said and done. Once Dother and Dian are dead, we can go out for drinks and have a good, long talk."

The same dread that would paint any man's features at those words tugged the corners of Kerdik's mouth downwards. "Talk? Is this something awful you've done to me, as well?"

My gaze fell from his eyes, fixing on my feet as I nodded. I shoved my hands into my pockets, though I was supposed to be displaying Kerdik's ring, as if that might encourage Dub to pop out of it. "Nothing on purpose. It was an accident that I didn't understand at first. I didn't mean to," I said, silently begging him to forgive me, too. I cleared my throat. "We can talk about it later."

Kerdik's eyebrows were furrowed together, concerned more than pissed. "Whatever it is, we'll move past it." He studied my guilty body language, my nervous shuffle as I kicked at a pebble. "Can I hug you, or is that wrong?"

I wanted to tell him to run while he still had the chance. I wanted to warn him away, so I didn't infect him over and over again. He had to get some distance from me if he was ever going to see me clearly. Lugh hadn't seen Brighde in years, and she was still bananas for him. I should have told him the whole truth right then and there, so he could cuss me out and ditch, but in the end, I was selfish, and nodded. I kept my hands in my pockets when his arms wrapped around me, for some reason fearing that I might fall to pieces if they moved to return the much-needed squeeze.

"Hey," he whispered when he felt me bracing myself from the affection I desperately craved. "Whatever it is, it's alright. Let's not condemn ourselves over an accident just yet, okay?"

"I killed your grandmother," I stated flatly, switching topics, so I didn't accidentally blurt out that I'd poisoned him over and over again from the very beginning. "I think I did the right thing, but even if I did, I'm crazy sorry it went down like that. I don't want to take anything away from you, but I killed her."

Kerdik rubbed my back, soothing the ache that felt

never-ending at this point. "Now, now. Let's not apologize for the most fearsome battle in the history of Faîte. You killed an immortal. Do you understand how impossible that is? That you had the presence of mind to finish the job... You amaze me. Don't be sorry for that. If anything, you can commiserate with me that Carman wasn't worth saving."

"Well, then I'm sorry for that, absolutely. She was hurting you." I pulled back so I could see his handsome face, glowing green in the barely-there dawn. I stood in his embrace, wondering if this might be our last one. "I don't like it when people hurt you."

Kerdik's mouth formed into a small smile – it was that same look he got when he thought I was amazing, though I felt far from it. "Well, after today you won't have to worry about that anymore. No one will harm me ever again."

I really, really hoped that was true. Of all the things I wished for Kerdik, a life where he wasn't thrown in harm's way anymore was at the top of the list. In the movies, this would be the part where we kissed, and started our happily ever after. There was too much weight in my soul, though. I had so recently been a Mrs. – I couldn't down-shift that fast. Kerdik deserved a whole person, and I was chipped and broken now. Plus, we had to still murder his uncle and his father, so this was definitely not our perfect kiss movie moment. A shiver ripped through me, and I felt the effects of too much talking to animals, coupled with insatiable hunger that still clawed at my insides.

"You haven't slept enough," Kerdik observed. "Go lay down. Dian and Dother will come when they come. There's no point in forcing yourself to stay awake in anticipation."

I shook my head. "Don't want to sleep yet. I'm afraid if I do, you'll be gone when I wake."

Kerdik looked like he was watching a three-legged puppy try to walk up the stairs. "Darling, I won't leave you. I promise."

I was about to protest further, but an electric current shot through my hand, making me jump back with a shriek. "Man your battle stations!" I shouted, taking my hands out of my pocket and hoisting my gilded ring finger up high.

Kerdik backed up, his palms raised. The onyx that had been stowed in his pocket was now clutched in his hand. At his side, Lugh had his bow and arrow in position, looking fierce and focused. I tried to remind myself that he wasn't going to shoot at me, though he was aiming too close for comfort. "Dude, do not shoot me."

Brighde made some catty comment, but I ignored her, readying myself for what I hoped would be the last hurrah from the Brothers of Destruction.

"Steady, now!" Cailleach called out to us, moving to Lugh's other side with her hands extended in preparation.

Black smoke emanated from my ring, and in the next breath, three men were standing between me and the others. Their heads looked around to assess their surroundings, and that was all the mercy they were granted before we pounced.

"Ah! Dub, what's happening? I can't see!" Dian exclaimed. Those were his last words. Lugh shot him through the heart at pointblank range, and Kerdik sliced a line across his uncle's chest with the base of the onyx. "Ah!" Dian's high-pitched cries fell on deaf ears.

Cailleach thrust a huge block of ice at Dother that she conjured up from thin air, knocking him backwards just as I jumped out of the way.

I pinned Dian's arms to the ground while Kerdik smashed his way through bone and sinew, until finally on the fourth strike, he pierced through his uncle's heart.

Dother tried in vain to help his brother, but he too had been struck blind. When his boot caught my side with a swift but unfocused kick, I held my ground, pinning Dian down until I had confirmation from Kerdik that the first Son of Carman had fallen, and wouldn't get back up.

"Run, little one," Cailleach cried, moving to take my place so I could escape in case things went south, as they had a tendency of doing. "Fly away, and we'll get you when it's all over."

I had every intention of doing just that, but Dother's flailing hands caught hold of my ankle just as I lifted off the ground. Pure and utter agony started at my foot and rippled through my entire body. I screamed when a million invisible needles pierced me through. He was the brother of Evil, and I understood just how firm a grasp he had on his unique gift. I lost my oomph and fell to the ground, slamming into the dirt with a thud that shook my bones. I'm pretty sure the sound I heard was my screaming, but I couldn't feel my vocal chords. The only sensation was my bones being electrocuted over and over again. I knew only pain, and couldn't grab onto any thoughts of escape, or the master plan.

Dother's voice was shrill, echoing out across the canyon. "Mine! Let me go, or I'll end your bride. Do you hear me, Kerdik?"

Everyone was yelling, but I couldn't pick out anyone's voice for very long. The grip on my ankle jerked, and my spasming body kicked him by default, giving me an inch of space so I could catch my breath.

Dother was livid. "Dub, what's wrong with my sight? Fix it, brother!"

I rolled onto my back just in time to see the arrow sticking out from Dother's chest. A second one thunked in right next to the first. His jaw went slack through a low moan. Dother's eyes were wide with the revelation that things had gone horribly wrong. He no doubt finally understood that despite emotional and familial pleas, Dub could not be trusted.

Sans Souci barreled through, rearing up and kicking Dother in the chest, shoving the arrows out through the man's back. Dother fell backwards, and skipped twice along the dirt, gasping in the pain that I hoped wracked his body with an echo of unending hurt.

My body was still in the aftershocks of agony, so I was powerless to take the onyx from Kerdik. I didn't want him to have to murder his own father, horrible as Dother was. I wanted to do it, so he could be spared that internal torment. "No, Kerdik! I'll do it!"

Dub seemed to understand my distress, and arrested the onyx from his nephew with the steady hand of a tribe elder. "This is my job, Son. Turn your head. I don't want you to see this."

Kerdik glared at Dub, and I could see the argument brewing in his stern features. This was his kill, but I could see the uncertainty begin to surface as Dother tried to struggle to his feet. "Do it quick." Kerdik handed the onyx to Uncle Dub and trotted over to me, kneeling down and putting his back to the scene. "Tell me when it's done," Kerdik whispered in my ear, after he helped my weary body to sit up in his embrace.

I was floppy at best, but kept my eyes open for him. We were trusting Dub with a lot – perhaps too much. I never knew how much tether to give him, but prayed we weren't dead wrong with this final leap. I tried to hold Kerdik while I watched Dub kneel next to his brother, but my arms were uselessly limp.

Dub gripped Dother's hand, looking like a doctor coming to tend to his terminal patient. Dub's black cloak was spread out behind him, his hood pushed back so I could see the strain in his eyes. "It's been too long you've tormented Faîte, little brother."

"No!" Dother cried out in shock at the betrayal. I could tell he'd been granted his sight again, because he blinked rapidly, his face twisting in confusion and fear when he finally understood that Dub was no longer his brother, but his executioner. "Dub, wait! Kerdik's twisted you against us! No!"

"No, Dother. It's you who's always been twisted." Dub raised the onyx over his head, and with one strong plunge, he brought the stone down on his brother, forcing a cry of emotional hurt and agony from Dother. The echoes of such an evil man sounding so wounded pinged my soul, and I did what I could to wrap Kerdik tighter in my arms.

One stabbing was all it took for Dother to cease his torment of Faîte. One stabbing, and we were free of his constantly looming threat.

Kerdik was an orphan now, for better or worse.

23

TAKING TIME TO WATCH THE SUNRISE

It was several minutes before any of us dared to speak. Everything I wanted to say would be the wrong thing, so I kept quiet, instead focusing on my breathing, and hoping that the echoes of physical anguish would alleviate. I was trembling from the pain still, and eventually me hugging Kerdik shifted into him holding me upright. "It's alright," he whispered. "The pain will go away."

I gave him a tight nod, wishing his promise did me a lick of good. I was beyond exhausted, but the battles, the adrenaline and the deep bone aches wouldn't let me sleep. I was on the verge of passing out, so I kept my movements to a minimum, not wanting to prove to all the big kids on the playground that I was the weakest link who needed her blankie and a nap.

"It's done," Dub announced what we already knew.

The two dead brothers laid motionless on the floor of the canyon, crimson spilling from their chests and dripping over their torsos. Their eyes were open, looking up at the slowly brightening sky, but seeing none of its beauty. I wondered idly if they would have appreciated the lovely sunrise, or dismissed it as something that didn't fit their master plans, and was thus deemed worthless. I wondered if I was guilty of that same crime.

Slowly, I turned in Kerdik's arms, crying out with each subtle movement. "What are you trying to do? Be still, darling. It's going to hurt for a while."

"I want to see the sunrise."

Kerdik smiled, and I was surprised he found the strength to look on me with such affection. "Of course you do. Let me help." He shifted me in his arms so I was sitting between his legs, my back resting against his chest. His arms were my shelter, encircling me to hedge me in on all sides. I shuddered as the pain rippled through me still, but I was able to keep quiet through it, so as not to ruin the mood that had become contemplative as the others joined us. Lugh plopped down next to us, and Cailleach joined on Kerdik's other side.

Brìghde sidled up next to Lugh, practically purring at the close proximity. He shot her a look of pure compassion, and I saw a flicker of their married life dance in his eyes. It wasn't flirtation, but a sweet respectfulness of all they'd been through – the good and the bad. He'd loved Brìghde, once upon a time. Though he didn't have those feelings now, I could see him appreciating the life that had once been, even though it was far from where they were now. "I can't remember ever watching the sunrise together," he said quietly to her.

"Maybe tha was our problem." Brìghde tucked herself into his half-embrace, taking the small offering he allotted her. Her hand rested on his chest, and Lugh closed his eyes briefly, savoring too many memories of a marriage he'd once treasured.

I wondered if one day, I would have such closure with Bastien.

Dub was impatient with our reverie. "I hardly think this is the time to sit around and watch a sunrise. What shall we do with the bodies?"

"Leave them for later," I ruled, the pain finally starting to mute to a more tolerable level. "Come sit with us."

Dub huffed, irritated with anything involving whimsy. "I don't have the patience for that."

We both knew that was a lie. The two of us had spent many nights watching various sunrises and sunsets, talking about nothing and everything as the hours ticked by.

"Uncle Dub?"

"Yes, Rosie?"

"Will you sit with me?"

It was the simple request that did him in, reminding him that he wasn't stuck in the ring anymore. There were actual sunrises here, and real beauty to behold. It took a few minutes of debate, but eventually whimsy won out, and Dub sat in the dirt with us. He was a healthy distance from the group, but still; it was progress, and I wasn't going to complain.

Sans Souci sat down behind Kerdik, giving his master something firm to rest against. Kerdik chuckled at being reunited with the horse he hadn't expected to see ever again. "That was some spectacular timing, old friend."

"It was torture, being away from you. I'll breathe easier, now that Carman's dead. No one's going to torment you again, Master."

I relayed the message, much to Sans Souci's displeasure that I'd been listening in (as if I could help it). Kerdik reached behind him and scratched under his horse's chin, bringing Sans' heavy maw over his shoulder to rest there. They breathed each other in for a few moments, watching the sunrise together with a sweetness that both of them had difficulty reaching on their own.

I loved seeing Kerdik with his horse. I hadn't realized there was a missing piece to him that was possible to reattach, but there it was. The surly animal nuzzled Kerdik, and I wondered how difficult the last couple decades had been for him, being trapped in Cailleach's cane with Carman. Talk about taking one for the team.

Cailleach kept her eyes on the rising sun when she spoke quietly to all of us. "My cane is useless now, so we'll need Rosie's ring to gather up any of the lingering higher magic."

Kerdik replied for me, firm but kind in his response. "She'll rest first, then I'll take her to Éireland. Round up all the Werewolves and Vampires, so we can heal them all together and be done with it."

"Grand. Give us two weeks to gather the infected ones. If it takes us longer than tha, then we deserve to live with whatever madness we've overlooked."

Kerdik nodded. "She'll be doing the same with Avalon after she finishes with Éireland. Then we'll be handling our own problems." He paused, his tone mutating with a slice of sharpness. "Callie? Brìghde? Do you hear me? The three of us handle our countries without putting that burden on the mortals. We've grown lax and apathetic. This is our chance to start fresh. Give Rosie a month, and then we do this without her."

I didn't know what to make of Kerdik's blatant declaration that I'd been an integral part in helping to heal Faîte. I didn't know how much of it had to do with me, and how much of it was the coincidence of me wearing the ring. Either way, I snuggled into his chest, marveling at the many pink and orange hues that were lighting up along the horizon. The sun agreed with us, that this would be a new day, and a fresh start for the land – perhaps for us all.

"Can this be done now? I'd like to get on with what needs to be tended to," Dub said with a clear note of irritation in his tone.

I threw my arms in the air in exasperation. "What

could possibly need to be done at this exact moment? Are they going to *Evil Dead* us and come back to life?"

"No. But I haven't been dealt with yet. I can't do it myself."

"Do what?" I asked. Other than Kerdik, it seemed I was the only one unafraid to converse with the last Son of Carman.

"One of you has to take the onyx and kill me."

That was enough to break us all out of our reverie. "Um, come again? How'd you jump to that?"

Dub looked incredulous, as if his reasons for asking to be euthanized were obvious. "I'm a Brother of Destruction. There's no place for me here. I don't belong in Faîte anymore. I'm not sure I ever did. This is how it should be."

Kerdik shook his head. "I'll not murder you, Uncle Dub. You're the only person in my family who's ever tried to save me."

Dub's face was stony as he stared up at the horizon. "I blinded your girlfriend. I'm not guiltless in tormenting Faîte when I was younger and more easily swayed by my mother."

I rolled my eyes. "Then stop being a jackwagon, you drama queen. If you don't want to be a bad guy, then don't be one."

Dub stiffened, affronted. "It's not as simple as all that. The people fear me. They don't need that in this new regime. This is your chance to start fresh with Faîte." He shook his head and stared at the sunrise, finally inviting the beauty to lull him, since he insisted this would be his last day of sunshine.

"Off yourself, then. None of us are going to do it," I ruled for the group.

Cailleach glanced at me sideways, silently asking why I was passing up on a golden opportunity. It was strange that such a powerful being deferred to me. I mean, what did I really know about super bad guys? All I knew was that I wanted to live in a world where people could redeem themselves, and make a change for the better. Dub proved he could change. The rest would be up to him, to decide what kind of man he wanted to be with his opportunity for a brand new life.

"You'll help Kerdik," I told him. "Dying is selfish at this point. Kerdik needs you to help him with Avalon. The people are scared. They want to know someone's looking after them, and they're too broken for Kerdik to handle everything."

Dub leaned forward to study my expression around Brìghde and Lugh. "You want me to clean up after the Fae now?"

My voice turned sharp. "Why not? Are you too good to help people?"

Dub scoffed, but didn't say anything one way or the other.

Kerdik kissed my temple, and pressed his cheek there so we could watch nature show off together. The sunlight was slowly spilling into the canyon, like a golden blanket that illuminated as it was shaken out. It was waking everyone from the stupor of survival we'd all been trapped in. There was the ethereal reminder that we could soon start living again – just plain living.

Kerdik twined his fingers through mine, thumbing my empty ring finger. We said nothing, but felt everything crackling in the air around us. There were too many points to discuss, and I was far too exhausted for such weighty conversations. I yawned, and he held me tighter, cocooning me in the arms I'd missed.

After the sun had fully risen and was seated in the sky to announce the new era, Cailleach rose to her feet. Her blue and gray robes were filthy with the red dirt and a bit of blood, but she looked glorious – fearsome and warrior-like. She was the picture of strength and femininity. It was hard to look away. A few of her blue dreads had come loose from the lace the rest were tied back in, and her countenance kept shifting from hag to young woman, depending on how the light hit her. "Come, Brìghde. There's much to do for Éireland." She hoisted her sister up, though Brìghde was reticent to leave Lugh's side.

Then Cailleach turned to me, leaned down and pulled me from Kerdik's arms. Her embrace was soft and maternal, making me choke with emotion I'd tried for so long to hold back.

I missed my mother. Lane was my touchstone, and I'd been without her for too long. Despite my pride-soaked need to be seen as a warrior who was competent enough to fight alongside the immortals, my head migrated to Cailleach's shoulder. For several elongated seconds, I simply breathed, letting my burdens rest in her capable arms. "Ye did marvelous, Rosie," she said in her gentle way. "When ye come back from Common, be sure to give us a visit."

I nodded, my arms wrapping around her to return the hug and feel her hump. "Tell me life gets better," I whispered, desperate for someone to dole out some hope that I could hold onto.

I could hear the smile in her reply. "Aye. Life gets much better. When ye come back in your second life, remind me to show ye the hot springs. We'll lounge around for days and forget all our problems. Who knows? By then, there may not be all tha many to forget."

I couldn't fathom an existence where I'd forgotten the worries I'd been bogged down with. It was so far beyond my current circumstances that it felt outside the realm of possibility. Still, I chose to trust the hope she offered, knowing I needed to keep a sliver of something shiny in my heart. I was dangerously close to crusting over with a glib acceptance that life would always find a way to be cruel. "Thank you. Thanks for everything."

"Aye, child." She met Kerdik's eyes when she stepped back from me. "I'll call for her once the Werefolk are rounded up. We'll make the healings as risk-free as possible for her."

"I appreciate that." Kerdik stood and extended his hand to Cailleach, but the gorgeous hag wouldn't have it.

She pulled Kerdik in for a hug I could tell he wasn't expecting. His eyes were wide at the embrace he clearly wasn't used to. It broke my heart a little to watch him be so unfamiliar with a simple embrace when it didn't come from me. I made a note to hug him more, so the act would someday become second nature to him. Cailleach whispered something in his ear, which made him gasp. "Truly?"

"You've earned it. I see tha ye love, and tha you're not a danger to Brìghde any longer. Be with whomever ye choose. Your curse is lifted."

Light shone in Kerdik's eyes. I knew Cailleach had freed him from the restrictions of not being able to make love without fear of turning the woman into a dragon. I didn't like any type of curse on Kerdik's shoulders, so I smiled along with him, enjoying the elation that lifted his posture. His lips brushed Cailleach's cheek in a gesture of putting the past behind them. "Thank you."

Brìghde moved to Lugh and kissed him square on the mouth before he could brace himself. She licked the outside of his lips, making me gag. "Come back for me," she breathed. The sound was husky and filled with PG-13 need.

"This is our goodbye, Brìg. Best accept it, and put me behind ye. I'll not be coming back to Faîte. I belong in Common." His words were clear in laying down a boundary, but Brìghde's eyes still sparkled with optimism and longing. "Go on, now. Éireland's waiting for ye."

Brìghde kissed him again, and I knew she was touching

his saliva, addicting herself all over again. It was going to be a long road to recovery for homegirl.

My head hung low at the reminder that I would have to confess to infecting Kerdik with my Gancanagh mojo soon. After Cailleach and Brìghde disappeared, I shoved my hands in my pockets and kept my eyes on the dirt. "Walk with me?"

"Of course. Be back in a few, guys. Lugh, pack up your provisions. I'll be porting you two back to the castle." Kerdik wrapped his arms around Sans Souci's neck and rested his head to the horse's thick mane. "Don't go far, old friend. How I've missed you."

"Master, master," Sans cooed. For how surly the horse was, he was a puppy for Kerdik. They were two peas in a pod, and I couldn't imagine how lonely they must've been all these years without each other.

Kerdik kissed Sans' neck, and then turned to extend his hand to me. "Come, darling. Tell me all the ways you love me."

If only we could have such unencumbered conversations.

24

DOCTOR DUB'S DIAGNOSIS

"**W**ho told you?" came Kerdik's dejected response after I confessed how I'd been unintentionally poisoning him to fall for me.

My eyebrows furrowed at his question. It was not the indignant telling off I'd been anticipating. My arms were wrapped around my middle, ready to stave off the verbal blows, but they never came. "What?"

"Who told you about your grandparents? I know it wasn't Urien. He didn't know. Did Morgan suspect what she was before the end? I'm sure Lane doesn't have any idea."

My jaw fell open. "You knew? This entire time, you knew I was poisoning you?"

Of all things, Kerdik laughed. When I balked at him, he covered his delighted smile and shook his head. "I'm sorry, it's just that you look as if you're about to tell me you've got two months to live or something. You're third generation Gancanagh, darling. It's hardly the arsenic you're thinking it is."

"Hello, you've seen what Lugh being Gancanagh has done to Brìghde. How can you be so flippant about this? I tricked you into falling in love with me!"

Kerdik must've hit some sort of seriousness maximum, because he couldn't stop laughing. "Oh, that's quite funny. Say it again. Tell me how devious you are in all of it. Tell me you've got your witch's cauldron and a lock of my hair or something." His shoulders shook with mirth, which only confused me. "Oh, I needed that. Thank you. Life was getting far too harrowing. Now, tell me what you really brought me over here to discuss. Why did you and Bastien separate?"

I glanced around incredulously, and threw my arms out for dramatic effect. "Because I tricked him, too! I poisoned him with my Gancanagh pheromones, or whatever. I told him that I found out one of my grandparents passed down the gene to me, and he said he was out."

Kerdik's features scrunched, perplexed. "No, he didn't. Bastien wouldn't leave you over a technicality like that."

"A technicality like mind-control? He has every right to leave. I even gave his ring back, because it shouldn't have been mine in the first place."

This sobered Kerdik marginally. "Darling, third generation Gancanagh is nothing like what Lugh's done to Brìghde. I knew your grandparents, and the lengths they went to in order to pass down the Gancanagh gene to their daughters. Nine daughters, and no sons. When I rounded up the higher magic, I could've scooped the Daughters of Avalon into the ring as well, but I didn't. The gift was diluted in them, and aside from the men they chose to take into their beds, their sweat was relatively harmless to most. Your Demi fellow was with Morgan, Avril, and who knows how many more of your aunts, but he doesn't crave them now. Demi told me that he craves only you."

I grimaced at the visual of Demi with my Aunt Avril and my mother, but Kerdik's logic began to crack my own. My frown caught on Kerdik's last sentence. "Demi doesn't crave me. We had a relationship, and it ended because he died prematurely. What we have is no closure. He woke up and I was married to some other dude. That's rough, no matter how you slice it."

"Demi can overcome your grand trickery, given time. That's more than Brìghde can do. It's been decades, and she still pines for Lugh." Kerdik reached out and took both my hands in his, swinging them between us, as if we were discussing dandelions. "I knew you had a bit of Gancanagh in you from the beginning. If you recall the first time I met you as an adult, we were in the cave I built, waiting out the storm. I didn't touch your skin for a while, but I fell hard for you from the very beginning. It was the sweetness of your smile, not your poison. Your magic has always been your kindness, Rosie. Never doubt that what we have is real."

I tilted my head to the side. "When we're apart, you're not like Brìghde? You don't crave me like a crazy stalker?"

The corner of Kerdik's mouth lifted up into a wry smile that had too much bad boy to it. "Well, I always crave you, but you can hardly blame the Gancanagh gene for that. If I was so addicted on a chemical level, I wouldn't be able to allow you to be with Bastien." His eyes turned serious, piercing into mine. "It was torture, to stay away from you, knowing you were in another man's bed. But I did it, because you told me it was what you needed."

I had no idea what to do with this new information. "You're not addicted to me?"

"Only in the usual love-of-my-many-lives sort of way. I'm mad for you, but only because of who you are, not because of who your grandparents were." He sighed, finally letting the whole truth out. "I'll admit that I do get a hit of a high when we kiss, or when I come into contact with your sweat. I crave you for like, a day or two with the strong unnatural way one feels when controlled by the Gancanagh. But that's all. It would wear off on Bastien in the same time, too. You've never had me so far under your spell that I didn't know exactly what I was doing. I've wanted you because of you. There's nothing more to it than that." He lifted his hand to stroke my cheek. "Bastien truly left you?"

I nodded, unable to keep the devastation off my face. "Do you blame him?"

"But he knew already he was addicted to you because

of how you feed from him. This is barely ten percent of that addiction's potency."

"But he understood that about our arrangement, and chose it. This was me tricking him. Unforgivable."

Kerdik pulled me into his embrace, leaning his chin atop my head. "I'll talk to him, and make him see reason."

I shook my head, squinching my eyes shut. "You're too good to me. Don't bother, though. It's my marriage, and it's over. It's what Bastien wants, so I'm respecting it. I'm going to Common for a while. Downshift a little from the Faîte drama."

"I give it a week before Bastien comes crawling back to you. Trust me. I know the madness it is to be separated from you. He won't last long before he realizes he doesn't care if he's being seduced by the magic in your makeup. He'll want you." Kerdik's voice shifted to a resigned tone of practiced patience. "And you'll take him back. You'll live out the remainder of his life by his side, and when Bastien passes as an old man, you'll come back to me. You're his princess, but you're *my* queen." He squeezed me tighter. "Promise me. Some days, it's all that gets me through."

"I promise. Though, you're wrong about Bastien coming back. I need to be in Common for a while. Clear my head. Be single. Blow off some steam. I'm barely holding on here."

"Lugh mentioned something about you staying with him. I trust I don't need to curse him with impotence?" The threat was heavy, and firm as a judge's gavel.

I blanched. "Don't do that to him. He's being a good guy and giving me a break. He has no one real in his life, Kerdik. Everyone fawns all over him in both worlds. Since I can't get taken in by his Gancanagh nature, I make for a friend he can actually trust. He needs a sister."

"A sister is fine. Lugh doesn't need a wife, and if he does, he doesn't need to look in my bed to find one. Are we clear on that? I share you with Bastien because I saw how strong your love was, and Bastien had his claim on you first. Do not underestimate my wrath if you find your way into Lugh's sheets."

I rolled my eyes at him and pulled back. "Deal. Lugh loves you, so you don't have to worry about that. I was Bastien's, and then I'll be yours. Until then, I just want to be mine for a while. I'm having a rough time with all of this, K."

He smirked at my informal address. "Then a holiday sounds just about right. You'll come back to me?"

"I always do."

He stiffened as the rest of the factors in my jumbled tower began to dawn on him. "But you're a Vampire! You need to drink Bastien's blood to survive! Come. I'll take you to him now and make him see reason. I'll not let you starve."

I shook my head and explained my assumption that Carman's blood cured enough of the darkness in me so that I could live on either blood or food. "It's a working theory, but I had a crapload of food from our packs, and it actually tasted like food instead of sand in my mouth."

"She's mostly correct," Dub confirmed, no doubt irked that I'd found a way around the limitation. "She can survive on food now, but there's still a minimal need for her mate's blood. I'd say she'll be able to cut down to a few swallows every couple of weeks."

My eyebrows rose with hopefulness. "Seriously? That's fantastic."

"Carman's blood can right a myriad of wrongs. The rest of the *Attelage* Vampires should be given a taste of the antidote if we're to keep things in order."

I yanked the conversation back from Dub, and shot him a look that told him "thanks" and also "butt out". I stretched a muscle in my arm before I continued. "Bastien's agreed to stop by the castle and donate blood once a week. Remy will send that to Common for me, and I'll have enough to live off of. Bastien's angry with me, but he's not spiteful. He doesn't want me dead." That last declaration was a wish of mine, and not confirmed fact. I truly hoped that after all we'd been through, Bastien could still see me clearly. I prayed that he still loved me, and didn't imagine I was some sinister monster who needed killing.

My chest ached with need for my husband, but I shoved that longing down, knowing that just because I wanted something to happen, didn't mean it would. My marriage was over, and that was that. I'd fought too much for my life. I shouldn't have to force my marriage to work.

Part of me knew that Bastien should've had faith in me – in us – but he just plain didn't. I would fight for Avalon when she was broken, but for this? I actually needed someone else to fight for me, and Bastien made it clear that he didn't want to be that guy anymore.

Kerdik twined his fingers through mine, and we walked together back to Lugh, Dub and Sans Souci, who snorted his disapproval at me. "You'll take Sans with you, right?" I asked the man at my side.

"Of course." Kerdik stroked Sans Souci's mane, and the horse practically purred his contentment. "That is, if he'll have me."

Sans stomped his hoof on the floor, and I heard his internal monologue swearing oaths of loyalty and love for his master.

I nodded my approval. "Good. Now you've got two solid backups. I worry about you when I'm not around to help."

Kerdik's wry smile made the corners of his eyes crinkle in a way I found positively endearing. "Only you would worry about me."

Lugh had my pack, his, plus the bow and quiver on his shoulders. "Are ye ready to get back to the castle?"

I nodded, and then locked eyes with Dub, wondering how to say goodbye to the man who'd haunted my dreams. I didn't know what to say to him. I mean, he was a bad guy in parts, but the best kind of person to have on your side in other respects. I wasn't sure if we were very close after all the time he'd spent in my subconscious, or if he was glad to be rid of me once and for all.

He didn't seem as torn as I did, and reached out to shake my hand. "After everything, it's good to see you in real life. Of all the minds to be stuck in, I'm sure I couldn't have picked a better one than yours. Farewell, little flower."

I wanted to shake his hand to seal his lovely words, but I merely stared at it, and shoved my hands in my pockets. "Thank you. I, um, recently learned I might be part Gancanagh, so I don't think I should be touching people on the fly. But thank you for saying all that. I'm glad Kerdik has you." It felt like the awkward conversation people must have with their significant others if they discovered they had an STD.

Kerdik briefly explained the unconfirmed theory to his uncle, who quirked his eyebrow at me. Kerdik sighed at my hesitance. "It's alright, Rosie. I've seen you touch people's skin before, and it was nothing like what Lugh can do." Then to his uncle, he explained, "She's a little skittish about the fallout."

Dub batted his hand in my direction, as if I was silly to be cautious over something so trivial as poisoning people. "Oh, that's easy to tell. You want to know if you're part Gancanagh? Do you need confirmation?"

My eyebrows rose. "There's a way to tell? Um, yes, please."

Dub closed the gap between us and pinched my cheeks between his thumb and forefinger, so my mouth popped open. He peered inside like a dentist, looking for... I'm not sure. Warts? A witch's cackle? Before I could brace myself, Dub's tongue darted past my lips, and licked the inside of my cheek. Like, licked inside my mouth. His lips caressed mine while I shrieked with righteous indignation. He managed to suck on my lower lip to end the weirdest kiss of my life before I shoved him away.

"Sick! Why would you do that? I'm your niece, you wang!"

The canyon walls trembled, and before I could stop Kerdik, a boulder appeared out of thin air in his hands, and lobbed itself at Dub, catching him in the abdomen with a loud, "oof!" Kerdik was livid. "You were in her head far too long, old man. She's not yours to keep."

Dub straightened and glared at the boulder that had walloped him in the stomach. "I trust the madness is out of your system, Son? I do not wish to bed your future wife." Dub shot me a smirk that made me want to punch him. "I was merely tasting her mouth. It's a surefire way to tell."

"Tell what?"

"To confirm that yes, Rosie is part Gancanagh, though it's faint."

Kerdik's expression mutated from livid to perplexed. "You can tell all that by tasting her mouth?"

"Sure. I'm sure if you taste Lugh, it's far more potent. No doubt I'll be craving Rosie for another day or two, maybe a little longer, but that's all. You can tell the difference easily enough if you know what to look for. There's that faint flavor that lingers." He licked his lips and shivered. "Like strawberries."

I don't know why that was the final straw, but I wound up and clocked Dub across the face, snapping his jaw to the side. I shoved my finger in his face, angry that we were even having this conversation. "Next time you want to go testing theories, you start off kissing Lugh, not me. I'm not up for grabs."

Dub chuckled at my moxie. "Now, now. Let's not get too worked up." His eyes gleamed with a flair for wickedness and play. "That can't be good for the baby."

My brain did a fuzzy static sound while it tried to process his words. As if he'd spoken another language entirely, my eyebrows furrowed together and the corners of my lips dragged downward. "What are you talking about?"

Dub's eyes darted down to my belly, and then back up. "I thought I was clear. You're pregnant."

I scoffed, as if that might dismiss the bomb he looked totally serious about. "Dude, that's some stellar doctor's exam. Shove your tongue down my throat, and you've got an all-access pass into my uterus? Nice try. You're screwing with me."

Dub didn't feel the need to quantify his doctoral qualifications. "I know things about the universe you couldn't even dream of. Make no mistake about it; you're pregnant. I'd guess you're a week or so along, judging by the flavor of your tongue."

"What? Dude, gross! I'm so over your mind games.

You're out of my ring now, so I don't have to listen to you. Kerdik, can you take me home? I'm tired, and I don't want to deal with your uncle any longer."

It was then I realized that neither Lugh or Kerdik were moving. They were both frozen on the spot, eyes wide and fixed on my stomach.

"Why didn't you tell me?" Kerdik asked quietly. It wasn't anger, but a brave face through sudden agony that he donned.

I tried to shrug it all off while doing a mental map in my mind. My birth control was a one-year shot that made traveling to and from worlds easy enough. I rubbed the back of my neck, and noticed I'd begun to sweat. "What month is it? Like, how long have we been down here?"

"It would be... May? June?" Lugh tried to work out the timeline, but everything blurred with the lifestyle we led out here. We were always on to the next harrowing event. Who had time for checking dates, or going to the doctor for a birth control update?

"You're lying," I guessed, with probably too much hope in the statement. "Tell me you're lying!" I wrapped my arms around my middle, but then moved my hands, as if that would make me not... I couldn't even think the word. I couldn't be...

Dub's features flashed with a rare glint of compassion. "Avalon's kingdom has an heir. This is good news, dear."

Kerdik's hand on my back spooked me, and I jumped back from the group. "It's not true, and that's not how you tell if someone's pregnant. I'm not stupid." The last sentence felt like a declaration I needed to make clear to myself, as much as to them. "I'm not stupid." My eyes met Kerdik's closed expression. "Will you take me home?"

Kerdik moved slowly, winding his arms around my waist with great caution, as if something had changed in the last two minutes. "Of course. You should lie down."

"Because I haven't slept in days," I reminded him, "not because of the other thing that isn't real."

Kerdik didn't say anything, but closed his eyes and pressed his forehead to mine. He held me like that, in front of the guys, not bothering to conceal the pain on his face. "I knew this day would come. I knew this day would come." He kept chanting it, like he was talking himself through the ordeal. "I promised myself I would congratulate you. I promised myself I would smile. Am I smiling?"

There was no trace of happiness on his face, only a deep sense of loss on the day he'd seen his father, uncle and grandmother murdered. I don't know why this seemed to hit him harder than everything else, but he remained quiet a little longer, as if that would make everything right again.

"Take me home," I whispered. "Please. This isn't real. Dub's screwing with me again."

Dub stepped back. "Kerdik, I'll meet you in Avalon when the sun sets. I can help you round up the Werefolk then." Dub pulled the onyx out of his pocket and extended his arm, presenting the gem to me. "Rosie, you should keep this. You'll be better at knowing when to use it than any of us."

I frowned at the fist-sized heart-shaped black stone, not wanting to touch it. "No way, dude. That's a family heirloom. It belonged to your mother. It's too important."

Dub picked up my hand and placed the stone in my palm, closing my fingers around it as much as they could stretch. "You're my family. You're to marry Kerdik one day, so you'll be my niece. Carman's granddaughter." When this explanation only made me uncomfortable, he added a brief, "You might be the only person in this world that I trust. I know your mind more than most. It'll be safe with you."

It was too much for one person to be trusted with, but since my plan was to move to Common, I wondered if Dub was right. The stone would be innocuous on earth. I nodded my thanks, and pocketed the gem. I tilted my head to the side, still not knowing what to make of the man who'd invaded my mind on too many occasions. "I'll make sure no one uses it."

"Very well. Off you go, then. I'll check in tonight to see if you need anything." Dub held his arms out to me with a smile, silently asking for the hug he'd grown accustomed to from me.

I glowered at him. "You've got to be joking. I'm not hugging you after you gross-kissed me."

My response only made him laugh more audibly. "Oh, little flower. I'm so very glad Kerdik extended your lifeline.

You do amuse me. I'll collect my hug another day." Then he bowed, which caught me by surprise. "Until we meet again, dear one." He straightened and gripped Kerdik's shoulder. "Carman's blood will have healed whatever damage might've been done to the fetus in the fight, but she should rest."

A storm of emotions was warring inside of me, but I said nothing as the canyon faded from view.

25

THE KING AND THE CURSE

I'd sworn Kerdik and Lugh to secrecy concerning Dub's assumptions about me being... I still couldn't say it, even to myself. I greeted the household, and left Lugh to relay the news of all the bad guys falling, my sight being back for good, the miracle blood we were thinking might give the *Attelage* Vamps some relief, and Dub returning to the kingdom as a good guy (fingers crossed).

I slept the day away alone in the bed meant for Bastien and me, and didn't wake until Rigby knocked on my door long after the sun had fallen. His eyes were round with fear, but his voice was ever the professional. "My Queen, if it's acceptable to you, your presence is requested in the throne room."

I rubbed the sleep from my eyes. "Sure. Let me just find my shoes."

Rigby let himself into my bedroom and shut the door behind him. "You have time. Perhaps you'd like me to draw you a bath?"

His oh-so-subtle hint that I looked like I'd been through a war wasn't lost on me. I didn't have the presence of mind to argue, so I nodded. "Sure. Thanks."

He didn't comment on the fact that I didn't put up a fight at the offer to luxuriate when there was work to be done, but his raised eyebrow told me he noticed my spirits were sufficiently broken. After he'd drawn a scented bath that was far too fancy for someone with hands as bloody as mine, I simply stood in the center of my mother's bedroom, lost in the simple task.

"My queen, where is King Bastien? I've heard talk of him staying elsewhere, but I know that cannot be true."

I opened and closed my mouth several times before actual sound came out. "Bastien and I decided to separate. Where did you hear he was staying?"

"Elsewhere," he repeated evasively, avoiding my eyes.

"At the tavern?"

Rigby didn't answer right away, but I knew it before he confirmed it. "Yes, my queen. But that doesn't mean he's taken another into his bed, like the last time."

Like the last time. I swallowed hard, feeling like a fool. "It's fine. He's free to be with whoever he wants." But he was my husband. He should be in my bed. Even if I'd accidentally controlled him, that shouldn't change us... or maybe it should. I didn't know which way was up anymore.

I didn't protest when Rigby linked his fingers through mine. "Your majesty, do you require assistance?"

I looked up at Rigby, seeing him, but not. "What am I supposed to be doing?"

Rigby took pity on me and led me behind the partition. Without a word, Rigby slowly undressed me, giving me ample opportunity to shove him away. His fingers were so well-practiced in undressing women that he didn't need to look at what he was doing. He kept his gaze fixed on my forlorn features, even as I stepped out of my filthy jeans. There was a pile of my clothes on the floor, and I stood before Rigby with utterly nothing in my chest, and nothing to cover my nakedness.

He was gentle with my fragile state, and led me to the bath tub. As if I was something special, he lowered me into the warm water, and let the flowery oils seduce me into a state of calm. When I made no move to touch the soap, Rigby picked it up and worked a lather into his palms. His hands massaged as they cleansed, soothing me from my inner turmoil. I wanted to bury myself in a heap of depression, burrow my way under the covers and let the night take care of itself. I would finally be given the space to grieve the loss of my marriage. I wasn't sure I deserved to lose it over such a technicality, but it was gone all the same.

Rigby helped me out of the tub once I was clean, and I stood there like Depression Barbie while he dried me with a plush towel. He brushed out my tangles, and styled my hair into a crown of dozens of braids. Then he dressed me in a crimson gown with heavy, flowing skirts that made me look like my mother. I even let him put a touch of dark pink lip gloss on me without a fight, not caring what I looked like, only that someone else could take the burden of deciding everything for once. When he showed me my reflection in a silver tray, I inhaled sharply at how much I looked like Morgan – regal and without a smile anywhere on the horizon.

I didn't feel anything but alone. I wondered if that was how Morgan had felt most days.

Rigby held his elbow out to me, and I consented to the escort. I wore red slippers, and didn't even have the whimsy in me to pretend I was Dorothy, wearing the iconic ruby slippers. I didn't have it in me to pretend at all anymore. I knew Lane would be sad at this, but anything beyond my own sadness was white noise.

It wasn't until I heard Urien's cries of anger and agony that I snapped into the present. My feet picked up, and I ran down the hall, my dress flowing out behind me. A few of the servants charged at the sound as well. Four guards responded promptly like it was, well, their job.

I bolted through stone corridors toward the throne room. I gasped when I saw Urien on all fours, heaving like a fifty-something couch potato who'd just been forced to run a marathon at gunpoint. Uncle Dub was standing over him, unperturbed. He waved off the servants, who shrieked at the sight of Dub so near their king. "He's fine. Just a little unfinished business. Nothing to see here, Rosie.

Go back to bed." Then Dub gave me a second, curious glance, perplexed by my appearance – as if me in a gown was a more disconcerting sight than my father on the floor, howling his distress.

"What happened to him?" The servants and even the guards were frozen near the doorway, afraid of the intruder they'd been taught to fear since birth. The boogeyman was supposed to have been locked up for decades, but here he was, traipsing around the castle like it ain't no thang. A few of the servants screamed, turned and ran. I pushed through and fell to my knees, touching Urien's shoulder to steady him. A warmth flooded into my right hand, confusing me. It was the most contact we'd had in... I'm not sure how long. "Urien, what's wrong? What's hurting?"

Dub crossed his arms over his chest, unruffled and mildly annoyed. "Oh, he'll be fine. He just doesn't like the taste of his own medicine."

"Run, Rosie!" Urien eked out through his panting.

Without turning his chin toward the others, Dub commanded them with a simple, "Out," and they scattered from the throne room that Urien had ruled with my mother so many years ago. Only Rigby remained, and he hugged the doorframe with a visible urge to leave me without so much as a "peace out." Even so, Rigs stayed, warning me with a look that this was a code red situation.

"What did you do to him?" I shouted, my gaze piercing Dub through.

Slowly, Dub lowered himself until he was crouching before Urien, his black cape billowing out behind him. He wore a cold expression that was tainted with a snide tease – as if he was trying to appear soft, but had little frame of reference. "Your father cast you out because you were other."

I stiffened at the painful recollection. "What did you do to him?"

Uncle Dub met my eyes without hurry, ignoring my father's pain. "I made him other. He's been infected with the Were curse. While your touch just now healed him from turning into a rabid Werewolf, he'll turn into a sentient wolf at night, just like your beloved Malone."

26

SHOULD I STAY OR SHOULD I GO

"You did what? How did you... Who told you to... What makes you think..." My indignation and horror couldn't mold itself into one coherent thought.

Dub frowned at Urien, and then gave me a scolding look. "I do wish you hadn't healed him so quickly. He hasn't even felt the full pain the other Werewolves have had to endure at the transition. He was partway there, but you stopped the fun. Pity."

I shoved Dub backwards. "What's your damage, Heather? The curses aren't supposed to be weaponized. Why would you do that?"

Dub shot me a menacing look that told me he didn't much like being pushed around. *Sucks, don't it, pal.* He huffed his frustration with me, as if I was the one being the problem here. "Because he's to rule Avalon with Duke Lot in your stead. I'll not have someone who could cast out his own daughter on the throne of Kerdik's land. A ruler without compassion is a bane to his nation." When my mouth fell open with no response, Dub softened. "You forget that I've heard your conversations. I've witnessed your life. I held you while you cried over your father's shunning, and then watched you rise above it all with dignity befitting a queen." His eyes narrowed imperiously at me, letting me know he would never be apologetic over this. "You wished me to be a better man? This is what that looks like. I'll not sit back and allow his sort of foolishness anywhere near a crown. Urien will recant his shortsighted policies, and Avalon will grow stronger."

I pinched the bridge of my nose. "Look, I appreciate where this is coming from, but you have to undo this." My father was shaking next to me, his arms barely able to keep his head from hitting the floor. Despite everything, I fell to my knees and wrapped my arms around Urien's middle in an attempt to calm him.

Dub let loose a low chuckle that made my spine straighten. "That you think you understand how a nation should operate better than I do is amusing."

"This isn't the way!"

"This is the *only* way. You're not willing to let sacrifices be made, unless they're your own. It's time to rule, Rosie."

I glowered at Dub. "Yeah? Then get the crap outta my house. How's that for laying down the law?"

Dub's chest shook with mirth. "I'll do as I please, and you'll thank me for the assistance. Do you think it's everyone I bother to avenge?"

"I don't need you to curse people in my name!"

Dub stood, and then flicked his hand at my protest, as if he was doing me some big favor. He looked exactly like Kerdik when he offered up a flippant, "It's no trouble."

I growled in exasperation. "Oh, you're the worst! How no one's dropped a house on you is beyond me."

Dub knelt down, and reached out to cup my chin with one hand. His voice was calm, and without apology. "Rosie, listen to me. Your father cast you out, along with too many others. If Avalon's to unite without you here, they need to trust their rulers. Urien's now one of the survivors of a curse. He'll be the pious king who saw the error of his ways. He'll welcome you with open arms, and the kingdom will feel treasured right alongside you. Can't you see they need that? You aren't the only one who lost a father in the mess of his bigoted decision. Avalon needs their father back, even if you insist you don't." Dub ran his thumb along my jaw. "But you do, precious girl. You do."

I willed myself not to get choked up at his words that left me feeling raw and vulnerable. I didn't flinch away when Dub leaned forward to kiss my cheek, but closed my eyes when his lips lingered on my skin. My lashes brushed against his cheekbone, and I inhaled the earthy scent of Dub. I wanted to thank him, but I didn't know what for.

Instead I said nothing, but Dub understood. He'd been in my head too long not to get me by now.

He stood, towering over Urien with an imperious glare. "I've bathed in your daughter's cries for far too long. You will not displease me anymore. You'll be the ruler Avalon needs, or I'll interfere again. You'll care for the whole and the broken alike. Do you understand, Urien?"

My father shook, not from fear of Dub, but from his body having gone through something that looked painful. "I understand. Avalon will be united, as you wish."

Dub had the nerve to pat my father on the head like a dog. "Very good." Then he turned to Rigby, who was still in the doorway, afraid to come to me, but not so cowardly that he left his post. "You. You're her attendant, yes?"

"Yes, King of Darkness." Rigby bowed his head, but his eyes never left Dub's. "What is it you wish of me?"

Dub rolled his shoulders back at mention of his old title, and I could feel the power trip flowing off him. "Your queen requires rest, and to be treated with great care. You'll make sure she has red raspberry leaf tea every evening while she's under this roof. You'll see to it she doesn't lift an object heavier than a quill."

"Yes, King of Darkness. As you wish it."

I shot Dub a baleful look. "Seriously? You're getting a little overbearing, here."

"If you want your attendant's head to remain on his shoulders, you'll take it easy." Dub made a pointed look down at my stomach.

I bristled and shot him a "dude, be cool" look. I probably wasn't pregnant, and didn't need him spreading that rumor around before I'd gone to a doctor in Common. Maybe two doctors. Maybe six.

"Undo this," I said again, pointing at Urien's stricken expression.

Dub smirked at me, and then vanished, like the ghost he always was to me.

"Condescending jackwagon!" I shouted to the spot he'd just been standing.

Rigby could only be expected to be a fly on the wall for so long. He moved fluidly through the room as he always did, and hoisted my father up. Urien's arm hung limply around his shoulders. I tried to take my father's other side, acting as a crutch to get him somewhere more comfortable. "No, my queen. If you wish to be helpful, call one of the guards. Tell them the King of Darkness has gone."

"I can help you," I insisted.

"The King of Darkness will end my life if you do! Go, now. Quickly. The king should be safely in his chambers when the moon has fully risen."

I was frustrated, but I obeyed, running to the hallway and shouting for someone to help Rigby. The soldiers were hesitant, but came at my behest, darting in to carry Urien to his room.

I wasn't sure what I was supposed to do, other than call for Jean-Luc. I mean, Urien probably didn't want anything to do with me, but he was in pain and didn't have anyone else. I didn't know what was the right thing to do, so I channeled my inner Lane, and followed that voice of calm confidence.

Though I knew he most likely didn't want to see me, I decided to go over Urien's head. I made my way to his room with Jean-Luc, pulling up a chair by his bedside to watch over him. I listened to Jean-Luc fuss over my father, keeping his assessments clinical and his eyes on the task at hand.

I watched sweat bead on Urien's cheek, wishing I could ease his pain. His expression was pinched with worry over the ache that seemed to be set deep in his joints. Though he probably didn't want me to touch him, I lifted his hand and started rubbing his thick fingers, hoping to alleviate a little of the discomfort.

"This is all normal for a first transition."

I nodded, though I didn't shift my gaze from Urien. "He looks... not well."

"He's afraid. Part of this is pure panic, and the other part is pain. His bones are readying to shift as the moon rises." Jean-Luc lifted my father's arm up, studying under the arm pit before dropping it back down. *"I need to lower his temperature,"* Jean-Luc said to me.

I darted to the wash basin in the corner and wetted a washcloth, and then pressed it to my father's forehead. He seemed out of it, in a state of shock as he stared at the ceiling with eyes so wide, I could see the whites around them. For the first time in too long, I was able to see my father up close. His face was more lined around his eyes than before, making him look far older. He had more prominent streaks of gray in his chestnut hair, which fell to the middle of his neck. He hadn't shaved in too many months, his beard growing a little scraggly around the edges. I couldn't believe Rigby would stand for such irregularities; my head dude was usually so on-point.

"So the king is Were now? What will that mean for the kingdom?" Rigby fussed over propping up Urien's legs on several overstuffed pillows.

Jean-Luc and I responded in like sentiments. "It means nothing. I'm a Vampire, and I'm still considered royalty. He won't be rabid. He'll shift at the high moon into a wolf, but he still has his regular thoughts. He's still him. And when he shifts, he'll be in a full wolf body, not half-and-half. He'll be like Malone."

Rigby met my eyes with trepidation. "How is he to rule when the moon is fully risen, then?"

For a sliver of a second, I actually debated offering to stay behind so I could interpret for Urien. I pursed my lips and held firm to whatever boundaries might remind me of my quest to get back to Common. "Duke Lot can handle the nighttime crises. Urien can help the kingdom during the day."

"But Avalon is so large, now that it's united. Surely Duke Lot can't handle it all by himself."

Jean-Luc cut through the polite dance Rigby was trying

to communicate. *"You cannot leave Avalon, broken as she is. You need to stay and help Duke Lot."*

I didn't think I could feel any further heaviness in my chest, but an additional bowling ball weighted me at the conclusion I didn't want shoved in my face. I didn't know what to do, so I chickened out and pretended I didn't hear Jean-Luc, which was probably the meanest I'd ever been to the man.

I couldn't stay, though. I knew if I did, it wouldn't be me in my body anymore, but a fraction of who I needed to be. It had been too long that Avalon had come first. My life was supposed to be my great adventure, but somehow Avalon kept taking top billing.

Still, while I was here and doing my healing thing, I could be helpful to Lot. I wanted to kiss my father's forehead, but I guessed he wouldn't want to be so close to my fangs. Emptiness shook me like a nickel rattling around inside a destitute tin can. I would never be enough for my father now, but I could be enough for Avalon, and maybe one day, for myself. I straightened, trying to feel like I had a handle on things. "Can you take me to Lot? I haven't seen him since I got back."

"Of course, my queen." Rigby perked up, no doubt assuming I would be staying. He moved around the bed and proffered his arm to me like a gentleman. In my ornate dress and fancy hair, I'm sure I looked like a true lady – the tea and opera and perfect eyebrows kind of woman. Inside, I was a rickety old truck that choked and spluttered every time the engine tried to turn over. The dress, the hair and the makeup were a solid disguise, and I welcomed the lie they told the world as Rigby led me down the many decorated hallways that were lit by golden candelabras. They claimed I had it together, that I had answers.

Oh, how very wrong they were.

27

LOT'S OFFER

igby left me to wait at the door, and then ran through the rain to the stables, where he summoned a coach for me to ride in. When the two horses sidled up to the back door for me, pulling a coach with grandeur to rival Cinderella's, I didn't give the chatty horses more than a polite nod. I didn't have anything to say in response to their excitement at getting to cart around the *Voix*.

Nightlife in Avalon diminished to a slow trickle of gatherings when it rained. The pubs were open, and I could see a few people sitting at tables through the windows, but most were in their homes, sitting by the fire to keep warm. I imagined them chatting about the weather, or holding their babies while the embers crackled in the hearth.

My gloved palm found its way to my abdomen, and not

for the first time, I wondered if any of it was true. My marriage hadn't been true, and now I was left to puzzle out whether or not I had a baby inside of me. I knew that if I did, I couldn't raise him or her in Avalon. A palace life was no way for a kid to understand how the world should work. Having servants and no fiscal limitations wouldn't churn out much more than a spoiled version of Morgan. Perhaps there were ways to finesse that, but I didn't know them. Draper had turned out alright, but I wasn't Lane. I couldn't be a good mother in this setting. If not for Kerdik, I would've died already. I needed to leave the magic, and find myself so I could create my own.

Rigby tried a few perfunctory proddings to get conversation going, but I was monosyllabic, letting the depression have me. We rode along bumpy lanes until we reached the barracks – a vast prairie to train soldiers, which was surrounded by a series of bunkers. The soldiers were doing pushups in the rain. I counted the rows, guessing there were over a thousand men out there, giving it their all while their captain called out the count that seemed never-ending.

As soon as my coach stopped in the mud a few feet from the tallest building near the entrance, the driver hopped down and unlatched this little hook under the door, unfurling a long red carpet, so I didn't have to walk in the mud. I blinked at the strapping man. He had black hair that was slick with the rain, but a professional smile that couldn't be dampened by the weather. "Thank you, sir." I'd seen him in the stables before, but any time I'd needed to go out, I'd just taken a horse without using a coach. "That was super way thoughtful. It's crazy muddy out."

Dude looked at me from under the foot-wide awning of the carriage as if I was the most confusing bug he'd ever seen. "Of course, my queen. Her majesty most high had me beaten if she got any dirt on her slippers. I wouldn't dream of letting yours get tarnished."

My eyes widened. "Oh, jeez. Well, you don't have to worry about that with me. You seem to really care about your job, to have stayed all this time with the throne."

"I would do anything for Avalon, my queen."

His sincerity struck me hard. He submitted to Morgan under such horrible working conditions because that's what Avalon required of him. I wished I could be as gracious. He was Avalon at its finest, even soaking as he was. "Avalon loves you, then, and I appreciate you."

That simple phrase seemed to lift his spirits, despite the dreary weather. He met my eyes with a promise burning in his. "I would serve you until my dying breath. Best day in ages, your grace. Thank you for letting me drive you."

"That'll be all for now. Keep the coach nearby. No telling when we'll be finished here." Rigby exited the coach, and offered his hand to steady me as I climbed down.

"Yes, Master Rigby."

The soldiers stopped their calisthenics and began

marching through the rain to salute me, standing in their muddy sweat-wear with looks of fierce loyalty and strength on their matching expressions. I wanted to thank them all for their service individually, but had to settle for a quaint, "Thank you for everything you do for Avalon. I see how hard you've been working to make sure our nation stays united, and that everyone who's been lost has a home."

I dropped Rigby's arm and clasped my hands together before me, letting them dangle and making me feel like a child standing before men. Perhaps that was a good thing; it had been so long since I'd felt young. My voice was clear as it rang out through the drizzle. "Duke Lot, King Urien and I will do our best to keep our land safe, so that you can be builders of Avalon, not just defenders." I closed my eyes, willing the right words to come. "With everything in me, I want the people of Avalon to be builders. I want you to be part of the reason this nation stands tall."

The captain called out three nonsensical commands, and the men all cheered. I nearly lost my composure and stumbled back at the cacophony of voices, but Rigby steadied me.

Lot trotted out with four guards from the headquarters. He wore his regal gear that he didn't mind getting stained with mud. The red coat of the royal outfit suited him well. Lot had always looked bred for the throne. He wore a smile of concern at my appearance, and greeted me with a kiss to both my cheeks. Then he took off his fancy coat and held it over my head to shield me from the rain. It was the nicest thing, and I nearly burst into tears at the display of sweetness and chivalry. My emotions were all over the place, but I did my best to keep my inner crazy tucked away from public view.

Lot waved at the soldiers, dismissing them to go back to their regularly scheduled fitness routine. He coiled his arm around my waist, while holding the coat above us both with his other hand. He seemed almost protective of my body as he moved me toward the main building, shielding me as much as he could from the rain. I tucked easily into his lean side, but let go once we crossed the threshold.

"You didn't have to get all wet to greet me. And now you're drenched and freezing. I'm sorry."

Lot's smile could light up even the cloudiest of nights. "Any day I get to see you is a good one. What brings you here?" His face fell in the next breath. "You're not leaving yet. Rosie, please just give us a little more time. We're not set up for you to go back to Common already. Please."

I glanced around at Lot's guards who I'd seen in passing, but didn't know all that well. "Is there somewhere more private we can talk?"

Lot's shoulders dropped with his low exhale. "Of course. Right this way." He led me to an office that was unoccupied, and instructed his guards and Rigby to wait in the hallway for us. Instead of taking the chair behind the large wooden desk that had too many pieces of parchment scattered across it, Lot took the seat next to mine. He scooted me close and turned my chair to face his, so that our knees were touching. He held my hands in his, and didn't hold back the earnestness in his eyes. "You cannot leave, Rosie. You have no idea how precarious it all is."

I frowned at him, frustrated that this was how things were starting out. I decided not to address his plea, but came to him with the reason I'd stopped by. "Did Lugh tell you everything that happened with Carman and all that?"

"He did. I couldn't believe it, but then Master Kerdik confirmed it. Don't think that doesn't frighten the entire household whenever he pops by." Lot squeezed my hands, making them feel dainty in his. "You actually killed an immortal?"

I didn't like the idea of being revered for murder. "I guess so. That's not why I'm here, though. Dub came to the castle."

"Dub?" Lot's eyebrows furrowed together. "The King of Darkness, Dub? Carman's son?" When I nodded, he hoisted me up out of the chair. "We'll get you somewhere safe. He'll not blind you again."

I shook my head, wishing there had been a solid debriefing that I didn't have to take part in. "Dub came into the palace to warn Urien that he needed to be a more compassionate ruler. He... He turned my father into a Werewolf, Lot. I mean, I healed him quick enough, but he'll still transition at the high moon. He'll have his regular mind, but be in a wolf's body."

Lot gasped, and then fell back into his chair. "Can't you

ask the King of Darkness to undo it? How is Urien to rule as an animal?"

I sank back down into my seat, keeping my voice steady so I didn't give away just how tired this whole ordeal made me. "That's what you and I have to figure out."

Relief swept over Lot's face. He tilted his head back and let out a "woo!" to the ceiling, making me jump. "I forgot you can translate for him when he's in his wolf form. You had me worried for a second there. You look so serious. I don't often see you in such formal attire, with your hair and makeup done. It makes you look older, and like you're about to drop something awful into my lap."

I didn't share in his smile, and slowly, Lot's grin died away into dread. "I can translate while I'm in Avalon, but that's not a long-term solution. I have to go to Éireland soon to heal the Vamps and Weres over there. When I'm finished doing what I can, I'm leaving. You and Urien need to work out a system or something, so it doesn't all fall apart once I'm gone."

"You've decided to leave, just when we've finally got a shot?"

"I'll wait until Avalon's a little more stable, but then yes, I'm going. I don't belong here. I can't live for Avalon for the rest of my life, Lot. Lane's in Common. I had a whole life before this that's going on without me."

"And what of Bastien's life? He belongs here. What does he have to say about this?"

"He'll be staying in Avalon. I'm going without him."

Lot's expression twisted, making him look like he'd eaten something sour and filthy that he wanted to spit out. "How long do you think he'll suffer being without you?"

"For the rest of his life," I choked out, willing my composure to hold. Each time I had to tell the sad tale, it felt like raking my fingers across hot coals. Still, I did it, confessing everything to Lot, including my obscure genetics. "I poisoned him. Without meaning to, obviously. I didn't know until recently, but he deserves to be around someone he actually loves – not someone he's been tricked into falling for." Before Lot could protest on my harsh ruling, I pushed forward toward the thing I didn't want to say, but knew I had to. "So I need to offer you an apology. When we first met, there were a few moments when I... and you... I'm probably making too much out of nothing, but I thought there were a few cute flirts here and there. They probably didn't mean anything to you, but anyways, I'm sorry. It was only that way because I probably poisoned you on our trip." My chest tightened, and I wished I could hide in a handy little hole somewhere far, far away. "I really am sorry, Lot. I didn't mean to trick you. I didn't even know."

Lot leaned on the arm of his chair, sacrificing his perfect posture to mull things over more comfortably. I gave him all the time he needed, knowing I was the one in the doghouse, and he was the one to decide how badly I needed to be kicked. "Did Urien know Morgan was Gancanagh?"

I shrugged. "Nope. I'd be willing to bet that Morgan didn't even know herself."

"And Bastien's left you? You didn't leave him, but you told him all this, and he left you?"

I nodded, trying to keep any emotion off my face. I'm not sure how well that was working, but I gave it a solid effort. "He's allowed to leave a party he was tricked into going to. It's fine. But I can't be here anymore, Lot. I'm hurting people just by touching them. Someone like me needs to be in a place where there's no magic. Lugh lives in Common, and he doesn't poison anyone into falling in love with him. He can be normal, and not hurt anyone. That's where I should be."

Lot frowned, puzzling through the story I'd had weeks to process. "But I touched your skin on our trek. Yes, I was utterly taken with you, but when we parted ways, I didn't follow after you. I was able to carry on with a normal life."

"That's because it's diluted with me. I'm third generation Gancanagh."

"Fascinating." Lot's eyes flitted to mine with a hint of a tease to them. "Forgive me for saying so, but oh, to be strung out on you. I can't imagine a more blissful existence. I try not to waste energy on envy, but how I do wish for Bastien's good fortune to have captured your heart so thoroughly."

I blinked at him, totally confused by his chill response. "This is the part of the conversation where you cuss me out and kick me out of Avalon. I don't think you get what I'm telling you. I straight up drugged you, dude."

Of all things, Lot sniggered. "So dramatic. It's fine, Rosie. Look at me. Don't I look fine? Am I scaling mountains to run after you?"

"No, but…"

"We had several lovely moments, and yes, I was perplexed over how long I pined for you once we parted ways, but I'm alright. Bastien truly thinks your entire relationship was a lie?"

"Would *you* like being controlled?"

"By you? I'm not sure I'd mind it," he kidded with an impish grin. "Bastien left, did he? That's a complete waste of a great thing. He's too stubborn for his own good."

I nodded, swallowing hard. "I'm not here to talk about whether or not my marriage ending was for good reasons. I'm telling you that I can't walk around with this kind of guilt. I can't risk infecting more people. I can't… I just can't, Lot. I think I've given Avalon my pound of flesh, and now I'm out. I'll stay long enough to heal the cursed people, but then I'm going."

Lot studied my features carefully, and his words came out measured. "I can't imagine you'd entertain it, but I put my token in on the day Morgan invited your suitors to make their intentions known. My offer to marry you is still on the table. That is, if Master Kerdik can be tolerant."

I stood, horrified. "It's already happening! I wore gloves

so this wouldn't keep going on, but I'm still doing it! I'm poisoning you!"

At this, Lot let out a loud laugh and clapped his hands. "You're too much. You're not bewitching me, Rosie, no more than you always have. If we were in Common, I'd be saying the same, no doubt. I know myself, and I understand your heart. Bastien is a fool – a prideful fool, but from the start he's been *your* fool, and I'm sure he will be again soon."

I balked at him, unsure when it was that I lost my hold on this conversation. "You clearly have no idea what I just said, or you wouldn't have offered to marry me. I'm dangerous, Lot, especially to a kingdom. If I'm controlling you, then what if I want to do something that isn't for Avalon's greater good? Look at what happened with my parents. Urien couldn't stand up to Morgan, so she friggin' took over and ruined the kingdom. I don't want that. I don't want to be that to you. You're a good man."

"I trust you, even when you don't trust yourself. But we can be done discussing it all, if you like. What can I do to convince you to stay in Avalon? The people rally around you, Rosie. Scattered as they've been? They're worn out from dealing with the curses, and moving and merging into a single nation. There are barriers of bigoted behavior still from when they were separate provinces. I need your help uniting the people."

I nodded, expecting as much. "I can stay for a little bit,

but then I'm gone, and you and Urien can handle Avalon without me."

Lot stood, sandwiching my hand between his. "You're unhappy here. I can tell we've called on you for too much. If this is what you wish, then I'll respect it. Please don't leave without setting a date to return, at least for a visit."

I hadn't considered coming back without impending doom being the thing that sucked me back in. My mind flitted over the many people I'd attached myself to over the time I'd spent in the land I was constantly trying to leave. Could I ditch Madigan? Could I really leave Lot forever? My mouth went dry when it dawned on me that because I'd be leaving without Bastien, Link and Quinn would have no reason to come to Common with me. They would stay in Éireland with Mad, or with Bastien in Avalon, and I would lose them forever. I loved Link, and my heart ached with a deep sadness at the thought of never being hoisted up in his arms again.

The thought of never seeing Urien again was a whole different animal. He didn't want to see me anymore, so it hardly mattered. But this would be final, if I left with no intention of returning.

"One year," I eked out. "Give me one year in Common, and I'll come back for two weeks. For every year you let me live my life in Common, I'll give Avalon two weeks. Would that help?"

Lot closed his eyes as if my response pained him. "Two

weeks? Not even a whole month you can stomach being near us? Were we all so terrible?"

I slowly shook my head. "No. You've been wonderful every step of the way. One month, then. After I leave, give me eleven months away, and I'll come back for a month every year. Is that fair?"

Lot drew me into his arms. "Very well. Thank you. I'll handle Avalon's problems during the night, and Urien can be helpful during the day. We'll make this work."

I wanted to rest my head on his chest and rest in the comfort he offered, but I pulled away. "The poison," I explained. "I don't want to infect you."

He flinched, like my words had grown a hand and slapped him across the face. "I understand." Then he cupped my chin and lifted my face so that I had no choice but to meet his eyes. "But you are no curse to me, Rosie. You're only my blessing. Always my blessing."

28

LUGH'S NEW SONG

The sun had risen by the time I reached the castle, and though the Werewolves were pouring in, bound and placed in the dungeon, I was barely upright. Though I'd slept the afternoon before, I begged off after only a dozen healings to get a nap in.

"Are you feeling alright, your grace?" Rigby asked, no doubt wondering why I was being such a wuss when there was clearly work to be done.

"I don't know what's wrong with me. I'm pretty exhausted. I just need a quick nap, and I'll be back to finish the rest of them."

"As you wish it, my queen." Rigby snapped his fingers to a couple attendants, and sent them to prepare my bedroom ahead of me. I couldn't imagine what they needed to do – I mean, any old couch would've been fine for me to crash in.

When Rigby led me to my bedroom, the bed had been freshly made, and a pretty floor-length nightgown had been set out for me. I didn't protest when Rigby helped me get changed for bed. My limbs were weighted, and my spirits impossibly lower than they'd been the day before. My time in Avalon was winding to a close, and as much as I wanted to rejoice in that, I was too exhausted to make it through an entire day without yawning my face off. Now that things weren't so harrowing, it seemed my body was catching up on the rest it had been cheated out of for so long.

Rigby undid my hair, and then had the grace to kiss my forehead before he left. We'd hit some sort of a sweet note to our relationship, and I was glad we seemed to have come full-circle.

I stared at the enormous bed, which had seemed merely large before I'd split from Bastien. Now that it was just for me, it seemed an ocean I didn't want to get lost in. I couldn't stomach the thought of sleeping in it by myself. It felt wrong somehow, so I pulled my pillow off the bed, and grabbed a blanket from the chest the extras were stored in.

I moved into the chain of closets, unsure of all the hidey-holes of my own bedroom. I picked an unused nook that had once held a portion of Morgan's huge dresses, but now stocked a few of mine. I laid out the blanket and pillow, and made myself a little nest on the floor under the hems of my many gowns. I wanted to be left alone in my sadness, which never seemed to leave me alone for too long.

After breaking down in the privacy of my closet, I finally was able to drift off to sleep, resting everything that ached inside of me.

~

"Jays, Prim! What were ye thinking, hiding like tha?"

Lugh's voice broke through my fuzzy dream, which slipped away once reality started knocking its way into my brain. "Lugh? What's wrong?" I blinked myself awake, unsure where I was for a moment.

"The whole household is going mad looking for ye." Then Lugh called over his shoulder, "I found her!" He rocked back and offered his hand to me, hoisting me up before he winced at my appearance. "Tell me you've been crying, and ye don't have a massive head wound. It looks like you're auditioning for a zombie movie."

"Oh, yikes. Just tears. Not zombie blood. Though that is the one monster Avalon's missing."

"I'll lodge a complaint with corporate first thing. Must get zombies to the party post-haste." Lugh moved into the bedroom and wetted a washcloth in my basin. Without asking me why I'd been a baby and cried myself to sleep, he simply cleaned my face for me. "Tha's better. I can't tell which looks stranger, the blood or the makeup. Either way, I like the look of ye when it's just your face."

"Thanks. I like your face without makeup, too. How goes the Vampire and Werewolf roundup?"

"We'll know when the moon rises, won't we? We've been bringing them in, and each night we think we've got them all, but there's always a few more the next night. But the numbers are going down, so it won't be too long before it's all solved."

"That's good news. You got your bags packed?"

Lugh's face broke out into a wide grin. "Tha's a relief. I thought you'd get back to all this luxury and decide Common's not for ye anymore."

"Dude, this place isn't me. You, me, Europe. That's the plan."

"A brilliant plan it is, Prim. But why were ye on the floor?"

I didn't know how to answer without sounding like a big old baby. "I didn't want to sleep in the bed without him," I admitted, wishing I had a cooler, more aloof answer.

The look of compassion mingled with pity on Lugh's face was the exact thing I'd been hoping to avoid. He pulled me into his arms, and for the first time in what felt like a hundred-thousand years, I sunk into an offered embrace. I'd wanted to hug back when people showed their affection, but I was too worried I'd infect them with my Gancanagh mojo. There wasn't that risk with Lugh, so I folded my body into his, exhaling the suck-it-up breath I'd been holding in for who knows how long. Lugh was safe, which was the only thing I needed, and what I'd been deprived of for far too long.

"It wasn't supposed to end like this," I whispered.

Lugh gently swayed back and forth, moving my hips with his in a slow rhythm. "Then it must not be the end yet. It'll be only happy endings for ye, Prim."

"I need to get to Common so I can see a doctor. I need to know if I'm... you know."

"Tha's probably best. We'll be stopping by your home in the States before we head off on our adventure." Lugh gave a stiff nod, but didn't stop dancing with me. He seemed born for charming the pants off of women – magical mojo or not. He couldn't turn it off, and I'd never want him to. His mere presence made my glib existence more delicate and precious. The simple dance made me feel like I was a woman with purpose, not a crushed tool that was still forced to eke out some semblance of usefulness.

Lugh pressed his cheek to mine. "We can go see your doctor before we leave for Europe."

"We?"

I could feel Lugh grinning against my cheek – a precious sentiment that drove straight into my heart like one of his well-timed arrows. "Aye. If I needed to see a doctor for something tha could be lifechanging, ye wouldn't send me to go alone. I'll be with ye – through the doctor appointments, labor, midnight feedings, all of it. I'm telling ye, Prim, your ending's going to be happy. I'm sure of it."

"I might need you to believe that for the both of us for a while."

"I can do tha." He pulled my arm out to the side and gripped my wrist with the tenure of a seasoned guitar player. There was no request to his hold that asked for permission, but a firm command that his instrument would sing for him however he wished. His fingers moved deftly over my wrist and the back of my hand, pressing a bassline into my skin that only he knew, and couldn't keep inside of him any longer. His other hand strummed my hip as he started to hum in my ear. I could feel the magic flowing through my body – the magic of art. I loved when Lugh composed on the fly, even more when I was his instrument. It made me feel useful and beautiful – like my soul had something lovely inside of it that was palpable to a savvy musician. Lugh was a man who appreciated art, and when he composed on me, it made my body hum with colors and brushstrokes. I became his masterpiece in hues of vibrant watercolors in the span of a song.

I wanted to be a masterpiece. Oh, how I wanted something delicate and lovely after all the grim brutality.

"'If only the rain didn't storm at your sadness.

If only the night didn't weep.

Then I could be glad my bed is so cold,

and I'm up with the moon while ye sleep.'"

I held onto Lugh, clinging to the solace he offered. A

shiver rolled through me when it dawned on me yet again that the great Lou Van Garden was composing his next hit on my body. "That was beautiful."

"Aye. It seems you're destined for only music tha strikes a stunning tune. It'll be okay, Prim. We'll figure this out. You'll be a grand wee mother, and I'll be the best uncle Common's ever seen. I'll help ye raise your baby, as long as ye let me pick the music he listens to. I'm a little afraid ye might turn on Justin Bieber when my back's turned."

I heard a gasp from behind me, and stiffened. I stepped away from Lugh and turned to see Rigby in the door, his mouth open in surprise. "Your majesty, are you with child?"

I let out a low groan and moved to the entrance to shut the door. "We don't know for sure, but Dub thinks I am. It's... I need to get to Common to let a doctor check me out."

Rigby's eyes were wide, and his posture straighter than usual. Every muscle in his body seemed tense at the news. "We have physicians, my queen. I'll summon Jean-Luc right now. Or if you'd prefer to wait for Remy, I can have him brought back from Éireland for you."

"No. I don't want anyone in Faîte to know. I've had way too many brushes with death to parade a baby around in front of people. If I am pregnant, no one's going to know about it."

Rigby gave me a stiff nod. "As you wish it, my queen.

But don't you think the kingdom could use some good news?"

I clenched my fists at my sides, instantly angry and overly protective. "My baby isn't news. My life isn't the headlines to perk up a dreary day. I'm not friggin' Britney Spears. *If* I'm pregnant, my kid comes first, not Avalon. I'm going back to Common after this healing business is all settled, and that's that." I pinched the bridge of my nose in consternation. "Not for nothing, Rigs, but only a handful of people in the world know about this. If anyone finds out, I'm coming after you."

"What did King Bastien say when you told him? Surely he won't stay away long if his child is being taken to another land."

"Bastien doesn't know about the baby, because he doesn't want anything to do with me. I can't imagine that wouldn't extend to what's baking in my uterus. He should be able to start over without me holding this over his head. I accidentally tricked him into marrying me. I'll not trick him into coming back. I love him, and I want him to be happy."

Rigby started to say something, but I'd hit my limit.

"I don't want to discuss this with you, or anyone! I'll be there to heal the others in the dungeon in a few minutes. Let me get dressed, and I'll see you down there."

Rigby had the sense to know when he was being dismissed from a conversation, and nodded to me. "Yes, my queen."

I let out a quiet string of curses as I shut Rigby out, and leaned against the door with my eyes closed. "Tell me that didn't just happen."

"I think a quick escape is best. How many can ye heal today?"

"As many as it takes. Help me pack what I need first, in case I pass out. Then if I get through all the healings today, we can just go, and I'll sleep it off on the boat to Éireland."

"Works for me." Lugh moved to the dresser and pulled out a few of my gowns to lay them across the bed.

"I don't need those. Where do you imagine me wearing them in Common?"

Lugh frowned. "A Renaissance fair?"

"Pass. Jeans and t-shirts only. I'll get the rest." I ran to the closet and changed quickly, throwing on a gown whose best feature was that I could do it up without help. The red material fell to my toes, and the gold bodice cut just below my bust, hanging loose around my hips so I didn't have to suck in my stomach all day. My cleavage was a little more on display than I usually cared for, but whatever. I didn't have a whole lot of options in that arena. It seemed the seamstresses all agreed that my mother's favorite feature was also mine.

I grabbed a traveling bag and started shoving everything I needed inside. I couldn't think of any mementos that I wanted to take with me, so I went with practicality. In one of the further back closets, I fisted a handful of jewels from the drawers of plenty, and stuffed them into a smaller velvet pouch. The gems meant nothing to me, but they would help Lugh and I extend our holiday as long as we wished.

"Ye don't need those," Lugh said from the doorway. "I've got money enough for as many lifetimes as we want."

I nodded, but took another handful, just to be safe. "I've got money in Common, too. When Lane took me to Common when I was a baby, we were homeless for a while. I don't want my kid to have to worry about that. I don't want to come back here because we're broke."

"Alright, alright. But tha's plenty. Do ye know how much a diamond like tha's worth? You're panicking, Prim. It's all going to be okay."

I shook my hands out, reminding myself that this wasn't a heist, and I had all the time in the world to pack up and go. Still, the desire to leave fueled me. I stuffed my pack with a couple pairs of shoes, and the clothes Lugh had taken from the drawers for me. I looked around the room, suddenly forlorn. "This is all practical stuff," I said, shaking my bag. "I don't have anything sentimental from Avalon that I'm taking with me. That's so sad."

Lugh tapped my ring finger. "You're taking Kerdik's promise of a better life with ye, and you're taking me. Tha's as sentimental as they get."

I tried to let his explanation soothe my unease, and nodded. "I guess that's good enough."

"I'll get us some food, and I've got your wineskin of

blood already packed. Are ye sure ye don't need any? It's been days since you've had any blood."

I rolled my shoulders back, reveling in the independence I'd desperately fought for. "After Carman's blood, I don't crave it so much anymore. I like it, but I can eat food and taste it now. I'm thinking I don't need as much blood, which is a good thing. If I don't have to use Bastien to survive, that's one point in my favor."

Lugh scratched the back of his head. "Wow, I'm glad tha's holding up. I didn't realize. Good, Prim. Then we won't have to work out blood shipments so often." His eyes flared with life. "We can really travel now."

A genuine smile broke out on my face, reminding me that somewhere deep down, I still possessed a sense of adventure. After everything, I was still me, and that was a beautiful thing.

29

WHAT I WANTED

The dungeon was dreary – that seemed to be the nature of places like this – but I had renewed purpose. The finish line was in sight, and I was ready for it. I wanted that new life. I wanted Europe. I wanted... to sleep. Lately it seemed like everything made me want to take a nap. Call it a long overdue adrenaline crash. I fought through the yawns that started after the tenth healing. There were at least thirty more to go, but I held my chin up and muscled through. Two guards held each Werewolf, so I wasn't as in danger of getting snapped at by their vicious-looking teeth. The memory of Bastien holding the Vampires steady for me to heal choked me around the throat, but I did what I could to keep going, despite my desire to break down every twenty minutes.

While I wanted to heal them all that night, the few Vampires in the mix sapped my energy and fried my nerves. I passed clean out from exhaustion, and had to be carried to bed by Rigby. I didn't even have the strength to protest being laid in the bed I'd been avoiding. I dreamt about my hand being chopped off, picturing Dian's evil laughter and the look of glee at mutilating me. I woke in a cold sweat too many times to feel rested.

I slept the day away until my stomach woke me. I'd been taking on the same nocturnal pattern as the Were-wolves, so I could heal them when they were fully turned. I was hungry, but I couldn't figure out what I wanted. I usually didn't care all that much, but the fruit and cheese platter turned my stomach at the mere smell of it. Before I could choke down a bite, vomit was thrusting itself out of my stomach, scaring me with how readily it came.

I was perplexed at my body, but then realized that this must be the morning sickness Lane had complained about when she'd been pregnant with Lucas. It had been such a happy thing when she was carrying her sweet baby. Even her mild complaints about morning sickness were cute. She'd been glowing with anticipation of the greatest moment of her life. Even when she talked about puking her guts out every morning for months, she told the tale with a giddy grin on her face, so pleased to be pregnant.

Me? I was just scared. I didn't have a husband in my life to hold my hair back, or run to the store in the middle of the night to get me ginger tea and saltines. I'm sure I could ask Rigby, but after I'd snapped at him, I didn't feel like it was right for me to ask him for anything. By Dub's calculations, I was nearly two weeks pregnant, and the doom was setting in. I didn't have that healthy dose of denial anymore, but began to embrace what part of me already knew. I was pregnant, and this was no place to raise my baby.

I washed up and dressed for the day, my stomach leading me to the single croissant on the side of the plate. It was filled with too much butter, which you'll never hear me complain about.

I hadn't been expecting anyone at my door when I opened it, and jumped when I found Urien standing just outside in the hallway, waiting for me. "Jeez! You scared me. How long have you been standing there?"

"An hour," he said, his regal posture and broad chest making him look every bit like Richard the Lionheart. "Are you feeling well?"

"I'm fine. What do you need?"

"A father has to need something to come visit his daughter?"

My eyebrows scrunched together. "Um, *you* do. Since when am I your daughter again?"

As if he'd been expecting my perplexed and frank reply, he didn't flinch away, but stood his ground. "I thought you might like to go for a walk with me before you start down in the dungeon. I've got a good hour before I turn into a wolf for the night."

I took a step back, wary of the offer. "Am I being punked? Why do you want to spend time with me?"

Though I could tell my honest concerns broke his heart, he didn't turn away. Instead, he extended his elbow to me. "Please?"

I shook my head, unsure what to do with the man who'd disowned me. "I've got work to do. Maybe after that."

"You work until you pass out. There is no 'after' for you every night. Please, Rosalie."

Too many things warred inside of me. I fiddled with the hem of the t-shirt I'd opted to wear that evening. I'd given up on the dresses that made me feel like a damsel, when I wanted to be a grisly construction worker who powered through until the job was finished. "No. Whatever you're up to, it's a trick. You want something from me, and I don't have anything anymore. I'm healing the Vamps and the Weres, and that's it. You and Lot can figure out the rest."

"I don't wish to talk business with you." His face fell. "You're really leaving?"

"Yup. One less Vampire polluting the air you breathe. Lucky day for you."

"Rosalie, I was wrong." Urien pushed out his apology in a gust, but his regal stature didn't suffer one bit. "I only thought of Avalon, and didn't think of you. I shouldn't have cast you out."

Anger I'd tried to suppress and label as hurt began to bubble up inside of me. "Are you kidding me with this? You didn't think of me or Avalon. You thought about your own fears. *Attelage* Vampires are Avalon, too! You didn't think of them – of us. They loved you. They wept for you when you were sleeping for so many years. They cheered for you when you woke up, and followed us to a new province. They paid taxes and helped rebuild the nation when we were all broken. Then they get infected with something that could've hit anyone, and you turned on us. Didn't stop to examine the facts, you just threw us all away. Now that Dub knocked some sense into you, you're all compassionate? I don't need your pity walk. I don't need you showing up here after all this time to tell me what I already knew. You were wrong. Good for you for finally realizing it, but I didn't need the validation, and I certainly don't need the apology." Venom rose up in me with a fury so fierce, I'm surprised the windows didn't rattle. "And I've never, ever needed you."

It was the meanest thing I'd ever said to someone I actually did need, and did love. I took a step back, shocked at the disgusting state of my soul. It didn't matter that I was the pretty girl now; my heart was utterly ugly.

Urien's downward tilted chin was unexpected after getting blasted with my sass. "Of course. I realize you don't need me, but all the same, I'm sorry."

I buttoned my lips for a solid fifteen seconds, lest I open my mouth and spew pure rancor all over him, or break down in a fit of childish tears that had no place here. When I finally spoke, my voice was low and even, like an evil queen who had a plan. "I wanted a dad so badly, and even when I found you and you were a vegetable, I loved you. I protected you, and helped bring you back. I gave you a voice when you couldn't speak. I gave you back your crown, hoping you would be good to the people who loved you."

He lowered his chin, but didn't speak in his own defense. "You're right. You didn't deserve that."

"Not just that, but you're in a position of authority. You made it okay for families to turn on their own. Quinn's whole tribe threw her out, and she didn't have Lane to run to in the beginning. She had no one, and you made that okay. I'm not the only daughter you abandoned. One day I'll get over what you did to me, but I can't forgive what you did to all of them."

He nodded, taking my anger with grace. "You're right. I never thought of it like that, but I should've offered them protection. Asylum. Something. I was afraid my people would be ravaged, so I cut out the diseased part, hoping Avalon could grow stronger."

"And how's that working out for you? You're living under my roof because I'm Lane's daughter, not yours. You can thank her that you and your precious pure people have a place to rest your heads. I took you and your province in, even though you were a bigoted fool. You're the diseased one, but I still sheltered you. I didn't learn that from you or Morgan." I shook my head, utterly done with it all. "And the thing is, all you had to do was be nice. That was it. I was already grown, already raised. All you had to do was laugh at my stupid jokes, and I would've followed you to the very end."

Urien met my eyes with sadness I couldn't quantify, but it seemed rooted deep. "We need you to stay, honey. Don't take your anger at me out on Avalon."

I stiffened, scandalized. "You're the one who taught me to never need, to never let anything crush you, because once you're a little bit broken, you'll be thrown away." I hated the emotion that rose in my voice, but some things just couldn't be helped. "I'm not leaving because I'm angry, I'm leaving because someone has to care if I live through this, and if I'm the only person, so be it! You may be happy to throw me under the bus so your life is easier, but I'm through with it. I matter, and I shouldn't have to tell my own father that!"

He held back none of the sincerity in his plea. "I'm sorry, darling!"

I started talking animatedly with my hands. "Good! Be sorry and change. I'm glad you got your head out of your ass finally. Avalon will be better for it. I've got bigger dreams for my life than this – than passing out by dawn every morning, and living in the same world as my ex. And you know what's funny, you've never even asked me about my dreams, what I want from my life. You assume my goal is to bleed myself dry so you don't have to work as hard. Well, it's not!"

He frowned, confused. "Bastien's not back yet? I

thought for certain he would've realized the error of his ways by now."

I summed it up as succinctly as I could. "Just another man who decided I didn't fit into his world. Can't fault a guy for that, can you?"

"Rosalie, that's not okay. He truly left you?"

I motioned between us with a jerky back and forth. "I don't want to talk about my life with you! I want to get away from you! Don't you see that? The time to help me was when my entire makeup changed. You could've taken the time to explain things to me, but you didn't. The time to help me was when I was walking into walls in the castle because I was blind, but you didn't. Do you have any idea how scared I was?"

"Bastien made me stay away from you! I wanted to debase myself and beg your forgiveness from the first day I came to stay here, but he wouldn't let me near you. Said I'd had my chance, and I'd hurt you too much."

"You threw me out of the house *I* invited you into. That castle belonged to me and Lane, and you took it, like a tyrant. If you want to debase yourself, go to Lot and thank him for taking in the daughter you abandoned, and the people who loved you that you threw out when they were confused and needed you most. I never thought I'd see the day when you were Morgan's match, but I lost my faith in fathers that day."

He clutched his heart, utterly woebegone at my fury. "Sweetheart, I was wrong."

I nodded, churning his words over to check them for holes. "Good. I'm glad you see it. It'll make you a better ruler. Spend some time earning back the trust of the families you tore apart by making it okay to abandon their own. Rebuild your nation that way. As for you and me? I'm out. There's nothing for me here, and a lifetime of cleaning up your mess isn't as shiny an offer as you're thinking."

"I want you to stay. I want to work this out."

"Again, what *you* want. Since you didn't ask, I'll tell you what I want. I want to sleep for a hundred years, and wake up when the problems of this world are long dead. I want to go home to Lane and hide in her bed until I get the image of my hand being chopped off out of my head."

"What? What happened to your hand?"

I waved off his concern. "Dian was being a butthole. Kerdik fixed it." I dug deep, unearthing truths I wished my father knew about me, but had never possessed the courtesy to ask. "I want to run away and call it 'traveling'. I want to be responsible for only myself, not thousands upon thousands of people, who all look at me like I'm supposed to know what the crap I'm doing." My breath came in shallow pants as I got more and more worked up. "I want my husband to see who I truly am beneath all the magical BS, and know that no matter what curveballs life throws at us, we both understand that we belong together." My pitch rose with emotion when my raw nerves began to expose themselves. "I want to be able to read any book I want, whenever I feel like it. I want to run far, far away from you and all of this, and come back when it's just me and Kerdik, and we can start over. That's what I want, and if you actually wanted to be my father, you would've already known all of that, because you would've asked me about who I was, and what I wanted out of life. You never loved me because you never knew me!"

I didn't want to hear his arguments or apologies. I didn't want anything to do with any of it. I stomped back into my room, threw on a sweater and pushed past him, going down into the dungeon to start my night of work.

30

FLOWERS FALLING FROM THE CEILING

With every night that I spent healing the Werewolves, it seemed another handful of them were brought in the next evening. I knew we were reaching the tail end of the curse, but it had been two weeks now, and I was still in Avalon. My packed bag laughed at me every time I walked past it, taunting me with the threat of never being able to put my escape route to good use.

Step two of the master plan to get Faîte back on track was putting Carman's blood to good use. The black oil-like cure was used sparingly, healing the *Attelage* Vampires with a single teaspoon diluted in a gallon of water. One shot glass-worth of the liquid was given to each Vamp, so they could lessen their need for daily doses of the blood of their mates. It turns out, I could get away with a couple of swallows of Bastien once a month, and be totally fine. I didn't have the rabid sexual desires anymore, and decided that was probably for the best. Avalon was in a state of flux, and after two addresses to the nation, I hoped they would be able to stand stronger together once the dust settled.

During both speeches, Lot and Urien stood at my sides while I preached a sermon on unity and family, claiming all was well in the castle with the royal family. It was a lie, a total lie, but the kingdom bought it. I told them how important family was, and that once my father had seen the error of his ways, all was forgiven between us. I didn't want to live two lives, but I also couldn't stomach the thought of my anger and resentment being the gift I left behind in the hearts of the Avalonians I was supposed to be caring for. I did my best to push my brokenness aside and pretend that I was loved, and that I forgave – though neither of those things were true. If Dub hadn't infected my father, he wouldn't have come back to me. I wanted no part of conditional, convenient love. My life was hard, and I needed someone in my corner who wasn't afraid of the fight when life grew too harrowing for the problems to be hugged away.

After a long, long day, Rigby escorted me to my bedroom, where he helped me out of my cumbersome red velvet going-out-in-public dress, and into my nightgown. I'd given up insisting that I didn't need help. Ever since he'd found out I was pregnant, Rigby hovered. "Is there anything else you need, my queen?" he asked as he pulled down the covers and helped me into the overlarge bed.

"No. I just need to take a nap before I go back to the dungeon. How many left to heal?"

"Only five, and that seems to be it. There haven't been any others found for two days. The Phare Dullahan have been scouring the country for more, but that might be it for you." He cleared his throat as he tucked me in. "A certain member of the Dullahan stopped by earlier to ask to see you. What shall I tell Demi when he comes back?"

Heaviness pressed me further into the mattress. Demi loved me, and I'd tricked him into the feeling. I wanted to curl up in his arms and see what sorts of hijinks he'd let me do with his detached head, but I knew I had to cut the cord. I couldn't keep Demi, as much as the idea appealed to my more selfish parts. Aside from being devastated that Bastien was gone, my body was freaking out with an ache for him. Our intense physical connection wasn't as rabid as it had been when I'd needed his blood on a daily basis to survive, but a portion of the longing was still there. A wicked thought traipsed across my mind, reminding me that Demi didn't need a head to satiate the unquenched parts of me.

I squashed that idea right quick, wondering when it was that I'd permitted thoughts of using someone as my mother had for such purposes. Guilt pressed down on me when Rigby touched his lips to my forehead, tucking me in with gentleness I wouldn't admit to needing. He was a pro, knowing how to handle me when I was a bull on a mission, and even when I was a delicate flower, pushed over at the slightest breeze.

"If you chew on the ginger root when you wake, you won't feel as sick before you eat. I've put some on your tray over here."

I thanked Rigby, and waited until he left before I got out of the bed and moved my pillow and blanket to my little nook in the closet. I hid under the gowns, letting the hems brush over my skin like feathery kisses that concealed my many sins. Oh, how I wanted a lifetime of hiding, of sleeping, of rest.

I had nightmares of trying to escape the Nain Rouge, shrieking myself awake when he tried to chop off my baby's hand.

"Rosie! Honey, wake up. You're having a bad dream."

I was disoriented and groggy when I woke, and it took me a few blinks to see the green glow that knelt before me. "Kerdik? What are you doing here?"

"I should ask you the same question. Why are you sleeping on the floor? I'm going to have words with your attendant about this."

"Rigby doesn't know. He thinks I sleep in the bed."

"Why are you down here? Up you get." He helped me to stand, letting me lean on his arm when my body took more than two sentences to wake up. "Darling are you sick?"

"No, I'm pregnant," I reminded him.

Kerdik's jaw tightened. "Yes, I recall. How are you feeling?"

I looked up at him, unsure how he expected me to be able to answer that. I was lost, turned around and completely devoid of the oomph I needed to get me through the day. I blinked, unwilling to gloss over my depression, or offer up a glib reply that assured us both that I was still in here somewhere.

Kerdik drank in the sadness that loomed in my eyes. He met my gaze with a studious glint that told me he was sifting through my emotions to find where I was deep down inside. "Darling," he cooed, thumbing my cheek as he pulled me into his arms. "Tell me what's been harming you." He brushed his nose across mine, his breath fanning my face and making me feel safe. "Tell me, so I can crush it, and you can sleep without nightmares."

"I'm leaving," I stated, daring him to challenge me on this point.

"I know. Lot tells me you'll be back one month a year. I'll be looking forward to those visits."

"I'm not raising my baby in Avalon."

"I assumed as much."

"I'm not coming back to stay until my kid is grown. I don't want him or her here. Avalon is no place for a baby."

"I understand. You want a life in Common. I've known that from the beginning. You promised me your second life, so I can be patient." He glanced back at the closet. "Why were you sleeping on the floor?"

I gaped up at him, astounded that he understood, that he knew me. That he knew this place – this lovely land he'd created – wasn't for me. What's more, he didn't beg me to stay, or take offense. He saw me, accepted me, and I loved him for it. "The bed reminds me of Bastien, so I don't like to lie in it."

"This bed?" he asked with a hint of charm in his voice. "This one here? It's a nice bed."

"It is."

"Awfully big for one little person." We stared into each other's eyes, saying things that didn't need words to muddy the waters.

I'm not sure who initiated the kiss that scalded my lips, but it crashed down on us with a fervency that neither of us could handle. It had been too long since I'd kissed him, too long since I'd made him moan for me when I sucked on his lower lip.

I didn't stop him when he ripped my nightgown over my head, and he didn't stop me when I unbuttoned his shirt and threw it across the room. "I have to lock the door," I explained when I pulled away.

"I've got it." Kerdik didn't miss a beat, but shot a spray of rocks and concrete from his palms, barricading us inside. He even mudded the windows, so we were lit only by the lantern's light, which he turned lower so we didn't get distracted by responsibilities or the many obstacles that had piled up between us on too many other occasions.

The high I got from his lips on my skin was heightened

by the fact that I hadn't been touched in weeks. My body was purring for him, and I didn't hesitate to finish undressing the man who'd been a touchstone during my time in Avalon. He'd been responsible for much of my growth, and had seen me through too many harrowing losses and joyful triumphs. Kerdik knew who I was, and didn't run from me.

Every touch, each caress felt like my skin was humming with anticipation. He was shy as he showed me more of his lithe body than I'd ever seen before, finally smiling with relief when I pulled him closer. I wanted to adore each part that made him the friend and the man I loved.

When he slid off my underwear and lowered me to the mattress, I knew that no matter what, I wouldn't regret this. My legs wrapped around his hips as I drew him to me, welcoming all that he wanted to be with all that I was.

"I love you," I whispered between sensual kisses as he hovered over me. Rose petals started raining down on us from the ceiling, and all around, flowers bloomed up out of the wooden floor. Of course Kerdik would create our ideal haven on the fly. He'd always been the romantic. Vines and soft petals tickled my naked skin, making goosebumps break out all over my body. He was so good at teasing me. "Kerdik, I need you."

"Oh, Rosie. It's always been you."

"Make love to me," I begged, needing to know every part of him.

Before life could tear us apart again, Kerdik kissed me, twining his fingers through mine so we could be connected as much as possible before we took that final plunge. "Promise that you'll come back for me."

"I promise. Promise that you'll let me go."

"I promise. I love you, darling."

I'm not sure whose cries were louder in the end, only that we didn't part until we were both sated, which took as long as we wanted it to. We were hurried and passionate. We were slow and sensual. Not a moment was forgettable or regrettable. He tasted every inch of my skin, and I didn't miss a moment of his. We'd been through too much to leave things so undone before I left him to find myself again. We made love over and over again all night long, until we both understood that when we finally parted, it wouldn't be the end of us.

31

BELONGING TO THE BROTHERHOOD

"You're green," Lugh observed. "I mean, literally green around the gills. I thought tha was just an expression, but you're looking peaky, Prim."

"Yeah? Well, that's what happens when you mix morning sickness with sea sickness. Tell me we're almost there."

"We're almost there," he lied. "The seals are pulling the boat slower than they should. They're probably hoping everyone sees they've been chosen to cart around the Avalon Rose. Can't fault the seals for showing off."

I groaned, gripping the side of the boat as I puked over the side yet again. Our boat was large enough to afford the two of us some privacy in our room near the hull, but not so big that we made actual good time getting to our destination.

When we finally reached land, I was barely upright. Lugh looped my arm around his shoulders, and escorted me toward the exit, where a whole army was waiting on the shore. I blinked at them through the porthole, doing my best not to look like I was about to ralph all over the place. "Dude, if this is an ambush, I forfeit. You're getting us out of the jam this time. It's your turn."

Lugh shook his head slowly. "I don't think we're in hostile territory. Have a look. They're saluting ye. Try to look like, I dunno, not this. You're here to save the day. Best give them a good smile when we get out there."

I did my utmost to stand on my own, but I'd puked more than any human or Fae should be allowed to. It was only at the sound of my favorite song that I started to perk up.

"Rosie, I love ye. Rosie, I care. Rosie, without ye, my heart's in despair!" Link burst into the vessel with a broad grin on his face. "Have ye missed me, wee Rose?" He grimaced at the sallow smile I mustered just for him. "Jays, what's wrong with ye?"

"This lass doesn't have her sea legs yet," Lugh explained. I was grateful he kept the bun in my oven a secret.

"Oh, babe. Here. Let your old Link help ye up. The lads are all waiting for ye, so best put on your brave face until we can get ye to my place."

"Is that where I'm staying?"

Link grinned. "Aye. I knew ye wouldn't want to stay in

the castle with Queen Aileen. She's a bore, but cares about the people more than Queen Shavon ever did, so tha's a plus."

"A definite plus." I was supposed to do the meet-and-greet with the new Queen of Éireland while I was here.

"Can ye believe Quinn actually got me to put down roots? She wanted a house, so tha's what my wife gets." Link was so proud that he'd landed a wife. I was proud of him too, constantly surprised that he'd been taken in by a nice girl – one of the nicest, in fact.

"Where is Quinn?"

"She's at the house. She's got a big surprise, and she didn't want to tell ye out in the open like this. Said ye had more important things to worry about than our... our surprise." His gaze fell to my stomach, and I instantly sucked it in, pretty sure that you couldn't tell by looking at me that I was knocked up. I mean, by Dub's calculations, I was only a month along.

The proud look, the settling down in a house, the grin that looked on the verge of bursting off Link's face... It wasn't all that hard to put it all together. "Quinn's pregnant! Oh, Link, that's amazing! Congratulations!"

Link threw his hands out into the air. "How did ye guess? Ye have to act surprised. Quinn made me promise not to tell. Said she wanted to wait until ye got settled." He bounded up to me, and despite the risk of me ralphing all over him, he threw his arms around me and squeezed. "Can ye believe it? I'm going to be a Da. Me! I'll be the first

Untouchable to have a child. I mean, other than Mad, of course."

I fought through nausea and emotional gut punches to produce a smile for the boy who I truly hoped would never grow up. I'd loved that about Link, but seeing him take to fatherhood so seamlessly? I loved him even more this way. "Luckiest kid in the world, to have you two. I'm so happy for you, Link."

"Bastien!" Link called through the boat, which had emptied at the wave of Link's hand. "Bastien, come on out and tell me you'll be the best uncle tha ever was."

I plastered my smile in place and took a step back from Link to grab my pack from Lugh. "Bastien's not here, but I'm sure he'll be over the moon once he finds out."

"Not here?" Link's face soured. "He sent ye across an ocean without him? I thought ye were waiting until Avalon was squared away before ye came to Éireland. Is it still chaos over there?"

"No, no. Everything's all tied up in Avalon. Bastien's just decided to stay behind."

Link's confusion turned stony. "Rosie, tell me what happened."

"Good news for the Untouchables, I guess. You don't have to worry about me anymore. Bastien and I decided to split up. I'll be going to Common, and Bastien will stay here."

"What?" he roared, his volume making me jump. "Is he alright? Is he wounded or something?"

"Do you really think I'd leave him injured? Of course not. He walked out on his own two feet, and I won't rob him of the choice." I held up my hands. "It's fine, Link. It's all fine. Really. After I finish up in Éireland, I'll be off to Common. I'm coming back to Avalon for one month out of every year, but apart from that, you can cross me off your list of things to worry about. Focus on the baby that's coming. That's super way exciting!" I tried to work up a good gleeful expression, but knew it was too fabricated to be taken at face value.

Lugh clapped me on the shoulder. "I'll wait for ye out there, Prim. Tha was a grand fake smile, by the way." He met Link's eyes and shook his hand. "Your pal Bastien is in need of a beatdown. Since he's Untouchable, I'll leave tha to ye." Before Link could get a grip on the conversation, Lugh exited the boat, giving us privacy for the conversation that never got any easier.

Link balked at me. "Tha's... Do ye really expect me to take tha as an explanation? Bastien left ye? Why?"

I glanced around the empty ship. "This is hardly the time to get into all that. I'm supposed to be meeting your queen or whatever. I'll tell you everything you want to know after Éireland's all squared away."

"I need to go get him. Can I take your boat back to Avalon?"

"No. You know I'd give you anything, but you can't take off on Quinn like that. She's pregnant, which matters more than Bastien and me splitting up."

Link frowned at the obvious information that I didn't want to spell out for him. "I'll take her with me, of course."

"Making a pregnant woman travel across the ocean like that? I can't imagine she won't spend the entire trip barfing all over you. Shouldn't she be taking it easy?" It was basically the same speech Rigby had given me yesterday morning before we'd set sail.

Link deflated. "Go back to him. Ye have to. Ye don't understand what he'll be like on his own. At best, he'll turn back into a hermit. At worst, I'll find him at the bottom of some bottle, and we won't be able to get him back out of it."

I tried not to let my tone turn sharp on Link. "Don't you think I'd still be with him if he'd let me anywhere near? He couldn't even look at me when we talked last."

"Is it Kerdik?"

"No, it's me. Plain old me. I'm the problem, and I already told you I didn't want to talk about this right now. Bastien's a big boy. He doesn't want to be with me. Happens all the time." I slapped my palms together, working up a good representation of a grin to fake that I was up for the job I came here to do. "So, anything I should know about the new ruler you all elected? How's this Queen Aileen handling the country?" I'd never been through Éireland without the protection of the Brotherhood, and wasn't sure how this would all shake out. I hoped my own royalty card would carry me through the journey, so I could get back to Lane without further incident.

"She's fine. Éireland will be fine. It's this I'm worried about." He pointed to my faked optimism with accusation. "When ye and Bastien split before when he slept around on ye, Mad and me were riddled with guilt that we'd left ye. Now you're telling me tha ye aren't my responsibility? Tha ye were only my sister because of Bastien?"

I shrugged and shoved my hands into my pockets. "I thought that's how it worked. Bros over hos."

Despite his frustration over me not giving him enough information, Link closed the gap between us and scooped me in his burly arms. "Ye wear my mark, so you're my wife. I didn't leave ye, even if Bastien did. Mad and me are still here, so you're staying with us."

Link's arms had always been a safe place for me, so I sunk into the embrace I'd missed, willing myself not to tear up. Just as quickly, I pushed myself back, remembering that I shouldn't get too close, lest I sweat on a man and infect him with my joy juice. Lugh hated when I called it that, but I thought it was funny. "Thank you. I would like to stay with you guys, if that's okay. I don't like sleeping in places where I don't know who's for me and who's against."

Link frowned at the hug that ended so abruptly, but didn't address the oddity. "We're always for ye, Rose. While you're here, I'll have someone come by and touch up your neck tattoo. Ye can hardly tell it's our mark ye wear."

I covered the scarring with my palm. "It's okay. You

don't have to do that. I know I don't belong to you guys anymore."

Link surprised me when he fisted the front of my shirt and yanked me to him. His nose was nearly touching mine, and his scowl was menacing as he sneered in my face. "What's gotten into ye? Since when do ye talk like tha? You're Untouchable because *I* say ye are. You'll get tha eyesore tattoo fixed, and I don't want to hear another word about it. They'll put my blood in the ink, because you're my wife. Aye?"

I nodded, remembering that Link was a teddy bear to me because he loved me, and not because he was naturally a cutie pie to all women. I always forgot that he was supposed to be terrifying. "Okay, Link. If you want me to keep the mark, I will."

"I do. Bastien can bail, but I won't. If ye need something, name it. If I catch ye holding back and not telling us what ye want, I'll be cross with ye." His nose was an inch from mine, his smile replaced by a menacing snarl. "Do ye want to see me get cross?"

I swallowed hard, unsure whether to laugh or pee myself in fear. "Of course not. If I need something, I'll let you know. If you want the mark to stay on me, that's fine. The tattoo's all janky now anyways. It would be nice to have it touched up. Can you make that happen?" Though he'd already offered, I made it a point to play along and ask for the favor.

Link nodded, his shoulders relaxing, now that it was

clear I would play ball. "Aye. Of course. Let me get your bag." He slung my pack over his meaty shoulder, eyeing me with concern and confusion. "Let's go. I can't wait to hear what's so big tha it upended such a good thing."

I played with the hem of my shirt, wishing I could leave without explanation, and let Éireland fend for itself.

32

SACRIFICING THE QUEEN FOR THE PAWN

The Were curse had hit hard in Éireland, keeping the bunker stocked with too many furry bodies. Malone was by my side through every healing, growling at the soldiers who didn't do a good enough job of holding back the Weres. I'd been bitten twice, and I began to see the lack of a large enough dungeon as problematic. It was the same building I'd been held in with the rest of the Vampires, and the place still stank of excrement and bile.

"This isn't working!" I huffed out, frustrated that I couldn't get near enough to anything except their heads, which had the fangs to snap at me. The wolves had been shoved in, three to a cage, which was far too many bodies for cells that were too small to be humane for one. I recalled what it felt like to be trapped inside, and couldn't imagine how scared the healed ones must feel when they were still stuck in the cells with the rabid ones I couldn't reach. The bodies of men and women with wolf heads were a disconcerting sight to begin with, but they'd whipped themselves into a frenzy, being cooped up as they were.

Lugh had his bow cocked and ready, angry that this was the best Éireland had done to prepare. "Back up, Prim. I'll not stand for ye getting bit again. Remy's going to run out of gauze if this keeps up."

"I've got enough gauze, but nowhere near enough patience to watch you get bitten again. Where are Brìghde and Cailleach? Can't they produce an herb to make them all fall asleep?"

Remy's suggestion was a good one, though not altogether useful. "I've already summoned Cailleach, and she hasn't shown up yet. I can do this without them. I just need to psych myself up." I narrowed my eyes at Lugh's weapon of choice. "You know, you pointing that thing this way isn't helping. If you miss, you shoot me, you know."

Lugh scoffed at the insult. "Miss? If I *miss*? Do ye know who you're talking to? Do ye understand tha I never miss? Jays, woman. Insult a man to his core, why don't ye. I'm Cross Shot, if ye don't properly remember."

It was hour one million of this whole process, and we were hitting that old married couple point in the evening where we bickered, but still called each other "sweetheart". "You can't shoot them, either. They don't know what they're doing!"

"I've hit my limit, Prim! I don't care if they know or not. I care tha ye survive this!"

"Fine! Go take a breather, and come back when you're less homicidal."

"*Ye* can take a breather, and come back when you're less *suicidal!*"

I blew out my nerves in a loud gust and cracked my knuckles. Squaring my shoulders toward the cage, I lunged forward and grabbed onto the first hand I could grip, squeezing for two whole seconds before claws scraped at my wrist when the wolf-man finally mutated into sentient wolf. Blood bloomed from my arm just under the bandage where Remy had fixed the previous slice. I swore, half in triumph, half in anger, and let Remy start cleaning the cut that was far deeper than I was hoping. I squinted into the cage, and then nodded with satisfaction. "Healed. That's one more down. Good."

"Grand. At this rate, we'll work our way through the lot of them in a month!" Lugh was exasperated at the lack of momentum.

I jabbed my finger in his face. "Dude, get some air. We're about to have a knockdown drag-out. You don't want a piece of me right now, sweetheart, I guarantee it."

Lugh glowered at me, and then turned his head toward the head of the guard, whose name was... I'm still not sure. Everyone called him Captain. He didn't seem to want to be identified by much else. Captain had dark brown hair cut short to his scalp, and a stern expression that was almost corpse-like in its ability to never shift. "Captain, this isn't working. The Queen of Avalon's been attacked too many times on your soil, under your watch tonight." His tone left no room for arguing, and no misconception that Lugh felt he was under any law he needed to respect. He leveled the order as if he was capable of commanding nations and armies. "Fix it!"

Captain kept his untouched expression in place when he spat back, "And what would ye like me to do? I was ordered to gather up the Weres, so I did it."

I touched my forehead in frustration. "This is inhumane! Look at them, stuffed inside. Wouldn't you panic?"

When I heard the tromp of boots that were heavy with purpose, I knew help was finally here. "What nonsense is it tha an Untouchable's had blood spilt on a Captain's watch? Do ye not understand politics? Do ye not understand the highest law?"

"Mad!" I called out across the long room, a genuine smile on my face. I trotted over to him, but stopped short of the hug I wanted to give the man who never needed to be touched. He quirked his eyebrow at the two feet of space between us, but said nothing. "I'm so glad you're here. It's good to see you."

"Grand. Who cut ye?"

I shook my head. "They can't help it, and you know that. They don't understand what they're doing."

"I know tha, but the Captain should know what he's doing. Ye got sliced how many times? Let me see."

I held out my arms with an it's-no-big-deal shrug. The rips in my skin were covered with bandages, but I still flinched away when Mad moved to touch me. I was wearing short sleeves, and knew I was sweating. I didn't want to poison him by accident. Mad studied my hesitance, but again said nothing. "I'm alright. We're all just frustrated that I can't get ahold of the Werewolves without getting bit. It's slow going."

"It's dangerous, is what it is," Lugh interjected his indignation.

"Aye. I'll take care of it." Madigan crossed over to the captain, and without warning, landed three hard punches to the man – one on his face, and two in his stomach. The Captain keeled over, and my screams were ignored. Mad fisted the captain's neck to lift his head. "For every mark on my wife, tha's one tha'll find its way to ye. Let's see how quick ye find a solution tha keeps her safe now."

The captain backed away, looking like a man who didn't want to receive orders, but preferred to dole them out instead. Still, the law of the Untouchables was the highest in the land, so he submitted, his eyebrows pushing together as he puzzled through how best to help the situation. "I could have her wait out in the hall while a few of my men wrestle one cell's worth of Weres into submission. If we've got a dozen soldiers, tha should be enough to subdue three at a time."

Mad lightly slapped the captain's cheek. "Tha's more

like it. Ye don't sacrifice a queen to save a pawn, especially not *my* queen."

My heart swelled at the bold declaration. I never understood how they could be so sure of me, but the loyalty of the Brotherhood ran deep. They didn't have many people they relied on, so they protected that trust with an iron fist. I worried who would look after Madigan when I was gone. I wanted to thank him for being so sweet, but when he turned to face me, his surly expression chased the levity away, and lowered my heels to the ground.

"Out," he ordered, pointing to the door. When he followed me into the hall, he glared at me, which was his invitation to spill my guts about why I hadn't hugged him.

I didn't take the bait, but offered up a smile of gratitude instead. We waited while the captain ran out of the bunker to summon a slew of soldiers to help. "It's good to see you, Mad."

"Aye. Why are ye acting strange?"

"Aw, I missed you, too. How's Annabelle?"

"Grand. She's helping Quinn around the house. Link said Bastien didn't come with ye. You'll starve without him. How come he's not here?"

"Actually, I found a way around all that. We brought a cure for the Vampires that'll let us survive off of way less blood and lots more food, so Bastien's off the hook."

"But why is…"

My voice cut with a sharper edge than I meant for it to.

"We can talk about Bastien in the morning when I go to Link's after I'm finished here. It's more complicated than a simple conversation, so let's just get through this."

Mad's eyes widened at the mood shift he hadn't seen coming. He pointed to the door of the dungeon with a stern look on his face. "Ye don't step a toe in there without me, understood?"

I gulped, and then nodded. "Thank you. I actually do need the help this time."

Mad glared at me, as if that might make me spill all my secrets. Another few seconds, and I just might've. Fortunately, the soldiers came to offer their assistance, bowing to Mad and me on their way into the room that was filled with gnashing teeth.

33

LINK'S PRIZE

"You're telling me that all this time, you've been Gancanagh?"

Lugh had taken the floor for most of the explanation, since I didn't have the gusto to expose myself more than the perfunctory facts. Lugh was the true expert on the subject, so he took over. "Aye, but it's diluted in her. She's probably sweat on both of ye at one time or another, and neither of ye were daft enough to follow her around like a lovesick pup. It's a small hit she gives men. Bastien overreacted to the whole lot of it, and bailed on the best thing that ever happened to him."

I frowned at Lugh, wincing when I scratched the bandage on my neck. The tattoo had just been to retouch what the Nain Rouge had burned away, but the process had been like a slow cat scratch after I'd finished a long night of work, in which I'd been bitten by wolves all night long. Fun times. "Lugh, you've got to stop editorializing. Bastien's allowed to have a reaction. He's allowed to walk out on someone who's been bewitching him into falling in love with her. He's allowed to be upset with me."

"When did ye find out?" Link asked, the veins in his neck tensed as he sat at the table across from me, and next to Quinn. I wanted to ditch all the boys and braid Quinn's hair, let her teach me how to sew or whatever, and girl-talk the day away. Unfortunately, business came first. Though I'd already braided her hair during the first few minutes of Lugh's explanation, so at least we'd done that.

Link's home was a quaint and cozy log cabin, complete with a wood-burning stove and a handmade "Only Love Lives Here" sign hung over the doorway that Mad snarled at every time he glanced at it.

"The Nain Rouge planted the seed in my mind when we were fighting him in Lugh's cabin, and Dub confirmed it for me." I pinched the bridge of my nose and leaned forward on the padded bench I sat on next to Lugh at the polished wood table. "I didn't know before then, and I'm sorry if I infected either of you." My eyes darted between Mad and Link apologetically.

Link's face soured. "I'm not ready to throw Quinn out for ye. Ye didn't infect me. I loved ye from the beginning, but not for myself. I loved ye for Bastien, and kept a sister for myself. Nothing more than tha."

Lugh shot me an I-told-you-so look, crossing his arms over his chest. "See? You're not poisoning people, as ye say ye are. It's too much guilt ye take on yourself. I have the ability to actually ruin people, but ye don't."

"I tricked Bastien into falling in love with me; he's allowed to be mad. He's allowed to leave something that probably wasn't real to begin with. Doesn't matter if I meant to, and I don't really want to discuss it with you all. I feel like I've told this stupid story a million times already, and I'm tired of it. It's my marriage, and it's over. That's all there is to it."

Link had plenty to say about this, but Quinn and Mad were quieter, more thoughtful. When Quinn finally spoke, it was with a gentleness only she could summon on command. "But how will ye eat, if ye don't have him to feed from? Rosie, you'll starve!"

I explained for what felt like the hundred thousandth time just what Carman's blood could do, and had already done for me. "So I don't need him as much. I wanted him, make no mistake, but I'll be fine on my own if I take a pint of his blood with me when I go. That should last me half a year or so, maybe more. I actually delivered a whole batch of the cure to Queen Aileen earlier today, so I'm sure the announcement will be going out soon enough. I brought a vial for Quinn, though, so she doesn't have to go in to the castle. It's in my bag. Hold on, I'll go get it."

Link's reaction to the news of his wife's impending cure was most unexpected. He stood, knocking his chair back in his upset. "No! There is no cure. Ye don't know what you're talking about. You're still Vampire. Don't come in here with something like this and wave it around in front of our faces. We don't need it!"

Quinn was quiet, but when she stood, it was as if she'd shouted. She wasn't showing yet, but the men behaved as if she was nine months along, and in need of bedrest and fainting salts. It was sweet to see Link's arm coil around her waist, and Mad stand to offer his arm to her, though she looked in no danger of actually needing the support. My heart ached to be cared for like that, but I kept my mouth shut, knowing that if they knew about my baby, they wouldn't stop until Bastien was pushed back in my direction, whether he wanted me or not.

Quinn met my eyes, searching for the absolute truth. "I want it. Where's the cure? I need it today, Rosie. Please."

"Of course." I made to stand, but shrank back onto my bench next to Lugh when Link started yelling.

"No! She needs me. We don't want your cure, Rosie!" His fury turned to genuine hurt. "How could ye do this to me? After everything, why would ye try to take my Quinny away from me?"

I balked at him, and simultaneously watched Quinn's voice and fight die down as she lowered herself back onto her chair. "Do you hear yourself? What if you're away for a week? What then? I'm trying to help your wife, Link. I wouldn't try to take her away from you. I love the two of you together. This will make her stronger, healthier."

Link's insecurity shot out of his mouth without a filter, his eyes tinged with desperation. "Do ye think we'd have ended up together if she didn't need me to survive? Do ye really think someone like me would've been able to hold onto someone as amazing as her without a little help from the dark magic?"

My jaw felt permanently dropped open. "Hold the phone. Link, she's not still with you only because she has to be. Can't you see that? Can't you see that she's over the moon for you, and that has nothing to do with how good your blood tastes?"

"Look at me!" Link thundered, showing his rare vulnerability as he threw his arms out to the sides. "Don't ye think I know my Quinn is out of my league? Do ye think I don't know tha? How could ye do this to me? Because you're alone, ye want me to be miserable, as well?"

I gasped at the gut-punch, a gust of my confidence leaving me in a breath.

Lugh held up his hands. "Jays. Obviously tha's not it. Rosie's trying to help the Vampires live longer, is all. If ye get held up somewhere, your wife's going to starve. Do ye want tha, mate?"

Link's irrational nature thundered through the log cabin he'd built for his bride. "I take care of my prize! I'd never let tha happen to her. Take your cure and go, Rosie. We don't need it."

I gaped at him, unsure how I'd overstayed my welcome so soon. I was exhausted, and hadn't been to sleep yet after hitting my maximum quota for healing the Weres. I could get through about two dozen before I had to beg off for sleep, but that didn't seem to matter right now. Link was furious with me, which I'd never thought would happen. I was ashamed, though part of me knew I had no reason to be. "Link, I'm sorry. I didn't mean to say anything that would upset you. I thought this would be good news. Don't you want her cured?"

"She's not sick! Her curse is the best thing tha ever happened to me. I don't care about the rest. Take it to the others, but keep it out of my house."

I was flabbergasted, utterly beside myself, but I knew when I was being shown the door. I stood, completely confused at how I'd managed to piss him off so irrevocably. Lugh was at my side, supporting me when my gait wavered due to my utter exhaustion.

I stopped at the door, turning slowly to steel myself. "Look, as much as I love you even when you're being a complete ass-butt, this isn't your decision. Quinn's the one who should speak for herself. If you love her, you won't rob her of her voice. Quinn, do you want the cure or not?"

I didn't want to put her on the spot, but I couldn't let Link lay down such a harsh edict. No way would I have been cool if Bastien had reacted like that. I watched her squirm at the attention, my face falling with the crushing defeat of women's lib when her voice eked out a meek, "If my husband says no, I'll not go against his wishes."

I wanted to argue with her, but reminded myself that if I did so, that would be me inflicting my will upon her, just as Link was doing. I was merely here to offer her a cure – it was up to her to take it. I'd controlled enough people without meaning to. "Okay. If that's what you want, I'll respect it." I met Link's defiant glare with a steadiness I willed myself to feel. "No matter how angry you are with me, I love you, Link. I've loved you from the very beginning. I'd never do anything to hurt you. I honestly thought I was helping, giving your wife a cure."

Link turned away from me, cutting me worse than the Werewolves had. "Mad, take Rosie to your place. She can sleep there."

"Aye. Come on, Rosie." Mad didn't blink at the utter shutdown of Link's affection for me, but I started to panic at losing someone I loved more than most.

"Link, I'm sorry! Please don't push me away! I would never hurt Quinn or you. You have to believe that I was trying to help you!"

"Help yourself! Are ye happier, now tha ye don't need Bastien? One marriage ruined is all you'll have, Rosie. Ye won't wreck mine, as well."

I gasped, stepping back at the well-aimed slash across my already beaten-up heart.

Lugh was livid, and bit back on my behalf. "Tha's out of line. We won't be staying with the Untouchables, if this is how ye treat your own. Mark her in the same night ye cast her out? Bastien's best friend, if ever I saw one. We'll be at the castle, working till she passes out to restore *your* land, and heal *your* sick. When ye come to your senses and realize what you've done, don't bother coming back. She'll forgive ye, but I won't. We'll be in Common long before ye grow up and realize all ye just lost." Lugh kissed my temple, and wrapped me in a hug, which was the only thing holding me together anymore. "Come on, Prim. I'll take ye to the castle. We're done with this world, anyway."

I sniffled into his neck, willing myself not to break down in front of people who didn't know me well enough to trust that I would never try to hurt them. I'm not sure if that was my fault, or theirs. Either way, we all lost in the end. "Okay. Let's go home, Lugh."

34

LITTLE ROSEBUD

Each night that I worked in the bunker, healing the Werewolves who desperately needed some compassion, I hoped Link would come back to me. I wanted him to say he was wrong, to take it all back. Each time the heavy door opened, my heart lifted in hopes it was his goofy grin rounding the corner. Then my spirits plummeted impossibly lower every time it wasn't him.

"Ye have to eat something, Prim. I know this much work makes ye feel barmy, but ye can't go skipping breakfast and lunch."

Lugh had taken it upon himself to be my mother, which was a sweet side of him I'm not sure many saw. He wasn't used to looking after anyone except for himself, but took to the challenge with grace Lane would be proud of. "I'm not hungry. You don't have to worry about me, Lugh. Really, I'm fine."

Despite my dismal mood, he persisted with logic. "You've got a baby to think of. Eat something, and I'll leave ye alone about it."

I ate seven grapes to make him happy, and then shooed him out of the room so I could sleep. That's all I did these days – work, sleep and try to eat. I hadn't seen the sun in days. I never visited the palace beyond the initial meet-and-greet with Queen Aileen, but took one of the bare-bones rooms in the bunker, so I could go right to work the minute I woke. It was slow going, but we were powering through. Lugh was extra finicky about working too much, insisting we stop at the first yawn.

My life was nothing like what I'd hoped or imagined for myself. I'd even cut myself off from animals, since they seemed to understand me, and I didn't want that. As soon as the Weres were turned into regular wolves, I smiled at them and showed them the door, where they were tended to by villagers who'd taken it upon themselves to care for the traumatized. I wanted to hug them all, but part of me couldn't handle the emotional tax that would need to be paid with each transaction of kindness.

I couldn't handle anyone being compassionate. Lugh was the only person in my life I let near me anymore, and that was because he was relentless that we were in this together. We were the only two Gancanagh in the land, and he clung to the notion of not being the only one of his kind anymore. There was no use pushing him away. Believe me, I'd tried.

Lugh snuck back into my room half an hour later to grab something from his pack. "Prim, are ye pretending to sleep?"

"Yes. Am I doing a convincing job?"

"Aye. Roll over. I'm bored of the howling down there."

I moved onto my side, letting him cozy into the single bed with me, spooning me as my knees pressed to the concrete wall. It was dank in the no-frills living quarters, but I didn't have it in me to complain. People left me alone in here, so I loved it.

Instead of pretending there was space between us, Lugh wrapped his arm around me and moved my hand to my stomach, pressing my palm to my navel. "How's our little Rosebud?"

I sniggered at the cute nickname. "Rosebud? I like that. Super sweet."

"Just like her mammy. Your belly's starting to get a little rounder."

I frowned. "Dude, how would you feel if I said that to you?"

"If I was growing a person inside of me? Honored. Besides, I'm fairly certain my belly *is* starting to get rounder, since I've taken to eating your leftovers, and you've taken to eating like a wee bird." He traced from just above my navel to the waist of my jeans. "Feel tha? It's your baby."

I nodded, unable to say anything. Lugh had given me enough space for a good chunk of denial, but this was his warning that sooner or later, I wouldn't be able to ignore my situation any longer. "I don't know how to be a mother. Lane made it all look so easy, but I know it wasn't. She was amazing."

"What do ye think ye won't be good at?"

"Well, I've never changed a diaper, for one."

"We can learn tha. Cross tha off the worry list."

"I'm not taking any prenatal vitamins. I'm fairly certain that's strike one right there."

His lips tickled the shell of my ear. "Your wee one is Fae, not human. Ye don't need prenatal vitamins."

"I won't have a job when I get back to Common. How am I supposed to support us?"

"You're my stylist. Done. Pick me out some old jeans and a faded t-shirt, and we're all set."

I sniggered at the idea. "You could be my Barbie."

"Not a bad arrangement. Besides, you're forgetting about the jewels we're bringing over. Ye won't have money troubles." He kissed the back of my shoulder, and slowly strummed his thumb along my stomach, playing my body, as was his way when he was thinking about something deep.

"What's on your mind, hun?" I asked nonchalantly.

"Lately? Getting out of here. Having a life again. I've made a list of all the things we're going to see before we settle back in with the band."

"Won't they be mad you've been gone for so long?"

"Nah. I told them I needed to take a leave of absence to

look after my terminally ill brother. They all understood. They're using a replacement while I'm away, who'll promptly leave when I return."

"That's the worst lie ever. Using death to ditch them? That's some bad karma coming your way, dude."

"Kerdik's the closest thing I have to a brother, and he's straight terminal for ye. No lie there. Plus, when I come back with ye, they'll forgive me anything. You've got tha way about ye. We're a bunch of misfits in need of a lass to clean up our act for. It's time."

"Hmm. I'm not sure a knocked-up groupie is quite the bargaining chip you're thinking it'll be." Our light chuckles filled the dank air, relaxing us both. I was so tightly wound these days; it was a relief to laugh. Lugh was good for me, and I wasn't so lost that I couldn't recognize that fact. I cozied into him and closed my eyes, smiling when he pulled the thin blanket up over us. "Whatcha thinking about?"

"How big your breasts are going to get after the baby comes."

I guffawed, blushing at the crassness only we shared. "You were not thinking that, you dork."

"I mean, they're already set for porn now. Add nursing to tha, and I don't think the guys will have a problem with ye staying with us."

"Good to know. I'll invest in some baggy sweaters first thing."

Lugh sniggered, and we both shivered when his thumb

traced the plump outer edge of my breast. There was nothing more to us than the light flirt, but it was just enough to mute the loneliness that clawed at us both. In the world that would die around us, we had each other to hold onto, and we didn't take that privilege lightly. We were the last two of our kind in Faîte – twin Gancanaghs to our core. He kissed my neck and inhaled, taking me into his lungs while my body arched against his. "I'm keeping ye up. Get some sleep." He blew a loud raspberry into the spot he'd just teased, making me shriek with laughter and lightly elbow him in the gut.

"Gross! You slobbered all over me!" I wiped off my neck, but no sooner did I get his spit off of me, did he lick me from shoulder to ear, like a dog. "Ack!"

We laughed and rolled in the sheets, tickling and teasing for no reason, other than that we were the only two who knew what it was to live how we did – afraid to touch, questioning every closeness. When I finally pinned him to the mattress, he leaned up and licked my chin just to be disgusting.

We didn't hear the door swing open. I only felt the whoosh of the hand before it gripped my hair and yanked me off my prey. "Ow! Dude, what gives?" My indignation was cut short when I was jerked up to sitting, straddling Lugh with a knife to my throat.

35

ENTRANCED BY LUGH

"I knew ye wanted him for yourself!" I didn't need a lamp to know whose voice it was. Molly's desperation was palpable. Her hands were shaking as she held me still, poised above the thunderstruck Lugh.

Lugh slid out from between my legs, which I'll admit, was pretty damning, even though we were both fully clothed. "Wait up, sweetheart. Ye don't know what you're doing. I wasn't with Rosie. Honest."

I didn't have to look at Molly to know she had crazy eyes. The once sane woman I'd shared girl-talk with was holding a knife to my throat and thinking I was macking on her would-be man. I kind of had let him cop a feel, and was admittedly too flirty with him for the outside world to look at us and see two friends, but I didn't want to die for it.

Molly's voice was hysterical, and laced with angry

tears. "Do ye want her, Lugh? She can't love ye like I can. She doesn't know ye the way I do."

It was the poison, for sure. She'd danced with him once, but her brain had been tricked into thinking she truly knew the man.

Lugh held up his hands slowly. "Of course she doesn't. Leave Rosie alone, and let's go outside. I fancy a long walk with ye, where ye tell me everything about yourself. Tell me how you've entranced me so."

"You're entranced by me?" Her voice squeaked at the end, and I knew if she was in her right mind, she'd be disgusted at the sound. She'd been cool when we'd first met, but it had all devolved quickly after Lugh accidentally sweat on her in the pub. "What about me do ye like?"

Lugh took a cautious step forward, and reached over my shoulder to touch her hair. "Ye have the prettiest hair. What's this color?"

"Brown."

He sighed like he was in a romance movie. "Brown, ye say? It's lovely. Tell me, do ye fancy a room with a window, or not? Have ye seen all the options here? If ye haven't, I'd love to give ye a tour. So many beds to choose from," he winked.

The blade trembled against my throat, and I felt a drop of blood trickle down my neck when Molly grew too excited. "I'd like tha." Then she seemed to remember the dastardly thing I'd done to her man, and gripped my hair harder in her fist, jerking my chin further up, so I was staring at the ceiling. "She was about to have sex with ye!"

Lugh shook his head, and I could tell he was coming up empty on viable reasons why the position she'd found us in was totally cool and easy to explain away. "No, no. Forget about her. I want ye in my bed right now." He met my eyes in a warning. "Rosie, get out of here and fetch us something to eat. My lass wants only the best this place has to offer."

I'd hoped Molly would let me go without incident, but after she removed the knife from my throat, she caught the look of loyalty Lugh and I shot each other as I reached for the door. She screamed at me to drop dead, and then lunged with the knife.

"Dude, I don't want your man!" I shouted, jumping back from the swinging blade. She slashed out at my heart, but I blocked myself with my forearms, so her knife slid across them instead. Blood dripped down my arms as I darted for the door, throwing it open and calling for help.

Molly wasn't finished with me, and tackled me from behind, knocking me forward. My knees hit the stone floor, and she landed atop me without mercy. I didn't want to fight her, lost as she was.

Lugh ripped her off of me, and slammed her wrist against the doorjamb over and over, until she lost her grip on the knife. A handful of guards came tearing down the corridor, and made quick work of arresting Molly. "She doesn't know what she's doing," he explained, following after them to make sure Molly wasn't prosecuted for attacking a queen, and an Untouchable, at that.

Remy was summoned, and he wasted no time at all lecturing me that somehow danger always managed to find me, and would I please be more careful.

I pursed my lips as he bandaged up my forearms. I didn't even care anymore if they scarred. It seemed I wouldn't be able to escape Faîte unscathed. I would remember clearly the danger that me being Gancanagh could cause the world if I didn't stay away from Faîte. The world was safe from me if I lived in Common, and I couldn't get there fast enough. I was a dangerous girl, and didn't take that fact lightly. "Can we go back to work? Are there soldiers around who can help hold the Weres so I can heal them?"

"There are enough for whatever you need, of course. But you don't need to push yourself."

It was mildly disconcerting to converse with a man who wore his head in a sling on his hip, but I didn't say anything about it, so Remy wouldn't feel self-conscious. I stood and slapped my palms together, willing the shaking to leave my limbs. I needed to give them purpose, so I didn't lose it. "Alright, then. Let's do this."

36

MALONE THE MIGHTY

"Are ye mad? Are ye trying to prove something by working yourself to near death?"

"I'm not dead. I just fainted. Big difference."

"Could ye give us a moment, Remy? I'm about to do all sorts of yelling."

"Don't hold back on my account." Remy frowned at me before leaving us to our fight in the privacy of our tiny room.

"What were ye thinking? Ye were in a knife fight and tackled to the ground. Ye take a day off when ye get stabbed. Ye don't go on a tear and work yourself till ye pass out. Did ye hit yourself on the floor? Did anyone catch ye?"

"Some guard caught me before I hit the floor. It's cool."

Lugh paced around the small room that was no bigger than a college dorm. "Is the baby alright?"

"How would I even know that? It's not like there's a

sonogram anywhere." I stared up at the ceiling in silent dread. "I didn't ask to be attacked, Lugh. I went to work because I want to get out of here. Also, that's the only place that's brimming with security. Molly couldn't get at me if I was with all of them."

He touched his chest with two fingers, his expression livid. "Ye scared me! When ye fell, I swear, my life flashed before my eyes. Ye have to be more careful!"

"Don't yell at me! It's your psycho stalker who started it, not me. I'm just trying to get us the crap out of here."

Lugh huffed as he flopped down, sitting on the side of the bed I was laid out in, resting his head in his hands. "I'm sorry. I know you're right, but I'm freaking out. Ye could've lost the baby!"

I softened at the man who'd grown more attached to the idea of my pregnancy than I had. It was often an abstract concept for me still, but to him it was life or death (which I guess it kind of was). I pried his hand from his face and lifted my shirt, resting his palm on my belly. "Tell your niece or nephew that you're done freaking out. Tell the baby that he or she is safe."

Lugh's shoulders dropped, and he moved to his knees on the edge of the bed, leaning over my body so he could hover above my stomach. The low lantern's light lit only part of his face, casting shadows on the fear he'd endured. He bent down and pressed his lips to my navel, making me squirm at the slight tickle. "I'm so sorry, Rosebud." He brushed his nose back and forth across my slightly rounded abdomen, giving me the shivers and making my back arch involuntarily. "You're safe if I'm around. I'm not going anywhere. Uncle Lugh's going to protect ye." He kissed my belly again, and I swear, my brain turned to mush.

"Okay, you can't do that."

"What?"

"You're going to confuse me, and I've got enough drama swimming around up in here." My hand orbited my head to indicate my near constant befuddlement that only grew worse the longer I tried to figure out my life.

"Confuse ye?" His scrunched nose smoothed out when he smiled at me with a tease to his lips – always that constant tease. "Ah. I knew it. You've wanted me for my hot body from the beginning. Would it help destroy the Lou Van Guarden fantasy if I farted on ye?"

"Please always offer to fart on me. Every girl's dream." I sighed, brushing a stray lock of his hair back from his forehead. "It's just that I'm used to life with Bastien, where we were going at it a few times a day. It's been a steep hump to get over – pun intended."

"I see. Well, I'd offer my stud services, but I don't think Kerdik would take too kindly to tha."

I blushed, wishing I'd found a detour away from this conversation before we'd landed here. "I wasn't asking, if you recall. I was telling you not to start my engine, because I'm at the edge of the cliff, like, all the time these days."

Lugh tilted back his head and barked out a laugh. "Tha's just cryptic enough to be ladylike. Well done, Prim."

After a few hours of sleep, Lugh helped me up, treating my body with more care than I did. After breakfast, we went down into the dungeon, where none other than Demi was waiting with the soldiers. I wanted to hug him, but knew I couldn't risk poisoning my old boyfriend. I wore elbow-length gloves now, courtesy of Lugh's shopping trip while I'd been sleeping last night. They gave me a little more confidence, and kept me from feeling like such a leper. Demi frowned at the handshake, but bowed without speaking his frustration. He was a pro, as always, tending to my needs without being asked. He opened doors, wrestled Weres, and made sure I always had water and something to eat. When I started to sweat from exertion after I hit eighteen healings, he gave me his handkerchief like a gentleman.

Exhaustion crept up on me, and I assumed once again that if I had the will to power through, my body would comply. Demi caught me before I hit the floor on my twentieth healing, and carried me to my dorm room. Though curing the Werewolves didn't shock me and hurt, it did make me sleepy when coupled with the animals talking pretty much nonstop.

Malone trusted Lugh with my safety, but no one else since he'd come back from rounding up what was hopefully the last of the Werewolves with the local Dullahan. When Demi laid me down in the bed, my wolf hopped up on the mattress and curled into my side, positioning himself between my body and the door to block any new people. Demi sat in the chair by my bedside, watching me sleep with his head resting on his lap.

Lugh was diplomatic when he shooed Demi out a few hours later. "The Dullahan need ye to check for more Werewolves prowling about when night falls again. We've finally got enough space to hold a few more, so tell them to gather up as many Weres as they can."

"Yes, sir." There was a heavy pause before Demi continued. "She's leaving after she's finished healing them, isn't she."

I kept my eyes closed through Lugh's response. "Aye. Best say your goodbyes when ye see her tomorrow night. We'll probably be gone before the week's out."

"There's nothing that can be done to convince her to stay?"

My heart clenched in my chest, but I tried to keep my breathing even, so they didn't know I was awake. Malone shifted next to me, keeping my front warm as I spooned his furry body.

"I'm sorry, mate."

The door opened, and the two went out, leaving me with Malone, who was too keen to be fooled by my fake sleeping. *"Are ye well?"*

I nodded, opening my eyes. Malone was the best teddy bear in the world – fuzzy, soft and affectionate. "How about you? Holding up okay? How goes rehabilitation for the healed Weres?"

Malone had been put in charge of taking the freshly healed Werewolves under his wing, offering them a kind word and a safe place to wait out the nights. They'd started calling him Chief Malone, which was fitting. He'd given up everything to protect me so we could restore the Werewolves to their right minds. I was glad he was getting his due reward. If anyone deserved a title and the largest pack in the world, it was Malone.

"It's going slow. Most of them are too turned around to make sense of much. They cry at night, scared they'll lose their minds again."

Some of the soldiers had taken to complaining about the excessive howling in the night from the healed Weres who now roamed around the bunker, but I didn't mind it. They were figuring out their lives, trying to understand how they fit into Éireland, now that their basic genetic makeup had changed.

"We need to give them a purpose. Their normal nighttime activities aren't an option anymore. What sort of things do you think they could do better than a normal Fae?" My mouth drew to the side as I attempted to answer my own question. "Hunting, maybe. I mean, if they put themselves in charge of hunting not just for their own families, but for all of Éireland, think of how heroic they'd be. Everyone would revere the warriors who bring home the food, don't you think? We could even get you a cool nickname – Malone the Mighty or something."

Malone rested his maw on my shoulder. *"Tha's not a bad idea – gathering for the whole country. There are so many of us now. We'd need to break into smaller packs, so we don't over-hunt in one area. Spread out where we get our food from."*

"I love that. And you'll need several leaders you trust to keep the smaller groups in line. Not dictators or anything, just someone to be accountable for the individual packs, and report to you."

"To me? Surely ye mean to Queen Aileen."

"Nah. She's still too green on the job. I trust you to look out for them. Besides, how's she going to hear their thoughts and concerns? You can listen to them in whatever form they're in. They'll need someone they can turn to. That's already you. Then sure, you can report back to the queen to keep everything above board. You up for it?"

Malone stammered his astonishment. *"I... um... I... Of course! Your majesty, ye don't have to do tha. I'm no one. I was a normal laborer before I turned."*

"So you were diligent in your previous life, and now you've given up everything to watch my back. What makes you unqualified to help your country?"

"There are many who are far more educated and eloquent than me."

"But none of them gave up everything for their country. You didn't blink an eye to stay with me. I've healed hundreds of Werewolves by now. Only you and your brother offered to stay with me to make sure every Werewolf had their fair shot at getting cured. You're a born leader, Malone. It can't be anyone else. Only you care about them enough to be in charge."

I could tell the sun was starting to rise because Malone's fur was getting shorter, patchier, and his nose shorter. He licked my face all over in gratitude, making me giggle like a little girl with her puppy. I kissed his neck, wrapping my arms around him so I could hold him as tight as I wanted. Though I'd gone to great lengths to seal myself off from the woodland creatures, Malone was my good medicine.

He laughed when I growled into his neck, pretending like I was his wolf cub and he was my pack leader. Neither of us were paying attention when his hind legs smoothed out, and in the next few breaths, he was lying atop me, a fully grown naked man, whose eyes grew wide with panic. "Forgive me, your majesty!"

I probably shouldn't have laughed, given that he was so embarrassed, but it was too funny. "I can't believe that's the only time that's happened since that very first night." I rolled out from under him, leaving him with the sheet to wrap himself in.

Malone's darker skin still flushed with a blush that hit his cheeks like a smear of strawberries. "Oh, I'm so embarrassed. Completely inappropriate. I'll report myself to the captain straightaway."

I covered my mouth to stifle my laughter. "Don't. It's

really fine. Oh, man. I needed that. I haven't laughed that hard in way too long." I instantly sobered. "Not because I saw anything humorous! You're totally all man, and nothing was funny about your body. Totally smokin' hot. I was laughing because of your face, and the situation." I smacked my forehead at my conversational bumbling. "You know what I mean."

It was Malone's turn to snort. "I do. And thanks." He smiled to himself, looking down at his sheet-covered portion. "The Queen of Avalon just called my body 'smokin' hot.' I'm fairly certain I won't be needing any other compliments for the rest of my life. That one's going to get me through for a while. Smokin' hot Malone."

We laughed together, until I realized he was still naked under the sheet. "Let me get your clothes. Down in the barracks?"

"Fourth room on the right."

"On it." I swung the door open, yelping at the sight of a towering man filling the doorframe. "Mad? What are you doing here?"

"Watching my wife stumble out of bed with some lad, apparently," Madigan grumbled, shooting Malone a filthy look. "Run," he warned Malone, who didn't need to be told twice.

MAD'S WIFE

Despite the fact that he was clad in only a sheet, Malone bowed his head to Madigan, and exited the room with his dignity severely compromised.

Mad glowered at me. "What's he doing, naked in your room?"

I leveled my finger in his face. "You don't get to care who's in my bed, but since you asked so nicely, I'll tell you that was Malone, my guard. You've met him. He's my Werewolf, and there aren't any windows in here. I didn't realize it was sun-up. He stays with me to guard me when he's a wolf. All you caught was an unexpected transition."

"Be more careful next time. Sun-up comes around every morning. Ye shouldn't forget something so predictable."

"Is there a reason you're here?"

Mad glanced down the hallway, and then moved into

my dorm room, scooting me backward as he shut the door. "Link was wrong to throw ye out like tha."

I gaped at him, astounded that he was admitting Link was capable of folly. "Wow. I wasn't expecting that. I wasn't expecting you at all, really. Thanks, I guess."

"I know ye weren't trying to break Link and Quinn up."

I shrugged, as if the whole thing didn't hurt one bit. "I would never do that. Sucks that Link doesn't know who I am, after all this time."

"I know ye." Mad met my eyes with a steady promise that told me not to question his loyalty, or his intentions. "I know ye wouldn't leave Bastien over nothing."

"For the record, I didn't leave Bastien. You've got that little fact reversed."

"So tha's it? You're leaving Faîte, and we're expected to just accept tha?"

I scoffed at him. "I'm not sure anyone cares except for you, hoss. And the fact that you care is a shock to me, to be honest. You'll be fine. You don't need me around." I took in the breadth of his shoulders and his wide chest. "Especially you. You've never needed me."

A rare flash of vulnerability crossed Madigan's features, confusing me more than if he'd thrown down and started rapping at random. He would never admit to needing me, but I saw it there, the glint of fear at being left alone to face the shifting world. "I don't want ye to go."

It was the equivalent of a bouquet of roses from the ineloquent brute. I didn't put up my same old argument of why I belonged in Common. Instead, I held out my gloved hand, offering up the most physical contact I could give him without accidentally poisoning a man I really did love.

"Come home with me. If ye don't want to be in Avalon, ye can stay with me and Annabelle."

I met his hesitant eyes with a glimmer of appreciation for the leaps and bounds it had taken him to get to this place. "As much fun as it would be to watch you try and figure out fatherhood, there's nothing for me here. My mom's in Common. My dad doesn't want me. My husband doesn't want me. My Link doesn't want me. I'm tired, Mad. Don't I deserve to be around people who want me around?"

"What of me? I just asked ye to stay."

"You know it would drive a wedge between you and Link. I meant what I said when I told Link I would never take anything away from him. If I stayed with you, knowing he hates me? He would come to your house less, or maybe avoid you altogether. He needs you, Mad." Most people thought it was the other way around, that Madigan needed Link to be his guide through normal societal inter-actions. But I knew that Link needed Madigan to anchor him, to ground him in something real. Link was only fear-less because he had Madigan to be terrifying on his behalf, watching his back and making sure that when Link leapt into something foolish, Madigan was there to pull him out and never say "I told you so."

I shoved my hands in the pockets of my worn jeans and

stared at Mad's boots. There was mud on them now, instead of snow. I wondered if Cailleach and Brìghde had finally reined in the climate issues in Éireland, so the people had four seasons, instead of just the one. I kept my eyes on his shoes as I spoke. "I didn't mean to hurt him and Quinn, you know. I wanted to help them."

"I know. Link can't see clearly. He's mad for her. Quinn wanted to take the cure. She asked me to come and get some for her in secret."

My jaw stiffened, now that I understood the reason for Madigan's unexpected visit. My shoulders dropped, and the lightness that made me feel marginally better since he'd come to visit was now crashing down around me. "Oh. I didn't realize that's why you stopped by. Of course. She's your wife."

Madigan met my eyes with a sadness we both shared. "So are ye. I wouldn't turn ye out like tha. Even if Bastien's being a fool. Ye belong to us."

I mustered up a brave smile. "Well, the good news is that I won't be a problem anymore. I'll be gone, and you can help Quinn with the baby when it comes."

"Right. Like ye could picture me with a wee baby."

"I can see you with Annabelle just fine. It's not all that different. You're a good man, when you want to be." I tore my eyes from him and cleared my throat. "Take whatever you want. All she needs is a swallow of the cure."

"Should she have more because she's pregnant? Or should she wait until the baby's out of her?"

I turned and shifted the sheets on the bed, so they didn't look so slept in. "Nah. I didn't have much more than a mouthful, and me and my baby are both fine."

As soon as the words were out of my mouth, I wished for a spatula to stuff them back inside. I froze, hoping Madigan had gone spontaneously deaf in both ears. "What did ye just say?"

I cringed, wanting to melt into the floor to escape the one thing I'd been trying to keep to myself. "Nothing. Bad joke. The captain's got a container of Carman's blood that he gives out to the Vamps who get brought in. You can get a vial of it from him. She'll be fine in no time."

I could feel Mad staring at me, like a bull readying to gore its prey. His voice lowered to a scandalous whisper, looking over his shoulder to make sure the door was shut. "Are ye pregnant? Whose baby is it?"

I brought my voice down to a harsh whisper. "It's mine, that's whose it is. And I didn't mean to tell you. It just slipped out. You can't tell the guys. I mean it, Mad. I'm so close to being out of here. I need to have this baby in Common. If Avalon finds out, I'll never be able to leave."

Madigan nodded. "So tha's why ye and Bastien split up, and why ye won't take my protection. Who got ye pregnant?"

I glowered at him, clenching my fists at my side. "My husband, that's who. Bastien got me pregnant, but we're over, so I'm leaving it all alone. So should you, if you know what's good for you."

Mad's face soured. "No way would Bastien let ye leave with his kid. I can't even picture tha." Light dawned in his eyes. "Unless he doesn't know. Ye didn't tell him, did ye." My silence confirmed the truth for him. "Bastien's going to have a kid, and he doesn't even know? Why? Why would ye keep tha from him? He never would've left if he knew it was his baby in ye."

I shrugged. "Maybe I want more than that. I told Kerdik about me being Gancanagh, and he didn't care. I don't blame Bastien for wanting out, but I also don't need to try and lure him back. If he wanted to be with me, he would be. I didn't leave him, Mad. Bastien doesn't love me, and I'm learning that the world still turns."

Mad sat down on the only chair in the room and leaned forward, resting his elbows on his knees. "Jays, this is so messed up. Ye have to tell him."

"I think the kindest thing I can do for Bastien is leave him alone. It's what he asked for, so I'm letting him go."

Madigan flattened his hand and turned it perpendicular to the floor, punctuating every few words with a downward motion. "You'll come back to my place, and you'll stay there. I don't want to hear no arguing. You're my wife, and tha's my baby. I won't sit back while ye take my kid to another world."

I didn't know how to tell the Tin Man with no heart not to have one when he'd finally managed to grow his own thumping organ from scratch. I worked up a smile, and covered my hand with his. "I love you, too. I've got this, though. You don't have to worry about me – about us."

"It's not a chore to care for the people who... Ye aren't a chore, Rosie. You're my wife, and I want ye to move in. If ye don't like Éireland, I'll bring Annabelle and go to the palace with ye in Avalon."

I knew there would be no arguing with him, so I gave him a lie he could hold onto for a solid week. "Alright, Mad. We can talk about that later. But I don't want Bastien to know. I don't want him coming back against his will. If he doesn't want me, I can respect that, and so can you. I know you're not crazy about keeping secrets in the Brotherhood, but I don't want you telling Link, either. Link kicked me and my baby out, so I'm staying out."

"Link wasn't thinking clearly! He was upset, thinking Quinn might leave him if she didn't have to stay."

"As complicated as that whole mess of crap was, I understood everything just fine. It's all okay, but it's my business, my adventure, and my story to tell, not yours. I'll tell Link when I'm ready."

"And just when will tha be?"

I moved to the doorway. "Probably never. Look, I've got a lot of work to do today. I'll see you next week, okay? We can talk about living arrangements then."

Mad narrowed his eyes at me. "I'm going to deliver the cure, and make sure Annabelle's fine to stay with Quinn and Link for a few days, and then I'm coming straight back here."

"What for? I'll just be working."

"Exactly. Working with Werewolves. You're pregnant, if ye hadn't noticed. Ye can't go getting attacked all the time like this anymore. Tha's my baby in there." He pointed to my stomach, and I started to melt for the sweetness he exhibited. It had taken a long time, but it was there – precious and fragile (two words I never thought I'd say about Madigan).

My eyebrows pushed together as I thought this over. Though Remy and Lugh had been urging me to pull back, I'd done my usual brushing it off. I'd been in such denial about being pregnant that I'd forgotten to factor my baby into the picture. But he or she was inside of me, suffering when I suffered, whether I was mature enough to deal with reality or not.

I bit my lower lip hard and silently apologized to my little guy or girl. I didn't know how to be a good mother, but I'd never learn if I didn't make this baby a priority.

Mad interrupted my breakthrough, touching the bandages on my arms with a scowl. "I can see you're being reckless, like always. I'll be back tomorrow. You'll take it easy until then."

"Yes, Mad," I replied with a humble bow of my head in his direction.

It wasn't until he left the room that I gave in to my panic.

38

GOODNIGHT, TIN MAN

"I don't understand why ye think ye can do this. There are fourteen more to go, and you've already maxed out on your quota." Lugh was frustrated as he led me out into the hallway, where we waited for Mad and the soldiers to let the next three Weres out of their cells. They needed to be restrained, which often took a few minutes.

I leaned on Lugh, breathing like a smoker trying to hike up a mountain. "It has to be done tonight. All of it. You don't understand."

"You're right, I don't. Ye said we could leave in a week."

"That's before Mad found out. The very next time he leaves to go check on Annabelle, we have to get out of here. The longer we wait, the smaller the chance is we'll actually be able to go!"

"I still can't believe ye told him."

"It was an accident! You try having pregnancy brain, and see what dumb things you blurt out."

"No, thanks. I'll take your word on tha. Ye really think we can just run, and he won't come after us?"

"He couldn't navigate Common with a roadmap and a Sherpa. The coach is packed, right?"

"Aye, but we'll make better time on horses without the coach."

I hugged my middle and rubbed my belly. I knew my baby wasn't in distress. The healings didn't hurt at all, they just made me overly sleepy because I was around talking animals all the live-long day. "I don't think I'll be able to be upright after I rip through the rest of these Weres. I can sleep it off in the coach."

"I won't say no to whatever gets us out of here fastest. Still, ye can't do this many healings in a day. We can wait one more night, Prim. One more night, and then we leave."

I blew out a loud breath of frustration, but conceded that he was right. Though I wanted to do all I could, I had my limits. "As many as we can heal tonight, then, so nothing holds us back tomorrow."

"Grand." When the door swung open, I gave Mad a smile that I hoped looked natural, and reached down to pat Malone on the top of his head. I strolled back into the dungeon and surveyed the scene they'd set up. Demi was holding one of the Weres, his head perched atop the cells so he could get a bird's eye view, while his body got down to business. It was a good system, actually.

The next night went just as smoothly, and I kept going until every single cell was empty. I hadn't passed out, but I was on the verge. Madigan carried me up to my dorm and laid me on the bed. I knew I would miss the feel of him. Even though he knew I had the ability to poison him with my sweat, he didn't shy away from touching me. He covered me with the sheet and held my hand for a brief moment. "Do ye need anything?"

"No. Just a nap, is all."

He made to let go of my hand, but my heart stuttered, and I clung to his grip. Though he was impossibly stronger than most superheroes, he bent down to sit on the side of my bed when I pulled him closer. "What's wrong? Do ye want me to get ye a healer?"

I shook my head, getting emotional when I realized that this might be the last time I ever saw Madigan. "You know I love you, right?"

He narrowed his eyes with caution. "Aye. What of it?"

I snorted at his predictable nature. "I just wanted to make sure you knew. Thanks for not throwing me out, even after you heard everything. Thanks for coming back to help me."

He nodded without saying anything, as if expecting the other shoe to drop.

I pulled him down so I could hug him, knowing this would be my last chance to make him uncomfortable for the greater good. I wrapped my arms around his torso, smirking at his stiffness. He was still terrible at hugging. As much progress as I'd made in Faîte, that was one battle I'd lost. I wanted Mad to be free, but he was ever confined to himself, confused at affection. I turned my head and whispered in his good ear, "I love you so much. Thank you for keeping me safe, and for caring about my baby." I closed my eyes, wishing for better words to come that might encompass all his loyalty meant to me.

I squeezed his neck as he sat up, taking me with him. His arms wrapped around me slowly, showing me that after everything, he'd learned the most important thing of all. "Aye. Thanks for being... ye know."

I smirked into his neck, understanding all that he couldn't bring himself to say. "And thank you for offering to marry me all that time ago. For making sure I wasn't auctioned off. I know I'm not always your favorite person, but every now and then, you're mine."

He pulled back, searching my face with confusion. "Do ye want me to marry ye? I'd do tha, if ye need it. I'll not bed ye, but I can put my name on ye easily enough."

I guffawed, wondering how I'd gotten that so wrong. "No, that's not what I was saying. I just wanted to tell you that I appreciate you." I tried to give him my most serious face, so he was sure to pay attention. "Listen to me, Mad. This is important. You look out for the Brotherhood at all costs, but every now and then, I want you to look out for you. Does that make sense?"

Mad rolled his eyes that this was what I'd been trying to say. "Aye. Go to sleep. You're talking nonsense."

I sandwiched his head between my palms and smooshed his cheeks, so his lips puffed out like a caricature. I smooched his lips, wishing I could take a portion of Madigan with me in my pocket forever. "Goodnight, Tin Man."

And goodbye.

39

DEAR AVALON

"Time to rally, Prim. The end is in sight!"

We'd traveled through the night, took a small rowboat across the ocean that was pulled by three seals, and caught two horses that I was able to sweettalk into giving us a ride to the barracks in Avalon. We were a little the worse for wear, but we'd traveled incognito for the most part, which was a huge relief. The horses had chatted with me all day, excited to be the ones to carry us on our adventure. I didn't tell them that we were going to be leaving Avalon for good, scared that they might decide to run off and take us far away, so we couldn't get to the exit. We'd stopped by the castle to take the stockpile of blood Bastien had been gracious enough to drop off for me, keeping our presence there as stealthy as possible. Jean-Luc had siphoned enough blood to give me at least eight months of space from Avalon, maybe even more if I was careful.

By the time we reached the barracks, Lugh was all smiles, but I was exhausted, and ready to fall off my horse. I waved to the captain and the soldiers, who we couldn't exactly hide from. I only hoped that when we made our way through the next world, word wouldn't travel quick enough to reach Éireland anytime soon. Lugh helped me to dismount, and it only dawned on me after the fact that I wasn't sure if pregnant women were supposed to ride horses. I hadn't exactly read a ton of baby books in my time, so everything was a shrug and a guess. I couldn't wait to be home, where Lane could help me make a plan, and a doctor could check me out to make sure my Fae baby wasn't flying around all wonky in my uterus, bumping into stuff and hurting herself.

Lugh walked behind me, following protocol of me being some bigshot queen, just in case anyone was a stickler for the rules. I shook the captain's hand, offered up a status report for Éireland, and asked to be let into the portal room.

"But your majesty, you can't mean... Surely you know we need you more than Common does!"

I offered up a wan smile, but no further arguments. I'd made a case for my freedom too many times to count, and I wasn't about to do it again. I decided I was done trying to convince people that I should be allowed to make decisions for myself. I had to just do it, and live with pissing people off.

I sighed, and realized I had one more goodbye to say. I pulled the captain into his office and shut the door. "Could you take down a dictation for me, Captain?" I hoped he wouldn't realize I was asking him to write the letter for me because I couldn't do it for myself.

"Of course." He got out his quill, not bothered at all that I was asking him to perform such a menial task. He sat at his desk, quill dipped and poised over the parchment, waiting for the words that felt stuck in my throat.

My last goodbye had been a long time coming. Of all the loves I'd left behind, this would be the toughest to stomach.

"Dear Avalon," I began. I cleared my throat, and wished for something more eloquent. I stood on the other side of the desk, facing the captain with my eyes closed as I pressed my palms to his desktop. "Of all the goodbyes I've had to say, yours is the hardest. I came to you an orphan, but you made me your daughter. We've been broken together, and strong at different times, so we could pull each other out of the trenches. We've seen each other through too much pain, and a lot of growth."

I pursed my lips, willing my heart to open one final time, so I could tell the people all they meant to me. After everything, they deserved me at my most honest.

"We've had each other, and I've learned that was the best thing about Avalon. Even when life tried to divide us, we found brothers in our neighbors, and made neighbors out of total strangers. We built up our country from the shattered fragments that even we sometimes assumed might always be a little bit wrecked. You're one nation now, and even though I have to leave, I'll come back. I'll expect to see that what made Avalon great is still there, going strong. You're my heartbeat. I thought I understood what life expected of me, but you taught me that I could do more, be more. You were always more – more than I anticipated, and more than I deserved." I swallowed hard, willing my resolve to hold. "Always be more." I cleared my throat and straightened. "With love, from the Avalon Rose. I'll return to you in eleven months. Until then, my heart beats alone, missing you every day."

I slung my backpack over my shoulder and kept my eyes averted from the thunderstruck captain, who spluttered out reasons why I couldn't leave yet. There was too much rebuilding still to be done. There were people still in need. The two provinces were in flux as far as unity went. All of it was legit, but I knew it would never end. I had to care about me. I knew if I didn't, no one would. Lot and Urien could unite the nation now. It would take some doing, but I wasn't leaving my beloved Avalon without watchkeepers to guide them to a better tomorrow.

Lugh followed my example of not answering the captain, and trailed behind me as I moved through the hallway, using my Compass to locate the exit I'd sorely needed. We had one backpack each, my wineskin of blood, plus Lugh's bow and quiver.

I wasn't expecting Dub to suddenly appear in my path, but then again, I rarely expected anything he did. Lugh made to greet him with a tight-jawed expression, but Dub shot him a look that told him that his words were very much not welcome in this exchange. "She'll be along in a moment." It was his polite-ish way of telling Lugh to scram.

Lugh waited for my "it's cool" nod before he moved along down the hallway.

"What's up your butt today, Uncle Dub?" I asked, letting him know that no matter how big, bad and scary he was, he'd never hold the upper hand unless I allowed it. He did me a solid and let me pretend that was how our relationship worked.

Dub's nostrils flared at my sass, and he covered my mouth with his palm. My first instinct was to shove him away, but his eyes were so intensely focused on mine that I hesitated when perhaps I should've pummeled. "I've been in your mind, and I know your thoughts. I know all you're capable of."

"Thanks?" I spoke it like a question, unsure if that was an accusation, a compliment or a threat.

He straightened, his hands migrating to my shoulders to ensure that I had his total focus. "You were not meant to lead an ordinary life. If you come back to me having wasted your years being average, I will be most disappointed."

A threat. Always a threat.

I tilted my head, gazing up at him as I tried to navigate his constant riddles. "Aw, that was almost sweet. Next time, lose the angry vibe. Tell me to go surfing and have a blast."

Again, his eyes held a warning that started to send shivers up my spine. "You are in my family now, so you will put aside any notion that being unremarkable is an option. It is not."

I glowered, unable to play nice if he wasn't even going to try. "Dude, you suck at goodbyes."

"If you return to me with unexploited potential, I will make it my business to help you rise to the occasion. I promise, you will not like my interference. Do not forget that I am the brother of Evil and Violence."

I shuddered, squirming out of his grip. "Stop with the controlling villain nonsense. I'll live my life how *I* want, and you'll say nothing more about it."

Dub's piercing look before he vanished would go on to haunt me for decades to come.

It took me several deep breathing exercises to calm myself down enough to meander to the well, where Lugh was waiting for me.

Lugh sat down on the dangling wide wooden plank at the bottom of the waterless well. I could tell he was nervous, despite his insistence that a quick escape was all he'd wanted. "Tha'll be all, Captain," he said, ensuring that we had a moment alone in Avalon before it was all over. Once the captain left and cleared any lingering ears from the hallway, Lugh worked up a charming grin. "Be a good stripper and straddle me, love."

I narrowed my eyes at his joke, but had no choice except to do exactly that. I played along, and made a show of sinking down onto his lap. I'm not sure when our friendship had migrated to the place where I could shake my boobs in his face, but he gave them both a playful nip with his caddish grin before I started using the pulleys to raise us up. It had been Bastien to get me out of here the first time, and Bastien again who'd lowered us down both times I'd ventured into Avalon. This final time was me, though. Lugh didn't even offer when he saw the look of determination on my stony face. I wanted to get us out, and I wasn't stopping until I'd freed us. This next stint would be *my* adventure, and I was determined to make sure the steps I took were my own.

My arms burned when the earth's sun finally kissed the top of our heads, welcoming us home. Both of us fell on our hands and knees, clutching the Montana dirt between our fingers and laughing that we'd actually broken free.

"We did it," I said, giggling with a breathless glee that finally we were away from the magic.

"Aye. Let's get as far away from the well as we can, though. I'll feel better once we're settled somewhere." He reached over and rested his hand atop mine. "We're free, Prim."

We didn't need any other words. We sat up, kneeling together in the dirt with matching grins on our faces. I couldn't stop smiling, not even when Lugh leaned in and kissed me. It wasn't a romantic kiss, but a private blessing between friends who'd seen too much together, and were about to start a life with backstories only we understood.

I staggered to my feet and hoisted him up, letting his chin rest atop my head as my fingers twined through his. "Ready to go home?" I asked, my free hand pressed to his chest.

"Darling, you've never said anything better. Let's go."

40

HOME SWEET HOME

I'm not sure what I was expecting Lane to do when I showed up on her doorstep, but after hour two of her sobbing on my shoulder, I called for reinforcements. I was pissed that technology had evolved while I'd been away, and she'd gotten a phone that had too many apps open for me to figure out. I handed the device to her, and between her sobs, she was finally able to call Reyn home from his day job.

Lucas didn't remember me, which only made me die inside a little bit. I'd been gone for too much of my nephew's life, and vowed to not miss so much again. I waited until he came to me, and dried his empathy tears that had appeared when Lane's had erupted.

Reyn's tears only lasted a good ten minutes, but he replaced them with questions that seemed never ending.

Where had I been, what had I seen, how was Avalon, how was Bastien. "Wait, where is Bastien? I'm confused. Is he on his way?"

I was grateful Draper came home then, so I only had to tell the whole awful story once. I didn't want to tell Lane that she was part Gancanagh, but there was no getting around that part of the retelling. I narrowed my eyes at Reyn, making sure he heard every word, and didn't punk out on Lane and Lucas. Lugh even positioned himself in front of the door to make sure no one bolted. "You fell for Lane before you two made it into Avalon, and that's why you're together. You live here, where being Gancanagh doesn't matter. Your marriage is real, Reyn. I don't want you thinking it's not."

Reyn quirked his eyebrow at me. "I know all that. I'm surprised you found out. Did you tell her?" he asked Lane, who shook her head.

I gaped at them both, floored that the big bomb that had wrecked my life was a mere conversation point for them. "You knew? Are you kidding me?"

Lane frowned. "I never knew for sure, but I guessed as much when Urien fell so hard for Morgan in the beginning. If you look, the pattern's there."

"And you never thought to mention it to me?"

"Mention what? That you're a quarter Gancanagh? Honey, I had a hard enough time conjuring up fake genealogy for us in Common, pretending we were part

Irish and French. I didn't think to educate you on your grandparents. You never asked."

"I never asked if…" I covered my face in my hands and let out a frustrated mini-scream. "Fine. Point is, I found out and told Bastien. He doesn't so much like the idea that I basically poisoned him into loving me, and tricked him into our marriage, so he asked for the ring back."

Reyn shouted his indignation. "No, he couldn't have! Rosie, you're mistaken. There's no way Bastien would do that. I've never seen him love anyone the way he loves you."

I tried to compose myself. "Then imagine how much better he'll be at loving his next wife." I forced the words out to try and sound aloof, but they cut me, and made everyone in the room wince. "It's fine. He made his choice, and we'll all respect it." I leveled my threatening gaze at Reyn. "Especially you. Bastien feels betrayed, so leave him be. I've hurt him enough."

Draper covered his face and muttered into his hands over and over how stupid Bastien was. For once, Reyn did not defend his friend. "I'll go to Avalon," Reyn said quietly. "I'll make him see reason. We're in the same boat, him and me. We fell in love with Gancanagh women. I can talk sense into him. He loved you from the first, Rosie. Before you even set foot in Avalon, he wanted you."

I shrugged. "Maybe so, but when he found out, he said that Roland was right all along. I'd bewitched him." I met my stepfather's gaze with a look that told him I was trying to be brave, and he needed to give me my charade. "Bastien's a big boy. He can make decisions for himself, which is exactly what he did."

"It's not right," Draper ruled, shaking his head. "I'll go, but not to bring him back. I'll go down there to beat him to a bloody pulp for walking out on my sister. If you had such a strong hold on him, *he wouldn't be able to* walk away. He wouldn't be able to ask for your ring back. He'd be addicted, no matter what you'd done. Being only a quarter Gancanagh can't be all that powerful, pumpkin." He shook his head. "What an idiot."

Lugh spoke up from where he'd migrated to stand near the hearth. "He's not wrong. I never put tha together, but my stalkers couldn't stop themselves for anything. If Bastien could walk away, he wasn't poisoned to the point of losing his mind. He was in control the entire time."

I studied the information, turning it over in my head to see how it fit into my messed-up puzzle. After a few beats, I cleared my throat. "Well, it's neither here nor there. Either way, Bastien doesn't want to be with me, and you'll all respect it." I switched topics, covering more of the broad strokes of Avalon and Éireland. I'm not sure how I got through it all, but I did, ending it with the Werewolf and Vampire drama that had finally winded down.

"Um, ye forgot the biggest thing, Prim," Lugh reminded me.

"What would you like to tell us about my daughter's life?" Lane asked with a hint of sharpness to her tone. Lane treated Lugh the way any mother would treat a strange man who showed up with her daughter in lieu of the husband. She was kind, but abrupt, confused as to how Lugh had traipsed into our lives without invitation. Lugh took no offense, nor did he attempt to win her over – he was the friend, after all, not the boyfriend.

"Oh, right. I'm baking Bastien's bun in my oven."

Lane blasted out a loud, "What?!" and jumped off the couch to wrap her arms around me. "Are you sure? Oh, baby!"

My slang was lost on Reyn and Draper, who looked lost in the sea of way too much information. "You're baking?"

Lugh translated for me. "She's pregnant. Maybe close to two months, by our guess. Prim, can I use a phone to set things up for us overseas? Ye have a passport, right?"

I nodded. "In my house, which is the one next door. Top drawer of my dresser. My phone was on my desk, I'm thinking. You're welcome to it, though it'll need a charge."

"Grand. I'll be back after I unpack. Mind if I take a shower?"

"Of course not. My house is your house. Make yourself comfortable." I gripped his hand. "We made it. We can rest now."

Lugh beamed at me. "You've never been lovelier than when ye say things like tha."

Draper frowned at Lugh, not needing any further information to make a decision. "No."

"No, what?" Lugh asked, confused.

"No. You'll not come sniffing around my sister when she's pregnant, abandoned and vulnerable. No. She's off-limits to you."

Lugh chuckled, not bothering to appear intimidated by my foreboding older brother. "Oh, tha was funny. Prim, tell him how badly ye want me."

I rolled my eyes. "At ease, Draper. Lugh's just a friend. He's a half-immortal, like me. We look out for each other, is all. He knows I'm not available."

Lane gasped and smacked her forehead. "You're Brighde's Gancanagh ex-husband! You're Cross Shot!"

Lugh nodded, and though she'd already been introduced to him, he stuck out his hand and shook hers. "Pleasure, Duchess. I'll be out of your hair just as soon as Prim and I can get things in order. No more than a few days." He bowed to her, and then left, leaving me to field all the questions that didn't seem to have an end in sight.

Lane's face fell to seriousness, and I almost laughed at how many emotions she burned through in such a short span. "That man is not taking my baby, or my baby's baby, in any kind of airplane. You're pregnant? You're really having a baby?" She started dancing on the balls of her feet and clapping, looking like a cheerleader.

Emotion swelled up in me, inflating my chest like a happy balloon. I nodded, for the first time feeling like this baby might be a thing to be excited about. I'd been nervous and confused for so long, I hadn't had much time to be able to just be pregnant and enjoy the ride. "I'm thinking I should probably go see a doctor tomorrow. Get a decent due date nailed down and whatnot. Make sure it's a baby growing inside, and not an alien or something."

"Today," Lane insisted, pulling out her phone. Before I could protest, she was dialing the family doctor, and using her motherhood powers to jimmy us an afternoon appointment. Of course she could do that. It was Lane.

Draper lowered me back onto the couch, taking great care, as if I was ninety, and in need of assistance. "Here, let's put your feet up. I'll get you some tea. How about chamomile? I don't know what pregnant women are supposed to have. When was the last time you ate anything?"

Instead of answering that question, I said, "Chinese food, please? Something non-Avalon, if we can. Is that okay?"

Draper got out his phone and ordered way too much food. I watched them overreact like cartoons, and finally found my smile.

"What's so funny?" Reyn asked, pausing his sweep of the living room for dangerous objects unsuitable for a pregnant woman.

"So this is what it's like to tell people you're pregnant. I've been keeping it to myself for so long. Only a handful of people know."

"This is what it feels like to be home, baby," Lane assured me. "You're safe now. You don't have to worry about a thing. I'm here, and I'll take care of all of it."

Lane plopped down on the couch next to me, and wrapped her arms around my frame. It had been too long since I'd been held by my mother, and with her love, finally I knew I was home.

41

JUDAH AND LOU VAN GUARDEN

"I can't believe she actually let ye get on the plane. It was touch and go for a while there."

I closed my eyes and did my best to feign comfort in the understuffed airplane seat. I'd never flown before, much less first-class international, but there I was, sandwiched between Judah and Lou Van Gaurden, sipping orange juice like a grownup. "Yeah, well, she sent a chaperone, so there's that." I elbowed Judah, who grinned.

Judah leaned over me to spout out his millionth fact about Lost and Forgotten to Lugh, who was taking the explosion of geekdom in stride. "Did you know that your fourth album went double platinum?"

"I think I heard tha somewhere, yeah."

"It should've gone triple. It was amazing. Your bassline on "I Never Knew"? Unreal. It's like you've got three hands."

"Well, I do. I've got the third one checked in my luggage."

Judah sat back, holding onto his armrests with eyes wide as saucers. "I can't believe I'm on a plane with Lou Van Guarden. We're going to Europe to go on tour with Lou Van Guarden."

"Ye know, if ye don't call the other lads by their full names like tha, they're bound to get jealous."

I giggled at the cuteness, relieved to have my best friend back. "I missed you so freaking much."

"Anytime you want to kidnap me and take me to Europe to go on tour with Lou Van Guarden, that's fine."

"You're sure work won't mind that you're gone?"

"That's the beauty of running your own company. I'm the boss, and I've got one whopping employee. I can take off whenever I feel like it."

"Nice of Jill to let you go."

"She couldn't get the time off work. She's not too thrilled that I'm going without her. But what's she going to say? 'No, honey, don't go on an all-expenses paid trip to Europe.' Well played, offering to take us both."

"I was being sincere. Lane was the one who insisted either you or Draper come to get me settled. I figured you could use a jailbreak more than Drape."

"You figured right."

I motioned to Lugh, as if I was a gameshow model, displaying the prizes. "Plus, it's Lou Van Guarden. If anyone should come on tour, it should be you. You know all the songs."

Lugh sniggered and twined his fingers through mine, resting our hands together on his lap. He'd foregone the armrest, so we could snuggle together more comfortably. "Darling, it sounds bizarre when ye call me by my full stage name."

"Well, we're in Common now. What should I call you?"

"Call me yours. Call me Bert. I don't care. Just don't be my groupie."

I mime-screamed and fanned myself, making him laugh, and Judah smile. We spent the million hours of the flight with me tucked in Lugh's arms, and Judah rattling off everything I'd missed while I was away. If only he understood that the most important thing I'd missed was him. Just him.

When the lights dimmed during the night on our flight, Lugh's hand under the blanket we shared traced up and down on my belly, relaxing me and giving me the shivers, as was our way. I was starting to show, and the more my belly jutted out, the gentler my family was with me. It was no small miracle that Lane finally un-superglued her fingers from my belly long enough for me to get on the plane. I'd spent a solid several weeks of her sneaking into my bed at night. I usually awoke to being sandwiched between her and Draper by morning. Despite all I'd been through, the doctor she'd taken me to assured us that the fetus was completely healthy, and that my little baby had been growing inside of me now for three whole months.

I stared out the window at the clouds, far more relaxed now that I was in Common, and going on my grand adventure with myself. Lately I found myself migrating to Lugh's arms, content that somehow, we were making life happen without the threat of Faîte bearing down on us.

42

LUCKIEST KIDS ON THE PLAYGROUND

"Dude, not for nothing, but do not name your kid Britney Spears. I saw the gleam in your eye. And not Posh Spice, either. Posh is not the name of a doctor or a lawyer. That is the name of the girl who never knows which dude's dorm she left her shoes in. No. Just no."

I laughed at Judah's assessment. "Hello, I'm naming my daughter Judah, obviously."

"Ha, ha."

We were celebrating finding out the sex of the baby. My baby. I had a little girl dancing around in my belly, making up jokes and goofy dance moves. It was totally surreal, but getting more real every day I settled into my new life. I was able to focus on actually being pregnant, introducing my psyche with the parts of me that were hardwired to somehow grasp hold of motherhood.

It was our fifth patisserie that day, and we were determined to figure out which was the best one in all of Paris. It was a hard sell, since every single one had something perfect inside, freshly baked and singing my song. The first time I bit into a macaron in Paris, tears welled in my eyes, which wasn't all that rare an occurrence these days, what with the pregnancy hormones. But that small pink cookie meant something to me.

My first macaron had been in the palace in Avalon. I recalled how I'd never tasted anything more perfect in all my life. With the loss of that world, I assumed such delicacies would be gone from my palate. Too many emotions flooded me as Judah and I sat at a quaint round table at the Ladurée. There was a sculpture of the Eiffel Tower made from the dainty cookies in the window. Inside, there lay an assortment of confectionary Heaven. The pricey shop boasted dozens of different flavors of macarons, and though the smaller bakeries had ones that tasted fresher, the variety here couldn't be topped. I wondered if Faith, Hope and Mercy were inventing new flavors still. Judah and I devoured as many kinds of macarons as we could stomach, which turned out to be around twelve apiece before we admitted defeat.

"I think my favorite was the licorice flavor."

I narrowed my eyes at him. "You're just saying that because black licorice is on my Pregnancy Puke List."

"Yeah. Found that out the hard way. Thanks for not making me hold your hair back while you ralphed."

"I know you're a sympathy barfer."

He sipped his café au lait, looking like a Parisian college student. His curly hair had been cut short, and his Buddy Holly glasses paired well with the green and pink scarf I bought him that he insisted he'd never wear. "Thanks for not being drunk all the time in college. Kind of funny that you've got your head in the toilet all the time now, when you're halfway through your twenties."

I snorted into my water. "Yeah, I guess I missed out on the getting drunk all the time phase. Too much studying, I guess."

"That is a problem."

I studied Judah's small movements as he people-watched from the picture window we were seated against. It was snowy out, and though it wasn't as bad as Éireland's winters, the arctic bite nipped at us all the same. "It's hard to think that I had like, half a year without you, and even more in Avalon before that. I was worried I'd changed so much, or you would've changed so much that we wouldn't fit."

Judah caught my gaze, and the corner of his mouth crooked upward. "And yet, here we are. I still remember the first time I met you, you know."

"You do not. That was a hundred years ago."

"I do. You were sitting in the back of the class, doing your self-protective thing. You had your shoulders hunched, and you were guarding your paper with your whole body, like you were afraid ninjas were going to come in and steal your History notes. You had your ankles looped around the legs of your chair." He demonstrated, instantly looking younger, more vulnerable. "You were so guarded back then. The only empty seat was the one next to you. Every morning, I'd come in and hope you'd look at me. I was so nervous. Everyone in that school was such a d-bag. I didn't play basketball, which was the big thing there. I couldn't do any afterschool activities because mom was always working. I didn't fit in anywhere." He traced the lip of his small cup. "Then one day your pencil broke, and I let you borrow one of mine. I caught a glimpse of your paper, and saw that it was mostly scribbles."

I shifted uncomfortably in my chair. "You didn't laugh at me. I remember that day. I was afraid you'd find out I was stupid, so I made Lane read the newspaper to me that night, so I could impress you with knowing about current events."

"First time I ever had a conversation about Iraq with a nine-year-old." He met my eyes with the same old soul steadiness he'd worn even as a naïve fourth-grade boy. "And you were never stupid. Don't say that about yourself." He cleared his throat. "You talked to me that day, which was the first time anyone in that school said my name. I never forgot that. It's a heady thing, to be seen as a person. You saw me, and even though you were bent on hiding, I saw you. Never looked back after that."

I let his beautiful words settle between us as we sipped our beverages, our stomachs protesting at the copious amounts of sugar we'd insisted we could handle. I set my water down and touched my finger to the side of the glass, wetting the tip with the condensation. "You sure you never looked back? Not even when I punched Billy the Bully? I really thought I might lose you that day. I thought for sure I'd let myself loose a little too much around you, and you'd bail."

Judah laughed. "Billy the Bully. Yeah, I remember him. And I remember that day. He'd called me 'Jew Fro' for the hundredth time, and it started to get to me."

"As long as it didn't look like it was bothering you, I let you handle it, but when I saw your ears turn red that day, I lost it."

Judah grinned at the memory. "You dropped that kid. One-Punch Rosie is what they should've called you."

"Yeah. That would've been better than 'That Dangerous Psycho Girl'."

Judah looked around the pristine shop that was littered with dozens of desserts that looked like little works of art. There was soothing French music playing gently overhead. "Never in a million years would I have guessed that we'd end up here."

"Eating cookies until I barf?"

He gave me a genuine smile, and I know he was picturing us way back then – two kids who were always on the outside of the cool crowd, so we decided to invent our own very exclusive club. "We're in Paris, Ro. We both got degrees. We survived Avalon. We got out."

"None of it would've been worth it, if it hadn't been for you. None of it would've happened, actually. Thanks for giving me your pencil that day."

His eyes sparkled with mischief and memories. "Thanks for looking at me." He held up his café au lait to make a toast, so I raised my water with a grin. "To Jew Fro and Remedial Rosie. Luckiest kids on the playground."

"I'll drink to that." We clinked glasses, and despite the worries of my life that still plagued me over raising my daughter, Judah reminded me to be in one place at a time, focusing on the beauty, instead of the duty. My shoulders relaxed as we stared out the window, watching the snow fall, and making it look like we were in our own little Parisian snow globe. "I hope my daughter's this lucky."

"See? That's what I love about you. After all you've been through, you still call yourself lucky. Don't ever lose that."

"I hope she finds her Judah."

Judah silently laughed into his drink. "If she's anything like you? He'll be the luckiest dude on the planet."

43

LOST AND FORGOTTEN

*L*ugh was usually with the band, practicing the songs they'd added while he'd been away. He was determined to re-establish "the vibe" as he liked to call it. He was worried that the dynamic would've changed with his absence and the addition of his substitute. But once the sub was paid and left, Lugh seemed to fit in seamlessly with his friends. You know, the Lost and Forgotten Sexy Six. Lugh had named the band after the Forgotten Forest and the Lost Village. I loved him a little more for the poetry of it all.

To his credit, Judah finally got better at putting a lid on his fanatic blurting. The guys were far more down to earth than I'd expected. I'd read articles about them throwing wild parties and getting kicked out of hotels for all sorts of illegal antics.

Lugh passed me my salad from the takeout bag. "We're older now, and half those stories weren't true. They just looked rock and roll, so our publicist spun whatever needed to be believed. Ye don't get to sell as many albums as we have by mucking about. Ye have to work hard to stay on top, which we do."

Finnegan McCabe, the lead singer, always sniffed his food before he put each bite into his mouth. "Now, don't go telling the lass all our secrets. She'll be expecting we sit around and play Bridge all night."

I shot Finnegan a smirk. "Hello, our room's right next to yours. I know you're not playing Bridge all night long."

Finnegan McCabe had a large flat in Paris, which we were staying at. Each member of the band had a home in different countries throughout Europe, so the whole group stayed there when they hit up each area. It was kind of sweet, seeing the brotherhood translated into the world of rock. The Sexy Six were pretty close, and had welcomed me and Judah in with open arms, surprised that Lugh had any friends outside of the band.

Finnegan high-fived me at mention of his many sexual conquests. "Ye want I should ratchet up the volume tonight? I've been telling them to keep quiet, so ye don't get jealous and throw Lugh over for me, but I don't have to hold back, if tha turns your crank."

I laughed as I fished out a napkin from the pile in the center of the long table. It was an oak dining room table that looked too fancy for takeout, but I'd learned that was how Finnegan preferred his house – plenty of expensive trappings, but a flare of commonfolk to it. His taste was a mix between eclectic folk musician, and a proper British grandmother. I leaned over and dabbed at the sour cream he'd gotten on his nose from smelling his food too closely. "There you go. Almost handsome now."

Finnegan growled like a feral dog and bit at my cheek. It was his way of saying thank you for not calling him out on his neurotic tick, but accepting his idiosyncrasies as part of who he was. "Have ye plundered the Shanzelize enough yet?"

I feathered my fingers together as if I was an evil villain. "I think I've hit at least half the stores as well as I'd like to. That still leaves the other half."

"No more scarves!" Judah moaned. "I only use the one, and you've already bought one for everybody back home."

I'd been enamored with the fancy varieties here, and had even learned to tie one – courtesy of a sales lady who had the glad eye for Lugh. "I want to do all the steps of the Arc de Triomphe again."

Judah groaned. "You keep saying that, but you're too pregnant to make it all the way up. The doctor said to take it easy. That doesn't mean go up three hundred steps. And it definitely doesn't mean you should drag me along for the ride."

I frowned, looking down at my belly that left no room for denial anymore. I was nearing the end of my second trimester, which meant that our Parisian trip would have to come to an end. "I still have two weeks left here, and I don't want to punk out on any of it."

Lugh's face fell every time Judah or I mentioned that our trip was finite. He was quiet during dinner, and despite the fact that the guys were waiting on him to hit the pub that night, he escorted me to our bedroom with care.

I wasn't as delicate as everyone was making me out to be, but being that I was the only woman living in the house of dudes, they all made a show of being sweet and straightening up. Add being pregnant to that, and they were on their best behavior – you know, like true rock stars. Finnegan had even rubbed cocoa butter on my belly one night and then read the baby seven French translation Dr. Seuss books he'd bought for my daughter. They were cute little domestic rebels between shows, the whole lot of them.

Lugh studied my movements with his arms crossed over his chest. "Do ye want me to stay home tonight?"

I smiled at Lugh as I strolled out of the en-suite bathroom in my pajamas. Despite the fact that it was freezing out, I was a furnace at night, so I wore a modest nightgown in the privacy of our bedroom. Lugh had brought me a calico cat to chat with during the day, so I'd be tired when the sun went down. Eleanor Roosevelt was curled up on my pillow, already purring in anticipation of sleeping with me and Lugh. I reached down to pet my fur baby, and her spine arched to get the most out of the touch. "No, no. You should go out and have fun. The guys need you to be you, but I brought a sweet and considerate gentleman back to them. That's only going to be tolerated for so long. I think I brought too much estrogen into the mancave. You need a break."

Lugh sat down on the side of the bed next to Eleanor Roosevelt and stared up at me. "Why do ye do tha?" He tugged on my arm, so I stood between his legs. I gazed appreciatively down at the man who had taken me under his wing at every turn. "Ye act like it's a chore to be around ye. It's not, Prim. What do ye need?"

I ran my fingers through his dark brown hair, smiling when his eyes closed at the luxurious touch. "I'm in Paris with my two best friends. What else could there possibly be?"

Lugh leaned into my hand and then stood, tugging down the covers for me and helping me into the bed. He slid in next to me as I blinked at the ceiling from my supine position, and covered my lower half with the sheet, as he did every night. In our little private time that was lit only by the dim lamp on the nightstand, Lugh slowly rolled up the hem of my white cotton nightgown. It had sheer lace around the bottom edge, and a line of matching lace near the top to accentuate my round breasts. The whole thing made me feel truly feminine. After the nights spent filthy, worn and exposed in Faîte, it was the little things that healed me, and made me feel like a person.

Lugh exposed my belly to the cool air, and started his

nightly ritual of rubbing cocoa butter on my skin while he sang to the baby. How he never settled down with anyone in Common was beyond me – until I realized that we were alike in too many ways. Lugh couldn't make long-term plans with a woman because he wouldn't age. He'd outlive them, and wouldn't be able to grow old alongside them. Apart from people who knew Faîte and understood what they were getting into, there weren't lasting relationships on the horizon for either of us. We clung to each other that much more – for better or worse.

Lugh tested out his newest songs on my daughter. "She's the best impartial judge. I can't charm her with my personality yet."

I grinned at the cuteness. "But how can you tell if she likes the song or not?"

His hand migrated to my navel, palming the baby as if we were both his. "I just know. Ye aren't the kind of girls to hold back." He settled into the spare pillow that he'd slept on every single night, his hand over my belly.

"What are you doing? Don't you dare get comfortable. You skipped out on guy time last night. You're not bailing on them again. It's not good for you to be cooped up with me for too long."

"Why not? I don't mind staying in."

"I mind turning you into an old man." I pointed to my belly. "This isn't your responsibility. You should be out having fun."

Lugh sat up with a frown. "But what if ye need something in the night?"

"That's what I've got Judah for. Or I can just get up all by my own self and get whatever it is I need. I'm not actual royalty here."

Lugh studied me, drinking in my features before he leaned down and kissed my lips. He did that at least once a day, and I never stopped him. "I wish I was in love with ye, Prim."

I chuckled at his melancholy. "I'm glad you're not. We're already in this for the long haul. This way we get to keep each other forever. Best friends till the end."

The corners of his mouth lifted. "I like the sound of tha. So long as Clarabelle gets her Uncle Lugh, I'm happy."

He was always trying out new names for the baby to see how they sounded. "Hmm. Pass on Clarabelle. Cute, but I can't see her punching out the clown who gets in her way on the playground."

"I'll keep thinking."

I sighed contentedly. "Uncle Lugh. Luckiest baby on the planet, right here." I lifted my chin and kissed him this time, adding a little tongue, just because we could. We were both lonely for the right one. Even though Lugh wasn't the right fit for me, we tried each other on from time to time to ease the ache that living so long alone left a person with.

Finnegan's fist on the door came at the right moment.

"Rosie? There's a lad at the door for ye. The doorman won't let him up without your say-so."

I frowned, wondering why the doorman wasn't letting Judah inside. Lugh was out of the bed in the next breath. "I'll go see who it is. Stay in bed, Prim."

I didn't protest, because Eleanor Roosevelt had a lot to tell me about her day, and I was too cozy in the bed. My lower back was being a wuss these days, so by the time night fell, I was ready to rest my aching hips.

When Lugh stomped up the steps on his phone, I tried to sit up, but looked more like a floundering cow than anything else. "Why did ye give him our address? She wanted to be left alone, and ye sent him right to our doorstep!" He hung up before he could say anything more acerbic. "They showed up on your mammy's porch, asking to see ye, and she just gave them the address." He threw his hands in the air, furious at the scandal I didn't totally understand.

"Who?"

"Lane!"

"No, I mean, who's downstairs?"

"Them!" Lugh paced the room, ignoring my furrowed eyebrows. "Do ye want me to let them in? I don't know what to do here."

I finally extracted myself from the mattress and put my hands on both of Lugh's cheeks, squishing his face just to amuse myself and refocus him. "Hey, Justin Bieber. Tell me who's here."

Lugh's eyes shone with worry that he was about to hurt me. "You've been doing so well. Of course he'd come back now to break ye all over again."

My mouth went dry, and my whole body stiffened. I croaked out my guess in a whisper. "Bastien?"

Lugh nodded. "And your Da."

44

WORST DAD CONTEST

J was suddenly on high alert. "Urien and Bastien are both here? They're downstairs?"

"They're on the street, actually. I didn't know if you'd want me to let them in."

The door was open, and my eyes caught on Finnegan in the hallway. "Who's Bastien?"

I pointed to my belly. "My ex-husband. He doesn't know about his baby."

Finnegan winced at the predicament I'd landed myself in. "I'll let them in, and then I'll take the lads to the pub. We'll be out late, so take all the time ye need. The house will be all yours for a few hours."

I moved to Finnegan and threw my arms around his neck. "Thanks, sweetie. They won't stay long. Trust me. Bastien will take one look at me, and he'll be gone in the next breath."

Finnegan's hand migrated to my butt and gave it a little squeeze. He was flirty with anything on two legs – men or women – but that was a new one. "Do ye want me to grab your arse in front of your ex? Let him see tha ye aren't pining?"

"I'll let you know if I need that. This'll be our signal, giving you the green light to grope me." I slowly raised my middle finger, giving Finnegan's chuckle a small smirk. Finnegan smooched my lips, his eyebrows waggling at the scandal he'd just gotten away with.

Every nerve ending in my body was standing at attention with the knowledge that Bastien was just outside. In Common. In Paris. I couldn't imagine why he'd come all this way, but I knew it couldn't be good. That he'd brought Urien with him? They wanted me to come back to Avalon, I was sure of it. Urien had brought Bastien as the bargaining chip, I was willing to bet.

Lugh seemed to be on the same page. "I won't let them take ye, Prim. You'll stay with me."

I stepped away from Finnegan, who went to go let in our unexpected houseguests. Glancing down at my belly, I started to panic. "Quick! I need a sweater. I don't want him to know I'm pregnant!"

Lugh arched an eyebrow at me. "Are ye thinking a sweater will make your belly invisible? Ye can't hide it, Prim. But sure, here." He handed me my red hoodie, which somehow only accentuated my belly more. I finally admitted defeat and threw on a pair of leggings, and then exchanged my nightgown for a fitted lavender babydoll shirt, knowing there was no way to hide the mammoth belly. And part of me was a little ashamed that I'd tried. I didn't want my daughter to think I was embarrassed by her, trying to hide her very existence. That didn't seem like something Lane would do.

But I didn't want Bastien to know. He would assume that I was again trying to trick him into staying, and I just couldn't handle the heartbreak of that anymore. He should've known that was never me, but he stuck with his fear, and let that dictate who he assumed I was.

I rolled back my shoulders and rubbed my belly to rally my daughter. I knew who I was, and I didn't have to prove it to Bastien.

Lugh twined his fingers through mine and squeezed as he opened the bedroom door. "Ye aren't going back to Avalon, Prim. No matter what they say, tha part of our lives is over for now."

I nodded, my jaw clenching to ward myself against whatever plea they had. "Absolutely. This is where I belong."

This seemed to ease some of Lugh's worry. His shoulders dropped to feign ease I wish either of us felt. I heard Finnegan and the guys leave with the bang of the door, and breathed a gust of relief that my drama wouldn't plague their lives too much. We walked down the stairs together, but Lugh moved ahead of me to greet the guests first, motioning for me to stay in the stairwell, hidden from view by the wall. "What are ye doing here?" he asked the men.

Bastien's reply was curt, telling me he was in no mood. "I'm here for my wife, not you. Why is she living here? She's got a home back in the States."

"She's on holiday, which, after all Faîte put her through, is the least of the luxuries she deserves."

"Fine. Whatever. I'm here to bring her back."

Lugh's bark came out aggressive. "She's not stepping a toe inside Avalon, do ye understand? She's allowed to live, which is exactly what she's doing. You'll leave her be, Bastien. And ye," he said to Urien, "I've no place for someone like ye. Either of ye, in fact, so ye can't stay here."

"It's freezing out there!" Urien countered, appealing to Lugh's humanity to be compassionate. "I came to see my daughter. I'm the King of Avalon, young man. You'll not refuse a request from a king."

"Why not? Ye both treated Rosie like she was fit to be used up and thrown away, and she was the Queen of Avalon! We're not in your land anymore, Urien. Get used to being looked at the same way ye despised your own daughter. There's nothing for ye here."

Bastien tried a different route, since he wasn't getting anywhere by simply demanding things. "Look, I'm not sure how much you know, but it's complicated. I need to talk to my wife."

"I know everything, because I've been by her side every

step of the way since ye tossed her out. She's not your wife, mate. Ye made sure of tha."

The surprise in Bastien's tone told me he hadn't been counting on Lugh knowing all that went down between us. "You've been with my wife? You and Rosie live here together?"

Lugh didn't hold back the sneer in his tone. "I was there when her hand was cut off. Then I was there for the nightmares about her hand getting cut off. I was there when she could barely lift her head because she was busy healing her father's land. I was there when she..." I knew he was about to mention something about the pregnancy, but luckily he bit his lip. "I was there, even after I knew what she was. Ye have no idea what it's like to be Gancanagh. My kind is afraid of ever getting close to anyone. Then when ye do manage a connection, ye live in constant fear tha they'll leave ye because they feel duped. Duped into loving ye back. As if a sweet piece like tha would ever have to trick a man into loving her."

"I was wrong, okay? I didn't know what to make of it all." Bastien's voice turned sharp. "And don't call her 'a sweet piece'." Bastien let out a long exhale. "It wasn't until Kerdik explained it all to me that I realized she couldn't have poisoned me." Bastien's voice rose to a shout that filled the flat. "Daisy? Baby, you didn't trick me into loving you. I was yours from the beginning. Gancanagh magic doesn't work in Common. I knew I wanted you the moment you punched me in the face when I tried to kidnap you. Before we were in Avalon together, I was yours."

I was frozen on the steps, confused and dealing with a storm of emotions. I didn't want to fall for his plea, so I braced myself against the love that should've come from him months ago.

Kerdik loved me enough to know I'd want the father of my baby back. He loved me enough to get over my DNA and do what was best for me and my daughter. I closed my eyes to steady myself as the tidal waves of life menaced my sanity. I wasn't sure what the right answer was, or if I had a reply to give him. After the months of silence from his end, a simple apology didn't seem to fit.

Lugh's voice was smug. "Do ye hear tha? It's the sound of nothing – the same sound she's gotten from ye for half a year now. How does tha feel?"

"It feels like I deserve it. But I didn't come all this way just to apologize, Daisy. I came to get you back. We belong together, and I shouldn't have questioned that."

Lugh was livid on my behalf. "And what of ye, Urien? I can't imagine what apology dipped in chocolate and gold ye must've brought."

"I'll not discuss my daughter with you. Your immortal status and your blessing from Brìghde might impress others, but I don't have the patience for this. Do you have any idea what a nightmare an airport is? I've travelled too long, and been through too much to be derailed by you.

My people need me, and I'm here at great expense to them. Step aside."

I heard a small scuffle, and hugged the wall as I sat on the steps, as if that might make me turn invisible. Panic seized me at my secret being found out by two people I didn't want anywhere near my private life. They'd both bailed on me. I couldn't stand for an ounce of that near my daughter.

I banded my arms around my belly, protecting myself from the onslaught of questions I knew were coming when Urien rounded the corner. "Rosie, I..." His eyes fell on my belly, and he gasped. "Rosie! Honey, when did you... I had no idea. Here, let me help you up. You have no business being on the steps like this. You should be sitting in a proper chair." He snapped his fingers at Lugh. "You. Where are her attendants?"

"You're looking at him. We don't exactly have a staff around here. I've looked after your daughter because she's my friend, and Kerdik asked me to make sure she had a good life here. Avalon's daughter is safe, no thanks to either of ye."

I don't know why my eyes did the scared "please forgive me" when my dad saw that I was pregnant. Part of me guessed that if he was the type to throw me out because I was a Vampire, then being an out of wedlock soon-to-be mother was probably also on that taboo list.

Urien's shoulders drooped when he took in my anxiety, and he closed the gap between us to help me up. "Sweetheart, it's alright. I'm here now. Everything's going to be okay."

I gulped, trying not to burst into tears. I didn't have the oomph to tell him off, so I simply nodded, letting him help me up off the steps. I was hoping he'd corral me to my bedroom, but he led me down the rest of the steps, revealing me to the one man who'd stolen my heart time and time again, refusing to ever give it back without a fight.

So here we were, ready to fight all over again.

My mouth fell open as pure Bastien filled my watery, bloody vision. Lugh handed me a black handkerchief from his pocket, which he'd taken to carrying around for me for my pregnancy-induced emotional moments. Though, something told me that I didn't need to be with child to tear up at the sight of my ex-husband.

Bastien had a beard that was at least a couple months old. It was two inches thick, and he looked unwashed and underfed. He was thinner, though not lacking in the muscle I'd always depended on. His flannel shirt was rumpled and dirty, and beneath the smell of his unwashed clothes, I inhaled the intoxicating scent of his blood – a vice I'd long learned to moderate. I could get by on a few swallows a month of his stored-up blood.

Only after a few wordless seconds did it register that equal amounts of shock were wafting off of him, as well. "Rosie, I... You're..." His eyes were trained on my stomach, his mouth agape.

"I didn't think you'd want to know."

"How could you?" His gaze hardened before I could make sense of his words. I saw a tear form in the corner of his eye before he angrily swiped it away. His fists clenched as he whirled on Lugh, his fists clenched. "Run," he warned in a low seethe.

Lugh had too much pride for a chase. He held his ground and jutted his chin out, inviting the beating that looked ripe, and coming his way. "Bring it, Bastien. I've been waiting too long for this."

"Gentlemen, you'll take your fight outside. There'll be no punches thrown around my daughter."

I didn't understand the sudden shift of rage, but when the front door opened, and Judah found himself standing in the middle of an impending brawl, I finally found my voice. "Everyone, chill!"

Judah jumped, his head whipping around to take in the newcomers and the hostile climate. He shook his head and then stomped the snow off his boots. "I knew vacation had to end sometime. Good to see you, Crazy Lumberjack who used to be Bastien. If you need a shower, we've got one you can put to good use." He grimaced at Bastien's smell, which I'm guessing wasn't too great up close.

Bastien turned his fury that was dripping with betrayal on me. "I begged you for a child, and you go off and make one with another man? How long were we broken up before you fell into someone else's bed? How long?" he demanded, but I was too dumbstruck to answer. It never dawned on me that he might assume anyone else was the father. When it was clear I was incapable of speech, he rounded on the guys. "Which one of you did this to my wife?" Bastien frowned at Judah, who held up his hands like he didn't want to get caught with the hot potato. "It couldn't have been you. The timeline doesn't add up." He refocused his rage at Lugh. "It's got to be you. I told you to run. That's the nicest I get today."

Judah met my eyes, telling me without a word that he had my back, no matter how this all shook out. "Bastien, you might want to have a seat. Lugh's not the father, though he's been there for Ro every step of the way." Judah was a good guy, and slapped Bastien on the back a few times, leading him to the dining room and pulling out a chair for him. "Ro, come on in. We'll give you two some time to catch up." Then Judah turned his beamiest grin on Urien, extending his hand to him. "So, I hear you're no better than my dad, abandoning your kid when they disappoint. Nice to see you again. You probably don't remember me, since you didn't give a crap about your daughter for the past two years. I'm Judah."

Urien glowered at my BFF, and shook his hand with great reluctance. "Yes, I recall your smart mouth. Get it all out now. I deserve it."

"Wow. That was almost the I'm-a-dirtbag speech I was hoping for, but perhaps two years of groveling would be best. You know, one year on your knees for every year you acted like your daughter wasn't worth your all-important time." Judah threw his head back and chuckled, as if they were old friends talking about shenanigans. "You know, my dad never knew me before he cut and run, but you actually got to know what an amazing person your daughter is, and you walked out. I'm not sure which of us wins the contest of who's got the worst dad. What do you think?" Then Judah batted his hand at Urien, as if they were in the middle of telling funny jokes. "What am I saying? Pregnant lady always wins. Enjoy your trump card, Ro. You win Worst Dad contest." Then he snapped his fingers in an "aw, shucks" kind of way.

I groaned at Judah's words, but didn't tell him to knock it off. Truth be told, if I ever came face to face with the man who'd abandoned Judah when he'd been just a baby, there wouldn't be many words – only fists. My bestie had my back, and I loved him for it.

Judah led Lugh and my dad outside, but only after Lugh checked in with me to make sure I was alright being alone with Bastien. Little did Lugh understand that Bastien would never raise a hand to me, but he'd pummel any man nearby who he thought might cross us. "You're safer on your walk. Could you grab my dad a jacket? He's used to Avalon's weather."

"Of course." His hand cupped my shoulder, and Bastien growled like a tiger. Lugh paid Bastien no mind, but leaned down to speak low in my ear. "Take him back if ye must, but remember tha ye did nothing to warrant him walking out, as he did. Ye can stay with me as long as ye like. Only go back if ye want to, and if ye trust tha he won't pull this rubbish on your daughter."

I nodded, putting my hand on his and meeting his eyes with a look that conveyed how grateful I was for his friendship. I trusted Lugh, which was saying a lot. After all I'd been through, trust didn't come easy.

When the men left, they took none of the tension with them, leaving it all to waft in the air between us. I never thought I'd have an ex-husband at twenty-five, but here I was, staring down the barrel of too much emotional baggage for one couple to stand.

45

BASTIEN'S DAUGHTER

"I don't need the details, I just need to know who knocked you up. Why, Rosie? How long did you wait before you jumped into the sack with someone else?"

I blinked at him, unsure which question to answer. "I thought you said you didn't want details. I think it's fair to say that when you take back your ring and tell me you want out, it can't matter to you who I sleep with."

"So it was Lugh. I knew it. Should've beaten on him while I had the chance. No matter. He's got to come home sometime."

"The only person I slept with was Kerdik, and that was long after you left me, and long after I found out I was pregnant."

Bastien sat back in his chair, his arms crossed over his chest. "Kerdik told me he slept with you. I was just seeing if you'd lie about it. So he got you pregnant? You've got a green baby swimming around in there?"

I threw my hands in the air, wondering when he'd gotten so bull-headed. *Silly me, he was always a mule.* I'd loved that about him in the beginning – that dogged determination that sought out the truth at all costs. Now that I was on the receiving end of his frustration, it was slightly less charming. "I feel like it should be obvious to you by now that you're the dude who got me pregnant. There's no question of paternity. It's you."

Bastien stilled, and for a moment, he seemed unable to move. My ex was a statue who didn't dare blink at me, but took in my rounder, curvier frame with new light. His chair toppled over and hit the floor with a thud when he ran over to me, kneeling before me and tugging up my shirt so he could put his ear to my belly. "My baby? We're having a baby?"

A layer of stone formed over my heart, walling him out as best I could. So many times I'd ached for the moment when he'd call us both his, but now that it was happening, it felt sour – tainted with too much neglect. "*I'm* having a baby. A girl, actually. *You're* not having anything, except a shower, maybe."

He scoffed at my firm line. "We're having a girl?" He clutched his chest as waves of revelation washed over him. His touch was heady, and reminded me of the luscious addiction we'd shared when I fed directly from him. He shivered against me, his skin sallow like a junkie's. I wondered what he'd debased himself in this time.

"Have you been drinking?"

He stiffened. "It's the Vampire/mate bond. Turns out, it wasn't just you who was addicted. I've been having a rough time. Living without you? Maybe if I hadn't gone cold turkey it would've been easier. For some reason, it's way worse at night. Couple that with the fact that I'm not your *Guardien* anymore, which means I can't sleep through any of this, and I'm in a sorry state." He shook as he pressed his lips to my belly. "I should never have left, Daisy. I was scared, so I ran, like I always do. But we were more than that – we'd been through more. I don't know why I didn't trust what we had. All I heard was Roland's voice, calling you a witch who mind-controlled me, and I lost it."

He was saying everything I'd wished he would come to me and confess, but it still wasn't enough. *I* hadn't been enough. Now that he was obviously addicted to my venom, he was back. Now that I was pregnant, he was back. It wasn't me he was here for, but himself.

I didn't have the heart to push him away, but let him rest his weary head on my lap. I ran my fingers through his hair, hoping to soothe some of the ache in his chest. While I couldn't justify letting him back in, I didn't wish pain on him. "What do you want me to do? Do you want me to feed on you, so you can get a break from the pain?"

With his eyes winched shut, he nodded his defeat.

"Please. Night's coming soon. It gets so much worse at night."

"Okay. Don't worry." I ran my knuckles over his cheek, trying to keep my breathing steady at the intimate touch I thought I might never have again. "Let's get you a shower, too. Do you have clean clothes in your bag?"

Bastien shrugged. "Clean enough."

I mustered a chuckle as I stood, offering him a hand up. "Come on. Let's get you washed. You'll feel better once you've had a shower." I led him up the stairs to the bathroom Lugh, Judah and I shared with Finnegan. The rest of the band slept on the main floor. Though we were alone in the house, I shut us in the bathroom, taking every precaution to keep Avalon out of my life in Paris.

"I shouldn't have pushed you away," Bastien said again.

I didn't respond to his words aloud, though my heart was on a cycle of mending and breaking, mending and breaking every time he spoke. "You can leave your clothes outside the door, and I'll wash them with the rest of your stuff." I set down a pair of Judah's shorts on the back of the toilet. "These'll be small, but they're only until your stuff dries."

He met my eyes, looking lost and completely without a plan. "You've been pregnant all this time? When I took the ring back, you had my daughter inside of you?"

I didn't know how to answer that minefield of a question, so I stuck with the blunt truth. "I didn't know I was pregnant yet, but yeah. I'm almost six months along. And she's *my* daughter, not yours."

Bastien didn't try to hide how badly my words cut him. That hadn't been my intent, but I didn't want to lie. "You can't keep me away from her."

"I didn't. You left. You didn't want us, so there you have it." I pinched the bridge of my nose. "Look, I don't really want to get into this right now. You're barely upright. When was the last time you ate anything?"

He was irate, but too feeble to do much about it. "Who cares about food? That's my daughter in there!"

"I care if you've eaten. I'm not going to drink from you if you're three seconds away from passing out." I turned on the water for the shower, and got it to the temperature I knew he preferred. He started undressing, and part of me knew that if I saw him naked, a big portion of my will to resist him would start to crumble. My libido was out of control.

I tried to scoot past him, but Parisian bathrooms were notoriously small, this one being no exception. I could smell his blood, the salt on his skin, and the piney scent that was purely Bastien. My sheets in Avalon had smelled like a mixture of us both, and I sorely missed the aroma of us together. I tried to hold my head high, as if being so near my own personal kryptonite didn't affect me at all. His fingers fumbled on his buttons as he slowly stripped, and I could tell he was trying to put on a show for me, but failing miserably. He was too worn and in the throes of six months' worth of withdrawal to seduce anyone. He met my eyes with a look of sheer defeat, knowing that he used to be strong, but those days were behind him unless I helped him stand tall again. He'd been such a bear of a man when we'd first met. I hadn't wanted to take that from him, and yet, here we were.

I took pity on him, which wasn't the same thing as sexual tension. I saw the defeat in his eyes when my fingers moved to undress him with no intention of a happy ending. "I'm sorry, Daisy. I'm so sorry."

"Shh." I removed his flannel, and then helped work off his undershirt. He kicked off his boots, and I undid his belt, letting his jeans fall to the tiled floor. Those simple motions made him wince, and I knew his joints were aching him.

Before his underwear slid down to reveal his perfectly taut backside, I leaned up on my toes and rooted around for my favorite spot near his neck, not wanting him to be in such pain. My fangs sank down into the meat of his shoulder, and my eyes rolled back when the taste of Bastien coated my tongue. It had been so long since I'd indulged, perhaps three weeks since I'd snuck a taste of the man who'd always entranced me. My libido flared to a dangerous level, and I feared I might tell him to forget our whole separation if he'd just throw me down on the bed and have his filthy way with me.

My daughter started kicking violently, keeping me from doing anything stupid. She'd done a few small movements so far, but this was sheer violence. She punched and rolled, making it known that she was a part of this equation, and Bastien's blood was affecting her, too.

Two pulls was all it took for Bastien's knees to buckle. I sort of caught him, but he was too heavy for me, so he still ended up on the floor. He didn't hit his head on the way down, so that was a plus. "Bastien? I didn't mean to hurt you. Was that too much?"

When he opened his eyes, his pupils were dilated, and he looked positively woozy. "You didn't hurt me. The opposite. This is the first time I haven't been in pain in six months." His chest expanded and contracted with none of the shakiness he'd exhibited before. "Thank you. I could barely think straight, it's been hurting so bad." He took a few seconds, but eventually stood and flexed his fingers. "Oh, that feels amazing."

"Shower," I reminded him, gathering up his clothes from the floor. I had to get away from him, or I knew I would kiss him and make a perfect mess of my situation. His naked body was right there for the taking, so I knew I had to get out of there. Before he could say anything, I all but ran out the door, my daughter kicking like a mini Chuck Norris the entire time. I drew in a deep breath when my belly hardened and grew uncomfortable in a way it never had before. There was a pain that lingered after her kicks, which was new. New and scary.

I bit my lower lip and stared down at my belly. "Steady, girl. It's going to be a long night."

46

NOT A CONTRACTION, AND NOT MY HUSBAND

I threw Bastien's clothes and my father's into the washer, appalled at how filthy Bastien's stuff had grown. He had a shirt in there that smelled actually moldy. Stairs took me a little longer these days, but I made it up with a bowl of leftover beuf burginion by the time the shower turned off.

My daughter hadn't stopped moving, which might not be something that normal mothers would be concerned about, but it was completely uncharacteristic of her, and every few punches, she got in one to my spine that was particularly painful. My belly was still doing that turning hard thing, married with a twinge of pain that didn't feel like distress, but more like something that shouldn't be there just yet. "Bastien, I brought you some food. I'll leave it here, just outside the door."

Bastien came out perfectly clean, and while he was

thinner, he was definitely the steady man I'd known, devoid of the shakes that had plagued him for too many months. What's more, he'd shaved. He touched his jaw, offering up a smirk that told me he appreciated my teenaged gawking. "I used your razor. I hope that's okay."

"Of course. Use whatever you need. You look more like yourself. That's good." I swallowed at the bulge in his too tight shorts, and didn't tear my eyes away until my baby kicked the sense back into me. I winced at the gut shot she took at my ribs, rubbing the small ache in confusion. My stomach started cramping again, making me short of breath.

"What's wrong?"

"Nothing. I just have to go make a phone call. You good with the food?"

"Looks great. You didn't have to do that."

"I won't let you starve," I promised him, offering up the same basic human decency he'd given to me when I'd needed his blood to survive. "Excuse me."

My girl roiled again as I slid into my room and shut the door. I bit my lip to keep from crying out, but the pain was getting worse. She was getting big in there, so each grand movement felt like a whale that was stuffed into a duffel bag, trying to squirm its way out. I felt around frantically on the bed for my phone, and dialed Judah. "Hey, you nearby?"

"Not really. Took a cab to the Eiffel Tower. I think

Lugh's plan is to dangle your dad off the top or something. Don't worry; I'll take pictures for you."

I cursed inwardly. "Okay. Cool. Can you guys do your thing and come on home afterwards?"

All levity dropped from Judah's tone. "What's wrong?"

"Probably nothing. Just a little pain. The baby's freaking out, rolling around and kicking like she's trying to make an early exit. Then there's these stomach pains that keep coming and going every few minutes."

Judah swore. "Are you having contractions?"

"No. I don't think so. Maybe. I can't tell. It just hurts, and I can't tell if she's freaking out in a bad way or not. I drank from Bastien, and she won't calm down. I mean, it can't be contractions, right? It's way too early for that. Don't worry. I'm just being a baby about it."

"Okay, since when has that ever been true about you? Finnegan and the guys are at the pub on the corner. I'll text him, and he'll take you to the hospital."

I closed my eyes, wanting to argue, but knowing my daughter's safety was of higher priority than my pride. "Okay. Thanks. But if he doesn't answer, it's fine. It's probably nothing." I winced when my girl heard the lie, and protested by throwing a mosh pit in my uterus. My belly hardened again, stealing the breath from my lungs with just how much a little cramping could hurt. "Judah?" With the single bleat of his name, I knew my BFF would understand how scared I was.

"Hey, do I sound worried? No way. Your girl's going to

be fine. She's just getting used to the fresh blood, is all. In the meantime, it wouldn't hurt to have a doctor check you out. No big deal."

I nodded, swallowing hard. My heart started to race when the inevitability of something being very wrong reared its ugly head. I tried to do my breathing exercises they'd taught Judah, Lugh and I in Lamaze classes, but it wasn't as easy to do, now that I was in actual pain. As the minutes ticked by, the discomfort grew worse, and I worried that something might be actually wrong.

"Daisy, are you alright?"

Of course my girl would pick that moment to pitch a fit. I leaned over on the bed and fisted the sheets, biting my lip through a groan. "I'm fine."

Bastien took a chance with his life and opened my door, taking in the scene with wide eyes. "No, you're not! Are you in labor?"

I shook my head. "No. It's too early for that. I'm only six months along. When I drank from you, it did something to me. She started freaking out, and she's not calming down. It's not labor. I'm not in labor. It's too early." I said the words like a warning to my daughter, willing her to calm the crap down for her own safety.

"Okay, where are my clothes?"

"In the wash."

Bastien ignored me and started rifling through the drawers, coming to Lugh's clothes. The jeans were tight on him, but I wasn't about to complain about getting a better view of Bastien's sculpted backside. He threw on a black shirt that was definitely too snug on him, and managed to locate clean socks and a zip-up hoodie that helped offset the you-know-you-want-my-body look he was oh-too-good at. He found my socks and shoes, and bent down to put them on me when the baby let up enough for me to sit down on the side of the bed. "Come on, hun. Let's get you to the hospital. I can't believe Remy let you leave Avalon with a baby in your belly!"

"He didn't know. No one did, except Mad, Rigs, Dub and Kerdik, and I swore them to secrecy."

"Are you kidding me with this? Mad knew? Well, that makes a lot more sense. Took a swing at me when I told him I was going to wait at the house for you to come back from Paris."

"Mad's in Common?" I rubbed my forehead. "Oh, jeez. He's going to get arrested for something stupid."

"Mad, Annabelle, Link and Quinn are all at the house. They were too afraid to get on the plane here. And something about Quinn being too pregnant to fly. I don't know all the rules." He tied my shoes for me, and I swear, I almost burst into tears at the sweetness. Actually, it was a debate between tears and kicking him in the face for leaving me to do this by myself for so many months.

"Bastien, you don't have to come. Finnegan's going to take me in. It's fine."

Bastien stood, towering over me and raising his voice to an angry shout. "Stop acting like I'm not part of this equation! This is *my* baby, and if I'd known, no way would I have stayed away as long as I did."

I stood and threw my arms out to the sides. "Yet another way I'm trapping you into staying with me. What would Roland say now?"

Bastien's jaw flexed with anger, but I was unrepentant. "I don't care what Roland would say. I care about what I want. You, Daisy. It's always been you."

"You don't get to come back when it's convenient, or out of guilt. You don't get to stay for part of us. You don't get to come back, and then walk out when you get scared. I won't let you abandon her, like you did me! Get out of here!" My girl kicked my spine, and my knees nearly gave out. I grabbed my back with one hand, and my belly with the other, my face twisting in pain.

Bastien's arms went around me, steadying me before I fell over. "Yeah, yeah. Yell at me all you want, just do it on the way to the hospital. Tell me I'm a rat bastard."

"You're a rat bastard for taking your ring back! I was more scared than you were, and you didn't give a crap about anything but your own fear!"

Bastien nodded, smiling at me. "That's right. I did. Dick move, for sure."

"Stop smiling like that! I'm mad at you!"

"Yes, you are. You're yelling, which means I've got a chance. When you were all cold and distant before, you weren't willing to even fight about it, but look at you now, ready to work things out."

"You're delusional!"

He pulled me so close; I thought he might kiss me. "I'm your husband. Say it."

"You're single," I retorted, making him chuckle.

I was livid that I actually needed him to keep me upright. He moved me slowly toward the hallway, and down the stairs, stopping only to fit my jacket around me and zip it up. It was too sweet, too protective. I was afraid if he kept it up, I'd sob all over him, and beg him to move back into our home.

Luckily, Finnegan was charging up the front stoop as Bastien opened the door. "Rosie, are ye alright? Judah called and said ye needed to go to the hospital. I've got a cab right here for us. In ye get." Finnegan took my free hand and helped me into the car, shutting himself in the back with me, which left Bastien to ride up front when I rudely slammed the car door in his face. "I see the reunion's going swimmingly. Finnegan," he introduced himself, leaning forward to shake Bastien's hand.

"You are not friends with him," I ruled, giving Finnegan my best fall-in-line face.

"Bastien," he replied from the front passenger's seat, taking Finnegan's hand with a tight smile. "I'm Rosie's husband."

"*Ex*-husband!"

Finnegan grinned at Bastien and rubbed his palms together with anticipatory glee. "Grand. Lugh's going to beat your arse for leaving this one. Me? I like a good show."

"Oh, you are such an asswagon!" I growled at Finnegan, glaring when he bit at my cheek in his playful way.

I wanted to shove him, but my girl wasn't having the drama. She rolled around so violently, that I was scared I might actually give birth in the back of the cab. Despite my desire for denial, I let out a cry of agony, hoping actual labor wouldn't get that much worse. I started to panic when I realized it definitely would.

Finnegan was terminally single, and it was no wonder why. Each time I screamed and squeezed his hand, he cried out like a little scaredy cat. "Hurry!" he insisted to the driver. "I don't want to see a baby get born back here! I'm too young to see this!"

"You're thirty-six years old, you baby!"

Bastien tried to calm me down from the front seat, but the more Finnegan freaked out, the more I began to panic, which somehow made the things that were certainly not contractions ten times worse. They couldn't be contractions; it was too early.

"Cross your legs, Rosie! Hold it in there until we get to a proper doctor!" Then Finnegan let out a girlish scream when my face screwed up as another non-contraction hit me.

My fear came out as anger, and splattered itself all over Finnegan. "The next time we do mud mask facials together, I'm posting that crap all over social media. 'Beauty Tips from Lost and Forgotten's Sexiest of the Six'. Calm down, you lunatic! I'm freaking out enough as it is!"

"I think I saw the head!" Finnegan cried out, his eyes squinched shut.

"I'm wearing leggings, you drama queen!"

"Get me out of this cab!" Finnegan wailed, giving me the urge to push him out of the moving vehicle.

When we pulled up to a red light, Bastien flung himself out of the car and threw open the back door, pushing his way into the cramped backseat.

Finnegan was all too thrilled to make an escape to the front of the car, keeping his eyes ahead as he bit at his nails. "Tell me when it's over!"

I swore at Finnegan, sweating and afraid that something was very wrong. Bastien sat sideways, and moved me to rest my back against his chest. With a steadiness he hadn't possessed an hour earlier, he wrapped his arms around me to hold my belly with both hands. "Easy, now. She's just excited her daddy's home."

"No! I'm the mother. I'm the father. I'm the decision-maker. You're the nothing, which is exactly what you wanted to be to me!"

"Keep on yelling, babe. You're going to have to push me harder than that if you're trying to make me go away."

I don't know why I trusted my worst fear to him, but it toppled out of my mouth before I could get ahold of myself. "Bastien, if she's born now, no way will she make it. It was biting you. That started everything going haywire."

"What sort of kinky shenanigans are ye into, Rosie? Biting, eh?" Finnegan commented from the peanut gallery.

Bastien stroked my belly, remaining calm so I could freak out. "Then we know what not to do next time. If she's not handling that, then we'll hold off until after she's born."

"But you'll be in pain!"

"So what? I want our girl to be healthy. I'm not so delicate that I can't stand a little pain."

I threw my hands in the air in exasperation. "You were shaking!"

"I'll survive, and now that we know we can't do that? So will she." My belly hardened and the agony was back, making me cry out as my arm reached behind me so I could grip his hair. I tugged on the follicles through the thing that couldn't be a contraction. Bastien didn't say a word about it, even as the agony eased. "Shh," he whispered in my ear when I started to whimper. "I'm here now. I've got you."

My heart felt pierced through at those three simple words that I'd tried to erase from my brain every night since we'd split up. "For now," I reminded us both.

"Forever." He kissed my temple, and kept his freshly shaved cheek against mine. "Do you have any names picked out?"

I shook my head, frustrated with myself that I hadn't

come up with something awesome. "I want her middle name to be Elaine, but other than that, I've got nothing."

"Hmm. Let me give it some thought."

"It's not up to you. I could name her Squidfish Elaine Avalon, and you'd have nothing to say about it. You left us, so you don't get a vote."

Bastien wasn't put off by the venom in my voice. "No, not Squidfish," he said, as if that had been a legitimate option I'd put on the table. "Something prettier than that. What about a flower name to match yours?"

I shook my head. "I don't want to name her after me."

"Why not?"

"Because I want her to be smarter than me. I don't want her to end up knocked-up, divorced, and in the back of a cab in a country where she doesn't even speak the language! I hate that I fell for your BS!"

Finnegan piped in from the front seat. "I can translate for ye, Rosie. I always do. I won't leave ye until Lugh comes. He's meeting us there."

Bastien took my acid with grace. "Be as mad as you want. All it shows me is that you're willing to work it out. Throw all the anger my way, Daisy. I deserve it, and I won't argue. I also won't leave, so get used to me being in your space."

I groaned at his kindness. It would have been so much easier if he had been cruel. It would've made him the one-dimensional villain I needed him to be if I was going to resist. "You make me absolutely crazy."

Bastien chuckled into my hair, kissing the tresses as if I was precious to him. When the next not-a-contraction came, he let me squeeze his hands as hard as I needed to, and didn't say a thing to deter my wrath. "How about Azalea? Like the flower."

"Azalea for what?"

"Azalea Elaine Avalon. For our daughter."

I cringed. "Darn you for picking the perfect name on the first try. Go away. Those get to be your only contributions. Sperm and the name, then you're out."

Finnegan whistled low through his teeth. "Jays, Rosie. Tha's cold."

Bastien fisted my hair into a ponytail and jerked my head back, so I was staring up at the roof of the car. His voice was low and unhurried, laced with a threat that stilled my rage. "Listen to me, and listen good. I'm going to be here every day for the rest of my life. You can yell at me and push me away until I'm old and gray, but I'm still not going anywhere. That's *my* daughter, and you're *my* wife. Suck on that, Princess."

His cold tone struck every nerve in my body, making me shiver with need for him. "If you think I'm just going to roll over and accept that line of utter nonsense, you're dead wrong. I'm not your wife. You made sure of that."

"And I'll be here to see my ring back on your finger. I'll stay by your side every minute until my last to make sure that ring stays where I put it." He tapped my belly as the cab finally pulled into the hospital, and started winding its way toward the drop-off. "And I'll be here to put another baby in your belly, and another. Azalea's going to want sisters and a whole pack of strapping brothers."

I glared at him when Finnegan opened the back door to help me out. "Say the right thing again, and I'll punch your friggin' lights out."

Bastien turned my face to his, pinching my jaw between his thumb and forefinger just to be controlling. "Stop turning me on with that kinda talk. These pants are already too tight."

Finnegan howled his laughter, but sobered quickly when another non-contraction hit me. He ran inside and grabbed an orderly and a wheelchair, helping me into it and throwing a fistful of cash at the cabby, who couldn't get away from us fast enough.

47

UPDATES ON AVALON

"I feel like I might be more helpful in the waiting area, away from all the... this." Finnegan eyed the fetal heart monitor as if it was an alien ready to wrap its tentacle-like IV tubes around his throat.

I took in Finnegan's skittish features with a smirk. "That's fine. Thanks for getting me to the hospital, man."

Finnegan didn't even offer up a parting wave, but literally ran out of the room, as if his shoes had caught fire.

Lugh kicked his boots up on the side of my bed, his hands laced behind his head while we waited for the doctor to discharge us. "This is all my fault. She wanted to meet her Uncle Lugh too badly, so she tried to make an early break for it."

I smirked at Lugh, grateful he'd dropped his plans to come. "Thanks for rushing over here. Pretty anticlimactic. You're a good friend."

"Anticlimactic is a good thing when it comes to hospital visits, Prim."

It had been an hour since my contractions had stopped, and all was well in baby land. I was ordered bed rest, which Bastien made the doctor write down the specifics of, in case I tried to worm my way out of the confinement.

Bastien was quiet in the chair on the other side of my hospital bed, studying me with too much clarity in his gaze. When I quirked my eyebrow at his scrutiny, he mumbled, "Your face is rounder."

I frowned. "If that's your idea of a compliment, keep on fishing, dude."

"I didn't realize how thin you'd gotten in Faîte. One thing after another came at us, so I stopped being able to see the details. You look healthier here. More at peace. It's all I ever wanted for you."

I mulled over his words, not knowing how to have the simplest of exchanges with him anymore. "I am more at peace here. I'm surrounded by music and macarons. It's nice. No one's trying to kill me or kick me out, so you know, bonus."

Lugh must have sensed we were about to hit the more serious swings in our broken journey that led us to this estranged place. "I'm going to go see how much apple juice I can pilfer from the cafeteria."

"I'll buy you apple juice," I offered.

"Stolen juice always tastes better. I like living on the

edge." Lugh stood and leaned over to kiss my forehead. "Take your time, Prim." Then he bent lower and whispered, "You've got a home with me, and plenty of money. Whatever decision ye make, be sure it's only what ye want. There aren't any other factors to consider." He squeezed my fingers. "It's our turn to live the lives we want now."

I pulsed his grip three times, silently saying "I love you" with my palm. When Lugh left, I tried not to be nervous at the very adult expression on Bastien's face. "How's Faîte holding up? What's the haps with Avalon?" I tried not to fidget, but since I couldn't run out of there, it was how my body compromised under my anxiety over seeing Bastien.

Bastien simply studied my tiny squirms in lieu of answering. "No."

"No?"

Bastien shrugged. "No. Faîte is going to handle its own problems for a while. No matter how good or bad it is, I didn't come here to suck you back into the drama of that world. You need this place. You need to be here for a while. Here, and only here." His eyes locked in on mine. "With me."

My jaw tensed, but I kept my retort low and calm. "You took the ring back. You left me. You didn't trust me enough, and in the end, you didn't see me clearly through the Gancanagh news. You didn't see me, Bastien. I don't need a husband who I have to constantly convince that I am who I am. You should've had more faith in me. After everything we've been through, I didn't deserve you walking out."

Bastien gave a succinct nod, but didn't respond for several weighted seconds. His elbows were perched on the armrests, and his fingers were tented in front of his mouth. "Agreed. As soon as I realized that, I knew I'd screwed up."

"I've been in Common for months. You should've put it all together sooner."

"You're right." He paused, his lashes sweeping shut at some painful memory. "I was detained."

My spine stiffened. "Who's dumb enough to capture an Untouchable? Are you okay?"

"Dub," he explained with a wry expression as he ran his tongue over his teeth. "I was drinking my weight in ale at the tavern, and he came in one night and tore me a new one. Nearly took the roof down with his anger. Then he blinded me."

I gasped, knowing just how devastating and scary that was. "Oh! I had no idea. I'm so sorry." And I truly was. No matter how angry I was at Bastien, I didn't wish blindness on him. "You must've been so frightened." I would have taken care of him. I would've picked things up off the floor so he didn't trip. I would've quietly held his hand through his anger. I would've dropped everything to take care of him – if only he'd let me. I wanted to apologize for not being there, but I knew it wasn't me who'd decided I wouldn't be his in-case-of-emergency contact.

"I was scared. I thought I understood what you went

through, but I had no clue. Dub left me blind in the tavern to figure my way back to the castle by myself. Then when I got there, Urien and Lot wouldn't let me in because the only reason that had been my home in the first place was because we were married. When we separated, I lost my stupid royalty title and my place to stay."

"No. Lot wouldn't put you out on the street. I don't believe it. That's horrible!"

"He didn't. He let Remy and Demi guide me back to my cabin in the woods." His eyes flicked to mine. "All that stuff I said about Demi pretending to be in love with you because it was his job? Well, I was wrong. Had to listen to his lecture the whole way home. He was grateful – actually grateful – to be poisoned by you. He said that if your whole relationship was a lie, then it was the best lie he'd ever lived, and he'd do it all over again if he had the chance. He told me I was stupid to leave you, and he was right." Bastien cleared his throat. "But it was too late. You were already gone to do healings in Éireland, and I was blind. I couldn't provide for you. I couldn't provide for myself! Remy took pity on me, which felt awesome, by the way, and made sure I had food. He looked in on me once a week."

My mouth was hanging open. "I don't know where to start."

"Don't start yet. I'm not nearly finished. After Kerdik stopped by to explain that your Gancanagh abilities are significantly diluted, and that you couldn't have pulled the wool over my eyes in the same way Lugh did with Brìghde, I knew I needed to get you back." He shook his head at himself. "But I'd blown it, and by then you were already in Common. Not to mention that I couldn't find you if I wanted to. I was blind, and Remy wouldn't take me to see you. He couldn't exactly escort me through Common, being headless and all." Bastien's eyes cut to mine. "Let me tell you the nightmare it is to communicate with a healer who can't speak when I couldn't see."

I grimaced. "Oh, jeez. I can't imagine how that would work."

"We worked out a system of tapping, but Remy only came by once a week to make sure I had food, and we didn't hang out when he stopped in. I'm pretty sure it was Lot who was sending it." Bastien spoke into his tented fingers. "Gave me loads of time to think. There hasn't been much time for that. Every time we get sucked into the Avalon drama, it's all action and no thinking. I could've done a lot better, Rosie. Not just the breakup, but from the beginning."

I didn't know what to say to this. It wasn't an emotional plea that I couldn't trust, but a lasting change that seemed to lower his shoulders as he approached our relationship with a bit more caution than the cavalier way he often dealt with things. "You weren't a bad husband. At least, not until the end of it all, of course. But up until then, I never felt cheated."

"Well, *I* know I shorted you. Made myself a little list of

all the ways I failed you as your boyfriend, your *Guardien* and your husband. I knew I couldn't get you back, so I started thinking about how much you'd sacrificed for Avalon. In the beginning, it was always about me: my stupid hang-ups, my mission, my friends, my status. But you made it all about Avalon. I never told you how much I admired that about you. That's when I realized I needed to get my act together. That was harder to do in the throes of withdrawal from your venom, but I still managed to get back on my feet." He cracked his knuckles one by one, his voice still steady and even. "When Dub came back, I talked to him about my epiphany, and my plan to help Avalon get back on her feet. He gave me my sight back, but only under the condition that I finish out my plan for Avalon before I went to Common to pursue you."

I touched my forehead, trying to keep up with it all. "Wow. That's a lot of information."

"For what a dick Dub is, he was right. I wasn't seeing clearly until he took away my sight. Then I understood how stupid and selfish I'd been. So I went to Lot and told him my plan. With his blessing, I started setting up support groups for Vampires and their mates all across Avalon. You wouldn't believe how many showed up. A few of the healers wanted to help out, so they were the facilitators. Healers make for excellent listeners, by the way."

"Are you serious? You set up a twelve-step program in Avalon?"

"Twenty-seven recovery groups for *Attelage* Vampires,

their mates, and friends and family to deal with the changes, actually. Then I set up groups for people grieving over their lost loved ones. Everyone knows someone who was killed in battle at some point. The healers were put in charge of more support groups. There are forty-five Grieving Your Losses groups."

I was too stunned for words, gaping at Bastien in wonder and confusion. I assumed he'd been drinking himself stupid in Avalon, glad to be free of me. That he'd taken all he'd learned in AA and turned it into a plan that helped our people? It was hard to remember all the reasons why I was mad at him; I was too busy being amazed. I'd been so focused on the evil supervillains that I hadn't put enough thought into the healing those that had survived would need. I'd walked out on Avalon when it was too hard to take anymore, but Bastien had stayed faithful, holding Avalon's hand when they couldn't find their way. "I don't know what to say. I should've thought of that. Leaving like I did... it was selfish."

Bastien leaned forward, resting his elbows on the side of my hospital bed, his hands folded as if he was praying. His expression was warm and earnest, contrasting with the cold and sterile environment. "No. You were smart. You have a baby in your belly. You were being a good mother, getting her somewhere safer. It's okay to have boundaries. We all leaned on you way too much. It was my turn to help out, so that's what I did."

"That's incredible. I had no idea you thought about that kind of stuff. You really put it all together?"

Bastien bobbed his head, and then cautiously reached for my hand. He rubbed my knuckles over his freshly-shaved cheek, his eyes closing tight at the simple touch. "Dub finally agreed to let me come to Common to find you. When he blinded me, he said you deserved a better man." Bastien shrugged. "He was right. So I learned to be someone you could be proud of."

I softened, running my fingers across his cheek. "I'm still mad," I admitted. "But I'm so proud of you for helping Avalon like that. That's beautiful, what you did."

"Trust me, Daisy. No one's angrier at me than I am. I got all turned around and didn't understand all the facts. I should've had more faith in us. I was wrong, and I'm so sorry."

I didn't argue, or say anything to brush off his apology. "I'm sorry you had to go through all that. Dub blinding you? Not cool."

"I've never felt so impotent. I hate depending on someone else for every little thing. I understand now that you were holding back how miserable you were." He'd been deliberate and collected in his speech, but finally his steadiness began to break. "I can do right by this baby, Rosie. Please. I know you hate me, and you have every right to send me packing, but if you could just think about it for a few days first. I don't have it in me to walk away from my baby. I just can't do it! I don't know how turned around I must've been to have walked out on you in the first place! Please, Rosie. I know you're going to kick me out, but before you do... Don't!"

I didn't know what the right thing to do was in this situation. I didn't want to let him back in my life, only to let him devastate my daughter if he got confused again. Looking at the earnest fire in his eyes, part of me knew it would be cruel to cut him off from his only child. After the emotional dressing down I'd undergone, I didn't have it in me to be cruel.

I closed my eyes, willing clarity to come to me. My voice was quiet when I finally answered his plea. "Okay, Bastien. You can be in her life." I shook my head. "But you broke us, and we're still broken. If you want to be a father, then it's your job to be the best one Common's ever seen. I mean it. If this baby comes out of me with a hump and a wonky eye, she's the prettiest girl in your entire universe."

Bastien let out a cry of relief and nodded while his eyes watered. "Absolutely."

I swallowed hard, voicing the thing that woke me up most nights with anxiety. "If she can't read, she'll be the smartest girl you've ever met, and you'll never let her think she's stupid."

"Of course."

"If she's born as the tiniest Vampire in the world, you'll help her figure life out, and make sure she still has oppor-tunities."

"Without a doubt. Thank you so much for this. I won't let you down."

"No. You won't let *her* down."

Bastien paused, and then nodded. "Of course. I won't let her down."

My breath caught in my throat as I began to panic. "Wait, could she really be born as a Vampire? I mean, I said it to make a point, but could it actually happen?"

Bastien wiped his eyes and smiled at me. "No, babe. That's not how it works. You can't pass down Vampiric traits. Azalea will be perfect, just like her mother."

My eyes were wide with all the things I hadn't considered. "I didn't even think to worry about that until just now! I'm going to be a terrible mother! I was only worried about the normal Commoner things that can go wrong with your baby. Did you know it's possible for your placenta to be too thin, or too thick? If it's not just right, the baby could die!"

Bastien stiffened. "What did the doctor say about your placenta. Is there something wrong with it?"

"No, but that's just one example of something that can go wrong. You should read some of these baby books, Bastien. They're terrifying!"

Bastien drew me closer to the edge of the bed and draped his arm over my belly. He rubbed the bump and kissed it, pressing his cheek to the side as he drew drags of relief into his lungs. "You don't have to worry about any of it, because I'm here. I won't let your placenta be weird."

I shot him a baleful look. "You can't control something like that."

"Maybe *you* can't. I'm Untouchable. That's just how we roll, baby."

I guffawed, then chuckled as my panic started to dissipate. "You're a dork."

"I'm *your* dork."

Part of me wanted to be his dork, and for him to be mine, but the wound was still too fresh. My voice dropped from the levity. "I still don't trust you, though."

Bastien hugged me around the middle. "Then I guess I'll just have to stick around for the next fifty years to change your mind."

48

HOME FOR CHRISTMAS

"You alright there, chief?" If I thought I was afraid of heights, it was nothing to Bastien, who was gripping his seat with white knuckles. Urien was lucky he turned into a wolf at night. I gave him a sleeping pill, so he dozed through most of the flight in his dog carrying cage.

"Airplanes aren't my thing," Bastien worked out.

I chuckled. "Well, just get over it. Isn't that what you told me when I was too tired to sit upright when we first rode through Avalon?"

"I was a jerk. Have I told you I was sorry yet today?"

"Only a dozen times. It doesn't start to register until you apologize twenty times. Then I begin to remember we may have had some good moments here and there."

Despite his desire to cling to the armrest between us, Bastien twined his fingers through mine. "I shouldn't have left you. You must've been so scared – pregnant and just learning that you were part Gancanagh. You were probably more afraid of yourself than I was." He drew my fingers to his lips, and gave them a little kiss. "But that's always been you – putting others first."

Judah pretended to barf all over me. "As great as your flirty little back-and-forths are, I'm watching a movie, and then going to sleep. Wake me if you actually take him back, Ro. Or if we crash to our fiery deaths. I definitely want to see that."

Bastien paled. "That's not going to happen. You're messing with me for bailing on Rosie."

Judah grinned at Bastien. "It's almost like you're starting to understand that when you married her, you married her family, and we all hate your stinking guts. I prefer my groveling to be done to the tune of the *Annie* soundtrack. It's gonna be a hard-knock life for you."

I leaned my head to Judah's shoulder. "Thanks, you."

"You're welcome, you. Don't go joining the mile-high club with him just yet. He's still in the doghouse."

I sniggered at the image of the tall and muscular man trying to get it on with bulbous me in the narrow bathroom of the airplane. "I think I'll pass."

Bastien rested his hand on my knee, tugging it gently toward him, as if he meant to take my right leg home with him as a souvenir. His possessive nature hadn't died completely, though his movements were tentative, as if he understood I could slap him away, and he'd deserve the rebuke.

Lugh had packed me with pepper spray and a pack of condoms. "For whichever route ye decide to take with your lad." The tears had been blinding at our departure, but Lugh was firm that he belonged with the band.

"Are you sure you don't want to come home with me?" I'd asked in the quietness of our bedroom.

"I'll be visiting on National Donut Day, and at Christmas, as planned."

I'd blinked up at Lugh, letting him wipe my tears away. "Saying goodbye to you is the worst! I love you, Lugh. Like, go the distance, love."

"I know. What a sorry existence you're about to have, with me so far away." His teasing smirk had made me chuckle, until he'd pressed his lips to mine, savoring this time, tasting my tongue in the privacy of our room. "I love ye, too, Prim. I'll be the man in your life who's..." He'd swallowed, and then tucked a lock of hair behind my ear. His eyes had watered as he tried to come up with the right words. "I'll always be the man in your life, so don't forget about me. Save a seat for me. Wherever ye land, make sure there's room for me in your life."

"I wouldn't have it any other way," I'd promised. Then I let him pull me closer, pressing my belly between us as he moved my arm out to the side. He held onto my wrist with authority that could make any instrument comply to his many whims. We turned slowly in a waltz that made me feel beautiful, instead of the clumsy mess I usually was these days. Then Lugh composed a tune on my body, making me his instrument, and turning our friendship into a song.

"I SEE IT NOW, TUNNEL'S ENDING LIGHT.

It's calling now. Calling for what's right.

And I can't ask you to stay. What else can I say?"

HE'D BEEN WORKING ON THIS SONG FOR A WHILE NOW, AND broke into the chorus I was well familiar with. We slowly swayed, two genetically enhanced freaks who were afraid to go off into the world separately, when no one understood our struggles quite like we did.

"ALL THE YEARS OF MY LIFE, FAR AND NEAR AND LONGER than most.

But you know that my dear, we're two of a kind.

And I hope you don't mind when I say that it hurts so damn much,

Now that you won't be here."

MY HAND HAD STAYED TIGHT INSIDE OF LUGH'S IN THE CAB on the way to the airport. Bastien remained cool about it, even going so far as to give us a moment to say goodbye when we were forced to part at the airport's check-in.

I knew I couldn't cry in public, but Lugh had been pushing the boundaries of my emotional hard limits. His voice had quieted in my ear when we heard his name being whispered, and then shouted in the terminal once he'd been recognized by fans. Lugh clung to me, knowing that when we let go, there would be no quick remedy to the distance. The chorus of the song he'd been wrestling with came again, quiet and unhurried.

"I KNEW WHAT WAS COMING FOR US.
    I knew it couldn't last.
    I knew you'd go your own way,
    but I never knew it would feel. Like. This."

A FEW ADORING FANS HAD TAKEN PICTURES OF HIM KISSING me goodbye at the airport. I'd cringed at our weird friendship being put on public display, but Lugh had grinned after he pulled back. "See? Now you'll have a grand photo of us together at our best. Maybe a few dozen, depending on how many cell phones captured us." He met Bastien's glare, but didn't shrink away. "Cheers, Bastien. Take her home and don't let her go this time. I'll see everyone in a few months."

I don't know how I got on that plane, but somehow, my

feet found their path away from Lugh. He'd been such a comfort, a balm for my battered soul. He'd been my safe place, my favorite friend, and now I would be without him right when life started to turn itself on its head yet again.

"Well, that was anticlimactic," Judah complained when we got off our plane and headed down to baggage claim. "No fiery plane crash? No mastermind villain twirling his mustache, trying to get us in his evil clutches? Common is boring."

I rolled my eyes. "Judah, if I haven't told you before, your jokes are awful."

"You have, but that one was spot on."

When I turned my phone back on, Lugh had sent me a dozen photo texts, including one of his lunch, which made me smile. He'd bought himself four brightly colored macarons, and promised he was sending a box of them to Azalea, so she didn't miss Paris too much.

"You love him," Bastien observed while he watched me check my phone as we waited for the carousel to start rolling out our luggage.

"Of course I do. He's my Judah for Faîte."

Judah frowned, and pushed his glasses higher up on his nose. "Hey. I'm your Judah for all the worlds, Hot Mama."

I snorted, and touched my shoe to the toe of his. "Of course you are, Pimp Daddy."

Urien strolled out of the men's room, carrying the dog crate he'd been snoozing in. He was wearing khakis and a cozy boutique men's cowel-neck sweater. He was just missing a pipe to complete the stereotypical picture of the ideal father. "I'm me again," he announced, meeting my eyes tentatively.

My father had been through too much. I studied the wrinkles at the corners of his eyes, and marveled that he had so few, given the life he'd led. He'd married a woman he'd grown addicted to, due to her Gancanagh genetics. She split up the kingdom, and put him in a two-decade-long coma. When he'd awoken, the world was different, darker. Then his best friend started dating his daughter, which, as much as I'd like to pretend is totally fine, I'll admit, is a little odd. He'd had to deal with his daughter murdering his wife, too. His old-school ways of dealing with the more dangerous magic were put to the test when his only daughter was cursed beyond repair. He'd missed two decades of the world evolving, which might've given him the chance to be more tolerant of my abnormalities. Then he lost the land he'd finally been given, and had to humble himself to move in with the daughter he was probably a little afraid of.

In all my sermons on compassion, mine had stopped the day he'd thrown me out. While I didn't condone his short-sighted behavior, even after his apology, I hadn't shown him compassion beyond that day. I hadn't tried to understand his fear, nor his lack of education on the last twenty-one years.

With no warning, I walked over to my father and

wrapped my arms around him. He dropped the cage and squeezed me tight, as if I was the buoy, and he was lost at sea without me to cling to. "I'm sorry I murdered Morgan. She was your wife, and I never apologized for it."

Urien clutched me, his fingers bunching in my hair, unwilling to let go under any circumstances. "You don't need to be sorry for that. You did what was best for the kingdom, and I never held that against you." He rubbed my back and rested his chin atop my head. "I'm sorry I couldn't see past your curse. The way I was raised... It's no excuse. I should've found a way to see you. That's all you ever wanted from me, and I didn't deliver. I'm ashamed of how I behaved, and I don't blame you for being ashamed of me, too."

I didn't argue with his self-loathing. He needed to change, for the good of Avalon. Instead, I focused on the future. "I want you to come to Common at Christmas every year. I want you to spend it with me and your granddaughter. It's not a lot of contact, I realize, but it's a start." My eyes darted to Judah and Bastien, who were watching like statues, uncertain if I'd been taken over by an alien or something.

Bastien's first and only instinct was to protect me. I watched his internal debate teeter between letting me have my moment of growth, or ripping me away from the man whose love had limits that had broken my heart. He fisted the handle on the baggage cart, meeting my eyes to let me know he was here, offering backup in whatever form I needed it. He let me call the shots, which, for someone as controlling and bossy as him, said a lot.

My father held me, and I felt his tears wetting my hair. "You want me in your life?"

"I think it's time we started looking ahead. Let's start with Christmas in Common with Lane. Baby steps. Plus, I'll be in Avalon one month out of each year to see the people and help out how I can. We can rebuild from there, if you're up for it."

"Thank you. I look forward to it, my girl." He kissed my cheeks, letting out a choked sob at finally having his family back. He'd isolated himself, and constructed a box he fit neatly into – pushing out good people so he could feel safer. Instead, he'd constructed his own prison. It felt like the first breath that ever was to open the doors and finally free him. I think that hug freed me a little bit, too. In the end, I realized my anger would only hurt me, and I finally decided I'd suffered enough.

Urien was reluctant to release me. "I have something grand to look forward to. I shall start studying up on Christmas traditions straightaway. Does Lane have any books I could borrow on the subject?"

I quirked my eyebrow at my father. "On the subject of Christmas? Only about a million."

Urien let out a nervous chortle. "I'm going to be a grandfather!"

Judah did Urien a solid and pulled up a website on American Christmas traditions for him, letting him scroll through the page so he could get properly excited about the best holiday ever.

Bastien postured next to me as he finished loading up the last bag. "Stay close," he warned, casting wary glances around. The open space held too many people, each bustling toward their own destinations.

I looked up at him with the first glint of the stars in my eyes I used to view him with. The protective thing really got me in my tender spots. I placed my hand on his, and leaned up to peck his cheek. He shivered at the simple touch I'd been withholding, steadying himself on the luggage cart. "You don't have to worry anymore, mister. We're home now. No one's coming for us."

Bastien met my eyes with a loyalty I needed to be reminded of, his passion burning through my clothes and reminding me that we belonged together. "Say it again."

"No one's coming for us. You're safe."

"No, the part about us being home." He leaned over and pressed his forehead to mine.

The corner of my mouth quirked up at the cuteness. "We're home, Bastien. This is where we belong."

He wrapped his arm around my hips, stroking my belly with his thumb. "You're my home, and I'm never leaving you again."

I didn't argue, because I wanted his words to be true. I decided to stop fighting the inevitable, and give in to the reality that Faîte handed us. "Do you still have my wedding ring?" I asked quietly.

I'd never seen Bastien move so quickly. He tore open his carefully packed bag, dumping most of the clothes on the floor. His determined fingers yanked out the ring in record time. He got down on one knee in front of my father and my Judah, asking the one thing I never imagined he'd have to guess at the answer to. "It's only you. Forever you. Please, Daisy. Will you marry me?"

I grew unbearably shy as the passersby in the airport stopped their busy schedules to gawk, letting out their "oos" and "ahs", and then clapping when I said yes. Bastien kissed my belly, promising our daughter that he would never leave her. Then he stood and kissed me, not holding back for the viewers. I was his – perhaps had always been his. And now finally, once again he was mine.

"Marry me and have my child," he pled between kisses, fisting his hand in my hair to let the whole airport know who I was going home with.

"Yes," I breathed, sucking on his lower lip, as if that was the one body part that might serve to anchor me to the planet.

"Forgive me. I was wrong, and I'll never be so stupid again."

"Take me home, Bastien."

With a smile on his face and love that seemed to beam out from his every pore, he nipped at my lips again, and whispered a grateful, "Yes. Of course I'll take you home."

With Bastien, it seemed I was in for a lifetime of "yes." Most days, all I wanted was more of the life we had – an infinite "yes" that lasted us through the many decades we would spend together. Bastien was determined to make good on his promise to be better to us, and I promised myself I would let him. Our love was the thing of fairytales. We were never again reckless with the gift we'd been given at the end of so many twists and burns.

We had each other, and in the long run, that was all we needed on our grand adventure through life.

49

THE PASSING OF TIME

"*P*ass the 'tatoes, pwease," Lily squeaked. No matter how old she got, she always squeaked. Her high-pitched voice grew operatic when she cried, so naturally, the guys completely spoiled her to avoid an ear-piercing "crisis". My granddaughter was four now, and her brown hair had been pulled into pigtails, the ends coiling into precious ringlets.

"Here ye go, sweetbean." Link held the dish of mashed potatoes with just the right amount of too much butter over her head. "Now, tell me who's your favorite uncle."

"Wink! Unka Wink! Gimme the 'tatoes!" She reached overhead, but came up two inches short, which seemed to be her lot in life.

Link blew a raspberry on her cherubic cheek, and then plopped a blob of potatoes on her plate. "Tha's right. Ye all heard her."

Madigan scowled at Lily. "Ye know he's just buying top spot. I bought ye tha crossbow, but Link gives ye potatoes, and he's your favorite?" He glared at the four-year-old, as if that would make her see reason.

Lily stared across the table at Madigan, her eyes impossibly wider. Her emotions were always washed over her face, and this time, I could see she was stunned and upset. "I thought Mommy said Santa gave me the crossbow."

Azalea kissed her daughter's head. "Santa did get it for you. Uncle Mad was kind enough to bring it over. Santa accidentally brought it to the wrong house. Silly Santa."

Mad glowered at my firstborn daughter, who was in her thirties, and old enough to hold her own. "I'm not playing this game. I didn't play it when ye were a wee one, and I'm not playing it for your little pipsqueaks."

Azalea was on the ball, as always. "You and I are going to have words about the kind of gifts Santa should be bringing a four-year-old. A crossbow?"

"I had one when I was tha age."

Azalea leaned into her husband and rolled her eyes. "Mark, will you deal with him?"

"Eat your potatoes, Lily," the accountant on her left said to their daughter. Mark held his own usually, but hadn't been able to find his groove around Madigan. Not like Mad ever gave him half a chance. From the time each of my children were born, the Untouchables formed a wall around them in whichever world they wandered to. Mark was a decent guy. Heck, with a dad like Judah, you couldn't go wrong. Still, no one would be good enough for Azalea – or any of my kids, for that matter. Bastien and I had been the least of their problems when our kids would bring home "study" dates back when they'd been in high school. The kids had worried most about introducing their significant others to their Untouchable uncles.

Though they'd grayed and their agile moves had slowed as the men reached the last vestiges of their sixties, they were no less terrifying. They moved easily between worlds now, but as this was the first Christmas without Urien, everyone cancelled their plans to come stay with us for the holidays. Children and spouses called off work, and even Lot made an appearance with his wife and their daughter with blonde pigtails, Yvette. Lot's wife looked like a legit Barbie, complete with a pinched, nervous smile and a penchant for high heels.

After dinner, Lugh arranged a picture of Bastien and I with our five grown children, all of whom looked a decade older than me. My daughters, Azalea, Marigold, Iris and Lilac all beamed out at the camera with their sole brother, Clover. Clover was the youngest in the mix, but was always tagging along with the uncles whenever they stayed with us, which had been often throughout their childhood. Most boys spent their middle school years playing basketball and video games. All five of my children spent their adolescence hunting with Mad, boxing with Link, studying business infrastructures with Draper, and practicing their bow skills with Lugh.

While most families went camping on summer vacation, we went to Avalon, so the country could know my family, and see that I still loved the people I'd bled so much for. We were a tightly knit family unit, even after Lane had passed two years prior to Urien's recent death.

Reyn sat with his grandson, trying to coax one more bite of food into the stubborn six-year-old's mouth. Reyn had grown quieter since his wife of more than thirty years had passed. Despite our attempts to bring him closer so he didn't drift, Reyn preferred to spend most of his days in solitude in his garage, building wooden toys for his grandson, and his many great-grandchildren. Lane had been the first Daughter of Avalon to die of old age, which I learned to be grateful for, though every day without her wisdom and goofiness felt like sandpaper scraping away at the surface of my soul.

Lugh met my eyes after snapping a few pictures for the mantle to replace the ones from last year. It was our tradition. Since we all knew what a fickle lover time could be, no one protested the cheesy grins. I left the hearth to stand at Lugh's side and peer at the shots he'd taken of us. "Ye haven't aged a day," he commented, his wrinkle-less face the only other one that hadn't changed.

It was a loaded statement, and one only the two of us could fully appreciate. There was a note of sadness to our extended lifespans that was hard to explain. "You haven't changed either."

Lugh brought me in for a tight one-armed hug that

said all the things we avoided speaking aloud. Bastien was getting older, but I wasn't. My time with my husband was finite, and though I had a life waiting for me after this one, I wasn't ready to say goodbye to my husband anytime soon. He had the best health regimen the finest doctors could prescribe, with Remy doing his best to prolong Bastien's vitality with Avalon's medicine. Lane and Urien dying had been a heavy hit I was still rebounding from. It was hard to explain the heaviness that outliving all your loved ones marked a person with, but Lugh understood. It was his lot in life as well, so we bore the pain together.

Lugh kissed the top of my head and pushed me back toward the hearth. "Come now. Let me get a photo of just the newlyweds." Lugh always called us that, and my fervent prayer was that it would never stop being true. Bastien and I were deeply in love, and treated our connection with more care than we'd given it in our youth.

I looked like I could be Bastien's daughter, but that never bothered us, even when people made nasty comments when we kissed in public. I was all his, and he would always, always be mine.

The next picture was of me and Bastien with our thirteen grandchildren. I never thought I could be so lucky. Each of them was a different brand of goofball that I treasured with all the love in my heart.

The next was of the Untouchables, including individual family shots of Quinn, Link and their two boys with their wives and children. Then Madigan and Annabelle, with her son, Madigan II.

Annabelle had made it her business to take care of her father with the same dedication he'd taken care of her when she'd been just a lost girl in the world. Her husband had died in a freak accident in Éireland after he'd cheated on her when she'd been pregnant with her only child. Mad never fessed up to it, but we all had a feeling the poor idiot's body was buried somewhere beneath Mad's bunker. She named her son after her father, who never once put her second.

The picture of Draper, Judah, Lucas, and me with Reyn grew sadder without Lane as the center. When Judah's mother passed fifteen years ago to breast cancer, Lane didn't waste a minute before she hired a lawyer and drew up adoption papers. Judah was legally my brother, though we didn't need a piece of paper to tell us that.

Draper moved slower than Bastien these days, and every time he winced through an ache in his knee from the arthritis that plagued him, I bit back a sob. I hated it when my big brother was in any pain, so a decent amount of my time was spent rubbing joint cream into his stiff limbs. Aside from the arthritis, he'd aged beautifully, taking women far younger than would be age-appropriate into his bed. They never lasted long; he moved on before they knew what hit them, shocked that the older distinguished guy with deep pockets would never settle down with his Anna Nicole.

There was a picture taken of the three Untouchables that, every year, jerked at my heart more and more. They stood like soldiers in front of the hearth, at attention for the first photo, and then with cheesy grins and their arms around each other for the second. Well, Link's arms were around Bastien and Mad. Mad was the statue that couldn't understand human contact, though he'd gotten better at it through the years. He hugged his daughter and grandson, though it was more of a checklist to make sure he was doing right by the people who adored him. Madigan never remarried, but Quinn and I wanted for nothing. When I'd broken my ankle in a soccer match (that we won, by the way) a couple years back, he'd moved in with us, barking at me each time I tried to get out of bed. There was never a leaky pipe or a rusty hinge in any of our houses. For all the grand gestures, it was the little things Mad did that made me feel treasured.

During the times where my marriage faltered, Mad and Link had been there, putting us back together when Bastien was determined we should fall apart. Link and Mad were my glimmer of light during some very dark times, and I never once took their love for granted. The Brotherhood remained strong until the very end – a thing that stood out as precious in a world that was often far too common.

The last picture was of Lugh and me, which we tried to smile through every year. Each time, the grins became more forced as we watched our family grow to bursting, and then start to lessen with time.

We had ten more rounds of pictures in front of the family hearth before Draper died in my arms, and fifteen before Bastien was confined to hospice. There were too many people to all fit into one hospital room, so my husband was sent home with around the clock care, so he could be with all of us until his last breath.

When that moment came, an iceberg cracked off from my heart, and floated out to sea, never to return. My flock of sparrows cried out through the house, announcing to the woodland creatures that their king was at peace, and I probably never would be again.

Link and Reyn had died a few years before, and a couple months after I buried my husband, Annabelle and I put Alzheimer's-riddled Madigan the Formidable into the ground, as well.

There is no measure of melancholy that can be quantified to describe the agony it is to bury so many insurmountable loves. I can only say that I lived through it all because it wasn't physically possible for me to die yet, not even of heartbreak.

The world lost many great warriors and loves, and I was there to bury them all, my face never wrinkling as my tears screamed in crimson stains down my cheeks.

~

"I'm not sure I'm ready for this." Lugh squeezed my hand as he voiced his nerves. The mountainous deserted area of Montana that housed the well to Avalon hadn't changed much, though I felt like I certainly had. I recalled my first trip down the well, straddling Bastien and hoping for a kiss.

It had been six months since he'd gone, which felt like an eternity of time, yet still like I'd just seen him yesterday. I pictured him giving me that "come punch me" face as he lowered us into the well. I'd been so scared of heights back then. Funny how our fears seem so precious to us at the time.

"You don't have to come, you know," I reminded Lugh. His hair was shorter now, but he'd been so famous in his rock star life that, short of plastic surgery, he couldn't start a new band. He needed a reboot, which was why when Bastien passed, he threw in his hat and told me he'd come back to Avalon with me. Now the arrangement would be split in the opposite way – with one month being spent in Common, seeing my kids, my grandkids, and my great-grandkids. The rest of the year would be spent ruling Avalon. Duke Lot had passed one week ago, which meant the throne belonged only to me now.

Lugh squeezed my hand as we stared at the well, and all it represented for us. "I know I don't have to come with ye, but I want to. You've made the last half a century bearable, Prim. Not sure what I would've done without ye."

"Man, that accent just gets thicker over time. I thought

hanging around me would make you easier to understand, but you're turning more Leprechaun every day." He chuckled, but we both knew I was doing shtick because I was nervous. "Tell me Judah will be okay without me. Tell me I'm not walking out on him."

Lugh pulled me into his arms. The feel of his affection had never changed, and in the quiet moments, that was a comfort we clung to. "Judah doesn't know who ye are anymore. He's got his kids to take care of him."

"He just went downhill so quickly after Bastien passed. One minute he's Judah, and the next minute he's fallen, we can't wake him up." I closed my eyes against the horror that was the forty-eight-hour period we hadn't been able to wake Judah. Then he'd come to completely confused, unaware of who any of us were, or how he'd gotten to this place of aging in his life. Dementia hadn't touched my Judah until he'd woken, but now it wouldn't leave him alone. It devastated me to see the sharpest mind in the universe dulled beyond repair.

"Ye put him up with the best in-home care possible. Avalon needs ye now. Tha's where we should be." When I didn't respond, he rubbed my spine to coax warmth into my body. "There'll always be a reason to stay. Keep Judah in your heart, and look ahead. What do ye see?"

"I see my kids freaking out when something goes south, and I'm not there to fix it."

Lugh chuckled, holding me tighter as he rocked me.

"Ah, but tha's ye looking behind still. Close your eyes, Prim. Tell me what next year looks like."

"You can finally use your bow without a permit. Mathews will be free to shoot at your command." I always thought it was cute that he'd named his bow.

He snorted. "Grand. I can't wait to be shot of paperwork. What else?"

"In a year from now? Maybe Avalon will start to heal from Duke Lot passing. They've been so united, so strong. People always think the time to worry about a country is when adversity hits, but really, it's the boredom that tells you who you are. They've had nothing but peace for decades, and they're holding strong, not squabbling over the little things. Now that Lot's gone, they need to be held for a while."

"Just like this?" Lugh rubbed my body as he rocked us from side to side.

"Exactly like this. Tell me this all gets easier."

"The fun things in life aren't easy, Prim. But I can promise ye tha ye won't be alone through any of it."

Lugh had moved in when Bastien started to deteriorate, helping me lift my burly husband and tend to the day-to-day needs. There were many days that I spent utterly broken. Lugh had held me together through my dark moments so I could be strong for Bastien, who'd been slipping through my fingers too quickly – always too quickly. Lugh and I had the stuff of a lifelong friendship.

Even after Bastien had passed, Lugh stayed with me. We shared several sad and quiet months together, holding each other through the pain of a life now behind us. I gave him my *lueur* the very first night, and we'd been inseparable ever since. Lugh was my *Guardien* now, and he took to the post easily. As much of a free spirit as he'd always been, part of him wanted to be anchored somewhere permanent.

Lugh kissed my lips as we held each other next to the well, sealing our friendship with a bond that had been there for so many decades. "Kerdik knows I took your *lueur*. He asked me to. Said he couldn't trust anyone else with your safety."

"Don't let me screw this up. We've been waiting so long for our shot. I think Kerdik's done being patient."

"I'm not sure anyone's learned to be as patient as him." Lugh kissed me again. His lips were soft, and filled with understanding we both needed. "Let's not keep him waiting anymore, aye?"

I nodded into his chest. "Tell me everything's going to be okay."

Lugh softened, stroking my hair just the way I liked to be touched. "Everything's going to be okay, Prim. We've gotten through one life together. Now it's time to start the second."

We threw our bags down into the darkness without caring how our things landed at the bottom. With a tear that trickled down his cheek, Lugh sat on the wooden seat that hovered over the empty well, beckoning me to his lap.

I clung to him with all four limbs, resting my head on his shoulder as he lowered us down into the darkness. We didn't speak a word as we descended, knowing there was nothing that could sum up the nerves, elation and devastation we shared. We were leaving our home that had taken us in when we'd been battered and worn.

I vowed to be strong for Avalon, and lead them on a path they would be proud to be part of. My adventure would be filled with love, kindness and determination, because in my journey through life, I'd learned exactly who I was.

I vowed to be strong for myself, so I could rest my head on my pillow each night without regrets.

When our feet tapped down on the soil, my heart was fluttering with nerves as I climbed off my *Guardien*, standing on my own.

I'd seen Kerdik once a year for decades when I came to visit Avalon, but he never looked like he did now, standing before me and holding a bouquet of his signature yellow roses. He wore the same chocolate brown slacks, pressed white shirt and charcoal vest, but there was a tightness in his eyes that belied his put-together appearance. He shifted his weight from one foot to the other, his usually self-assured expression vulnerable with nerves. The other visits had been while I was still married, and I'd had my whole family with me. He'd been "Uncle Kerdik" and had treated my children with gentleness he would've bestowed upon his own kids, if he'd had any.

This was different. It was just me this time.

We stared at each other while Lugh busied himself gathering up our bags. "Good to see ye, Kerdik. Are those flowers for me? Ye shouldn't have."

"Shut up." Kerdik shot Lugh a withering look, and brushed his sky-blue hair back, his anxiety getting the better of him.

Lugh left us to our awkward reunion, strutting out to the military salute Kerdik had arranged for my return to his homeland. I could hear Remy and Demi calling my name, but I couldn't tear my eyes from the man standing before me.

Kerdik swallowed hard, studying the many conflicting emotions that warred in my eyes. "I was so sorry to hear of Bastien's passing. He was a good man."

"Thank you. It was hard on all of us." I glanced at the perfect thorn-less roses – Kerdik would tolerate nothing short of the best, nor any chance I could get hurt. "Are those for me?"

"Yes. Sorry. I think I'm a little nervous." He thrust the flowers at me, and I saw his arm tremble a little. His voice was quiet, as if he was afraid the next words he whispered might shake the earth if he wasn't careful with them. "Have you finally come home to me? Is it real?"

I nodded, timid in my declaration that had taken us a lifetime to get to. "If you'll still have me."

"Always, Rosie. Always." Kerdik's apprehension left him with a cry of elation when I fell into his embrace. The roses scattered on the floor around us, but the kiss we'd put on hold for too long couldn't be postponed another moment. His lips were insistent, and quivering with emotion that pushed grass through the concrete floor of the military building. The soldiers jogged out of the barracks to give us privacy when the walls started to shake. The buildup of too much love had been put on hold for far too long.

Kerdik kissed me, pushing me up against the wall with passion I needed to feel in every inch of my body. I didn't like the polite exchange filled with awkward glances. We'd waited too long to suffer though that.

"Your mate's passed on, so you can choose a new one." He unbuttoned his crisp white shirt, yanking open the collar to expose his neck to me. "Bite me, Rosie. Make me yours."

I paused the kiss to gape up at him, marveling at the man who'd been so irrational and infuriating in the early stages of our friendship. "You still want me? After everything I put you through, you'll still have me?"

Tears sparkled in Kerdik's eyes as he held my face to meet my amazed stare. "I would have waited a thousand lifetimes for you. Now that it's our chapter together, I want to be yours in every way I possibly can. Make me your husband. Make me your mate. Bite me, Rosie. I'm utterly dying for it."

I hadn't fed directly in months, though I'd drank on and off from the supply I'd syphoned from Bastien just before he'd died. The prospect of Kerdik providing my basic sustenance felt like a rite of passage from one life to the next. While we could've (and perhaps should've) waited for a more private or romantic setting, I leaned up on my toes and ran my tongue from the tip of his shoulder up the slope of his neck, searching for the spot that called out to me. While Bastien's had been the back portion of the meat of his shoulder, Kerdik's neck screamed to be bitten. Just above his collarbone on the right, a pulse point taunted me with an invitation to fall down the rabbit hole with him.

After everything, I was finally ready for the fall.

My two sharp incisors bit down, welcoming the blood of the man who waited for me, who'd seen me grow and change, and who now would sustain me through whatever life would hurl our way. Pure and delicious Kerdik flooded my senses, and a feeling of completion overwhelmed me, welcoming me to my new life. His blood tasted of oranges and cloves, coating my tongue as he let me drink as much as I wanted.

Oh, how I wanted.

Kerdik shouted with surprise, elation, and then seconds later, desire, as my venom trickled through his body, sealing the addiction we had the rest of my life to satiate. "I can't wait another second! Rosie, I need you!"

"Then take me, Kerdik. Make me yours."

With the army of Avalon waiting outside of the building, Kerdik walled us in with an impromptu forest that kept the outside world from walking in on our reunion. We stumbled over the grass he'd grown on the fly to cushion our tryst as we crashed into each other. Too many emotions mixed with the venom, making waiting for a bed a thing of total excruciation. The kiss took on a life of its own, our frantic and barely-controlled movements outlined against the flower-lined concrete walls behind us. We were together, and that seemed to be the only thing in Avalon.

It was ten minutes before Lugh grew impatient. He was the only one with the stones to interrupt our total lack of self-control. "If ye think you're being subtle in there, ye might want to see what you've done out here, Kerdik. Take her to the castle, where ye can bed her all ye like."

Kerdik was exactly as beautiful as my memory of him, the green glow making every muscle seem altogether other and elevated from the norm. We reluctantly parted, shivering with the smallest brush against each other. He took my hand in his and kissed the ring that never left my finger in all the years we'd been apart. "Shall I take you to your kingdom, my queen?" He caught himself at his words, emotion seizing him. "Finally, you're my queen."

I leaned up on my toes and fisted his collar, bringing him down to meet my lips in a kiss that was slower this time, less frantic. "Take me home," I whispered, reacquainting myself with the feel of his arms around my waist.

Kerdik's lopsided grin made him look high. He hooked

my hand through the crook of his elbow and said, "My darling, I've never heard you say anything sweeter."

We followed after Lugh, meeting Uncle Dub at the exit. I wrapped my arms around my uncle, giving him a squeeze that he returned with an indulgent chuckle. "I think Avalon's never looked more beautiful than it does when you're here. Look at all you've done." He opened the door, revealing what had been a prairie mere months ago, but was now utterly covered with every kind of flower at the height of full bloom.

I gasped at the sight, taking in the fragrance that was so fresh and luxuriant, it nearly bowled me over. "Kerdik, did you do all this?"

Kerdik looked just as surprised as I did, and scratched the back of his neck bashfully. "Uh, sort of. I didn't mean to. I guess I got carried away in there."

I laughed, picking a handful of pink snapdragons to play with. "I love it. I love you."

Kerdik chuckled at his lack of control that only seemed to happen around me. "I'm glad to hear it. Shall we, my dear? I can't wait to show you the improvements I've made to our kingdom. I've added some things I think you'll be pleased with." He frowned. "I hope you'll be pleased. Occasionally the enhancements need tending to. The magic twisted up a little, but it's nothing I can't sort out."

I could hear an ominous note in his voice but talked myself out of assuming there was something to dread around every corner. This was my second life, not my first.

I quirked my eyebrow at the new development, but said nothing, since we had about a thousand sets of eyes on us. The soldiers stood at attention on either side of the road we were to walk down. Remy and Demi had been standing at attention, but broke forward and hugged me when I beamed at them. I never imagined I'd get to keep them in my second life, but the bodies of the Dullahan didn't decay. They would remain the men I'd counted on for too much to call them merely friends.

I folded my fingers through Kerdik's, and stepped further out into the sunshine, greeting the world that welcomed me back as Kerdik had – with open arms.

"Tell me you're happy to be back here with me," Kerdik whispered as we walked with our chins high, like the royals we were.

I squeezed his hand, following Dub, who marched before us. I glanced back at Lugh, Demi and Remy, who watched our backs (though there was no hint of danger). These would be my people, and this would be my new life. "So long as we're together, I can't imagine anyplace more perfect."

We walked through Avalon with the entire militia escorting us through the land. Avalon had grown so much since I'd first stumbled through her unending riddles and bottomless mysteries.

I'd grown so much, and knew life would demand yet more from me as I figured out this next chapter. But that's the beauty of a new adventure – so long as you take people you love with you along on the journey, and refuse to lose yourself along the way, you'll always land exactly where you're meant to be.

Love the book?
Leave a review.
And if you think this story is finished,
you are super way wrong.

50

OTHER GIRL

*H*ere's a free preview of *Other Girl*, Book 12 in the *Faîte Falling* series, which introduces United Kingdom folklore.

In which Rosie has led an ordinary life,
and Dub punishes her for it.

IF THERE WAS ONE THING I WISH I UNDERSTOOD ABOUT LIFE after all these years, it would be a how to tell who's telling me the truth and who's on Santa's naughty list. After 85 years trying to figure out the basics like that, you'd think I'd have a clue.

"Now, now, if you keep fidgeting, I won't be able to

brush these snarls out of your hair," Camille chided me in her stern but gentle way.

I forced myself to sit still, biting my tongue to keep from spouting at her that, even though I still looked twenty-three, I was actually in my eighties. But since Camille was forty, she treated me like I was her daughter. That seemed to be the way of most of my relationships.

I wasn't so sure how much I was liking Camille yet. I had a natural distrust of personal attendants after the ups and downs I'd gone through with Rigby. Still, Kerdik insisted I have a handmaiden, and apparently, Camille was the best in the business.

"Sorry," I offered, unsure how to tell her that I knew how to brush my own hair without sounding rude.

It was no great surprise to find that as soon as I crossed over to Avalon to start my second life, Kerdik would pull out all the stops. The many-storied castle had once belonged to my mother (and then me, and then my father and Lot, and then just Lot, and now once again me along with his daughter). It was bedecked in gold and the vibrance of nature. The stone walls had gilded fixtures to match the hand-painted borders along the floor and ceiling. Golden vases had been sawed in half long-ways, and then affixed to the walls so they could be filled with flowers of every kind and color.

That was a new addition since I'd lived here last, and I knew I would soon become addicted to the luxury. I loved living in a home with fresh flowers. Walking out into the hallway revived me with a breath of nature, relaxing and refreshing me each time I made my way through my home. I wasn't sure if it was overkill that would die down once the newness of my arrival wore off, or if that was just how my fiancé rolled. I had a feeling it was the latter. My guy had always been just the right amount of a little too much.

"Master Kerdik wanted to make it clear that anything you wish for, you should simply ask. If I cannot solve the problem for you, then he will get you what you require."

Camille had said as much to me three times already today. "Thanks. Really, there's nothing I need. I mean, what could there possibly be to complain about? You all thought of everything."

I mean, everything. Kerdik had stocked my bathroom (that's right, no more tub in the corner with a partition. In the last sixty years, Avalon had graduated to indoor plumbing, thanks to the aqueducts and the evolution of time). He'd snagged all my creature comforts from my sporty-traveling-goofball life in Common. I don't know how he found my brand of shampoo and managed to get it here, but dude was thorough.

Camille moved her hand over her tight bun to smooth back her dark brown hair. She rolled back her broad shoulders before attacking one of my tangles that was being particularly stubborn. "The master wants you to be comfortable here, and to think of Avalon as your home."

That might take some doing. I'd had decades to deal with and move on from the legit PTSD Avalon had given me. Add that to the fact that my husband of nearly six decades had only been in the ground six months. I wasn't sure what therapeutic magic my regular shampoo and conditioner might hold, but the fact that Kerdik was willing to go to such lengths to make my transition smoother said volumes. We would take better care of each other this time around.

I blew out a nervous breath when Camille ruled me presentable and took my hand to lift me from the chair. I felt like a Barbie, all dolled up for the crowd, but stiff and wearing an expression that felt plastered in place. I hadn't done an address to the nation since last year, when I'd come with my granddaughter Lily and my BFF Lugh on my annual visit to Avalon.

I tried not to let my nerves show, but something about trading in my soccer shoes for legit ruby slippers gave me a sense of unease. I knew the bile churning in my stomach would only grow more wretched until I got my speech over and done with.

Three knocks of a fist and two trills of fingertips on the wooden door let me know that Lugh was outside. It was our super-secret knock that we liked to pretend was unduplicatable and belonged only to us. We had lots of little quirks like that. Being the only two Gancanaghs in Avalon made us cling tighter to each other.

When I moved to open the door, Camille frowned at me. "No, your majesty. You don't open doors here. I'll get it."

"It's just Lugh."

Camille stepped back from Lugh when she saw his frame filling the doorway. The note of hesitation in her eyes wasn't missed, but she quickly covered it with a stiff smile and bowed her head. "Good afternoon, Cross Shot, sir."

Lugh took her caution with a practiced smile, the corners of his eyes tightening only slightly. In his homeland of Éireland, he was revered for his never-failing aim with his bow and arrow. His rakish good looks didn't hurt matters, either.

Here in Avalon, though, it was a different story. Gancanaghs had been extinct from the land for decades, so truth gave way to the gossip of lore. The game of telephone that time played turned facts into a thing of fantasy fiction. But the truth of it was that Lugh's sweat excreted a poison that made any woman who touched it go bananas for him. I mean full-on *Fatal Attraction* stalkerish addiction to my bestie. It wore off eventually, but the poison was life-ruining in many cases. He had to be careful.

We both did.

Lugh strolled into my bedroom, his brown eyes widening at my appearance. He covered his mouth, chuckling into his black riding gloves and pretty much asking to be punched. "Is tha ye, Prim? I can barely tell with all the fanciness you're dressed in. Ye look... I mean..."

Arms akimbo, I glared at Lugh. "There had better be a compliment somewhere in there."

He couldn't stem the sniggering as he fished for something nice to say on the fly. "Lovely, as always, Queen Rosie the Gentle."

"Oh, shut it."

"No, no! I say ye should wear this getup to the movies next time we go. Are ye wearing a bustle?"

"Not anymore, I'm not!" I frowned at Camille with a note of pleading. "I told you this was too much. I don't look like me at all."

Camille gave Lugh a wide berth, her eyebrows pulling together. "Master Kerdik said to get you the best of the best. That's exactly what this is. It's the same style Duchess Yvette insists on."

"And I appreciate it, but the people should see *me* – not some version that I can't recognize in the mirror." I tried to find my manners and stop being such a princess about everything. "I'm sorry, Camille. You're doing a great job. We'll find our rhythm eventually. Until then, can I pick something else out?"

"Something befitting a queen, yes. Duchess Yvette's dress will be in line with the one you're wearing. It's the most opulent of styles."

I held Camille's gaze a few beats, realizing that she was a bit more strong-willed than Rigs had been. Part of me still missed Rigby, the man who'd turned out to be my faithful attendant. At his request, he'd been buried out back near the well. It was the same one he'd thrown me down while following Morgan le Fae's orders. Though I'd forgiven him long ago, I knew by his burial request that he never forgave himself.

There was an elegant gentleness to Rigby, a sense of always being in control without being controlling. With Camille, there was sometimes the hint of a battle of wills I could see us falling into, where she knew best, and I would be her daughter who obeyed. It's hard to get people to treat you like a true adult when you look like you belong in the dorms.

I wanted us to be friends, to understand each other. She seemed like a decent person. Perhaps I wasn't giving us enough to time to settle into a groove.

I fixed an easy smile on my features. "I think Duchess Yvette's earned the right to stand out. Lot's daughter has done a fantastic job in the transition from her father ruling, to now her holding the crown in my place. She can wear the extravagant dress." I moved to the closet and tugged on a red gown that was made of silk so soft, I couldn't help stroking it. My walk-in closet was actually a series of rooms with more space for clothes than anyone truly needed.

Lugh waited in the bedroom while Camille helped me in the closet. She tugged the burgundy and gold material over my head. It was heavier than theater curtains and set some of my curls loose. The bustle was so stiff, it actually stood on its own when Camille helped me out of it. I had some nice lift and shape to my butt from decades of soccer;

I didn't want to look like I was walking around with a horse's backside from the bustle.

The long crimson sleeves were fitted to my elbow, and then belled out toward the wrist. The bodice was fitted to my curves, which the silk did nothing to conceal. The square neckline wasn't low enough to make me feel like I might have a wardrobe malfunction in the middle of my speech, but it certainly left no question that I was a woman frozen in her prime.

The silk of the elegant, flowing skirt kissed my toes as I moved out of the closet to get the go-ahead from Lugh. "So help me, if you laugh at this one, you're wearing it for the rest of the day."

Lugh's chortles died down as he took in the girl he'd palled around with for the better part of a lifetime. His eyes were kind, but when Camille moved back into the closet to hang up my huge Queen Elizabeth dress, he did an exaggerated scoping me out, looking me up and down with a sly smile. It was laced with things that would get him slapped, if I didn't know him so very well.

He was my *Guardien*, and I was his charge. There wasn't a thing about me he didn't know, and there was nothing about him that I didn't adore.

Lugh's sexy toothpaste ad smile died when I reached for the gloves on the golden table and slid them on. He shifted his wide gait to the side as he studied me. "Ye don't have to wear those."

I tried not to acknowledge the sadness in his tone. "It

makes everyone more comfortable around me. I don't mind."

He flexed his hands inside of his own gloves, no doubt cursing the lengths we went to so we could keep our poison from harming others. "You're only a third-generation Gancanagh. Your poison doesn't last in lads more than a few days. It's nothing as dangerous as mine."

"That's a few days where a man might think things that could ruin his life. A few days is more time than it takes to wreck a marriage. I care about the people in my household. I won't risk mind-warping them into loyalty."

There was a palpable melancholy in his eyes as his shoulders drooped. Before he opened his mouth, I knew he would utter the word, "Complicated." It was one of the things we both loved about Common – our Gancanagh mojo didn't translate up there. We could be ourselves. In Faîte, we had to be careful.

Lugh cleared his throat. "Tha's much better, without the giant dress and bustle. Ye look like..." He shook his head as the corner of his mouth lifted once more. "Ye look like the lass who could unite a nation, tha's for sure."

"Aw, thanks. So do you."

Lugh snorted at my joke and opened his arms to me – an invitation to drop the formalities and just be us for the span of a few seconds.

I cleared the gap between us and folded my body into his arms, sneaking a quick hug while Camille was in the closet.

Lugh was dressed in fitted black slacks, a white dress shirt under a red military jacket. There was a golden crown-shaped medal on the breast, denoting that he served me. It was such a strange thing to employ your BFF, but Lugh and I had a good rhythm. I was used to seeing him in ripped jeans, old t-shirts and cardigans my daughter Azalea knitted for him. She'd had quite the crush on her Uncle Lugh in her teen and college years.

He stepped back when a knock sounded on the door and served as my butler to usher my fiancé into the room. Kerdik was Lugh's oldest friend, and someone he'd gone to the mat for time and time again. "Impatient to see your bride?" Lugh teased him.

No one teased Kerdik, and I loved Lugh a little bit for the humanity he was always trying to inject into my main man's life.

"One more week," Kerdik confirmed, a smile touching his eyes. "I don't know why my patience lasted so many decades, but now that I must wait a week to marry my bride, it feels like a hundred more years."

"Aw," Lugh cooed, and then followed it up with, "Barf. Ye can start up with tha cutesy stuff when I'm out of the room."

Every time I encountered Kerdik since I'd come back to Avalon to stay, a million emotions welled up in me. It was hard to pick just one to declare how I felt. I was used to Bastien, my husband who had died in his eighties. It was strange to be swept into grand kisses or to be hoisted up in capable arms. I wasn't used to not keeping track of my guy's meds. I didn't have to make sure Kerdik was sleeping enough, lift him to go to the bathroom, bathe him, rub cream into his aching joints, shave him, or help him dress for the day.

While Bastien and I still made love up until the week he'd passed, Kerdik's lithe and agile body teased me just as much as it confused me. Though Kerdik's form should be familiar to me, since we'd gone to the rodeo before (decades ago, but still), I was nervous around him. I felt confused and a little shy. I knew I wasn't cheating on Bastien by marrying Kerdik, but though we'd had a lifetime to process our arrangement, it was all feeling a little fast. My first life was barely over, and here I was, pledging my second after being back only a week.

During our many girl-talk sessions, Lugh suggested it was because my whole relationship with Kerdik had centered around us restraining ourselves. Now that there was nothing holding us back, I needed time to adjust to the reality that it wasn't wrong to be with Kerdik. In fact, it was the exact right thing.

Kerdik's green skin was a beacon of beauty, beckoning me ever closer to the man who had been the king of patience. I was clumsy around him now, dropping things and blushing like a dummy, when I should've been throwing him on the bed and having my filthy way with him. There was a dashing gentlemanly sweetness about Kerdik. He possessed a sensitivity to all the things I would never admit to aloud. He knew I was struggling to find my footing in this new life. As much as I loved him and did want him, my head was spinning from all the change.

He looked me over with sheer contentment in his gaze. "Even better than I pictured you."

"You're exactly how I pictured you," I teased, motioning to his standard chocolate-colored slacks, crisp white dress shirt and charcoal vest. "Can't stop perfection." My face soured. "Top. I meant to say 'top'. You can't *top* perfection."

See what I mean? Who wouldn't want to get with all this awkward sexiness? I cringed at myself. What was my deal?

Camille came out of the closet and bowed. I noted the deference I'd seen around the castle and out in Avalon. It was a welcome shift from the pee-your-pants fear Kerdik incited when I'd lived here last. The whole exchange was far more balanced now, after decades of him helping Avalon, showing up to solve problems instead of lording his superior, well, everything over his subjects.

"She's ready, your majesty," Camille said with her chin lowered.

"Well done, Camille. She's just missing one thing."

Using people's names in conversation was new for him in the past decade. The simple displays of courtesy went a long way with the people, and spoke to my heart, assuring me that Kerdik could be kind.

Camille looked like she might have a stroke. "She insisted on not wearing the bustle, your grace!"

"Not that. The crown." Kerdik moved over to my closet and fished through the many hidey-holes until he found the white gold sparkling tiara that was encrusted with aquamarines and diamonds. With a gentle kiss of my lips that made my knees turn to precarious Bambi legs, he placed the crown on my head. With a smirk that told me he knew the effect he was having on the butterflies in my belly, he wound a few of my chestnut curls around my ear. Then he extended his hand to me, looking like a classic gentleman. "Are you ready, darling?"

"Yeah. I mean, I shink tho." I shook my head, flustered as the butterflies started doing haphazard cartwheels. "Think so. I meant to say I think I'm ready, yes."

My ring sparkled on my right hand as he walked by my side through the hallways. We moved slowly toward the second-story balcony that faced the rolling greens of Avalon, with Lugh following behind. Though I'd never taken my ring off to clean it, the aquamarine square center stone that was hemmed in by twin sets of three-diamond clusters still shone with brilliance and opulence – two words that made perfect sense to Kerdik.

Just before we walked out onto the parapet so we could address the nation, Kerdik stopped us a few feet from the row of guards. He was careful as he turned me so we could have a semi-private moment. "Rosie, are you alright?" he asked delicately. Kudos to him for not saying, "Rosie, why you be crazy, girl?"

I nodded, unsure how to answer that question. "I think

so. I'm just nervous, is all. The whole public speaking thing is… It'll be fine, right? If I burp in the middle of my speech or forget all the words, the sun will still rise." I grimaced that I said "burp" to someone as polished as him. Queens didn't talk like that, but here I was, being a huge dork again, wondering what the heck he ever saw in me. I'd given hundreds of speeches to Avalon, but still felt like a flunky trying to fake her way through a public speaking class every time. Add that to the fact that I was on permanent idiot-mode around Kerdik, and all my insecurities I thought I'd put behind me long ago started swirling.

Kerdik didn't seem put off at all, but still had that same look of rapture when he drank in my features. As if I was something special – a queen who never said "burp".

"I'll make sure the sun rises. You don't have to wow them; they're just excited you're back. Happy to have a queen again."

I nodded, swallowing hard as Kerdik pulled me into his embrace, letting me feel the steadiness of his leonine body as his arms held me with tender affection. Oh, how badly I'd wanted him to hold me. It seemed we were always surrounded by people, though, or talking shop as he caught me up on all I'd missed in Avalon. At the end and beginning of each day, I just wanted the man I loved to hold me. I needed him to remind me that everything would be okay, and eventually, so would we. So would I.

My whisper was timid as I leaned up on my toes, tugging on his collar. "Tell me I'm enough for them."

Kerdik's shoulders loosened that this was the crux of my nerves. "You're all they've been talking about. The Avalon Rose, come back to them at long last. They will adore you, as they always have. As I do." His fingers trilled on the small of my back, dancing over the spot Bastien had claimed like a territorial pit bull, and now was up for grabs.

My heels lowered to the stone floor, and I willed bravery to find my features. "Thank you. Okay, then. Let's do this."

Kerdik held my hand and led me past the guards. We waited for the ruling Duchess Yvette to announce us, and finally Kerdik strolled with me out into the sunshine of Avalon's warmth. I braced myself to greet the people, who cheered so loudly, I jumped backward.

Start Book 12 in the *Faîte Falling* series,
and read *Other Girl* today!

ABOUT THE AUTHOR

USA Today bestselling author Mary E. Twomey lives in Michigan with her three adorable children. She enjoys reading, writing, vegetarian cooking, and telling her children fantastic stories about wombats.

While she loves writing fantasy, dystopian, and paranormal tales for her readers, Mary also writes romance under the name Tuesday Embers, and cozy mysteries under the name Molly Maple.

Visit her online at www.maryetwomey.com, and sign up for her newsletter, so you never miss a new release.